W9-CAL-170

The Midnight Guardian

The Midnight Guardian

A Millennial Novel

S ARAH J ANE S TRATFORD

St. Martin's Press ✺ New York

This is a work of fiction. All of the characters, organizations, and events
portrayed in this novel are either products of the author's imagination
or are used fictitiously.

www.stmartins.com

Library of Congress Cataloging-in-Publication Data

Stratford, Sarah Jane.
   The midnight guardian / Sarah Jane Stratford.—1st ed.
     p. cm.
   ISBN 978-0-312-56013-3
   1. Vampires—Fiction.   I. Title.
   PS3619.T7425M53 2009
   813'.6—dc22

2009016927

First Edition: October 2009

10   9   8   7   6   5   4   3   2   1

For Allie . . . with eternal thanks

The Midnight Guardian

𝔓𝔯𝔬𝔩𝔬𝔤𝔲𝔢

Berlin. Midnight. March 1936.

"Well, Kunz? Do you think it's true?"

"Nonsense. Fairy stories. Grandmothers' folktales."

"But the Führer must believe it, too," the younger man insisted. "Else why arrange those secret squads we're not meant to know about?"

"Creating more work, isn't he? Preparing for the great days to come."

His comrade nodded but still looked nervous. He had a sense of being watched. Worse, he had a sense of being smelled, even tasted. The street was quiet, and surely no one would dare to confront the SS, not if they knew what was good for them. Yet still . . . he was sure someone was stalking him.

Kunz lit a cigarette. His companion's chat annoyed him. He thought he might ask to switch to a daylight patrol.

The sound of breaking glass in an alley made both men jump despite their strict training.

Kunz drew his pistol. "Who goes there?"

No answer.

He motioned to his fellow officer to keep watch on the street while he inched toward the alley. The younger man nodded, hating the shaking of his hands, wishing he hadn't heard the stories, wishing even more that he didn't believe them.

Kunz rounded the corner, hoping to face a few drunken anarchists, or perhaps some particularly foolhardy Jews. He was disappointed to find nothing but a girl.

He was about to chide her for whatever she'd just broken, but her playful smile stopped him. She was very young, perhaps only fifteen. Her stick-straight black hair was cut in the severe bob that had been so fashionable a few years ago. He wondered why a girl who was otherwise so smartly dressed wouldn't wear her hair in more stylish curls.

"What are you looking for?" she asked, with a strangely knowing smile. Kunz felt his stomach contract and his ears buzz with a delightful hum. The girl sauntered closer, her eyes glittering hypnotically. All thoughts of duty to his patrol vanished.

She put her hand on his cheek. The touch was cool, almost liquid. He thought his face might melt into that little hand. He didn't know if he was leaning toward her or she was drawing him in. He hoped it was the former.

A scant centimeter from her lips, he felt a blazing heat against his half-closed eyes. He jerked his head back to see that the girl's eyes were swollen and glowing red. A scream began to rise through his larynx, but the sudden, piercing pain in his face changed it to a hiss. He tried to run, but felt the flesh tear from his skull. Her hand had turned to a claw that held him fast.

She smiled again, and something like a gargoyle reared up from inside her face, bulging hard under the skin. Long, shiny white fangs burst from her gums, and in the brief moment of realization that his companion had been quite right, he felt the fangs sink into his neck and proceed to suck him dry.

The younger officer, meanwhile, was sweating, though the night was chilly. The feeling of eyes on him was so strong, he was sure they were leering at his bare flesh instead of his spotless uniform, and he had to fight the urge to wipe them away.

"Kunz? Kunz, what is it, what's taking so long?"

His voice sounded too small. He wondered if he was the butt of a joke. He knew Kunz wasn't the only one who thought he was a fool for believing in vampires, and it would be just like Kunz to team with the others and have a bit of fun at his expense. If he sounded too frightened, they'd never let him hear the end of it.

Squaring his shoulders, he ignored his jumping stomach and rounded the corner.

"Kunz! What's the—"

He was just in time to see Kunz's empty body drop to the pavement like a rag doll. The vampire grinned. Blood dripped from her teeth.

"You look frightened. If it's any consolation, he tasted of fear. Then again, so do you all. The quality of German food has gone into a marked decline since this Third Reich began."

The trembling officer raised his gun. "Vampire! Vampire!"

"Yes. We shall give you credit for observation."

But she hadn't spoken. The voice came from behind him. A hand reached around and twisted the useless gun into a pretzel.

The officer turned to gaze at a male vampire. One red eye winked.

"But you, you never hunt in pairs." The young man spoke automatically, echoing the words of his grandmother.

The vampires laughed.

"It's our anniversary. Things have been grim, so we thought we'd push the boat out."

With that, the male vampire bit into the officer's neck, taking a slow drink. He pulled away, rolling the blood around in his mouth as he clenched the terrified man's lips in a pinch to keep him from screaming.

The vampire shook his head regretfully.

"A perfectly terrible bouquet. But waste not, want not."

And he resumed his meal.

The female circled, smiling, enjoying the sight of the life draining from the officer's eyes. As his consciousness was fading, he registered something strange in the female's eyes—fear. She wasn't looking at him anymore.

The male released him and he landed with a hard thud that shattered his cheekbone.

"Gunther. Paloma. I would not have expected to see you in Berlin." It was a handsome, although plainly Jewish, man who confronted the vampires. A wooden stake was strapped to his thigh, marking him as a true hunter, a man of the old ways. The Nazi hunters were a very different breed.

"Leon. We hardly expected you, either." Gunther, his face reverting to its human features, sounded genuinely concerned for the man's welfare. "It's not safe for you anymore, surely?"

"We have made . . . arrangements, the Nazis and I."

The vampires exchanged a glance, taking note of the hunter's wry face and angry, shamed eyes.

"You can still leave," Paloma insisted. She could not keep her eyes from the stake.

"If you think so, you don't know them."

"Leon, Leon, we are not your enemy now. You must know that." Gunther's tone was gentle and placating.

"I do. But you aren't the ones who can help me and my family. Not enough. I'm sorry."

With surprising speed, he snatched one of Paloma's hairs. The act roused the vampires and they growled, moving in for the kill. Leon drove the stake into Paloma's heart, dissolving her into dust that choked the dying officer, even as Gunther's horrible wail ruptured his eardrum. He tried to crawl away from the ensuing fight but was too weak. Leon secured one of Gunther's hairs with one hand and staked him with the other. The dust swam into the officer's eyes.

Leon briskly assessed the man's wounds and shook his head.

"I wouldn't save you even if I could," he murmured.

"Quick work, Arunfeld." Another SS officer, wearing a highly polished Iron Cross, strolled up to Leon. "And here you told the lads those older vampires made for a nasty fight."

Leon tucked the vampires' hairs more deeply into his pocket, avoiding the officer's eye.

"Possibly I caught them by surprise."

"Ah! You mean they thought you would align with them, rather than us? Or is it just that you hunters don't bother with the older vampires so much? Funny, the way you all know each other. Why don't you have dinner parties?"

Leon smiled, as he knew he must.

"Well, the Reich values you, Arunfeld. It's good work you've done, training the Nachtspeere. You and your wife, of course. Such a loss."

The dying man saw the hunter's fingers flex, as though hungry for a weapon.

"We were . . . asked . . . to serve our country." Leon demurred. "We knew the risks."

The officer's eyes flickered. Whether he was amused or offended was hard to gauge.

"We should tend to these bodies," Leon announced, watching the dying man's eyes fade.

"Indeed. An unfortunate waste. But this vampire scourge is nearly past."

The officer headed for Kunz's body while Leon bent over the nearly dead man and hauled him over his shoulder. The last thing the young officer heard before his final breath sputtered out of him was a heavy, sorrowful sigh and the beginnings of a prayer that, he was sure, was what those cursed Jews spoke for their dead.

He knew full well it wasn't for him.

Chapter 1

Berlin–Basel train. August 1940.

There were three young SS troopers in the dining car, all vying to buy the lovely young blonde a drink. Didn't she know a finger of schnapps was very healthy before going to bed?

Brigit smiled, taking care not to look any of the men in the eye, willing a blush onto her cheeks. These men weren't the problem, anyway; it was the other one, slightly superior, marching past them again, fixing her with that unchanging steely glance. She'd seen his eyes on her not five minutes after boarding, and they'd lingered just long enough to beg the question. Now, here they were again, cold and merciless.

Whatever he knows, it's too much.

The sense of apprehension clawed at the back of her neck, but she ignored it and carried on gently fending off the sweet yet insistent attentions of the younger men. Perhaps the sergeant just didn't like to see men flirting with a silly Irish girl. If they were going to dispose of their off-duty time so frivolously, it should be with good German stock.

"Gentlemen, please, let the young lady go back to her compartment. You see she doesn't want any schnapps."

His voice was low but authoritative, with a hint of condescension. Something that might have been a smile teased about his lips but came nowhere near his eyes.

The men glanced at him—after all, he was only a sergeant. But they nonetheless inched away from Brigit to gauge her reaction. She hesitated, unsure which way to play this game. She could say that perhaps one drink would, in fact, be very pleasant and hope that the sergeant went away, thinking no worse of her than that she was a tease. Or she could pretend some gratitude to him and seize the opportunity for the solitude she was craving. She only had to hope that he wouldn't accompany her, and that he didn't suspect anything, however unlikely that seemed.

Offend none of them. You can do it.

She cast around a dazzling smile.

"It is a bit late. Perhaps you'll forgive me this evening, and I'll say good night?"

The sweetness in her voice and sparkle in her eye assured them that all was not lost, that for as long as she and they were on the train together, their chances were very good indeed.

The effusion in their wishes for her good rest was almost touching. Another time, she would have laughed.

She gave the cold-eyed sergeant a pleasant, even slightly grateful nod and slipped by him, willing him to simply glare at her receding back.

He let her take five steps down the corridor before following her.

"Fräulein," he called, "a moment, please."

Damn.

She smelled nothing immediately dangerous in him, but it had been many months since she could really trust her senses. There was certainly something in him worth her concern. Possibly an alert had been given out to watch for someone of her description. Or, of course . . . she wished there was a way to find out, and to know exactly how detailed the warning was.

She wondered if she detected a frisson of annoyance in his face when she stepped back against the wall of the corridor as he approached. A small stroke of luck placed her directly in front of a panel. He could not easily scan the window for a reflection, not if he wanted to tread with any caution.

"Is there a problem?"

She put her head to one side and gazed up at him earnestly. The tiniest vibration in her throat was meant to cloud, and even soothe. Or, at the very least, distract. But it didn't seem to work. Not well enough, anyway, which had become par for the course.

"You are very young, Fräulein."

There was almost definitely a sneer in the statement, but that could have many meanings. Brigit willed her expression not to alter.

He smiled suddenly, startling her.

"I am Sergeant Maurer," he announced, his tone generous but his eyes still flinty. He was looking at her too hard, as though hoping to see the shadow of a fang behind her lips. She forced herself to breathe.

"You should be careful, you know, traveling like you are. Alone."

No mistaking the emphasis on that word, or the brief smirk. Brigit inclined her head, curious.

"Perhaps, I mean to say, 'unprotected.'"

The intense desire to show him exactly how capable she was of protecting herself swelled up inside her with a hot rush.

"One can hardly feel unprotected with so many fine officers on board."

There was only sweetness and sincerity in her melodic voice, but Maurer looked neither pleased nor flattered.

But is he fooled?

What he wanted, she could tell, was to touch her, and she almost wished he would, wished he would find an excuse to lay a hand on her skin. Maybe then he'd think twice, be cowed, step back. Think he must be wrong. It would not be what he might expect. The chill of her body was not the iciness of mythology, the cold of death. It was more like a pleasant coolness, and not wholly inhuman. To touch, or, happier, be touched by Brigit, was like sinking a hand into a bowl of fresh cream. A man could roll over and be enveloped in that sweetness. He'd never want to be released. It was a touch she could control, but even at its coldest, it still imparted calm. A promise, an idea of comfort, however illusory.

He didn't touch her. Instead, he jerked his head, indicating for her to walk on. Hands behind his back, he accompanied her to the door of her compartment. She turned to him, a cheerful smile lighting up her features.

Wouldn't I just love to show you my other smile. The one that would drain the color from your face and tug the high scream into your throat before I reached out and . . .

"These are dangerous times, Fräulein. A girl like you wants to be careful."

Brigit tossed her golden curls and gave him an arch look—the confident seventeen-year-old adventuress, thoroughly enjoying her hasty trip home.

"Thank you, I can manage."

Still polite, even friendly. Still acting with infinite care.

She slid the compartment door shut behind her and leaned against it, listening to the measured tread of his steps as he marched down the corridor.

And we thought this would be so easy.

It was anything but easy, with so many minefields to navigate. Even at her most innocuous, she engendered scorn and envy from other quarters by traveling in a compartment to herself, dressing in expensively tailored clothes, and possessing such an astonishing beauty. She looked like an arrogant, overprivileged chit dripping in excess. Even the ruse of being Irish was of little help. She was a question mark of a girl, in one way too many.

She cast a glance around the dark, quiet compartment, checking again that everything was in place, that her well-cut blue coat was still hanging with casual insouciance over the mirror. There was something about the train's efficient amenities and highly polished veneer that irritated Brigit, despite its manifold comforts. The money poured into the Reichsbahn, the surety of the superiority of their trains, it all seemed too indicative of the entire manner of capricious thinking that had landed her here, watching, waiting, wondering.

"British trains are warmer anyway, no matter what anyone says."

It was not her habit to murmur out loud, but the sound of her true, suddenly dear, British accent was a tiny comfort. It was just about the only thing around her that was still familiar. And it made her feel less alone. She almost marveled at the speed with which her world had been upended and shattered. Two days. An absurd little speck. Or two days, nine months, and one year, to be more exact. Either way, the enormity of the upheaval was easier to bear when tempered with fear.

No, not shattered, that's not fair.

Her real world, her whole world, was waiting for her, and she could feel him.

Eamon.

The cherished name echoed in her brain, and she didn't dare even whisper it. She had to retain her control.

Her eyes studiously avoided the upper bunk, where the precious, volatile cargo she was toting was stored. She checked the door again to make sure it was locked. Not that it was any sort of real fortification, but even illusions were welcome now.

Brigit sat by the window and slipped off her shoes. Rubbing her feet, she cracked the blind just enough to peep outside. She concentrated on emptying her mind and enjoying the dark countryside. Her well-trained eyes could discern beauty in all that blackness.

Funny, how much light there can be in darkness, if you know where, and how, to look.

Funny, too, how surprised she was at her own surprise. If there was one thing she knew, it was how quickly one community of men could destroy another. It was one of the easiest acts a human could commit. She and all her kind often thrived on that destruction. Besides, she'd done her own personal share of havoc-wreaking, there was no denying it.

It wasn't even the first time she'd had her own little rug yanked out from under her, but this was very different.

It's not just me, now.

Nor was it over. At no time in her long life had she ever been in such protracted potential danger, a situation in which so much of her strength and abilities would have to be channeled in a manner unsatisfying, to say the least. And if ineffective, well . . .

I can't fail. I will imitate the action of the tiger, stiffen the sinews, summon up the blood. There is no other option.

She repeated it out loud, attempting to assure herself. She would throw herself into it, and hope for the best.

Berlin to Basel, at the Swiss border; through Switzerland and across Vichy France to Bilbao; a boat to Ireland; a boat to Wales; a train home. She laid out the steps of the journey in her mind like dominoes. It was easier to apply cold logic to the proceedings than to dwell on details like the length of the journey, the long hours of daylight that comprised a European summer, the delays that must characterize wartime travel, however determined these new rulers were to keep things normal and briskly efficient, and the presence of armed guards throughout the train.

If only she could tell if he knew. What would give her away? She seemed to breathe, to blush, her hair shone and her eyes sparkled. And he wasn't a hunter; he wasn't trained in the finer arts of detection. He wouldn't discern the skin, the touch, the whisper.

And you have to be one of us to read the history in our eyes.

History. Confounding, exasperating history. Lessons learned over and over, and never learned at all.

Still. It's not over yet. None of it.

From two cars away, she could hear the rhythmic *click-click* of the striding boots. She fought down the hot surge of impatience, the rising bile at the Nazi gall. How dare they patrol up and down the corridors all night long, as though the train were a prison? She supposed they fancied they were providing comfort and security for the slightly uneasy passengers. Who, at this stage in the journey, were almost all Germans, bathed in the warm certainty of their nation's power and absolute justification for the violence and despair they were wreaking on their weak, insolent neighbors. Still, however untouched they yet were by the war, one could not exercise too much care. Besides, this steady marching gave the soldiers a feeling of importance. Their brethren were holding sway in Poland, had broken down France, and were now battering England. Soon, they, too, might have more impressive dominion than this sleek, sumptuous train. But until that time, they would assert themselves however they could, and so they patrolled.

Irritants. Brigit shook her head, almost amused at this reduction. Her marvelous strength, so close to useless. The powerful demon she had to soothe and lull into slumber. She caught the scent of Maurer returning, his steps slowing, but not stopping, outside her compartment. So recently, so very recently, a man like this would already have been a memory. Now he was a man to be feared.

A man. To be feared. *Oh, Eamon, where am I?*

Quickly, silently, she put on her silk pajamas and tucked herself into the narrow bed. Who knew but that they might find some excuse to knock, even enter? At no point could she be seen as doing anything unusual. Her situation was already absurdly delicate. She was in no position to take chances.

Chapter 2

Calais–Cologne train. November 1938.

Otonia always insisted that there was no such thing as a sudden crisis. As ever, she was right. The vampires had seen this possibility coming over six years, but had hoped the circumstances wouldn't get so dire. Still, it was a wrench. Barely two weeks ago, they were going about their nightly business, enjoying their lives. Now, this select group was on a train heading for Berlin via Cologne. No matter what Otonia said, it felt sudden.

Easy for her to talk, anyway. She's still in England.

The five of them were certainly quiet enough. Except for Mors, who steadily hummed in a manner that Brigit was beginning to find grating. He was excited. Mors thrived on action. It was he who'd insisted they take some sort of action late in 1916, when things were starting to look particularly bad, and he maintained for years afterward that if they'd done more, and sooner, it would have made a difference. Brigit suspected he was right. Mors was an ancient warrior. He liked a fight, and having something to fight for.

He winked at Brigit. She smiled quickly and looked away, feeling his eyes still on her. Mors was her best friend, except for Eamon, and her oldest. *My first real friend.* He was exasperating, but undeniably powerful, and she was glad of his company on this mission. Not that there was any question of his participation; indeed, he was their de facto leader, although a few in the tribunal had wondered at the wisdom of that, fearing he might be recognized. He was one of the most legendary among them, more than two thousand years old, and with his shaved head and earrings (which, at least, he'd temporarily removed), he was distinctive. But strong. Very, very strong. He could move like lightning. His cunning and seductiveness were the very foundation of vampire lore. He was a master of controlled chaos. They could do this thing, because they had Mors.

Not that the rest of them were slouches. Their little group was only five in number, but their combined strength could overcome an army.

Except that's not how we're playing this game.

Brigit shook the thought from her head as though it were a gnat. It wasn't just their physical strength that was in play, it was the accumulation of their intelligence and skills. Received knowledge. That would win the day.

It had to be millennials, of course it did. Brigit knew that, as did Eamon, as did they all. The mission needed that level of power. There was a new skin a vampire stepped into as he crossed the threshold into the thousandth year of undead life. An extra layer of immortality encased him like paraffin wax. All those hundreds of thousands of nights consolidated into a burnished shield under the skin, coating all the still organs and every idle vein, through to the bones. It would take a specially forged stake to kill a millennial, and few hunters knew the formula. Indeed, few even believed in the lore of such very ancient creatures. It seemed too incredible to be true.

They never understand. They always think it's just about strength, about the seduction and the kill. They know of our loves, but they think that's just about endless lust. They know nothing of our actual lives.

Living one thousand years was not only about eating well and avoiding hunters' stakes and blades, or accidents involving fire and bad timing. It was about cultivating a powerful motivation for life. One found interests, remained constantly curious, developed the mind. And there was love. Pure, deep, earth-shattering love. *It gives to every power a double power.* The alchemy of all this created something close to an omnipotent vampire. It was just as well the human world was generally ignorant of their existence. The fear would be overwhelming.

But it meant that Eamon couldn't join them. Nor Cleland's Padraic. Next to her, Cleland was staring out the window with an air of determination. His hand, resting on his thigh, rhythmically twirled a sovereign through his fingers. Brigit watched the sovereign's path for a few hypnotic moments, then shifted her focus back onto nothing. Cleland was regarded as the exemplar of tragedy in the vampire world, a mantle considered all the more respectfully deserved because he shrugged it off. He'd endured the loss of great love as both human and vampire, and now, just over one hundred years into a new relationship, was being called upon to leave it for who knew how long.

Not too long, they'd all determined. The Nazis were arrogant, and this weakness was one they could easily exploit. They were only too well versed in the nature of human arrogance. Careful flattery and a few well-placed dispatches should allow them all to infiltrate the party with ease. The males would impersonate SS officers, the females would ply their particular wares, they all would sow seeds of discord, confusion, and chaos. They would break the party's back from the inside, and the Nazis wouldn't know what had hit them.

Brigit had her doubts about Meaghan, though. This wasn't really the sort of thing for which she was suited. She looked across at Meaghan, who was, as ever, huddled against her partner, Swefred. They were unlikely millennials. For that matter, they were unlikely vampires. Few vampires fit the description spun by humans, but the one thing they did all irrevocably have in common was a demon deep inside them. And while each demon was a bit different, it was cut of the same hellcloth. That was what gave them vim and zest. It made them hungry. Both Swefred and Meaghan were quiet, retiring even, and rather humorless. Swefred, at least, had a dashing air—there was just something about the swoop of his brow and his slightly crooked nose that made him interesting and gave him edge. But Meaghan, when she wasn't quiet, was fretful and petulant. Brigit had never liked either of them. Everyone in the tribunal got on well enough, as was the vampire way, and Otonia insisted on congeniality, but at home, it was easy to avoid Meaghan. Now, here she was, right across from Brigit. They'd been traveling only two nights, and already Brigit was impatient. It didn't help that Swefred and Meaghan were so close and affectionate. Never mind that they'd have to work separately on arrival, Brigit wished Otonia had ordered them not to touch in public at all. It felt like a slap, watching them.

Well, I hope she has it in her. I hope she knows what she's doing.

There wasn't much choice. Otonia could not leave the tribunal and looked far too Greek. Leonora looked too Jewish. And Ramla was pure Egyptian. There were no other millennials in England. There weren't even any others left in Europe, not since the last war. So Meaghan it was.

She was pretty, certainly, with her strawberry-blond hair and enormous green, catlike eyes. But she looked frail. Brigit suspected the Nazis were more interested in women who brimmed over with health, exuberance, and possibility. On the other hand, Brigit had to concede that Meaghan was perhaps the least likely of all of them to arouse suspicion of being a vampire. That was all to the good.

It was particularly advantageous that the Nazis believed Germany, and perhaps the whole of the Continent, to be purged of vampires. It would never occur to them that a team of vampires might descend into their midst with the single-minded goal of bringing about their destruction. Their guard would be down. But what they'd managed to achieve already worried Brigit.

The vampires who had sought refuge in England were afraid. A vampire should be apprehensive about hunters, but to be truly afraid of humans was wrong. It upset the order of things. Europe had become toxic, alien. Forbidden.

Cleland believed in staying out of hot spots. At the final meeting, he demanded of Otonia: "And you really think we must do this?"

"1919," was Otonia's quiet answer.

Yes. 1919. No one could accuse that *annus horribilis* of being a sudden crisis. Vampires had seen the human world torn apart many times. And as much as they thrived on the elixir that was human chaos, the demons inside drawn to it like a siren song, there was some chaos that was too much. The aftermath of the Great War wrought more destruction than hunters ever could. The war had severely depleted the vampires' food supply, and would have repercussions for a whole human generation; so that for the first time since those awful few years after the Black Death, there was a vampire famine, which inevitably led to friction, and then another great, shameful vampire war. The Continent's tiny cadre of millennials had tried to stop it, and were cut down, to the

British tribunal's shock. If such a thing happened once, it could happen again.

The human world had recovered its numbers and even its financial woes seemed nothing it couldn't overcome, but the rise of Hitler unnerved the vampires. They suspected that they debated more vociferously than human governments as to how to manage the rising tyranny that smelled so suspiciously of total annihilation. Then, ten days ago, came Kristallnacht, and an end to the debate. Otonia, who had seen the waste of human civilization many times over, saw the broken glass as a prelude to broken bodies. She decided that Mors was right to want to intervene before another human war could break out and once again cut a swathe through their food supply, and no one disagreed. It was not the vampire way to involve themselves in human affairs, but rather to enjoy the human world for its amusements and delights. This was different. This was defense of what both humans and vampires held dear—although the humans did not count among their own delights their status as delicious, and necessary, food. This time, the vampires were determined to preempt the devastation.

"No one wants another war," Otonia reasoned.

Of either kind.

But they had another, more personal, reason to depose and destroy the Nazis. At first, they hadn't believed what the refugees were telling them. It was just too preposterous. Of course, humans had always wanted to eliminate vampires, but for those who knew of their existence, it was tacitly understood that eradication was impossible. A lofty goal for a different world. Vampires were. Their numbers could be tapered, the damage they did kept minimal, but there was no cleansing the earth of them. Even if every human on the planet were made to believe in them, to know vampires walked among them, it would stop nothing. One might as well wish to rid the world of nightmares.

Yet refugees had come from Germany, France, Belgium, Austria . . . on and on and on. Not many from each country. Some were so shaken and befuddled that they could not accept the idea of safety, and soon fell prey to British hunters and even sunlight. With their world upended, they no longer knew who they were.

Wolfgang, the oldest, the last survivor of the proud Prussian tribunal, explained:

"These Nazis are intent upon blood purification. It's not enough to clear Germany of Jews and homosexuals and other humans they don't like, they want to eradicate vampires, too. We are a blot on human society and we must be purged."

"They hardly seem the sort who would believe in vampires," Mors scoffed.

"Are you joking?" Brigit asked. "They're obsessive, megalomaniacal fantasists. What wouldn't they believe?"

"The only sort who believe in us are pragmatists who respect the shadow realm. And history. And not even all of them can extend their minds so far. I don't say I'm bothered. Keeps the hunt lively."

Wolfgang cut across their smiles.

"Oh, they believe in us. They know their legends. They have trained a special squadron of hunters. Clandestine, not even all the SS know of it. The Nachtspeere, it's called."

"Night Spears?" Otonia was puzzled. "Surely 'stakes' . . ."

"They like the idea of spears, the Nazis. And these hunters. You've never seen anything like them."

"I do not follow," Otonia said.

"The Nachtspeere are quite young and very foolish. They have nothing else in life, so they are most useful tools for the Reich. Single-minded. They have been assured that with each vampire death, they are paving a path to a kingdom of heaven on earth. The greatest empire yet seen, because it has no blemishes." Ignoring Mors's snort, he continued, "And they were taught by the true hunters."

Now he had their undivided attention.

"How the Nazis found the true ones, I do not know. I would not be surprised if they befriended some Irish, but we only learned of the Continental hunters. Possibly one or two came of their own accord and named names. Most are unwilling. But they have told some secrets; they have laid the foundation. With a few lessons and a mighty government behind them, these zealots have wiped Europe clean of the undead."

Eamon leaned forward. "How do you know all this? How are you so sure?"

"I barely survived an attack on my home. Our tribunal was scattered. I thought it was a random attack—German hooligans. No Prussian hunter would use such artless tactics. I went to Berlin. I was a witness. I-I captured one. A true one. I tortured him until he told me all." Wolfgang looked up at the sound of a hiss. "It was the only way."

His voice trailed off. Ulrika, his new partner and the last of the Berlin vampires, took his hand. Otonia gave his shoulder one quick touch, then stood and took in the whole of the tribunal at a glance.

"So, we have a true enemy."

"An enemy that has had the good luck not to tangle with millennials," Brigit pointed out.

"We can fix that." Mors grinned.

They'd begun to understand what the refugees meant when the boat docked at Calais. There was a chill that had nothing to do with a foggy November night. Meaghan muttered something only Swefred could hear, and he put an arm around her and whispered into her hair. The other three concentrated on buying the train tickets. They wanted to keep moving, swiftly.

France felt like a nation holding its breath. Watchful. Apprehensive. But not enough, Brigit decided. There was still too much to enjoy. And there was some kind of faith she couldn't place, some variation on the age-old certainty that everything would be all right because it always was. Except when it wasn't.

I suppose we should be grateful for constancy.

Zipping along through the countryside, Brigit began to sense something even more infuriating. Many of these provincial people knew, or suspected, that Nazi hunters working undercover had been systematically scourging France of its vampires. They approved; they liked it. A vampire-free France had been an ideal for centuries and had now been achieved at no cost to the French. There were many who wondered what other benefits the Nazis could bring, so long as no one made much fuss.

Disgusted, Brigit made her way to the back of the train where Mors stood alone, leaning on the wrought-iron gate, watching a long-invisible England disappear further into the mist.

He smiled at Brigit. It never failed to amuse and yet vex her that he almost always knew exactly what she was thinking, and today was no exception.

"Well, perhaps they're not so wrong. What do we do for them, really?"

"Give them the stuff with which to scare their children into behaving."

"And nightmares, don't forget nightmares."

"A little abject terror is good for a person."

"Too right. How else do you know you're alive?"

Brigit's laugh was stopped short by the sight of a church spire. Norman, and lit in a majestic orange glow, it radiated surety and solidity to the market town.

"I almost want to make ten vampires, just to upset their precious pleasant order."

Mors smiled his most wicked smile.

"Feeling energetic, aren't you?"

"And angry."

"Save that. You'll need it later."

What he really meant, they both knew, was that she had to be careful. Brigit was possessed of a kind of fire inside that was a unique beast, separate from the demon. Time away from Eamon was not likely to keep it tamped down. It had exploded twice in her life, and nearly killed her both times. Mors knew how to guard her, but they'd be working far apart every night. She placed her trust in her control, and the essence of Eamon that clung to her. She was determined it would be enough.

The smell hit them like a blunt object as soon as they crossed the border into Germany. Brigit inadvertently dug her fingernails into her palm, a reaction as much to the reeking air as Meaghan's low whine and shudder.

They had to change trains for Berlin. Stepping out onto the platform, Brigit had a strong sense of walking through a curtain of ice water. She and Eamon had once traveled to Berlin to see Beethoven debut a new symphony, and they'd enjoyed themselves. The food was a bit hearty, perhaps, but lined the stomach well for the crisp autumn nights. There were pleasant cafés for lingering, reading papers, and savoring the marvelous coffee. To be sure, there was a stridency about the people that one didn't see with the French, and certainly not with their beloved British, but there was nothing to make a vampire uneasy.

This was quite different. Blinking away grit, she inhaled coldness, trepidation, and what she could only imagine must be the smell of impending catastrophe. It was Eamon, not herself, who had a sense of things coming, so she hoped it was just a fancy. The others, after an initial wrinkling of noses and shiver, had recovered their mantles of businesslike indifference. Except for Mors, who was casting a bold eye over a pretty young woman. She was blushing, but seemed to enjoy the look.

Lots of luck, my friend. The train's due in ten minutes.

The other waiting people, well-wrapped in winter coats, noticed nothing. Brigit studied them. Just civilians. Looking ordinary. Tired, perhaps, and impatient for the train, but nothing to cause alarm. They were just people. Simple, small, edible people. But not appetizing. The vague uneasiness in a few, the whipped-up lather in too many others, it didn't smack of anything digestible. Brigit told herself it could be worse. And it had been. The Civil War, that had been bad. And countless other times.

Maybe I just don't care for foreign food.

She meandered down to the end of the platform and leaned against the railing to better stare out at the empty track. In her mind's eye, she followed it back to Calais and then across the Channel and home, to Eamon.

Feeling the danger of that thought, she turned the other way and looked instead toward Berlin, to the lair Ulrika had described, and the task ahead. She closed her eyes to better summon her strength. Then it happened. As surely as if she had turned her eyes inward, she saw the apprehension in the demon. It felt something akin to fear. It had the power to thrive on fear, although it generally chose not to use it, preferring to gain strength in sensuality and desire. That the demon could lose its nerve had never occurred to Brigit. She chose to be cross. She had not spent so many years learning to be mistress over that inner beast to let it assert itself through faintheartedness now. Its fear would feed on her, and she wouldn't have that. It and she would go home again, once they had completed their work.

Mors had disappeared, but Brigit studied the other three, wondering if they had taken any stock of their demons. It wasn't the sort of thing she could ask. The demon was each vampire's own personal creature, that innermost part of the self in that other world. It was them, and yet not them. In the human world, with their human faces on, it was as though the demon did not exist. Not that they pretended it did not, it was merely that there was no acknowledgment. They were two different creatures, and neither was human.

Brigit pressed her fingers to her eyelids, collecting herself. When she looked up, she saw a man watching her curiously. She tossed her head and smiled at him.

"Just a bit of grit in my eyes."

"Ah, yes. Inevitable. But the stations are much cleaner now, wouldn't you say?"

"Oh, certainly."

Did he really think so? It didn't seem any more clean than the French or British stations, and a damn sight less cheerful, too. However, she nodded politely and moved down to rejoin the others. Her first insincere conversation in Germany. She wondered how many more she would have before she could leave. The thought nearly made her smile, but it was interrupted by the screeching arrival of the train.

Mors swung up behind her, whistling. She turned to him with questioning eyes. He winked.

"Got a toothpick?"

"Seven minutes. I'm impressed. And what about teeth marks? Tracks covered?"

He edged her farther into the dark corner and raised a hand—one fingernail stretched out long into a blade-like talon.

"Throat slit. Which is why you shouldn't struggle when being mugged. Why parents don't teach their children these things, I don't know."

He flipped open his coat just enough to show Brigit the woman's handbag.

"Extra identity, which you'll probably need. You can thank me later."

"Such a giver you are. So, a violent crime in a peopled train station.

How shocking. Here I thought the Nazis had established themselves on a platform of law and order."

"Scandalous, isn't it?"

Brigit hesitated, then had to ask.

"And the taste?"

Mors had just started toward the others. He paused and turned to look at Brigit with some resignation.

"Well, we didn't come here for the food."

Indeed.

The train was a local and unbearably slow. Brigit rubbed her wrist absentmindedly, then gazed down at the pink mark she'd made.

Pink. Her skin turned pink under his hands, his mouth. The blood that lay so still under her flesh always rose with eager obedience to meet his touch. She followed the path of his hand up her leg, her thigh. He nipped the inside of her knee and she moaned, clutching the sheets as his mouth slowly worked its way upward.

More of her body yielded to him, to his insistent tongue. A tiny pocket of her mind wanted her to pay closer attention than she ever had, because this might be the last time, the last time that she was lost in such perfect ecstasy. But Brigit did not want to think such things. Eamon's mouth now trailed up her stomach, closed around her left nipple. His eyes, warm and sensual, rolled upward to see the heat in her face. It was a look and a gesture that never failed to inflame her further, and she groaned with the exquisite pain of wanting more.

And there was more. And more. And she didn't care what anyone might think—she was not going to bathe the scent of him out of her hair before the journey. But she wasn't leaving yet. Not yet. She held his face in her hands and concentrated on the feel of his skin, the sheen of his eyes, the curl of his mouth. She had known him the moment she'd met him, but she would memorize him yet again. Even through the glaze of tears that she couldn't keep from clouding her eyes.

"Eamon. My Eamon. My most beloved."

She woke suddenly, wondering if she had spoken out loud. But only Mors was looking at her. She shifted her gaze away from him, and her thoughts away from the dream. It was easier to think about Mors. Mors was very different from the rest of them. Nearly all had been notably beautiful humans, and young, quite young. Few were older than twenty-five when made, because most of the chosen, men and women alike, were virginal and comparatively untethered to life. Mors was, the guess went, forty. Possibly older, perhaps younger, it was difficult to say. He had certainly been a soldier. A Roman general, they thought with some certainty. His way with a sword, or even a pair of swords, was terrifying in its power and artistry. In his occasional moments of restlessness, he sought out hunters to fight and dispatched them with his big, easy laugh. His was an untold history, though there was no one who didn't wish to learn it.

In any case, his face betrayed some time. Which could, Brigit supposed, make his association with four people half his age look questionable. On the other hand, he covered his shaved head with a fedora worn at a rakish angle and had a way of shouldering his greatcoat that made him seem to swagger even when lounging in his seat. In fact, far from looking distinctly older than the others, he simply looked roguish, powerful, a man who would naturally draw acolytes. Swefred and Meaghan existed separately from the group, Mors plainly had as little interest in them as they him, but whatever Brigit and Cleland might be to this older, knowing man with the ironically cocked eyebrow and curving, amused lips, that was another matter. One that gave some novel pleasure to those observers so disposed to lurid speculation.

Theirs was to be the next stop, and Brigit was impatient. The sooner they were settled, the sooner they could begin. Ulrika's detailed instructions for getting to the abandoned lair played out in her mind and she was grateful for their intricacy, and for being rather tired and hungry. It meant there was no mental acumen left for wondering what Eamon was doing right this moment.

Extra distraction arrived in the shape of a startling smell. A young man, sweet and intoxicating, lurched past them toward the lavatories. All five pairs of eyes rolled toward him, intrigued. A spy, Brigit guessed, tapping him for Belgian. And a virgin, too, or at least not very experienced. On his way to meet a woman in Berlin. Desire and happy anticipation ran high in him. One good potential meal amid all the unappetizing lumps they'd encountered so far, and he'd have to go free. Mors sing-songed out the window: "Going to be a loooong holiday."

Despite the late hour, the station was busy and no one noticed the attractive, well-dressed group of five, who, while they had sat together on the train, now peeled off to various points around the station. One of the ladies headed for the powder room, another to the newsagent. One of the men needed a quick pick-me-up at the bar before going home to deal with the wife—honestly, such a relief to have business in Paris, such a bother to have to go home to snapping wife and squalling children. The barman understood only too well and they swapped stories with spirit. Another man thought he might just as well get his shoes shined. The third was a tourist and roused the sleepy clerk at the information desk to inquire in painstaking German if he could take a bus to his hotel, or should he hail a taxi?

The strolling guards usually noticed lovely young women who were traveling alone, but if the guards on duty had been questioned later, they would have sworn no single women had left the station all night. Nor men, for that matter. The vampires knew how to move with hot swiftness, clinging to shadows. Only one guard thought he saw a glint of something in the corner of his eye, but decided he'd either imagined it or it was a spark going off, or something equally innocuous. He'd never have guessed it was the rhinestone brooch on Meaghan's felt hat.

Two hours later, they all arrived at the lair. It was an idle section of the U-Bahn, with the extra advantage of never having been completed, so there was only one entrance accessible by humans. Over time, the vampires who had lived there had dug an extra tunnel that wended down into the sewer network. This was kept blocked by a concrete slab that you'd have to be at least a double centennial to budge. Even the stairs led up to a blocked entry, and then a conveniently sheltered yard behind an abandoned butcher's shop. Brigit was surprised, what with the war machine revving up, that valuable property like this wasn't being put to use; but the entire area was run-down and just enough on the city's edge to be unappealing for anyone to want to work, much less live there, unless there was absolutely no other choice. She could understand why vampires had thrived here for so long. Ulrika had assured them that neither Nachtspeere nor true hunters had ever come any-where near the lair.

"The Nachtspeere, they're interested in action, not subterfuge. They want to get us when we roam. They certainly don't want to spend much time in forethought."

Brigit was unconvinced. The Nazis seemed to like convenience, and what could be more convenient than to find the homes of vampire families and simply throw firebombs in them at midday? For true hunt-ers, of course, this was both unsporting and anticlimactic. A tactic saved for the last resort. One didn't go through all that training and prepare for battle and death, only to kill a vampire without even looking at it first, showing it the face of its doom. This was not like war. A born vampire hunter lived the calling as an art. These wormy Nazi thugs who dared term themselves hunters were not interested in art, the refugees made that perfectly clear. But they were only too keen on seeing the eyes of their vic-tims before they dissolved.

Bastards. Souls of geese that bear the shape of men.

The place was musty, with the feel of a home that hadn't been lived in for a long time. Even when vampires had been there, it was nothing like the lovely underground castle in London. Meaghan sniffed and looked fretful, but the others set about lighting a coal fire in the main room and airing the beds.

"I don't know about you lot, but I'm almost tired enough to sleep hanging upside-down from the ceiling," Mors joked.

Even Meaghan smiled at that. Some humans did get the funniest notions. Personally, Brigit loathed bats and found it insulting that anyone thought she might have an affinity with the filthy beasts, never mind partly being one.

Besides, what a waste of time sleeping would be if you had only parts of your own self to wrap up in?

Wishing she hadn't thought that, Brigit concentrated on picking out her own pocket-sized chamber with a single bed. The less space to move, the less she might notice the body that wasn't there with her. The body that had wrapped itself around her every day for more than seven hundred years.

Brigit pressed her palms tight against her temples. She gulped hard, and even drew a few breaths. The body's memory allowed the act to be calming. She wiped her hands on her skirt and was perfectly steady when she headed back to the main room, where Mors had called on them to gather.

He'd thoughtfully filled a thermos with blood from the girl at the train station, and now poured it out into five goblets. He grinned as they all held them aloft, watching him.

"To the mission," he announced, with a solemnity that startled them.

"To the mission," they repeated, and drank. It wasn't very tasty, but it was still warm, and filling. Better than trying to sleep on an empty stomach.

"A little bit cheerier, all of you! Come on, this isn't so bad. We'll be home soon." He looked steadily at Brigit and Cleland as he said it, his confident grin large.

They nodded, even smiled, but carefully avoided one another's eyes.

Chapter 3

London. November 1938.

Everyone was being so kind. Suggestions for theater outings and concerts and the late-night museum shows and all the things he and Brigit partook of so readily flowed in every evening. Eamon was touched and grateful, but, for now, preferred to be alone. Padraic felt the same. Eamon, feeling his responsibility as one much older, had asked Padraic if he maybe wanted to attend a scientific lecture at King's College. Padraic and Cleland liked that sort of thing. He'd smiled at Eamon's invitation, the first smile he'd managed in a week.

"You wouldn't stay awake ten minutes." He grinned.

"Oh, I don't know. I could probably manage a good half hour for science. One of your strange numbers things, though, that would put me right out."

"And they say musicians have an affinity for mathematics."

"Not this musician."

Padraic smiled again, and nodded.

"Thanks, Eamon. Another time, maybe?"

Eamon nodded, too, and left Padraic to his studies.

He prowled disconsolately around the West End. There was a lot of nervousness in the air. Londoners felt sure war was coming, and very likely soon. They were almost forcibly enjoying themselves, both to stave off apprehension and to laugh as much as possible before humor was sucked out of the world again. Eamon smiled. He liked their determination, their stoutness. It was the sort of thing that made him proud to be British.

The theaters held no allurement for him tonight. He couldn't imagine going to a show without Brigit. They'd been going to theater and concerts together for hundreds of years. How could he sit in a theater, how could he concentrate on a show, never mind try to enjoy it, without his Brigit by his side? Unthinkable.

Instead, he walked slowly up Charing Cross Road, vaguely wondering if there was a letter waiting in the post office box they'd gone to such pains to secure. Eamon knew it was too soon for anything to have arrived. He preferred to enjoy the anticipation than experience the flatness of disappointment. Otonia had also devised a series of codes they could use for communicating via telegram, but this was only to be resorted to in an emergency. Picking up telegrams required visiting the office in person. She was sure they would eventually be able to steal their own telegraph machine, but until then, all steps must be taken to avoid suspicion.

Two businessmen walked past Eamon, heading for a club.

"Say what you will about Hitler, you can't deny he's a man of action. Imagine what the stock market would look like if Chamberlain could manage that much action."

"Shaky, I would think. I prefer steadiness in the market myself. I think I'll be putting my money into shipbuilding. Mark my words, it will yield a fortune."

"I would guess aeroplanes. Rather wish the war would start already, if we're going to have it. Great bore, waiting."

Eamon turned to look after them, incredulous. What a peculiar thing, to be considering one's money when the cost of war was human. Perhaps the general public found it easier not to think about it too deeply. He supposed it was useless to expect real understanding, even though the Nuremberg Laws had been printed in the papers and discussed with properly expressed abhorrence before turning to the home news. Everyone approved of the Kindertransport, but quietly agreed that it should have its limits. In spite of the vast improvements, it troubled Eamon to realize that little had changed in the overall attitude toward Jews in Britain since he himself had been a member of that community some eight centuries ago.

Contemplating the breadth of general prejudice, he'd remarked to Brigit back at the time of the Russian pogroms that it was almost a shame Jews weren't vampires, as some stories had it.

"They'd be a damn sight safer, anyway."

"But still dead, the way those devils want it."

"There's always a catch, isn't there? Of course, if death is coming anyway, at least as vampires, they could fight."

He knew his logic was muddled, but this was not an area in which he could think with his usual clarity. As a Jewish vampire, made on the eve of the York massacre in 1190, he still had a tenuous tie to that segment of human society. The Jew-haters were wrong: Jews were not bloodthirsty and there was no good reason to link them to vampirism, which in any case was so much older than any established religion. But Jews made excellent vampire companions. Theirs was one of the few human groups of which Otonia was aware that had no theory of an afterlife when the human body was spent, so that an observant Jew, once sired, would always retain a shroud of humanity. In one of his songs, Eamon described it as the bitter-sweet weight of a partial soul. It was indeed as though the soul could not wholly depart but must cling to the animated body it had known, sharing space with the newly lodged demon. The demon was as powerful as in any other vampire, but that fragment of soul gave a Jewish vampire a different sort of light. They were often called the only beating heart of the community. Their lot was not the easiest, because, as Brigit liked to joke, "You eat as heartily as the rest of us, but you feel guilty afterward." Not entirely true, more that they felt a little melancholy, but it was the idea. Still, they were loved, they were respected, and they were equals, and that was generally such an improvement over their human experience, beyond the Jewish community, that they were prepared for the trials of undead life.

The "millennials only" rule for this mission made sense, but it rankled nonetheless. He hated the idea of not doing anything. Eamon was energetic, and he liked to be active. There were some foolishly vocal Nazi sympathizers to tease and pick off, but they were so inconsequential as hardly seemed worth the effort. Eamon wanted to make a difference.

Even worse than the sting of uselessness was the prickly feel of impending chaos. He couldn't literally see the future, not exactly, but even in his human days, when something explosive neared, he could sense the vibrations, the way some animals knew when a natural disaster was approaching. It had bloomed on his making, and intensified over the centuries. He'd gotten the feel of the plague coming, not it precisely, but something that meant the vampires had better be prepared. So they stole a few sheep and pigs from all the local farmers—most of whom would later be dead anyway—and maintained them in a hidden shed. It wasn't anyone's favorite solution. Animal blood has not the same nutrients and potency. Some of the new ones had argued strenuously for the stockpiling of plump humans who could be made to last. With not a little asperity, Otonia had reminded them that such torment was not the vampire way. Arousing a bit of fear during the chase, if you fancied, was acceptable and could add a pleasing spice to a meal, but to kidnap and feed from a human for months on end was an act even the demon would repulse. The animals didn't provide quite enough, the vampires had to ration, but it kept them alive. Theirs was the only circle in Europe that remained whole, and thus the tribunal only enhanced its influence.

This time, Eamon wasn't yet sure what they should do, but there was a weight in his abdomen that told him the war was likely unavoidable. Which meant that Brigit and the others were not going to succeed, were putting themselves in danger for almost no reason. It was the damndest thing about humans. Their will would always win out, if it was strong enough.

No, no. We've never tried this. I'm just upset because I miss Brigit. There's no reason they won't accomplish all we hope, and more.

A slow grin spread across his face.

Those poor brownshirt bastards. They won't know what hit them.

Despite the chill, the streets in Soho were crowded. There was the usual rush to nip down a quick drink, or tuck in a chop or even just a sandwich before one had to be at the theater or concert hall. The people who were out only for supper, or were headed for a private engagement later and thus had more leisure, regarded the desperate ones with happy, haughty amusement, even though they themselves might have been in the same predicament the night before, or would be so the following night. For himself, Eamon preferred to get a drink after a show, when its pleasures or horrors might be discussed at length. As to eating, well, that was a show all onto itself. One generally guaranteed to be pleasurable.

He began to hum as he strolled, smelling the air, searching. It was one of the only things he and Brigit did—any vampire did—alone. Hunt. Eat. A few occasions called for a shared feast. The monarch's birthday. Winter Solstice. But for most meals, it was a dance you danced as a single. To your own music.

"Literally, in your case." Brigit smiled.

This was true, but it wasn't a typical tune. Hardly even music, really, more like a code. Eamon's hum swirled into the air like a spider's web, spreading out and out in concentric circles, wending its way through dingy alleys until at last it secured a moth.

About half an hour later, he felt a note hit. She was two hundred yards ahead. He felt the girl's head turn, wondering, interested. She smelled of stealth. He stopped humming when he turned into the alley and leaned against a wall, watching the girl, who was now focused on the back door of a grimy pub. When a drunken young man came out, tugging his hat low, she set upon him, skillfully relieving him of a pocket watch. As she made a play for the purse, however, he noticed her.

"Oy, get off! I ain't interested," he barked, assuming she was a streetwalker.

"No harm trying." She grinned.

He made a disparaging gesture and staggered up the street.

She held up the watch, squinting at it in the dim light.

"Not quite nine." Eamon helpfully announced from behind her.

His hand was on her mouth as she whirled around, muffling her startled scream. His gentle smile and soulful eyes calmed her. But they were also intriguing. There was something about the smile that suggested a man who was not entirely innocent. She liked that. She also liked how well dressed he was. If she could inveigle him somewhere private and distract him, she could probably walk away with a month's haul.

Centuries of experience with stalking the demimonde told Eamon her thoughts, and they never failed to amuse. The silly pickpocket, like so many before her, did not seem to notice that it was she who was being led somewhere private.

They walked, his hand stroking the small of her back. Shivers ran down her legs. His eyes rarely left her face, and she felt herself falling into them. Nervous, she switched her gaze to his lips, whose curl enchanted her. It seemed almost certain that the strange, seductive sound that had entranced her was coming from them, and if they could make that sort of magic without even touching her, the idea of contact was so enticing as to be unbearable.

How they'd ended up in a dark, deserted corner, she neither knew nor cared. She liked the feel of him, liked the feel of herself with him. His hands, pulling her body into his. And that mouth, that mouth! It didn't meet her own hungry lips, but teased around her ears and jaw so that her knees were buckling. She felt her entire body turn liquid.

There was a sudden pressure on her neck, something that might be pain except that she wanted more, wanted the heat of his embrace to melt her even further, wanted him to take every last bit of her into that amazing mouth. His fingers were firmly, yet tenderly, massaging her spine and neck, and if she had realized that the effect was to manipulate all her blood down his throat, she still might not have minded.

Eamon carefully lay down the empty body, smoothing the girl's skirt over her knees, although not before using it to neatly dab his lips. He stood, and sighed—the same reflexive action, as so many times before, the body's memory of how to express a twinge of regret. The waste of a life, and yet he needed it to continue his own. A conundrum. Sometimes there was something small he could do, as atonement. He liked that. He searched the girl's jacket carefully.

Ten minutes later, the drunken young man was struggling to fit his key into the lock at his family's house. His mother opened the door with a frown. But the scold died on her lips and her eyes widened at something unexpected over her son's shoulder. The man looked behind him, apprehensive.

A good-looking fellow with a peculiar smile was casually twirling *his* pocket watch. He handed it to the astonished young man.

"I'm feeling generous tonight. You oughtn't drink so much, though. You're going to need your strength for the fight ahead."

And, with a polite nod, he was gone. The young man exchanged a glance with his mother. Suddenly cold, he ducked inside.

It was a pleasant, if long, walk through Camden Town and then up Malden Road on the way to Hampstead Heath. A human would grow weary before even going a quarter of the distance, but vampires liked to stroll. Besides, they could always move faster, if they needed to. It was still early, though, and Eamon wanted to take his time getting home.

On Parliament Hill, he gazed down upon the city, the way he and Brigit had for so many centuries. He still marveled at how it had grown and changed. He adored its lights. Life was there, and adventure, and promise.

The lights in Berlin cannot possibly be this warm.

There were some among the younger vampires who saw the mission as an adventure. Even Mors probably felt that way, Eamon mused. Mors still had a tremendous appetite for danger. It was presumed that creatures of the night fed on danger as readily as they did jugulars, but this was really only true the first hundred years. After that, a vampire made the distinction between danger and risk. Unless that vampire was Mors, in which case it was all wonderfully intoxicating.

Eamon adored risk, too, but over the centuries he and Brigit had become less inclined for it. There was too much else to do. Eternal life opened one to a wealth of possibilities. As a human, Eamon's natural aptitude for music was something he and his family could never dream of affording to indulge, but as a vampire, he'd learned to play the rebec, then the violin, and a small host of other instruments, although his passion was for those two. He liked the feel of them in his hands, and the way the bows danced across their strings. When music hall began to be popular, he had to expand to the piano.

"You just can't play George Formby on the violin, not if you want to get the right expression."

"Or hit the right note." Brigit smirked.

And while George Gershwin lent no end of entertainment to violin experimentation, that wasn't quite the same, either. Piano it was. For some things. Music and Brigit. So long as he had them, he had the whole world in his still heart.

The tribunal made its home in a castle deep below Hampstead Heath. Otonia liked the view, and the fresh air. The current millennials often marveled at how well she had chosen the location, which had been pure wilderness at the time—Kenwood House came later. She had sensed that London would become the center of the civilized world, and she'd spent too many years in the center of things, or waiting for there to be things again, never mind a center, to let events overtake her. So southward from Yorkshire they went, and hadn't had much cause for regret.

Eamon slipped through the hollow tree that marked the castle's entrance. Not that a human passerby would see it was hollow—the vampires had built a cunning sliding door once the Heath became popular for roaming. Even if a human did manage to get in, they would never find the other door at the base of the trunk, or work out how to open it.

The apartment he and Brigit had shared for so many centuries was warm and cozy. Eamon stirred the fire in their book and music room and sank into his own squashy armchair. If he squinted, he could just make out a depression in the cushion of Brigit's chair, still there after a week of emptiness. He hoped it wasn't an illusion.

He opened his latest book, then realized he couldn't remember anything from the last chapter. He didn't want to read anyway. His sketching things were in the corner, but that didn't bear thinking about. There were his instruments.

The only real comforts now, that's what they were. They were his friends, the pretty little piano, the Amati violin, and the rebec, that odd little curio, the precursor to the violin, played while propped awkwardly on the thigh. The instrument that had started it all for him, and for Brigit. They all missed Brigit, too. They were the only ones who really understood.

That wasn't fair, of course. That was selfish. He was restless, so restless. He needed more distraction.

Eamon knew Padraic was probably in the castle library—a library any book-loving human, especially the collectors, would give a ransom just to see. Otonia had stolen books back in her early days, and acquired more as she went along, and others joined her. So works that humans thought lost, or didn't know even existed, could be found in that cool, enormous room. To say nothing of first editions. Also the complete works of Shakespeare. Some folios were even signed by the author.

I don't want conversation, I want . . .

Well, a host of things. None of which he was going to get, not now. He practically snatched the Amati from its rest and cradled it under his chin. The bow purred under his palm.

Where will we go tonight, my friend?

The bow touched the strings, and spun out a memory in melody.

Brigit. Brigit, and the sound of her laugh, the sound of a sudden rain on a midwinter's night. The two of them, skipping and splashing through the Thames, jumping from boat to boat, until many of them cracked. Leaping up to catch onto bridges and daring the lightning to come closer. Mocking it with their own energy and light. Chasing the storm all the way up to the top of the heath. Collapsing on the grass, sides aching, but still laughing. Rolling down the hill. Catching her as they rolled, turning her over so she would land on him and not the muddy ground. Tangling her wet hair hard between his fingers . . .

The Amati played on, a sweet, erotic melody that ran rings around him, chased its way through the castle, lightly touching here and there on open ears, promising the happiest of dreams as the notes flew up and out into the pale air until they hit the faint sun rays just tickling the earth. There, like eddies, they swirled up, up, up . . . and out into nowhere.

Chapter 4

Berlin–Basel train. August 1940.

Brigit took advantage of the prolonged evening train stop to stretch her legs in a brisk stroll around the small, well-shaded platform. She bought two bars of chocolate and a newspaper from the tired-looking newsagent, who did not return her smile, and tucked them into her hard leather Hermès bag. The warmth of the evening was not unpleasant, and she made a point of taking several deep breaths, as though relishing the fresh air. But the only person who noticed her was a harassed young mother shepherding two squabbling little boys—twins, by the looks of them—in crisp sailor suits. The woman seemed to take Brigit's beauty and calm as a personal insult and sneered as she passed her, muttering something unintelligible under her breath.

Fighting back a giggle, Brigit continued her energetic walk. After all, a healthy young fräulein needs her exercise. Get a bit of circulation going. Again, Brigit felt a laugh rising. She wished the demon could swallow it.

It was being out in the air that was making her giddy. It gave the illusion of freedom. She forced herself to concentrate on the soot and grime, the smell of too many cigarettes and sweat under summer tweeds. This was no atmosphere for exhilaration. In as much as she knew she should look at ease, a young woman on a great adventure, she must also look capable and self-contained. A woman with responsibilities, who took those responsibilities seriously. Balance. And balance was something she had worked at her whole life, so she was hardly in new territory.

But I am. Oh, Eamon, I am.

At least this line of thinking squelched all the smile right out of her. The whistle sounded, and, in no mood to wait for the next call, she decided to board at once. The sooner she was out of the air, the better.

At the door to her car, the porter was assisting an elderly, slightly deaf couple with their luggage, and they kept shouting at him to be careful. Another new passenger, a bony young man in dark-rimmed glasses, smiled pleasantly at the old woman and held out his arm.

"May I give you a hand getting on the train, madam?"

The woman recoiled from his arm as though it were toxic.

"Don't you be thinking you can get my handbag, you little rat! Army too good for you, is it? Off on a pleasure jaunt instead of fighting for the glory of the Fatherland? Army knows what to do with rotten thieves like you, mark my words!"

The man blushed and tried to apologize and back away. The porter made a gesture at him over the old woman's head, implying that bad old bats like this were not worth anyone's time or energy.

The bat in question was not yet done with the unfortunate young man.

"Look a bit Jewish, don't you? I thought we were clean of Jews here."

The young man was indignant.

"Perhaps if you weren't going blind you could see I'm Catholic."

The small group of passengers waiting behind the old couple laughed. The woman, seeming to choose not to hear the riposte, carried on abusing the porter.

Deeply irritated, Brigit headed for the next car down. As she got on, she glanced back at the throng and saw the couple finally board. The insulted young man followed, too proud to let the porter take his case for him. Brigit let her senses wash over the man, feeling that he might be a good meal possibility. Worth further investigation, at the least. As she was contemplating this, she caught sight of a middle-aged man in a heavy silk suit carrying a shiny black doctor's bag, who, she was sure, had his eye on her. And something about that eye, its cold and calculating assessment of her and everything about her, made all her organs shrivel. He turned and marched into the train. Two handsome young men in uniform tagged after the doctor like obedient pups, reverently bearing his books and baggage.

Brigit decided to linger in the empty lounge car before going back to her own compartment. She wasn't in the mood to wait in the corridor while the beleaguered porter attempted to settle the cranky old couple. Neither did she feel like getting any closer to that doctor and his eye.

Maybe he wasn't studying me. Maybe he was just staring into space. Middle-distancing.

But she knew that wasn't it. The look was harsher than anything she'd seen in even that Sergeant Maurer's interested, icy face. Harsher, and more triumphant. Which, if it meant what she hoped it didn't, could spell a level of danger she wasn't sure how to navigate. This uncertainty was more unsettling than the doctor's look—she couldn't get used to it. Her faculties were clouded. She would have to eat soon.

Not that it will help much. Damn it.

What would have been ideal was a meal at the station, but she was not alone enough to draw one in, and in any case, there hadn't been any likely candidates. There was a trick to picking someone out in a public place, both the vampire and meal had to be unobtrusive. The prey must give off the sense of a person who wouldn't immediately be missed. It wasn't enough for them to traveling alone, they had to be unnoticeable. Anything else could rouse suspicion. And while her status as an innocent young woman was helpful in case of questions, it slowed her down when tracking food. Men engaged in the business of travel, especially during wartime, had a mind less tuned toward such lively possibilities. Furthermore, she had to be careful using allurements, because someone, like the mother with the twins, might observe the action and thus create a scene. It was all right for Mors, people would expect a silly girl to be attracted to a sexy, smiling man, and if she was later found dead and the man long gone, well, it was her own fault, wasn't it? Her parents hadn't taught her sense. A beautiful woman smiling encouragingly at a man, however, and drawing him away from the public eye, she was more likely to be remembered. It was best not to be spotted when looking for food. Especially given the circumstances.

The body would have to be disposed of. Even to stage a suicide was risky and might delay the train. She would have to find someone traveling alone, wheedle them away somewhere discreet before their stop, eat, and then toss the body out the window once the train was going again. The staff would assume they had disembarked. By the time anyone waiting for them alerted authorities, the train and Brigit would be long gone. As for when they found the body, well, she would just disguise the marks and hope for the best.

She smiled at the lounge attendant, gave him a perfunctory, expected order, and headed back to her compartment. There, she took off her hat, gloves, and coat and sat down to compose herself for the upcoming trial of dinner. She would prefer to remain here, with a door closed behind her, listening to the reassuringly musical breathing of her dangerous cargo. But she knew that those who thought it right she appear outnumbered those who thought it more appropriate that she remain ensconced in her compartment. For now, it was best she please the majority. Their opinion held more sway.

When she knew she could avoid it no longer, she changed her dress, smoothed her hair, and checked that her seams were still perfectly straight. She desperately hated to leave the compartment so unguarded but had little choice.

"I'll be back soon," she announced with determined cool, bolting the door behind her and thinking foolishly of the humanly impenetrable entrance to the castle under Hampstead Heath.

In the corridor, Brigit could smell the maligned young man in his compartment, only three doors down from hers. She smiled, fancying that he was looking for a smarter tie before going into the dining car, as a way of regaining his dignity and establishing his status. Or else waiting until he was sure the nasty old couple would be done eating. Brigit smelled the rest of the car. It was empty. Passengers were eating, or smoking, or playing cards, but no one else was in their compartments. She decided to seize the prospect.

The whisper started low in her throat. It wasn't to seduce, only to intrigue, meant to be felt, rather than heard. A drop cast in water. A sound to start a thought. Not anything rational, or coherent, but the beginnings of a stir that would ultimately be desire.

The door was partly open and she could hear muttering. She tapped shyly. He put his head around and stared at her.

"Yes?"

"Hello. I'm sorry to bother you, but wasn't that just awful with that woman? I thought you handled it brilliantly, I'm sure I'd have made a mess of it. I'm rotten with confrontation, just rotten. I'm Brigit, by the way, how are you?"

Dazzled and flustered, he hesitated, but seemed to grow more confident under the assurance of her bright smile.

"Um, hello. Fine. No, fine. Yes. I'm Kurt. Horrid old woman, wasn't she? Oh well, I suppose we have to be patient with them."

They shook hands. Her throat emitted the tiniest vibration under her hesitant look. It decided him.

"Can I offer you a drink? I have an excellent bottle of schnapps."

"Lovely."

Brigit was amused at how quickly he produced two glasses, as though he'd been expecting to play host sooner rather than later. Very likely, his intent had been to impress a man who might be persuaded to become some sort of patron, as Kurt did not give off the air of a fellow with any knowledge or experience of girls. Polite, yes, but reedy and pale, with too-slick hair and a rather putrid tie. A man who wanted to do well but had a little more money than taste or education.

She clinked her glass to his, her mind ticking over possibilities. She had to ask the right questions, draw out all the pertinent information, assure herself that he was easily disposed of and would arouse no inquiry.

"So, Kurt, since it isn't the army for you, where are you going?"

"I tried for the army, but they wouldn't take me. I've got an irregular heartbeat."

"What a funny coincidence, so do I."

"Really! Well, so I'm going to Paris. I hear they need Germans who speak French to manage businesses, or they will, once the race laws are in place."

He didn't notice her blanch. He nattered on about how he really wanted to be an artist, and was hoping he might open a gallery—she hardly registered any of it.

The race laws. In France. Why should I be startled? If liberté *is quashed, why should not* égalité *follow?*

Kurt had opened a sketchbook and was proudly narrating the thread of his artistic journey and boasting of his skill. Brigit oohed and aahed admiringly, glad that Eamon couldn't see the drawings. He would have killed Kurt just for their rottenness. Eamon was, in addition to his brilliant musicianship, a very fine artist. He drew likenesses of all the vampires in the tribunal and everyone said there was no need for a reflection when you had one of Eamon's drawings.

"I've always loved the Paris galleries." Brigit smiled. "I'm sure you'll do well there. Not that I know art, I mean, but I think yours is awfully good."

"It's all a matter of opinion. A fine, educated young lady like yourself, of course, appreciates the better things in life. You know what's attractive."

"Do I?"

"You must. You see it every time you look in the mirror."

She giggled, an embarrassed girl.

Bloody men. He knows he is no man if with his tongue he cannot win a woman, and thinks an obnoxious dollop of flattery will get the gold.

"I can see you're refined," he went on. "You've probably gone to opening nights and salons and all the best concerts. And dined and danced in some of the finest places afterward, haven't you?"

He was wandering into jealous waters, wanting her, but wanting her wealth and privilege more, suspecting that she took it for granted. He knew the difference between an English girl and an Irish girl, and that the Irish one, for all her money and beauty, knew what prejudice was, had suffered indignities. But his well-trained arrogance trumped any innate empathy, and he was certain she didn't know real injustice, nothing like what he and his friends and family had endured during the Weimar years.

Mortal fool.

Another tiny vibration in her throat settled him. He reverted to pure enjoyment of the charming creature smiling at him with such strange, sparkling eyes.

Brigit was reaching for him now, the demon millimeters under the skin, fangs barely starting to slip out from under her human teeth, when there was a clamor of loud voices and running feet in the corridor. A sudden shout and a tipsy young man stumbled through Kurt's door, so that Kurt and Brigit jumped and exclaimed.

The man and his friends paused to take in the tête-à-tête and grinned lasciviously.

"Sorry," he chortled with an uncoordinated wink. He backed out and their loud laughter echoed all the way to the next car.

Attempting to recover his aplomb, Kurt downed the last of his drink.

"Can I tempt you to dinner?"

They'd been seen together, and drunk though the young men were, she was still memorable. A new plan must be forged. Brigit forced a grin and rose, patting down the sulky demon.

"Consider me tempted."

The dining car was crowded. They had to squeeze in next to another man, who seemed undisturbed so long as he could continue his steak in peace. But he looked up when Kurt started talking about art again.

"The trouble with the Expressionists is they have no interest in beauty. There's no point in creating art if you're not going to create a thing of beauty. Don't you agree?"

Their dinner companion cut across Brigit to respond.

"It's been a problem with art for years. We're blessed in the Führer, he's clearing out all that degenerate rubbish. Foul stuff. I haven't wanted to take the wife to a museum in years. Who would?"

It transpired, much to Brigit's annoyance, that the man ("Herr Eberhard, and a very great pleasure") had taken over a Berlin gallery and was looking to purchase in Paris. No longer Kurt's first object, Brigit was forced to play the part of the girl caught up in the important conversation of men. They ordered dinner and a bottle of wine, and Kurt smiled at her, a man who could hardly believe his luck.

Brigit's mind was working feverishly. It seemed certain the two men were on the same schedule, and the more they bonded, the more the hope of this meal was dashed. She ate her goulash mechanically, casting trial sniffs throughout the car for anything else likely, and wondering how best to disentangle herself from this pretentious and insulting conversation.

That was when she saw him. The doctor, oozing a confident chill. He ate alone. Ostensibly, he was skimming a medical journal as he lingered over chops and coffee, but she felt his sharp little eyes rising to her.

He's trouble. Just what I need. More trouble.

A sudden heat swelled up inside her—the desire to rouse the demon in full and kill every man in the car. To eat no matter how much it would choke her and then go on and on and on until . . .

Exactly. Until what? You're stuck. You have a job to do. Concentrate on that. Never mind all this rubbish.

If only it were that easy. If only she weren't so alone.

"What do you think, Brigit?"

The interested smile had never left her face, but she had absolutely no idea what Kurt was asking.

"I think it's all simply too marvelous!"

Kurt beamed and turned to his other useful new friend with a triumphant air.

Through the corner of her eye, Brigit saw the doctor finish his coffee and exit the dining car. His eyes never left her, and hardly blinked.

Chapter 5

Berlin. December 1938.

"At least we can still space our meals, to a point. That's something."

Brigit nodded. Cleland was right, it was something. They had to hoard what few blessings there were and guard them carefully. Millennials could go nearly a week without food and still be perfectly sound, although ideally they fed well every four or five days. The band of five was discovering, however, that tension and pressure stoked the appetite. They were pleased to eat more Nazis, although nervous about too many disappearances being noticed. More troubling, however, was the flavor. Nazis were nearly indigestible. The taste of hate was hard to swallow.

But they could still space their meals.

Mors, of course, had the easiest time procuring a good uniform that fit him, but as Cleland pointed out, he'd had extraordinary luck.

"When a major from Freiburg decides to get stinking drunk and collapse alone in an alley on his first night in town, he's really just begging to be eaten, isn't he?"

So Mors was lucky, because no one had yet met the major, but the photograph on his identification card was harder to alter than expected. Thus far, he'd managed to avoid having to show it to anyone, but he wanted Swefred to hurry up and find a way to make the dead man look more like the undead man.

"You couldn't even try growing out some hair?" Swefred grumbled.

"Easier to erase his."

This was true, although it was cumbersome. Swefred was interested in technical arts and had developed a fascination with photography. Which, of course, was useless with vampires, so he devoted himself to tweaking pictures and the results were often interesting. He was sure he could alter all the identity cards they were able to steal to look well enough like each of their own selves, it only required more time—time they weren't sure they had. Brigit and Meaghan had mingled their way into several parties, and from what little they could glean, determined that the Nazi machine was even more well oiled than the refugees had described.

Mors thought it was very inconsiderate of the major whom he was impersonating, this Werner, to be in such a restricted sphere as tank warfare. He didn't understand why it limited his prospects—surely he should still be invited to the better evening parties? How else did anyone expect to conduct real business?

At meetings, that was how, and during the day. Times had changed. Plans were not discussed over brandy and cigars at evening parties. Or at least, no plans to which any of them had yet been privy. Women in particular, it seemed, were not much trusted. Women who asked questions, even less so. Confidence would have to be earned, slowly.

A wealthy general was celebrating his daughter's engagement with a party so lavish, it was said he'd spent a Jew's fortune. Which, Brigit suspected, was literal. From what she knew of General Pfaff, he was one of the few truly stupid men in the party. The sort who'd risen to a position of power through a bit of luck and his wife's money. The sudden acquisition of a factory could only be due to the Jewish owner's hasty flight from Germany. Brigit took some comfort in the assumption that the general's utter lack of management skills would spell the end of that bit of fortune for him within a year.

In the meantime, he was currying favor with a choice guest list, which worked well for all the millennials. The males were going to scope out wives who looked bored and might be susceptible to delicate attentions, the females were looking for men who might be on the rise and open to the possibility of a mistress.

Brigit was glad the party was not a formal seated dinner. They could circulate with abandon and she could wear a cocktail dress, rather than a gown. That was one thing she really liked about this new century, as problematic as it had been. Fashions had changed to allow her to show off her magnificent legs. What with the curving high heels, the seamed stockings, and the silk dress that danced around her knees, she knew any man who ran his eye up one of those seams would follow it in his mind as high as it went.

The humans may be more ruthless than they were in 1914, but the clothes are better.

She carefully ran a bone comb through her silky curls and guided mascara over her lashes. As ever, she smiled to herself at the reaction a human woman would have to the prospect of grooming without a mirror. Indeed, grooming was one of the first things female, and even male, new ones fretted about, and yet it was so easy. The reassurance of beauty was all that was needed to keep one happy; liberation from the reflection was generally welcomed once accepted.

"When you can't see yourself, you begin to see yourself," Otonia liked to say in her enigmatic way.

Mors preferred to be more blunt.

"I know I look fantastic, what more proof do I need?"

Brigit's human community had been tiny and rugged and no one there even knew what a mirror was. She had only ever seen herself in water before her making. It wasn't until Eamon had drawn her that she really came to know her own face. A curious sensation, seeing herself again after so many centuries. Blond, blue-eyed, curling pink lips and strong white teeth—of course she was a natural for this mission.

"Trust an ancient Briton to look like an ideal German fräulein," Otonia laughed.

As a going-away gift, Eamon had drawn a new picture. The two of them together, tiny smiles playing around their lips, deep love in their eyes, even though they were gazing out rather than at each other. One might almost think there was something fascinating that was more worth their attention, but the way their eyelashes touched, their hair mingled, betrayed the real truth. When all was said and done, they were for each other only and always. Eamon drew his face from memory, a good memory for one who hadn't seen that face in nearly 750 years. A beautiful face. More than beautiful—compelling, even mysterious. Brigit had memorized that face over centuries now, and still saw something new whenever she looked at it. She liked that.

They each took a different route to get to the general's house. When Brigit arrived, the only one of their group she spotted was Mors, who was chatting outside with two SS privates. They seemed to be manning the entrance to the party, which struck Brigit as at once extreme and laughable. They were not asking for identification, but they were consulting a guest list. To their credit, they looked abashed by the absurd duty. Trained to defend the Fatherland, and here they were acting like doormen at a first-night gala, with only an Alsatian to lend them an imposing air. Brigit wondered if they were being paid. She assumed Mors's Major Werner was on the list at least; he was distracting the men so the other four could enter unmolested. Or perhaps he was genuinely interested in the dog who, far from being ferocious, was lapping at Mors's hand as though the vampire had offered him bacon.

It was a curious thing, Mors's rapport with dogs. Part of his inimitable legend. The vampire mythology often had it that other creatures of the night, both real and imagined, ranged with the undead, but it wasn't true. For one, none of the imagined creatures existed, for another, foxes and owls and other such nocturnal beasts kept a respectful distance from the vampires. They had their own quarry to hunt, and their own path. They knew the undead for what they were. Besides which there was an unwritten contract: Beasts do not keep other beasts as pets. As ever, Mors was different.

He loved and respected dogs, and they him. His affection was for the unwanted mixed breed he could rescue either from a life of servitude or a painful death. Dogs thrived under his care, and lived many years longer than they should, ranging at his speed, loving the night. No one knew how he did it, surely he could not gift them power? Brigit had always wanted to ask, but kept her counsel.

Still, every twenty years or so, the dog would die. The vampires wondered how Mors could bear it, bonding so closely to creatures to whom he would, too soon, have to bid good-bye. His swaggering insouciance made some think it didn't touch him, but the love he showed his pets was real, so whatever happened in him when one turned and took its final separate path was for him alone.

"Get in here!" Cleland's directive, echoing in her skull, roused Brigit from her reverie and she ambled up the steps, quite unnoticed.

Slipping into character, she hesitated at the door, looking around nervously as though for a female friend she was to meet. Her eyes accidentally met those of two young men ogling her appreciatively. She gulped hard and looked down, smoothing her skirt over her hips in a manner guaranteed to make them notice just how invitingly curvy those hips were. Turning from them, she feigned surprise at the smiling appearance of a square-faced colonel bearing two glasses of champagne.

"Good evening. I saw you standing here alone and without a drink and thought these two afflictions must be immediately remedied."

"How kind of you! Thank you so much."

"You sound like a Heidelberg girl."

"Do I?" she answered, an artless girl playing at being mysterious.

Heidelberg, hm? Well, that's handy.

The Roma claimed that a vampire's mastery of many languages and fine arts was part of the evil magic of the demon. The tribunal was more of the opinion that once your mind was relieved of the minutiae and shackles of human life, it expanded to its full potential and allowed you, if you were so inclined, to dive headlong into education and erudition. There were vampires who were better read than the greatest human philosophers could ever hope to be, although the vampires were fully aware of their unfair advantage.

The millennials happily pressed that advantage, speaking flawless German in accents that did not betray their roots. The colonel was nattering on and on about his one day in Heidelberg and the hills and the castle and the beautiful countryside. Brigit sipped her champagne and wondered if he was the sort to let a girl get a word in edgewise.

"I'm a Bavaria man, myself. We're a hearty lot, love music."

"Oh, so do I!"

"Do you play and sing?"

"No, neither. I just love to listen."

"A perfect audience."

He gave her a repugnant wink. A stout woman wearing something that looked like an evening dirndl waddled up and slipped her arm through his, smiling beadily at Brigit.

"*Grüss Gott*. I am the colonel's wife. Have we met? You look unfamiliar."

Good.

"I am Brigitte, madame, and pleased to meet you. Your husband was just saying how much he loved music."

"Ah. Was he? How lovely."

The colonel flushed, and Brigit enjoyed the seed of discord she'd planted. Even a colonel can't give his all to his country when he's trying to prove to his wife that he's as faithful as ever.

Brigit wondered, however, if perhaps she was wrong about these priorities when a general cleared his throat to get the colonel's attention. The general jerked his head toward a corridor and the colonel extracted his arm from his wife and barely looked at either unimportant woman as he marched after the general.

Left alone, there was nothing to say. The colonel's wife looked Brigit over, concentrating on her legs and breasts. Brigit smiled pleasantly, which made the woman shudder and, with a quick nod, a vestige of politesse, hurried back to the little clique of wives that Swefred and Cleland were attempting to amuse, with what Brigit noticed was only middling success. Thus far.

Helping herself to a canapé, Brigit stopped to be amused by a spotty boy, perhaps seventeen, who was being far too familiar with a bosomy waitress. The uncomfortable waitress bustled to Brigit's side and almost begged her for an order. The boy gave Brigit a supplicating look she couldn't understand—surely he knew she would side with a pestered female?

As she looked down her nose at him with haughty amusement, she caught a whiff of the stake in his modified crossbow. Nachtspeere. This almost-child following whatever direction his hot loins led was a Reich hunter. Brigit held his gaze longer, allowing him any opportunity for recognition. There was none, and she sensed he was carrying the stake out of nostalgia, because Berlin was clean. Furthermore, he was only in attendance as a courtesy to his fond supervisor. Brigit narrowed her eyes—the hunter's skin mottled under her pitiless sneer. He looked down and slunk away.

He does not know me. He has absolutely no sense of what I am.

The boy tried to save face by joining in conversation with Mors and two other men. After what looked like several unfortunate sentences that were wearing patience thin, Mors turned and caught her eye.

He knows none of us. They have not studied the legends, not to any use.

The pleasing knowledge that the British millennials were such total strangers to the Nachtspeere was only a small compensation for the sudden lack of valuable targets. Brigit wandered the dining and drawing rooms, sipping at her drink and giving halfhearted sniffs here and there, as though prowling for food. The corridor down which her colonel had disappeared was dark and tempting. She affected fascination with the unnecessarily graphic hunting prints lining the walls and studied each one with great care, clearly not noticing she was drifting farther and farther away from the allotted festivity space.

The door was left carelessly ajar, as though certain that no one who was not invited to this far more private party would ever dream of crashing. There were twenty-four men gathered, with cocktails, and they seemed to hew to the old idea that the business of domination was to be discussed at parties.

"If the Führer says Poland rightfully belongs to Germany, I shan't argue. The countryside is marvelous. Shame about the people, though. Rotten workers."

"Exactly what the Führer says. So we shall remind them that they are in fact German, and they'll start working again. They'll work as if their lives depended on it."

"Which they will."

Good-natured laughter greeted that smiling comment, and drinks were refilled.

"How we ever could have lost Poland in the first place is beyond me."

"Having so many Jews in Germany made us weak. We won't make that mistake again. It will be good to have more breathing room."

"We'll need it for all the children the Führer wants us to have."

A florid middle-aged officer popped open a champagne bottle and sent the cork sailing across the room. It landed at Brigit's feet as surely as if it had been a guided missile. She glared at it, but when she looked up to meet the commingled hostility and curiosity facing her, she was the sweetest, loveliest, most artless young fräulein any of them had ever encountered. Her girlish blush and giggle was charming, musical even, and softened nearly every hard eye.

"You must forgive me, gentlemen, I did not mean to intrude, I was only wondering where all the handsome men had disappeared to."

Deeply embarrassed, she blushed again and laid her hands over her pink cheeks, not daring to meet any of the pleased, laughing eyes. Some smiles were indulgent, others, taking note of her curls and curves, were something different. But the diversion, delightful though it was, still needed to be removed. An officer nodded to a younger man, assigning him to the duty. The man gave one brief, courteous nod in response and turned to Brigit.

"Permit me to guide you back and get you a fresh champagne."

She giggled and took the proffered arm, allowing her thumb to brush his wrist so quickly, it was surely an accident. She sensed the shiver deep inside him, and was pleased.

His name was Gerhard, and he smelled of ambition, which in itself was nothing unusual for young men in Berlin, but there was a particular air of determination in him, something that might be described as fangs. He was certainly looking at her as though he'd like to eat her. She suspected it was less because of her perceived tastiness than his push for greatness. A woman like her, such a visible prize, would be a boon to parade. Ambitious, unattractive men always gravitated toward the most beautiful women. And Gerhard was unattractive. Brigit wondered how much even his mother loved his sharp-boned face. He held his shoulders back in an unnatural stance that was probably meant to convey authority and a soldier's power, but it was clear his main hope was for no one to see how scrawny and concave his chest was. His blond hair was dull and lank. His almost-white eyebrows rendered his face nearly featureless. They were thickest around his nose, and here they tilted up most unfortunately, giving him the look of a perplexed peach. His eyes were small, and there was so much eager acquisitiveness in them, no room was left for cheer or warmth. Gerhard bore the look of an efficient paper pusher, not a candidate for the inner circle, but his mind was quick and his manner ingratiating without being oily. His success with women was nil, but he knew exactly how to work a man to curry favor and had set himself well on the path to greatness, regretting only that it must be so tediously slow.

Brigit could hardly believe her luck. He was in the Ministry for Weapons, Munitions, and Armament and must be privy to the sort of documents that could prove useful. Gerhard would be easy to work, she could tell. She would hardly have to expend any strength at all. He handed her a glass of champagne and she let her fingers touch his as she accepted it, with what could only be interpreted as greater intent.

He left her at the threshold to the ballroom, where she was tickled to see Swefred, Cleland, and Meaghan all dancing with what looked like sure bets. Even better, Mors was talking to a captain, who had arrived late and was greeted by Gerhard. Gerhard smiled at Brigit.

"I shall see you soon, then, Brigitte?"

"I look forward to it."

There was no question of Mors accompanying the two men back to the circle of power. Brigit was proud that he looked smarter in his uniform than any other uniformed man there—and no one could miss it.

It's called panache, you fools. And you'll never have it, even if you live two thousand years. You have to be born with it.

Mors turned his head just enough to meet Brigit's eye, and winked. Her grin was broad and she couldn't resist whispering something only he could hear:

"Knock them dead."

They compared their various successes back at the lair. Mors, of course, had gained acceptance and respect, and the men he'd talked to had laughed so hard at his jokes, they hadn't noticed his evasion of their questions. Cleland had enchanted the restless wife of a junior propagandist. Swefred had befriended several important journalists. And Meaghan was being hotly pursued by a rising star in the Reich Chamber of Culture. Brigit laughed scornfully when she heard that.

"Culture! They've chased out all their best artists and musicians, how much work could there be to justify an entire Chamber?"

"He says they are very busy." Meaghan sniffed defensively.

"Probably hunting down more artists to send into exile."

"No, trying to factory-grow new ones to suit the enforced tastes," Mors countered. "They probably keep a cauldron in the cellar—throw in some spices and *phoom*, instant artist. The ultimate alchemy: the creation of creativity. Ah, clever, clever Nazis. Give a stir, and marvelous: a musician! Dip the ladle and out comes a playwright! Dip again and there's an actor, prepared to declaim in a stirring baritone whilst turning out his leg to its finest angle. He finishes with a flourish and oompah, oompah, oompah, the orchestra strikes up a rousing march. Ooh, they do like a good march, don't they? What a delicious concoction. But there's a catch, there's always a catch. These avatars of efficiency forgot a crucial ingredient! Playwright! Actor! Musician! Painter! Curse the luck but don't they need hearts? And souls, yes, in the last analysis, they need souls. This soufflé is doomed to collapse. And that, that is their great failing, isn't it? Ooooh, yes, whatever that Speer fellow may have in mind, the greatest empires are remembered for their culture, and this piddling would-be empire is sadly bereft. Poor deluded things. I'd put them out of their misery now, if I were a kindhearted sort, but it's such fun to watch. And we do need our entertainment in these strange times, don't we?"

Swefred stood, and put an arm around Meaghan.

"Some more than others. The sun's coming up. We're going to bed. Carry on if you like, I'm sure you can go on in this vein for quite some time."

"Oh yes, I can play with myself for hours on end."

Swefred and Meaghan left the other three to their laughter.

Brigit's warm smile lingered in her eyes, even as she shook her head at Mors.

"It's not true, though. You know it isn't. The Roman Empire was perhaps the most powerful the world has ever seen. And they had buildings and sculpture, yes, but nothing like the Greeks. Their plays, their poetry, it was all derivative. No one cares."

"They had fine music."

"No one remembers it."

"I do."

"But that means nothing. You don't count. It's history's count that matters, and by history's count, what made the Romans great was their ability to reach a hand far around the globe . . . and squeeze."

Mors was silent for half a moment.

"I do like you when you're figurative."

She turned away from him and he reached out and took her wrist.

"They won't get the chance. Even if we weren't here, think of how powerful our blessed England is."

A swell of pride rallied Brigit and she grinned at him.

"But we *are* here. England may save her strength."

Cleland spoke then.

"We did well tonight. We made good ground, for them to lie in."

Before Brigit tucked herself up in bed, she pressed her hand tight to the drawing of herself and Eamon, willing it to vibrate warm under her fingers.

Oh, my Eamon. I will play this game like a champion. And I will be home with you. Very soon.

For the first time since Otonia had announced the plan, Brigit went to sleep with a smile on her face.

Chapter 6

London. December 1938.

Even after a third reading, the letter still trembled in his hand. Eamon didn't know why he was so upset. This was the plan, after all, and it was all going forward exactly as expected, so what difference did it make? This Gerhard certainly sounded like a live one, the perfect dupe for Brigit's abilities, and with such excellent connections, the path to success looked golden. And, of course, Brigit would have many ways of working with such a man, ways of making him sure he'd touched her when he hadn't. So there was no reason for Eamon to feel jealous. But he couldn't help it. She would be smiling at Gerhard, talking to him, listening. For purposes of destruction, but still, he would get her attention. And he, Eamon, was not there to be the arms she came home to every day before dawn. If he were at least there, he could be a receptacle for all her frustrated energy. He could bathe her clean with his eyes and his tongue. He could pull her into him so that she would melt. He could keep her safe, and cool.

He tucked the letter into his breast pocket, hoping to stow his vexation as well. Otonia had reminded him that Brigit's control was excellent, that she would manage it all beautifully and he would do well to focus his worry and attention where it could do more good. "Besides, Mors is there. He saved her the first time and could do so again, if it came to it. But I do not believe it will."

Yes, Mors was there. But despite his longer association with Brigit, he did not have that level of connection to her. Eamon, more than two centuries her junior, had been tied to her even before his making. In all these centuries, they'd grown wholly attuned to each other, and he could sense what she was feeling from miles away. If there was trouble, he could be there faster than Mors ever could, despite that vampire's legendary speed. Mors and Brigit were friends, close in a way a human brother and sister could be close, but when Eamon, still as his human self, had looked into Brigit's eyes, he'd seen life there. Hers, and his. Their lives were in each other's guardianship, as surely as was their happiness. And here he was, safe and comfortable and useless in London.

Too moody to think about eating, he resumed wandering the streets. The night was raw and wet, and people scurried from cabs and buses to doors as quickly as they could, struggling to keep umbrellas and spirits intact. Two men were having a heated debate over who had gotten to a cab first, and the disgruntled driver was just waiting for the way to be clear so he could speed off and leave them to their argument.

Eamon watched the men for a moment, then couldn't resist interfering.

"Why don't you see if you're going the same route? You could share the cab."

The driver, interested, turned to gauge the men's reaction.

"Fair enough, just to save trouble. Are you heading Chelsea way?" The more polite of the two waited for a response from his adversary.

The man studied Eamon with a distinctly nasty smile. Eamon realized he'd had a little too much to drink after work, and needed more outlets for his contentiousness.

"Which are you, a Jew or a queer?" asked the man. "You must be one of them, they're the only ones who suggest strange men getting together and saving money."

Both the driver and the Chelsea-bound man were disgusted and took advantage of the other's new showdown to shut the door and drive off. Before there could be any shout of protest, Eamon was in front of him, his gentle smile intimidating. The man hadn't realized how tall Eamon was, how much power was in his shoulders and arms. He wanted to step back, or yell for help, but was frozen to the spot. No one noticed them.

"As it happens, you can't really call me either," Eamon informed him helpfully, His voice singsonged in a cadence that sent a sudden warmth and buzz through the bustling passersby, but left the man feeling as though he'd been clouted round the skull.

"But you shouldn't insult anyone in such a way. You know that, don't you? It's just not polite."

And he pressed his hand on the man's shoulder, nodded, and strolled away through the gathering fog.

Later, though, in the hospital, when the doctors were struggling to repair the man's shattered clavicle, he couldn't remember how he had been injured.

Waste, waste, waste. Eamon clutched the back of his head and swayed precipitously in the winding stairwell leading to the library storage room.

I should not have done that. I should not. He's young enough still, and able-bodied. I'm too upset, it's clouding my judgment. I'm lonely. I'm not good when I'm alone.

Anyone would comfort him, if he asked, would remind him that they were only creatures, that no matter how old and circumspect they grew, this was still the sort of behavior to which they were prone, and besides, it wasn't too terrible an injury and the fool deserved it. Perhaps. But it really wasn't for them to police the human world, to overly interact—it upset the balance.

Except where we have to, of course. That's different.

He hoped.

His insides were roiling. He thought he was going to be sick and pressed his cheek against the cool stone, closing his eyes. A peculiar sort of guilt was coursing through him and he couldn't stop it. It wasn't about the man he'd injured, or his inability to assist on the mission, or the familiar ancient ache, the one that had plagued him with varying degrees of intensity for centuries. It was something new and disgusting to him. Outwardly, everyone knew he was frightened of that strange fire inside Brigit, the one only he seemed to know how to control. But there was another fear inside him. She might change. She might come back and not be his same darling beloved. He was being unfair, he knew it, hence the guilt. But how long, how long could they all eat people so full of hate and fear and anger? With no other variance to the diet, or to the air surrounding them, even if they didn't have to breathe, what might happen? The refugees might never be the same again. Could his Brigit be marked in the same way?

Please, Brigit. We are so right together. We've worked so hard to get to this place. Don't be different. Don't grow from me.

The age difference between them rarely touched him. What was 274 years when they had lived nearly three times that together? It only mattered now, because age gave her a strength he didn't yet have. But he knew where she was weak, too, weaker than he, and who else could protect that?

Then again, what if she doesn't really need me?

Hating himself for that thought, he reached down his shirt and pulled out the ancient locket he always wore. A lock of her hair lay coiled inside.

I know you. I know you so well. Your hair was long and anarchic then and your eyes were wild and you were a lonely, hungry thing. You were buried in darkness and lost in air, as though you were Caliban and Ariel together. You were Brigantia and before that, you were human, and all those years you were searching, searching, and your search ended at my eyes.

He knew. He knew it all. She had opened up her history to him as if from a treasure chest, and he'd absorbed it as readily as though it had been his own. And the parts she couldn't see, he knew through his own powerful inner eye. To replay her from the beginning, to feel the whole of the story, to remember yet again what he knew so intimately, to keep her present, even when far away . . .

He pressed the locket to his lips, and concentrated.

One thousand and twenty-three years before, a tiny Brigante community continued to live in the manner of the ancient Britons, curiously untouched by either Roman or Viking, though the latter was now thriving in the city they called Jorvik, only a half-day's walk away. Whether because their hillside welter of shallow caves and farmlets was too unworthy to settle and tame, or because they were wholly unnoticed, no one knew or cared or discussed. Only some of the names that had blown through with the various invaders stuck in the minds of these people, which is how the prettiest of the younger maidens among them had come to be called Hilda.

No one could have known when she was born how apt the name might be, for there was a hot, warring spirit inside her. Her temper was frightening, particularly because it was so unpredictable. Some wondered if it might be an ill omen, and there had been a few attempts to sacrifice her, if that was perhaps what the gods wanted, but she had outwitted every endeavor. Or, as the elders put it, the gods had intervened. They couldn't understand where such anger had come from, and concluded that her mother must have been too near a fire when Hilda was conceived. The women took care ever since to keep their distance from the flames during such delicate moments.

Adulthood had not improved her temper, although it was noticed that she was as quick with a sharp laugh as a nasty word. At seventeen, her parents were several years' dead and there had been no siblings. People were less afraid of her than they had been—she was just part of the scenery, the prettiest and most interesting part. No man was intrepid enough to disrupt her solitude. Even if she could be chased, she was not one to be caught—she could run faster than even the strongest youth. They admired her, though. She liked to climb trees and stare out over the land. The sun glinted in her golden hair and her eyes were the color of the sky she studied so much. She sometimes seemed not entirely real.

Only the healing woman, Ceana, who had taken some care of her, knew of Hilda's passion for herbs, and especially the things that could grow in the night. Had anyone else known of her creeping about in all that fearsome dark, she would have been banished for sure. But Hilda saw nothing to be afraid of in the dark. Things happened then. There were creatures, some that could never be seen but were wonderful to hear. During storms, there was lightning, which thrilled her to the core. And there were things that grew. Herbs had power. They could chase sickness out of you. Some could even blow away despair with their scent. There was no anger in her when she was among the herbs, coaxing them gently out of the earth.

On hot summer days, she liked to walk to the mouth of the spring that fed their river. She filled a flask with water, to which she then added some sprinklings of rosemary, having discovered it made for a pleasant drink. Then she climbed a tree and looked out at the faint rising smoke that indicated Jorvik. Hilda had little patience for Vikings or, anyway, the stories thereof. For all her temper, she saw no reason for violence until provoked, so men who used violence to plow through the world were automatically distasteful. Still, the idea of the Vikings intrigued her. They had come from somewhere else. They could make things happen. They thrived in a place that the smoke suggested was active, and perhaps even interesting. No, it *must* be interesting. Lively. To step into the city would be to step into a world where perhaps the days were not guided by invariable sameness. If she did not suspect that a lone girl wandering into a city would be instant prey for men of action, she would go directly, without a single regret.

She also wondered what lay beyond the world of the Vikings. There was that other thing she yearned for, that which seemed wholly unattainable. She didn't know the word for love, but knew there was something she needed that was bigger than the city, the river, or the forest. She might have been comforted knowing that poets had written about such desires, even if she was certain she couldn't achieve them. As it was, she only knew that there were moments of joy and longing that she wanted to share with someone who could understand, who could speak a language that went beyond words, and knowing such a person would never be there for her sometimes constricted her heart so much she thought it would burst, and she had to bury herself in foliage, lest her sobs be heard.

This day, however, she only sighed. Tears and wishes made no difference. She walked home slowly, by the river, enjoying the squish of the mud between her toes and the play of sunlight on the water's surface. There were pleasures in her world, and she was not the sort of girl to discount them.

Six months later, a band of Vikings was traveling far too late for a dark winter's day. They stumbled down into the hills, but would not have found the community had it not been the winter feast day and a large ceremonial fire blazing. Perhaps, if no one had screamed, it might not have gone quite as it did. There was food enough to feed the community and a horde of hungry Vikings. But there were screams, there were invocations. A fiery log was thrown. So it went.

Hilda found the sound of screaming repulsive. Why scream when you could fight? What good did screaming ever do anyone? And she swung a log, and the sound of it making contact at the back of the man's head through his matted hair—the thick crunch—was intoxicating. He fell at her feet and she snatched the sword from his fist.

But in the space of a moment, two things happened that changed her course. The blast of fury within her, useful at last, seemed to make sense and almost calmed her with the realization that it was this, this that she wanted. Action. The tininess of this life was what fueled such frustrated passion. She wanted to be out, to be running through the world, doing things. Learning. Living. Actively hunting for something that might be called bliss. There was nothing here for which she wanted to stay and fight. She was meant to fly.

The second thing that happened was that her eyes, glowing with the delight of awareness, were seen. And she saw that they were seen. Only a human girl who had spent so much of her life exploring the darkness could have spotted those eyes. Though she didn't know what they really were, she sensed what they intended. Capture.

No. Oh, no. I have not come to this moment to be tethered like a slave to some brutish man. That is not the life I'm going to have.

So she turned and ran.

For some years afterward, her thoughts often wandered to that run. What she must have looked like, to eyes that could see so much better in the dark than her own. The strong back, the slim waist. Miserly bits of moonlight occasionally flicking over a flash of leg under the ragged cloak. The tangle of golden curls flying straight out behind her as she tore through the woods, as fast as a wild young mare. She was the ultimate temptation, a feral creature whom it would be a pleasure to domesticate. And the attractive look of her was nothing compared with that intoxicating scent. The herbs she grew, the determination and the laughter deep within her, all wafting out like a heady vapor. And, of course, the rage, the searing rage that tickled around her pores and spelled pure allurement for the sort of temperament that had been drawn to her even before she'd swung that log. The scent lingered . . . was the flaxen rope through the labyrinth.

There was a shallow cave near the river, by the place she liked to fish, and it was here she took shelter. Finding it in the dark was nothing, and she slipped inside and headed straight for the mossy corner that formed a pleasant nest. There was a puddle just beside it, and she bent over to splash her face. The drops were still in the air when her distorted reflection startled her. Not because of it, for she had seen her face in water many times, but because it was light enough that she could see. There was a torch. She had been followed.

Her instinct was swift and impressively sure, but his hand clamped around her wrist just as the sword grazed his stomach. The man grinned. He wasn't dressed like the other Vikings, and there was something in his face that made her think he was even more foreign than they were. It was unsettling. She didn't find him attractive, but she couldn't tear her eyes from him. What she could do was glare, and so she did. Whatever he planned to do, there was no chance she was going to let him enjoy it.

"What a funny, volcanic girl you are. Yes, this is the sort of heat one could enjoy for years."

She didn't know what he meant, but the tone was making her want to vomit.

"I'm Aelric. Tell me your name."

"You're going to take what you're going to take, but I will give you nothing."

He seemed to find that funny. Which in turn made her more determined to kill him. He must have sensed it, because he wriggled the sword from her fist and slammed it into the cave's rocky wall.

Hilda had never known fear in her life, but now something prickled under her scalp. That wasn't human strength. There was something else happening here. The night was cold, but sweat pooled under her arms.

He smiled, and it was an unexpectedly sweet smile. Hopeful. He whispered and caressed her in a manner that would melt any artless, impressionable virgin, but though Hilda was certainly a virgin, her nascent fear morphed to amused condescension, combined with scornful resignation. As she had ever expected, this was what it came to. Such stupidity. Such a waste. Wasn't there more than this—somewhere, anywhere? And couldn't he hurry up? All this hot breath at her neck, hands kneading her spine. A new impatient fury welled up inside her. He seemed to be growling, like an animal. She felt as if her organs were expanding and she was going to spew molten rage and she hoped he'd drown in it. She hadn't even felt the bite, and she'd ground her teeth into her inner cheeks so hard, it was her own blood she tasted, more than his, when he'd slashed his shoulder and pressed it into her mouth.

There was but one coherent thought running through her head, pulsing so hard as to overwhelm any other sense:

You won't own me, you won't own me. You'll do whatever you will, but you won't own me. You won't. You won't.

And one final "you won't" was the last human thought she ever had as she dropped into her death sleep.

As with any sort of phenomena, there is a ritual involved in the making of a vampire. A powerful, long-lived vampire is always made under certain laws. Were Aelric even the sort of vampire who listened with any level of attentiveness, he would still not be given to following a prescription, particularly one laid out by Otonia. He stayed with the tribunal only because he innately knew he didn't have the ability to lead a small family of his own, and no reasonable family would adopt such a brash, vain, foolish vampire into their midst. It was only the protection of the tribunal that had allowed him to live some fifty years, and even that was astounding to Otonia.

But nothing was so astounding as the fortune that made the vampire who had been Hilda. There could not have been another lucky star in the universe the whole of those twenty-four hours—it must have all been on her. There were so many chances for her to have gone wrong. Aelric hadn't realized that the heat in her when he'd bit was fury and scorn. And he was almost too late with his blood offering—his blood was still wet on her lips when her eyes closed.

He'd done a poor job of burying her, not paying attention to the rocks in the soil. Digging one's way out of the grave was supposed to be hard—fully half a vampire's virility was gained in that dig—but if it took too long, a vampire could become faint, could even starve to death. But she was strong, and the anger she'd died with was still bubbling inside her, and she impatiently hacked her way through. A vampire should be born with passion, with desire, not anger, but it was the anger and the stubborn soil that combined to give her the strength of a centennial on her rising. The hunger for blood and life was not the delicate interest it should be, but a raging storm, so that when Aelric stupidly held out a hand to help her out of the dirt, she pushed past him, knocking him down.

He tagged after her as she strode with perfect instinct to where she knew food was waiting.

"How about I capture a nice morsel for your first meal?"

It wasn't that he didn't know you're supposed to let your hatchling find their first meal, there was just that in her that made him revoltingly eager to be solicitous. The age-old dance of foolish men and women—the less interested a woman is, the more a man tries to please her. Even a vampire wasn't immune. But she'd carried over her human disdain for help, especially of the male variety. The only answer he received was a snarl, one that couldn't have been more intimidating if her fangs were extended. He finally paused and waited, anxious and intrigued, watching as she descended the hill toward her former home.

Bodies lay scattered about, and the Vikings were still there, drunk and carousing, as though a whole night and day had not passed. One young Viking sat by the fire, peeling burned flesh off a roasted pig—of which there was plenty, now that the community was mostly dead. *Swine for the swine.* The thought made her chuckle, and the chuckle made him look up. He smiled. The leader had said some of the hiding girls would return once they became hungry, and here one was. A slim blonde who might be beautiful under all that dirt and grime. A body of infinite possibilities. Glittering eyes. A bath and an hour or so with a comb, and she'd be quite the tasty tidbit.

"Well, pretty girl, you must be starving."

A shifty smile played across her mouth. He was taken aback.

"You don't actually understand me, do you?"

She did, although not quite as he meant. Still, it was all she needed.

He held out the meat to her.

"Have some. It's fresh. Go on, take a taste."

And she did.

The dig. The meal. The name. These were the formula. Not all vampires chose new names on rising, but even that was a choice, to keep your human name. Your maker might give advice, but only if you asked. This was not like parenting. You were partner to your maker, and that was a different thing altogether. The name you chose marked you, helped you as you grew into yourself. Hatchlings who wanted their makers to name them rarely lasted long.

Some knew this by instinct, but most because their makers explained on the way back to the lair. She knew by instinct, which Aelric ought to have sensed. He suggested she be called Fleta, because of her speed.

She stopped, and looked him in the eye. Now that they were equals, and that she had fed, she could truly assess him. He was weak. Headstrong, sweet, and foolish. His occasional good instincts—and she had certainly been a good instinct—were as nothing to his poor ones, and they were dominant. He had made her in loneliness, for there was nothing in him that invited the trust and friendship, much less love, of the others. He was a member of the tribunal because he was a vampire, because no vampire would ever be forced to range alone, but that was as far as their protection went. She pitied him, but she could see how he would be a hindrance. Her knowledge and self-awareness were expanding by the minute, as though now that she was stripped of the need to take in oxygen, she was instead inhaling the wisdom of the world. It introduced her to a new feeling—giddiness. She felt big, and all-encompassing. She felt like a shout.

"My name is Brigantia."

"What?"

She answered automatically, because it wasn't his voice she heard.

"Brigantia. Our local goddess. You will call me by no other name."

And he would never have dared to try.

To be made was an intimate act, and it was expected that yours would be an intimate partnership. It was meant to be a symbiotic relationship. Perhaps, in time, one would move on from the other, but this was rare. The dark kiss was meant to open the door to deeper, hotter kisses. Just because the blood no longer coursed through veins did not mean it couldn't boil. As surely as maker and made shared blood, they were meant to share bodies.

Brigantia knew her duty, felt her obligation, and wondered, too, if it might make a difference. She suspected not, but thought it would be unfair not to give it a chance. Being a virgin didn't have the same mystical weight for a vampire as it did for a human girl, so there was nothing to make her feel any particular regret for the lack of fervor in her as she rose from her warm bath and threaded her way through the caves to Aelric's nest. No one asks for the dark gift, but once bestowed, it is usually welcomed and received with gratitude. She knew she'd entered something special, and was grateful to Aelric for having chosen her. She just couldn't help wishing someone else had done the choosing.

One lonely candle burned on a table in the corner of the poky cave. Aelric, wearing only a short tunic, took her hand when she entered and pulled her into the candle's light. It took a few tries, but he managed to unfasten her cloak at last and ogled her, his mouth hanging open.

She looked into his eyes and tried to see herself through them. Her only interest in her body had ever been what it could do—its appearance seemed a pointless thing to notice. Now she traced the long sinewy muscles of her legs, the satiny skin, the droplets of water still clinging to the few delicate golden hairs that covered her body and made it seem as though she glittered in the pale light. A flat stomach. Full, high breasts. A long neck. Sturdy arms, powerful shoulders, nimble fingers. His hand reached around and cupped her bottom appreciatively. For his sake, she was pleased her body was enjoyable, but as he inexpertly explored it with first hands and then mouth, a chilling sting ran its way through her like a wasp.

The pain that seared her on his penetration was not a human virgin's pain, not the mixture of hurt and happiness that marked such an occasion when it was its best. What Brigantia felt went far beyond the physical, tugging her skin from behind. She knew what this ought to be, knew it was a sacred, special thing, that her heart should open as readily as her legs, and with the same warmth. But her legs opened only because

Aelric wanted them to, and her body forced warmth against her own in-clination, as protection from further pain. Brigantia thought she would have welcomed more physical hurt so as to anesthetize her from the tor-turous places her mind was journeying. Once again, Aelric stirred fear in her, and this was greater, because she knew her fate was sealed. Every predawn would mean this, mean a giving over of her body that should be a delight and instead only remind her how alone she still was. Alone, and maybe deservedly so.

He nipped at her several times, gently, with his human teeth, a kind of atonement for the other bite, bites that were meant to inflame her passions rather than suck out her humanity, but she noticed none of it. She needed this to be over, before he saw her tears.

After fifteen minutes that felt interminable, he climaxed, groaning across her in ecstatic defeat. The weight of his body, both warm and cool, was not such an unpleasant thing, and she stroked his damp hair with unforced gentleness. Even still, she suspected he knew, or at least sensed, that this was not a coupling of hearts. He was a fool, but he could not be so wholly insensible.

Aelric raised his head to look at her. He'd been so eager. Those curves, that hair . . . he'd thought she was a creature in which to get com-pletely lost. But for all her inner heat, she was inexplicably cold. And yet, when he rolled onto his back, she looked down at him and smiled, and the smile was warm. It was the first tender expression he'd seen on her face, and it made her look so beautiful, he thought he felt his heart beat. Per-plexing creature. She brushed his sweaty hair from his face, patted his cheek, and swept a cloak over her shoulders.

"Where are you going?"

"I want to feel the air."

"It's nearly daylight. You have to be careful. Don't go."

"I will be back."

At the main entrance to the network of caves, she sat, tucked her knees under her chin, and stared out at the dark wilderness. The stars were gone, but the sky was still black. Finally, a chance to think, to absorb all that had happened. There were some whispers of regret. Had she known that the dull morning of two days ago was the last glimpse of the sun she would ever have, she might have paid it more attention. *For as long as I live,*

I must remember that daylight is a beautiful thing. It frightens me, and it will kill me, but I must remember it is beautiful. She knew she would miss seeing blossoms turn toward the nurturing sun, seeing all the true colors of every plant that thrived under her hands, the rainbow gift of nature. And yet, she had always loved her nighttime gardening, touching buds that chose the blackest hours to unfurl. She wondered if something in her human life had known this was coming, was intended, and had prepared her. She had never heard the lore of vampires, but felt curiously unsurprised at her fate. From this realization, her mind played out the monologue of all new vampires, although none of them knew it was a sort of script.

My human self is dead, is gone. Parts of it are still in me, perhaps always will be, but there is a demon there, too. Humans are my lifeblood now, my livelihood and prey. I am solely of the night, from now until always. Until never, whenever that will be, and I hope it is thousands of years away. I would not have chosen this life, but it has chosen me, and I embrace it. I will make this a good life. These are my people now, my family. I am cleaved to them.

But from there, her thoughts took a turn unique to her, and down a path she wished she didn't have to follow.

I have no love for Aelric, though he is my maker. I am grateful for the gift, and even his desire, and I pity him in all his well-meaning and foolishness, and certainly I never pitied anyone as a human, but he is not the one onto whom I can pour all this love that lies so heavily in me, like waste. No. I cannot love him, and I never will. And he . . . he has no love for me. He thinks he does, and that is sweet, but he only loves an idea. He'll never see me, whoever I am now, and whomever I'll grow to be. Have I slipped from light into eternal dark, only to be kept from love? Isn't love the only genuine light in this darkness? Or perhaps that is just my mark. As girl and now as creature, I'm not made for love.

The sky was turning navy. It was time to go. Aelric was keeping the bed warm for her, and that would be pleasant. This was important. Still, as she turned her back on the rising sun and slipped down the tunnel, she wondered how it was that a heart which was no longer beating could feel as though it might break.

Eamon roused himself, wiping his wet face. He hadn't tumbled down the rabbit hole of Brigit's history in centuries, but that world was more vivid than some of his own memories. Her pain pricked him. He wanted to break through the hourglass and rearrange the sands.

He had no envy of Aelric, of the bond he had shared with Brigantia, of the years they shared a bed. Perhaps it would have been different if she'd loved him, but the only thing Aelric had that Eamon would have coveted was the chance to look in her human eyes. And since that would never have been possible, he dismissed it. He knew, too, that it wouldn't have been the same. The deep blue eyes that met his nearly three centuries later had been shaped by life. They were marked less by that hunger and fiery rage than by loneliness. There was a vast knowledge of humanity in them, and a seductive intelligence, and a scintilla of something like terrified hope. Aelric had seen the glow of human life, but Eamon had seen something more. Something which, under his hand, had evolved.

Don't lose that, Brigit. Don't come back without the sparkle.

"Eamon? Are you all right?"

Padraic had come up the stairs and was looking at him, worried.

"I'm fine, thanks. Just musing."

Padraic nodded and held out his hand to help Eamon up. Eamon didn't meet his eye and said nothing as he turned and hurried to his own tower. He hadn't realized how much he'd needed to feel a friendly hand on his, even for a moment, and he wasn't entirely sure he could bear it.

Chapter 7

Berlin–Basel train. August 1940.

A heat wave had rolled over the land. Brigit could feel her hair starting to go limp. She couldn't remember ever being so hungry and uncomfortable. The demon was restless, anxious, clawing away at her tissues. There was nothing else for it. The time had come to take a risk.

The water in the tiny bathroom remained stubbornly warm, but she flicked some over her neck and arms anyway, telling herself it provided relief. There was the problem of leaving the cargo unguarded yet again, but that could not be helped. The time was long past when she could space her meals. Any more of a drain, and she'd be as delicate as the cargo. Tucking her hair in a snood and sticking a defiant silk camellia behind her ear, she strode out of the compartment.

Had she not been feeling so unwell, her knees probably wouldn't have buckled so visibly when the blast of light from the sunset hit her right in the eyes on exiting. The blinds were usually lowered this time of evening to prevent glare, but someone had raised the one outside her door. The light seared her skin and the demon roared, nearly popping out her fangs. She ducked her head and groped for the blind, lowering it quickly.

Dabbing her brow and trying to regain her composure, she sensed a faint odor but saw no one nearby. She felt sure it must be the doctor, but she had no idea why. These people prided themselves on logic, and where was the logic in sending a doctor after her? If that was what they were doing. There were other possibilities. Who could have described her well enough to make her a target with such unerring precision, she couldn't imagine, but it seemed safest to think they had guessed and were trying to garner absolute proof before closing the trap.

Well, where are you then, little cowards? I have just shown a great weakness, aren't you pleased? Don't you want to dance round me like a funeral pyre?

She stalked down the corridor, fury and hunger pounding in her ears, her fingers twitching, wanting something to rip. Kurt was not in his compartment, and she suspected him of being closeted with that Eberhard swine, happily planning their meteoric rise through the art world. Deciding that caution could be carried only so far, she added their deaths to her list of things to accomplish before finally getting off the train. There would be leisure for a plan, once she could think properly. Once she . . .

"Fräulein!"

Maurer strolled up to her, grinning. A stuffy woman in an absurd hat sniffed as she shuffled around Brigit, and cast a glance at the sergeant that suggested he should not waste his time paying attention to such trash. Maurer took no notice; his eyes were firmly fixed on Brigit. They glittered.

"Are you enjoying your journey?"

His voice was polite and genuinely interested. Brigit was thrown. She had no idea what to make of him. She decided it was best to play along, and play up her assumed role: a spoiled, silly girl. The sort he was bound to get bored of sooner rather than later.

"I am, but it's taking quite a bit longer than I had thought. These stops are awfully long. Shouldn't we have reached Switzerland already?"

"Indeed, indeed, deepest apologies, but you must realize how much caution must be taken, how carefully papers and even luggage must be checked. There is a war on, you know, and there are spies amongst us. We cannot be too careful. And I'm afraid those British have managed to damage some rails with their bombs. That is slowing us considerably."

Brigit found herself in the odd position of cheering her native country and being cross at the timing of its prowess.

"Yes, but I thought surely the German trains would be efficient, even during a war. I might as well have cycled to Bilbao!"

"That would have been something to see."

"Another time, maybe I will. But really, it's so miserably hot, I can't think about such a venture too long, even as a joke."

"Yes, the heat is bad. Wouldn't we all be happier if we could wear less clothing?"

Brigit had no more energy to create a blush, but she spoke with proper outrage.

"Sergeant Maurer! I'm afraid that's really no way to talk."

"Come now, Fräulein. Girls who dine with artists are known to be open-minded."

A giggle threatened to burst from her cheeks, and she quickly twisted it into a snort.

"Perhaps in Germany, but that's hardly the case in Ireland."

Her modulated tone lessened the insult and made it sound instead like an apology for her poor, benighted island nation. There was, however, still a warning glint in her eye. To her shock, it seemed to arouse him—he grasped her wrist and jerked her up against him, hissing in her ear.

"You should let me in your compartment, let me take a bath with you, that will keep you cool, if indeed you're not cold already."

"How dare you!" She made to pull from him and he wound his other arm around her back, gripping her hip.

"You should be careful, you know, you and your little friends. Perhaps if you're nice to me, I can take care of you. Wouldn't you like that? Wouldn't you like me to take care of you?"

"I can take care of myself well enough, thank you. Myself and others, I'll have you know."

"I know that's what you think. But you may think wrong."

"I'll take that under consideration. Now, if you'll excuse me . . ."

The sound of running feet and giggling children startled them both, and he pushed her away from him. They stood, glaring at each other as a small cluster of boys ran past them, followed by their flustered nurse, who was feebly calling to them to stop and please behave like nice children.

When the ruckus had safely descended into the next car, Maurer caught Brigit by the chin, jerking her head so she looked in his eyes.

"You are being watched. You're intelligent enough to know that, I think. So perhaps you should be asking yourself whom you want watching you: them, or me?"

"Oh, so I have options?"

"Things can be arranged."

With a greedy sneer, he ran a finger down her throat, dangerously close to where, by all rights, a pulse should be pounding. She bore her eyes hard into him, struggling to keep his concentration on other possibilities. He winked, pulled away, and strutted down the corridor, whistling off-key.

I swear, if I stayed in the bath for a year, I would never wash off the feel of all these monsters.

Shaken and nauseous, Brigit limped toward the observation car, desperate for fresh air, hoping that the platform's awning would provide enough shade from the lingering sunlight. She found the nurse and the rowdy boys waiting impatiently for a table in the dining car. One boy set up a shout as Brigit passed, making her jump. The other boys laughed with gleeful malice and the nurse smiled a grim apology. Brigit could see that the woman hoped to engage her in conversation, yet no matter how sympathetic she might feel, she simply could not marshal the strength or wits to equal the effort. Luckily, another of the boys shouted, hoping to see the pretty lady jump again, and the nurse set about rebuking them all.

"Excuse me," Brigit muttered, hoping she sounded rueful about making an escape, and carried on toward the back of the train. Since the chastened boy's flat "sorry," addressed more to the floor than her back, would likely not have been heard by a human woman, she felt safe ignoring it.

The observation car was blessedly empty and the train had just turned enough so that they were heading southwest and Brigit could contemplate the gathering dusk behind the train at leisure. She supposed she could thank Maurer for the slight delay that guaranteed this advantageous position, but she thought she might have dropped her sense of humor somewhere along the line.

What had he meant, the insinuating toad? His words ran in a continuous loop through her exhausted brain. "Cold already," "little friends," "being watched," well, that last was unnecessary information. But "if you are not cold already"—a stupid phrase if she'd ever heard one, and yet laden with portent. He was surely hinting, although he may have been referring to the coldness of a girl who rebuffs a man's advances, who won't bestow even a light kiss where it seems due. That must be it, she reasoned, because otherwise he was at once attempting to seduce and threaten what he knew to be a vampire, and no man in his right mind . . . On the other hand, she was being watched for several good reasons, and he might know how tied were her hands, how incapable she was of unleashing the demon. As such, perhaps she was irresistible, perhaps the idea of touching a body so full of power, otherworldliness, one that reached back through wave upon wave of history was a temptation worth giving in to. Perhaps.

And what of the groups of people watching? "Them or me"? Which set of "them" did he mean? His superiors? Unseen operatives? Or did he know of the doctor and his attendants?

And "little friends." A phrase that made her feel the chill in her blood. She would like it to mean Eamon, or Mors, or Cleland. The entire tribunal. The demon inside her, however numerically inaccurate that was. Anything but the obvious. Anything but the precious, precarious cargo. The one thing she was determined to protect that couldn't protect itself. If Maurer, if anyone, had a thought that meant compromising the safety of that cargo, there was nothing she would not do. The thought of his hands on her body made even the demon want to vomit, but if it had to be that, instead of his bloody death, she would do it.

It's too much, it's too much, it's too much. How am I supposed to go on?

She filled her lungs with a mass of arid air, held it, then expelled it over the countryside. The act brought no relief.

Too bad there isn't a finite amount of oxygen in the atmosphere. At least I could take pleasure in stealing someone's breath.

Eamon's music, that's what she needed now. If he were here, he would play and sing a song to clear all the cobwebs and chase the fears of impotency and doom right out of her. She hummed softly, in her own unmelodic way, searching for a thread of Eamon's magic lingering somewhere inside her. It was gone. She'd used it up.

The door slid open behind her and a sturdy, broad-shouldered woman strode onto the platform. Her lips were pursed and her neck was thick, giving her the impression of a fish. On seeing Brigit, she smiled widely.

"Not so hot this time of day, is it?" Her manner was eager, a woman desperate for sisterly companionship.

"It's a bit better, yes."

"I think there might be a lake, where I'm going. I'll like that, I've always wanted to spend time at a lake in the summer, see."

"You don't know where you're going?"

The woman brayed with laughter.

"No, this wasn't exactly a planned trip."

She leaned in confidentially, clearly bursting to share her story with someone, and who better than a complete stranger?

"My fiancé sent me a letter from Bern, see. Well, my former fiancé, I ought to say. I knew he wasn't interested in fighting, see, but I didn't realize he'd go so far as to leave Germany. Don't mistake me, I liked him for his cowardice. You'd have to be mad to marry a man ready to go off and be killed, is what I think."

"But surely the war will end soon, and there's no danger of anyone else being killed?"

The woman's expression was fond, as of one who knew the way of the world.

"You're young, of course. I'm twenty-six, see, and I've seen some things. My name is Elsie, by the way, what's yours?"

"Brigit."

"Irish, aren't you? Lucky you, coming from a neutral country," she carried on blithely, not noticing Brigit's quick bristle. "Well, the Führer hates war, of course, but those horrid Jews are having to complicate everything. It's only because of them that more fighting is happening. Them and the communists, of course."

Brigit studied Elsie's oily face and pale, piggish eyes. They held that damn spark of certain superiority. This pathetic woman, abandoned by what was no doubt a relieved man, must know somewhere inside herself how worthless she really was in the grand scheme of things. But no, the

Nazis had lifted that burden from her in their bizarrely magnanimous manner. Brigit ran her tongue under her teeth, feeling the tips of the fangs start to descend.

Elsie chattered on, as though Brigit had asked her a question.

"So sure, Jews should be able to be destroyed easily enough—I don't know why the Führer doesn't just set my granny on them, that would be something to see, all right, but what I really mean is that too many men will be taken away from their duty to us women. I want a quiet life on a farm. I want to raise lots of children, not because the Führer says we should, but because I like the idea of it, always have. All this needs a steady man, you see? A strong, hardworking man who takes care of the business side of things and takes care of me and all of us. If you have a man like that, you'll never be hungry, see?"

Brigit had a brief vision of a brood of empty-faced, empty-headed children waddling around after Elsie. The fangs slipped another millimeter.

"But surely, if your fiancé has left you . . . ?"

Another braying laugh rolled out of Elsie. Brigit could smell old onions on her breath.

"I just didn't want him to have the last word, see? Saying he'd only ever agreed to it because his mother liked mine, but now she's dead and he could do what he pleased and was damned if he'd marry a fool cow like me. He wanted a new life, is what he says, see, and whatever it says about him, running off from a fight, well, it's his life, isn't it? I'm amazed the Swiss let him in, but apparently he's already married to this girl, and how he managed that, well, I can't think, but if he's not mentioned me, she's going to get a bit of a shock, I think!"

Elsie's beady eyes were twinkling.

"What does your family say about this? They couldn't have just let you go off after him all on your own, and during a war, no less."

"Oh, the war. That's just over England now, isn't it? But I didn't tell them, why should I? They'd have tried to talk sense into me, and that's never been worth anyone's time and I'm quite right anyway. Besides, I'm not going to go back. Whatever he's done, he's done, but I'm sure I can find me some young Swiss farmer who likes the look of a girl who isn't afraid of work, see?"

Brigit saw. No one knew where Elsie was going and no one was expecting her. She'd aroused no interest on the train and was not memorable enough for anyone in her compartment to notice if she didn't come back. Or, by the time they did, for anything to be done. There was nothing appealing about her as meals went, but she was, essentially, being handed over on a platter.

The demon couldn't even be bothered to turn Brigit's eyes red. The fangs flew out and Brigit clamped her hand around Elsie's mouth, although it wasn't really necessary, as Elsie didn't even have time for a gasp of surprise before her fat neck was pierced and the blood started pouring into Brigit's dry, desperate mouth. Brigit ate like a greedy child, swiftly sapping the strength out of Elsie so that she hardly struggled at all. Brigit dug in deeper, clutching at her prey as if hoping the blood might seep in via her pores. The taste was not so terrible as might have been expected, and the strapping girl was full of decent blood. When Elsie was dry, Brigit closed her eyes, feeling the blood coursing through her, replenishing her brain, her skin, her senses. Plumping her up. It was not the full and pure restoration she would have liked, but she never expected that. It was, however, a relief. She wiped her lips on Elsie's collar and took a long breath. This time, the oxygen took hold and calmed her. For the first time in days, she felt a little bit like herself.

Quickly, she tended to the body. Popping a talon out from under her fingernail, she slashed at the bite wound so that it looked like a knife attack. The bloodstains on the collar might prevent anyone from examining the rest of her blood, although probably not, but Brigit couldn't spare that a thought. She heaved the body over the railing and down an embankment. It bounced through the trees and landed in a pile of brush. With luck, it would not be found for several days, and the work of the weasels would hamper the investigation. Elsie's small bag had dropped to the floor and Brigit riffled through the contents. It held only some papers, a compact mirror, and a hopeful lipstick that had seen nearly no use. Brigit used it now, even knowing the color was not ideal, then crushed it between her palms, sifting the powder onto the tracks. The mirror followed. The papers she tucked into her jacket pocket to be wetted and destroyed in private and the bag she flung with gusto into the air, knowing it would land in the next county. A quick hand over her hair assured she was groomed as per usual and she slid the door back open, feeling quite equal to whatever new hurdle this maddening journey was going to present.

Brigit's renewed strength and confidence wobbled precipitously as she reached her own corridor and saw three men outside her compartment door. One of them turned at the sound of her heels and muttered something to the other two. The stoutest moved forward, a courteous smile on his face, his hand extended in greeting. It was the doctor whom she mistrusted with such a passion.

"Good evening, Fräulein. I am Doctor Schultze. I hope I did not startle you. I have been wanting to speak with you for some time now."

"Have you? And you thought it was acceptable to come to my door, when we might so easily have chatted in a common area?"

It was more of a remonstrance than a snap, because this girl's inclination, however supercilious she may be, was to look on most men with a friendly eye, at least until they gave her reason to look otherwise.

"I thought perhaps a bit of privacy would be appreciated. But yes, that was presumptuous of me. I hope you can find it in yourself to be forgiving."

There was no discernible sarcasm in his smooth and overcareful English, and his smile was perfectly pleasant, but it was all such an obvious ruse. Or perhaps the doctor didn't know that, with the proper proximity and faculties, she could sense that his lackeys were hunters-in-training, which put a whole different gloss on the situation. She sometimes forgot how little they really understood of her abilities. It was an advantage, and she had to embrace advantages.

At least it's only me they're after. That's something.

Although as to that, she couldn't be sure. The main thing was to expect that all possible disasters were on the table, that way she was less likely to be surprised.

"I was actually on my way to get a drink, Doctor. Perhaps you'd care to join me? You and your friends?"

It was only with the greatest effort that she didn't refer to them as "little" friends. He glanced at the two men, as though only just remembering they were there.

"How very rude I am being! It must be chatting to a pretty girl that does it, for I ought to have introduced my young interns straight away. Weber and Lange, and they are as ready to be at your service as am I."

Each man shook her hand, and she wondered if they were assessing its temperature.

The joke's on you, little men, because between the weather and the meal, I'll feel human to the touch for days.

"And, I am so sorry, but may I ask your name?"

"McRae. Brigit McRae."

"So very charming to make your acquaintance, Fräulein McRae. Let us indeed repair to the bar. Unless, of course, there is anything you wish to do inside your compartment first?"

"No, nothing that can't wait."

Weber and Lange exchanged glances, but tagged behind Brigit and the doctor obediently.

The doctor waited until Brigit had swallowed some of her wine before starting to explain his purpose.

"The fact is, Fräulein, I noticed that you seemed unusually pale and drawn for one so young and rich and of a healthful weight. It is presumptuous of me, of course, but I could not help but be concerned. Perhaps you are under a great strain?"

His smile was solicitous, but the absurdity of the lie made her want to pop out a claw and rip off his unctuous face. Which, she realized, was the idea. Not the face ripping, but the claw. They wanted evidence. She wondered why they didn't try to stake her then and there, without these nonsensical preliminaries, but undoubtedly they had something bigger in mind. A capture, a public execution, or something else, something diabolical. If there was one thing she'd learned in the last two years, it was that these Nazis did not tend to think small.

That they didn't know how to best weaken and overpower, much less dispatch, a millennial was little comfort. The doctor's eyes were greedy. Brigit knew a prize when she was one. Worse, there was no sexual yearning, not from him or the would-be hunters. That made it trickier.

"I think I'm quite well, thank you. I've always been a pale girl. Ireland isn't known for its heat waves."

"You should take advantage of the European summer and get some sun."

"Can't exactly sunbathe on a train."

"No, but you should take a stroll on the platform at the next day stop. I am sure it is healthier not just for you, but—"

"She's got some color now."

Schultze glared at Lange, and Brigit blinked, having expected him to be too well indoctrinated in his role of silent intimidator to actually speak. Weber simply gaped at his companion, then stole a glance at the doctor, eager for a cue.

Lange was studying Brigit with interest. She wrinkled her nose and turned back to the doctor.

"The heat, you see, is quite exhausting for me. And, of course, I have my responsibilities. Your concern is gratifying, Doctor, but I am, as you observe, a healthy girl and think I am quite capable of maintaining that all on my own. Now, if you'll excuse me, I have business to attend to."

As she hastened away, she could hear the three men muttering, but her feelers were not strong enough to glean any words. Not that it mattered. They knew. They probably knew everything. But how, how did they know? The plans had been so good and careful. And a doctor, why on earth would a doctor be the one they sent after her? There must be something more to it, to all of it. Or perhaps there wasn't. Perhaps it was just yet another twist in the giant morass the Nazis were making, into which the world would descend.

Perhaps it is simply madness, with no method. No method at all.

They were approaching Stuttgart at last, and Brigit began to feel exhilarated, hoping there might be a telegram waiting for her. She'd been able to send Eamon a message before getting on the train and, if all had gone according to plan, his reply should seem to have originated in Berlin. But if they knew who she was, and her business, then it might have been intercepted. She was sure, however, that Eamon knew where she was, and what she was doing. She could feel him, feel the energy he was marshaling toward her. She knew he would give anything to be there, to partner her through this nightmare, but he would stay in London, as he had all this time, and follow her journey in his mind. Yes, she could feel him, but she wanted that telegram. Desperately.

To her great rage, Maurer appeared almost out of nowhere as she reached the train's door as it slowed, giving her no chance to use blinding speed to reach the office before anyone realized she'd even disembarked. She calmed herself as best she could—far better he be with her than sniffing around her compartment and the unguarded cargo. He strolled with her as if by right, ignoring his lack of invitation, and grinned.

"Walking alone again, Fräulein?"

"It would seem otherwise, Sergeant Maurer."

"I don't believe in squandering opportunities."

"How prudent."

And at the first opportunity, I am going to kill you.

"Is this just a little ramble, or are you wanting something? A newspaper, perhaps, or some chocolates?"

"You're a bit inquisitive, Sergeant Maurer. I can't say as I like it."

"You're a girl who invites questions."

"And if I choose not to give answers?"

"Well, I suppose we all are free to make our own choices."

Certainly. Unless you're Jewish, French, Polish, Roma, communist, homosexual . . .

"But you'd be wise to accommodate me, little Brigit."

She knew the red glow swirled in her eye, even as a fang caught her lower lip, but she was past caring. Few passengers were embarking here and she had, at best, five minutes to conduct this business and was not about to be stopped. She reached up so her lips were nearly brushing his ear.

"Would I? Would I be wise, little man?"

And she blew an idea through him, reveling in this brief return of some of her abilities. It wouldn't last, and he might guess later, but she needed to do what she needed to do.

There was no time to enjoy the sight of him lumbering back to the train, slightly drunk and dazed with wondering if the nurse tending to the unruly boys might really be hoping to meet him in the observation car once the children were safely in bed. The telegraph machine was whirring busily in the tiny office and the slim, stooped man tending it whistled as he prepared messages. He looked up sharply at Brigit's ringing "Excuse me?"

"Well?"

"I'm expecting a telegram. Miss H. Morris."

The man appraised her briefly, then skimmed the neatly sorted file of recent telegrams. His fingers rested on one near the front. He paused, and ran his eyes up toward Brigit again.

"From Berlin?"

"That's right."

He looked at her, then the telegram.

"From a Mr. Jakes. That's an English name, isn't it?"

"I suppose it could be, but he's Irish, like me. My cousin, actually. He's there on business."

A slightly raised eyebrow told him that this girl's cousin was a member of the IRA and working with the Reich, trying to give them useful information in the fight against the British. He smiled, and slid the telegram across to her.

Brigit almost skipped back to the train, tucking the precious telegram deep in her jacket pocket. The message had gone through! She had words that came from Eamon pressed against her side! She lay a hand on her pocket, as though the telegram might fly back out and into the office. She fancied she could feel it purring under her fingers.

As she entered her corridor, however, Maurer was there. He was doubled over, rubbing his temples, but still there. A porter brought him a glass of water and glared at Brigit, as though certain the sergeant's sudden illness was all her fault and hoping for an immediate and harsh rebuking of the Irish girl.

"Is something the matter, Sergeant?"

Maurer straightened up and jerked his head at the porter, who slouched his shoulders in disappointment and trudged away.

"A momentary headache, a bit of dizziness. Nothing to alarm yourself with."

"There is a very charming doctor on board—Doctor Schultze. Shall I help you find him?"

He studied her face, which she kept absolutely motionless.

"No, thank you. That seems unnecessary." He smiled suddenly, and much too brightly. "Is he concerned for your health, this doctor?"

Brigit cursed herself for having mentioned him.

"He said something to that effect, but as anyone can see, I am quite the vision of health."

"That's good luck for you, isn't it?"

There was a sneer playing around his upper lip that she desperately wanted to scratch right off.

"I am not a girl to trust in luck. That's why I never wish it on anyone."

He leaned in with a shadow of a wink.

"Don't get too comfortable . . . Fräulein."

"No. I do not expect to soon reap the harvest of perpetual peace. If you'll excuse me . . ."

A couple anxious to get home to Barcelona approached Maurer and peppered him with questions in a mix of Catalan and broken German. With a delighted smile at his predicament, Brigit slipped into her compartment, determined not to lose another second before reading Eamon's words. She bolted the door behind her, slid down to the floor, and unfolded the telegram.

Dear Coz. Have received note of travel change. Have informed Auntie. Will make all arrangements. Contact from Bilbao with boat info. Flat good enough don't fret. Safe travel. Love. Jakes.

She pored over it again and again, hating its necessary brevity, loving its proof that Eamon knew where she was, what was happening, and that he and Otonia were hatching a new plan to somehow smooth the arrival in Ireland. Of course, they couldn't do much, but knowing, knowing, that was something. It had to be.

"Flat good enough don't fret," well, she knew what he meant, but wished he could remember that, despite all his patient explaining, she could never summon musical notes into her head the way he or Mors could. F G E D F. The beginning of one of his many songs about her. Which one, though? But it didn't matter. Having committed the contents of the telegram to memory, she soaked it, along with Elsie's papers, in the lavatory's tin cup, ground the wads into grimy crumbs, and sent them snowing out the window. F G E D F. Maybe it would come to her in a dream.

Chapter 8

Berlin. March 1939.

The suppers with Gerhard had become mind-numbingly routine, with conversation nearly as bland as the meal. He was unsurprisingly stolid in his choice of food and so scrupulous about cleansing all the plates of every crumb that Brigit suspected he'd been severely punished as a child whenever he didn't finish a meal. Despite his hearty appetite, Brigit didn't get the sense that he enjoyed food. Rather, he saw eating as a necessity and a duty, the way he viewed much of his life. His only passion was for power and, increasingly, Brigit.

Yet he, like all the other party members the vampires were so carefully cultivating, was circumspect and cautious in the extreme. Even Mors, moderately ensconced as he was, found it difficult to get the full access and information he wanted, never mind the opportunity to wield some influence and forge a clear path to destruction. Something was wrong, but the vampires couldn't seem to discuss it. Talk would confirm their concerns. Brigit was sure that Swefred and Meaghan had been convinced of this possibility all along and were taking some grim satisfaction in the lack of success, as it validated beliefs only they had held. Yet they seemed to be working as hard as the other three, and so Brigit made an effort to be charitable, assuming that her bitter thoughts were just an offshoot of her general dislike of the couple, her frustration with Gerhard, and her gnawing desire for Eamon.

Some mornings, as she was struggling to fall asleep, she thought she could hear the soft rumble of Swefred and Meaghan making love. Their room wasn't really close enough to hers for that to be possible, but she sensed it anyway and hated herself for it. This business of getting into an empty bed, alone, and knowing that she would wake up alone, often as not with tear-stained cheeks and damp thighs, was as draining to her as the minuet in which she was discreetly attempting to guide Gerhard. Perhaps if that dance found its rhythm, she might feel less despairing.

Increasingly, she and Cleland were finding excuses not to be alone in the same room. Whatever empathy they might offer each other was nothing to the fear of falling into the discussion of the men they were missing. Brigit knew the only way she was getting through the days was without hearing the magical name "Eamon" being spoken by anyone. Even Mors, whose tact could rival Attila the Hun's and whose subtlety was often compared to an anvil landing on the head, moved delicately around the subject of the missing. Whether it was out of his affection and respect for her, or because the whole of him was engaged in the mission, Brigit neither knew nor cared. She fairly wallowed in gratitude.

Reports from home were sketchy at best. They couldn't set up a post office box in Berlin, as the Germans asked far too many questions. Even retrieving telegrams too regularly was eyebrow-raising. Worse, it seemed every telegraph office was perversely located in a spot not accessible by sewer and with no shade, so as the afternoons grew longer, options shut down. At least they could send letters home once a week. Brigit loved to think of Eamon entering the bright central post office in London, so easily reached from sewers even in summer, and finding a letter from her in the little brass box. But she did wish she, or any of them, had more encouraging tidings to tell. This total lack of progress made no sense.

The demon would like to rise fast and strike hard and then sprint back to London posthaste. Organize an invasion into a major meeting and kill them all: Hess, Speer, Göring, Himmler, Eichmann, Goebbels, and leave Hitler for the last. Eat none, of course, because that would be poison, but execute swift, violent slashes that, one might hope, would bring about a decisive end to this Reich. It seemed so tantalizingly possible, and perhaps, back in 1934 or so, it would have been. But there were too many pitfalls. Meetings took place during the day, in so far as they all were privileged to know, and under heavy guard. The Nazis were confident, with a power Napoleon would envy, and yet left nothing to chance. Brigit saw them all as nothing but horrid little schoolboys, still entranced with the idea of gangs and secret hideaways . . . only they had the muscle and arms to back them up, and the imposing Reichstag was none too secret. Yet there was something infuriatingly childlike about the boundless cruelty of their ways; the enjoyment those in power took in being huddled up in an opulent room planning an empire built on blood and intimidation and the bullying pleasure those who guarded that room took in their supposed power. The millennials all knew that the weak, given some privilege and proximity to greatness, would always be the more dangerous in their way, having so much more to prove.

The millennials had even more to disconcert them when Mors reported that some Nachtspeere were among those who guarded the corridors of power. He could not be sure, because even the gentle, subtle probing he'd done had been risky, but just the idea was enough to give them pause. The Nazis were enamored of their certainty. It drove them. And if there was one thing of which they were certain, it was that Germany, Berlin in particular, was thoroughly cleansed of vampires. Possibly the Nachtspeere were kept at duty because of lingering superstition, but it seemed more likely the Nazis wanted to make sure the crack squadron they'd trained so carefully still felt indispensable. The demon prodded Brigit anyway, reminding her that the Nachtspeere, as far as they knew, had neither weapon nor skill that would dispatch a millennial, but this hardly mattered. They couldn't be sure, that was one consideration, and they didn't know how many true hunters remained in the Nazi sway and might be ready to pursue them, should they have a hint of the millennial presence. They could overpower everyone in the building, but what then? How on earth could they guarantee themselves a safe escape? The U-Bahn tunnels and the sewers did not allow them to travel during the day as freely and widely as they would prefer. Even getting to the Reich headquarters would be fraught, and then there was the matter of getting inside. Only Mors would be allowed to enter with anything like ease. The picture made Brigit bristle, imagining how much he would welcome the challenge, how well he would rise to the occasion, how recklessly he would court death and danger. It didn't matter that the Nazis were clever, that they might go so far as to blast holes through windows and walls to let in pure sunlight. He'd go out with a roar and take as many with him as he could snatch.

But are you ready to die, my dear friend? Are you really ready to die?

She knew the answer, and she knew, too, that it wasn't the right question. Was she ready for him to die, that was more apt, and she knew the answer to that as well. Not here, not now, not for this.

So there they were. Possibly they could find a faster way in, but it seemed only too likely that they wouldn't get out, and that wasn't the point of this venture. They were meant to survive. Their power was immense, but they weren't wholly invincible, and so they must still be careful. Infinite care, always infinite care. They were here to strike back, and what was more, to make Europe safe for vampires again and maintain the health and safety of vampires in the world. They had to remember this. Too many millennials had already died in the aftermath of the human war. Not one more could be spared. Not if they intended to thrive.

Brigit stabbed an overboiled potato with more venom than she intended, and Gerhard interrupted his droning monologue to stare, surprised.

"I'm so sorry, my dear, am I boring you?"

"Oh! Oh, no, no, I just . . . it's just so frustrating, waiting for things to happen."

True enough.

Gerhard beamed, clearly thinking she was referring to his career path. He gave her hand an approving pat, full of affectionate condescension.

"I understand your frustration, dear, but we must be patient. Look at our beloved Führer, and imagine if he were not patient, all those years ago. You see what patience has gained him? Wait and watch, it won't be long now, and you and I will be going to all the best events and I will be able to do marvelous things for you."

She squeezed his hand.

"I don't need any of that, but thank you. You are so very sweet."

"As are you, my dear, as are you."

A leer crept over his face.

"Perhaps, my little Brigitte, there are some things for which there is no need for patience?"

His thumb rubbed her palm meaningfully. She giggled, blushed, and made to pull away.

"Gerhard, please, not here." She looked around, worried lest anyone observe this vaguely inappropriate behavior of a rising young officer. Silly of her, of course, and betraying her small-town roots, but no man could help be charmed.

"Are you worried someone will report your dalliance to your auntie?" he teased, grinning. He rarely made mention of her home life because it was of so little interest to him, excepting that its laxity freed her up in the evenings to see him. An orphan, she'd left Heidelberg to tend a reclusive aunt on the outskirts of Berlin and learn nursing, but soon found her aunt was a full-time job. Fortunately, the old woman retired early and didn't care where Brigit went in the evenings, so long as she was home to make breakfast. There was a housekeeper who could manage things if there was any trouble. Of course, the arrangement wasn't quite as simple as he might have liked. The old woman held on to her money with a fist worthy of Jews and steadfastly refused to get a telephone. She was also strict about visitors and so paranoid about burglars she forbade Brigit to so much as give out her address. Brigit was given no opportunity to make friends and there was no other family, so it was not expected she would receive any letters. Strange woman, but Gerhard understood. She'd come up in a hard time and mistrusted everyone on principle. More than likely, she was not even going to leave Brigit any money. He didn't care. Brigit seemed to like him a lot and want to see him as much as possible, and since it seemed no trouble to her to trot down to the corner shop and phone him, he was content. He had enough work to do without fussing about courting a woman. Not that he considered himself to be courting. They both knew he was in no position to do that, not yet. No, he was cultivating a mistress, although he was a bit frustrated with the amount of effort it required. These dinners were all very nice, she looked well on his arm, and her kisses and body were divine, but she would only allow him to take her to his office, not his flat, and she asked more questions about his work than he was comfortable answering. It was exhausting.

"I don't want anyone to think I'm that sort of girl, is what it is, and if your landlady saw us, well, she wouldn't think too highly of you, either, would she? And you can't afford that."

"You are too sweet, my Brigitte, and clever, too. You know that the guard at my office will only think better of me, if he ever sees me bringing you inside."

"You mustn't joke! It would be awful to get caught!"

This wasn't true. Many of the men were married and carried on their peccadilloes in their offices. Gerhard was a bit low on the rung for it, but no one would give it much thought. She seemed to enjoy the idea of subterfuge, however, and he liked indulging her.

Her eyes were wide and reproachful. It touched his heart and fired his loins.

"Let's go."

He paid hastily and seized her hand, almost dragging her out of the restaurant.

Ten minutes later, they'd slipped past the night watch, hurried upstairs, and locked the door to Gerhard's little office behind them. Brigit lit up as she always did and Gerhard wondered why she never tired of her eager exploration of his desk and files.

"Oh, Gerhard, I do love how, well, *official* your office is! Of course, it should be much larger, and more grand, but they do seem to be appreciating you, I think. What are the chances they would allow you a personal secretary?"

"None as yet, not while I'm just a lowly assistant." He laughed.

She wagged a disapproving finger at him.

"You mustn't even joke about being lowly, not when we both know it's quite, quite untrue. Perhaps you aren't yet where you ought to be, but you know how important you are."

He smiled, reveling in her sweet ignorance and simple pride. If she continued to please him like this, he might, someday, reward her with marriage, although it was hard to imagine, not unless the impossible aunt decided to endow her, and that would have to be substantial enough to overcome the stigma of a poor education and shadowy background. However, there was no point in considering that aspect of the future. The only future in which he was truly engrossed was that of his career, and the only present that intrigued him tonight was Brigit's curvy body.

Although her blood was obviously hot for him, she couldn't resist carrying on with silly games. She snatched up a notepad and pencil and, her back straight and legs crossed, made ready to take dictation.

"Now, let's see . . . Dear Doctor Todt, I have noticed a lack of new rifles being designed in favor of those that were used in the war. I believe this is a woeful oversight and one that could be easily amended were the right man put in charge. . . ."

He was standing over her, his knees nearly touching hers, his face smiling but insistent. Gently, he took the pad and paper from her hands and made to pull her to her feet. Instead, to his delight, she reached up and wound his tie between her fingers, tugging until his face was level with hers.

He couldn't get used to her kiss. True, he had almost nothing against which to compare, but there was something unnerving about her mouth, almost as though she were digging into him. Every time she kissed him, he had the strangest sense of her being suddenly far older than she was, and someone else altogether. Part of him wanted to pull away, even run away, and never see her again, but he knew this was a mouth he couldn't leave.

Her hands wrapped around his head and he sank to his knees. Somehow, her fingers were in his mouth and her lips teasing around his ear. She exhaled into him, and he collapsed back onto the fine wool rug, spent, the pleasures of her body continuing to course through him long after he'd enjoyed them. He drowsed pleasantly, feeling her warm weight curled on top of him.

Brigit skimmed papers quickly and meticulously while Gerhard lay in his stupor. The power of her whispered scenario seemed to ebb with each tryst. Sooner or later, she would have to go much further in truth, unless she finally got information they could use.

Most of the drawers were locked, and Gerhard hadn't let slip where he kept the key. She couldn't break the locks without giving herself away, so had to make do with what papers were accessible, and once again, they were nothing but the most tiresome orders.

Orders, orders, orders, they do love their orders.

Suddenly, Brigit came across a set of orders that made her sit down hard. She had to read them all several times before they began to make any sense, and even then, they made no sense. How had Mors not heard about this? How had none of them? How was it possible?

She glanced down at the blissful Gerhard.

"You can't be serious, can you?"

He stirred slightly, but slept on.

Brigit replaced the papers and lay back down, even though she really wanted to throw him out the window. The sooner she woke him, the sooner she could get home and they all could get to work.

"When?"

Brigit answered the flat inquiry with bitter sarcasm.

"Czechoslovakia next week. Poland in September. Autumn is a fine time to start a war, especially with a country with whom you have a non-aggression pact."

"He denounced that, or don't you remember?"

"Yes, well, and they signed one with Denmark, do you think that means anything? Something will certainly be rotten in that state, you mark my words. This war is coming, the plans are well in motion, and what the hell are we going to do about it?"

"I am trying, but what can I do, really, when my man is involved in culture?" asked Meaghan, her accent fretful and petulant. She folded her arms and fixed her eyes on the teakettle. Swefred laid a hand on her shoulder and looked at Brigit and the others resignedly.

"I wondered. It's the questions the journalists haven't been asking that have been worrying me. When I pointed out to the one fellow I'm supposedly friends with that he seems to be doing nothing more than regurgitating the party line in print, he was, shall we say, surprised. As though he couldn't imagine his job entailing anything else. I think they're rather proud of what's been accomplished, and this great future. They want to keep extolling it in the papers."

"Or they're too terrified to do anything else." Brigit was disdainful.

"Not without reason. But what we need to do is penetrate the inner circle."

His eyes swiveled to Mors as he spoke.

"I don't want to take all the fun from everyone."

"Since when?" but Cleland winked at him. He turned to Brigit with a placating tone. "Masses of Germans have been saying for years that there ought to be a total German empire again, that the Danzig is rightfully part of Germany, just like Austria. Come on, you remember von Bismarck." Brigit mashed her lips together and glared at the ceiling. "Well, what did you expect?" Cleland continued, a bit more heated. "You've seen empires in their infancy before. Did you think they'd detail all their plans in the newspapers for the world to read? Put it to an international vote, perhaps?"

"Don't be exhausting. All I want to know is why we didn't already know this, why we didn't already stop it. It's getting a bit late to interfere."

"This hasn't exactly been a stroll in St. James's, has it?" Cleland snapped. "These people aren't fuzzy little bunnies, either, you might have noticed."

"We've been doing our best," Swefred added, almost as petulant as Meaghan might be.

"Have we? Have we really? If we had good fake propaganda, confused people, we could create chaos. That was the plan, wasn't it?"

Cleland and Swefred exchanged glances, riling Brigit further.

"Well then, what the hell are we doing? What are we doing?" Brigit demanded. "We're supposed to be so clever, so capable, so powerful, what are we doing? How are we breaking their backs if they're getting ready to mow down Poland? I've hardly gotten to even eat anyone really worthwhile, we have to be so damn cautious. What? What do we do now?"

"She's right," Mors interjected, laying a hand on Brigit's tensed forearm. "We should have made more progress by now."

"It's hard to make progress against such determination," Cleland protested. "They're so sure they're right, and they're so loyal to each other, and the party, and him. I think the Goddess of Discord herself would have a hard time turning this group on each other. We must be cautious, and clever."

"But we cannot be total slaves to caution," Mors pounded the wall for emphasis. "We cannot, lest we lose yet more and then more. Indeed, as the lady says, what is our purpose but to thwart such actions? We must be true to our very selves, and ruthless, ruthless and bold. Ambition! Ambition . . ."

"By that sin fell the angels."

Even Meaghan gaped at Swefred. His face was impassive, inscrutable, and Brigit wondered if he'd gone so far as to make a joke. It seemed so unlike him, but, she reminded herself, she had made a point all these years of not getting to know him too well.

Mors recovered from the surprise of the interruption and grinned.

"Verily, aye, but we were never angels. Nay, not even bright still. We may cling safely to our ambition."

"So what then? What do we do?" Brigit knew it was now she who sounded petulant, but there was something unsettling creeping into her skin, and she wanted a plan to which she could cling with new passion. Mors locked eyes with her, sending a spark through the room.

"There is a great Prussian general coming to Berlin soon." Mors spoke in a hypnotic purr. "One of the most famous heroes of the Great War, but a star long before then. He's been critical of the Reich, but apparently has changed his mind, and is now to be one of the top commanders and advisers. They think it's going to make a tremendous difference."

Brigit interrupted.

"So you *did* know they were preparing for war!"

"No, my impatient Yorkist. I knew they were preparing for an empire, and that is not necessarily the same thing, as the Anschluss demonstrated."

Brigit grumbled and folded her arms. Mors continued.

"They are arranging quite the fete for General von Kassell, and he will speak to a select group. It will be in all the papers." Mors paused to wink at Swefred. "He will arrive laden with treasure. One wonders where on earth it was amassed, but never mind. Wouldn't it be a shame if he and all his honor guard were assassinated before the festivities began? And troubling, too, because who amongst them could even think of such a terrible plot, let alone carry it out? Indeed, if the sabotage is made to look as though committed by a crack team within the party, well, can a spine so bent ever again stand tall?"

Even Meaghan and Swefred looked interested.

"So when? When is he coming?" Brigit felt as impatient as a child, but didn't care.

"Late in May, is the word so far."

"But that's ages from now!"

"Gives us time to plan it properly, as Otonia would have it."

The others nodded, pleased, but Brigit couldn't shake her disquiet. She needed to do something, now.

"I'm hungry. I think I'll go out."

Cleland glanced at the clock.

"Slim pickings this time of night, Brigit. It's pushing close to dawn. Are you sure you want to risk it?"

"I can't wait."

She could feel the others looking at one another, and hear the silent questions, but she didn't care. She needed more than a meal. She needed a kill.

The night was chilly, and felt much more like midwinter than early spring. Brigit prowled discontentedly through the frosty, bluish haze. Spring. The days would soon be getting longer, giving them even less of an advantage. They ought to have come earlier in the autumn. But back in November, they thought they knew what they were doing and how they would carry it off. And though they hadn't admitted as much to one another, or even to themselves, they'd tacitly assumed the mission would be accomplished by now and they would be home.

She wondered about this plan of Mors's and the effect it might have. If they did it right, it could indeed be the strike they hoped for. Something definitive, something to throw the Nazis off their game, to keep them from gaining their much-sought prize. But she wished they could do it now.

No. I wish it were already done.

As she reached the business district, she began to send out inquiring sniffs. After half an hour, she started to worry. Cleland had been right, this was a foolish time to try. In London, there were always the after-hours clubs and parties and salons to enjoy, but here, despite the glorious dream of a society that they were supposedly bringing to fruition, there was nothing so fun. The happy hedonism of the Weimar days was long gone, as were the days when men like Mikhail Bakunin or Aleksandr Herzen might look to Germany as an inspiration for the democracy they hoped to cultivate in Russia. Perhaps the people were confident, and felt strong, and had an outlet for their energies and something in which to believe. All this, yes, but theirs was a dour world. Of course, she only walked by night and wasn't privy to much beyond the scope of the mission, but it seemed to her it was only their little clique of vampires who laughed with anything like sheer pleasure in this strident city.

What a turnup for the books, if history could record it. A great new world indeed, where only the undead experience unadulterated joy. I'm embarrassed for you.

She giggled. The giggle turned into a gurgle as a sniff caught at last and she scampered happily toward her prey.

Two night watchmen outside a bank vault had purloined some good gin and were happily toasting each other's future success as they climbed up the ladder. They toasted the inner circle, the Führer, of course, the Fatherland, and all its most luscious blond daughters. It may have been the effect of all that gin, but one watchman was sure he saw the glittering head of just such a blonde winking at him from down an alleyway. A sweet whisper sounded in his ear:

"Komm her, mein Schöner. Ich hab' was für dich."

Well, if a blonde with such an intriguing voice had something for him, who was he to keep her waiting?

His compatriot hardly noticed him get up and head down the alley, and probably just thought he was going to relieve himself. Which, in a way, he was. He chortled, almost skipping up to the blonde, who was so beautiful he nearly stopped breathing. She was like something out of a film. Yes, things were definitely turning around in his life. It must be the uniform. Women were notoriously helpless for a man in uniform.

She stroked his face. Her hand was cool, almost cold, but the touch electric. Her fingers danced through his hair, teased down his neck—how could such a young, open-faced creature, with such a delicate smile, be so experienced?

He hadn't realized they'd been walking, had no idea where he even was, but her lips brushed his ear and made his knees tremble. The whisper she spoke was unintelligible, perhaps musical, something from an old song. It was enthralling and yet unsettling. But not so much that he wasn't still melting under her light touch.

Brigit smiled, looking at him. Young, handsome, overflowing with ambition. And he was no angel, either, and was about to fall. This paragon, an Aryan ideal, a simple watchman who would be in the Gestapo soon, if he parried his connections well and curried enough favor. He was just the sort to break down doors, beat the defenseless, and rip apart families, then go home and dandle his own children on his knee. Brigit looked further into him, and smiled even wider. Yes, and then put them to bed, make dutiful love to his wife, and sneak out to steal a few hours with his current mistress. And every Sunday, he'd enter the church with a proud, clean, self-assured heart.

The smile stretched, and she held a hand to his chest firmly, making sure he saw it all. The rising red in her eyes, the jagged cheekbones bursting from under the smooth skin, the spreading jaw that accommodated her shiny, well-kept fangs. He shook his head, too frightened to scream, sure he had simply slipped into a gin-soaked nightmare. He had a whole plan for his life, he was the shining hope of his family, and in a country cleansed of undesirables, he could go far. Could, and would. It was not, it could not be about to be quashed, snuffed out, and in such an impossible and ignominious way. No. Everyone knew the Führer had purified the land, that no vampire walked in Germany anymore and never would again. Impossible. His head continued to shake, almost of its own accord.

Brigit gripped his head and forced it to nod. With one last grin, she sank her teeth into him, loving the gasps of anguish, loving the feel of his body jerking in hopeless desperation. She sucked slowly, wanting to draw out the pain, but it had been a long time since she'd killed a man using pure fear, and she'd forgotten you needed a taste for it. And as for the taste of him, well, it was perhaps the worst yet of all the food they'd been eating. His callousness, arrogance, superiority. All that, spicing the fear and the fury, scorched her esophagus. She choked and his blood spurted out through her nose and down his back. She pulled away, sputtering. If Eamon could see this, he would be rolling on the ground with laughter. The watchman slumped against the wall, not dead yet, and coherent enough to look at her with a bleary eye and smile.

"Choking on me, vampire? Good." And he laughed weakly.

Brigit wiped the blood off her mouth, now set in a hard, thin line. She seized the watchman by the cheekbones and jerked him up to face her.

"Challenge me, will you? Mock? This, this is nothing. I promise you, what I have inside me is far more frightening and destructive than anything stewing in your soul. Mine is the never-ending nightmare, or don't you know?"

Even as she said it, she wondered fleetingly if it was true. Something in his eyes told her he wasn't so sure, either, and it made her eyes blaze harder. She dug her fingers more deeply into his cheekbones, feeling them splinter under the pressure.

"Don't you know I could feed off you for a month, if I wanted?"

He managed a shrug, not dropping his eyes from hers.

Well. Courage. I certainly didn't taste that before.

However, she wanted him to know, to understand, the way she wanted all of them to know what sort of fate they might be bumping up against, the longer they stayed on this path. He was sputtering, and she could see him working up enough saliva and blood to spit in her face. She pinched his lips so that they poked out like a duck's bill.

"Didn't your mother ever teach you to have respect for the dead?"

With that, she snapped her fangs through his lips, silencing him. The pain and the heat from her eyes made his own water. She summoned more of the demon from under her flesh—an inch-long talon extended from her index finger. She poked it into him, just above his nipple, and slowly ran it down, down, down, into his inner thigh. Her red eyes burned into his agonized ones.

She pulled away from him, ripping open his lips. Using just her forefinger and thumb, she neatly broke his jaw. He was past screaming now, and clawing desperately for the relief of death. His hand clutched at her coat in a silent plea. She leaned into his ear again for one last whisper.

"Yes, I could keep you alive, conscious, in this much pain, for a month. And I wouldn't lose a wink of sleep over it, you can be sure." She paused, letting the words sink in. "But I won't. Because unlike humans, we don't inflict pain for fun."

The gratitude came rushing into his eyes and she nodded, satisfied.

The rest of him went down much more smoothly.

Czechoslovakia went down without a whimper, German Jews were stripped of yet more rights, and a ship full of refugees was turned away from the States and sent back to Europe. There was nothing in the news to rally the vampires. General von Kassell's arrival was delayed, only adding to the exasperation. At last, however, he was on his way, and they were ready for him. The event was to take place on June 21, which amused Mors.

"Delightful. A midsummer night's nightmare."

Von Kassell was arriving in one of the Führer's personal trains. A woman Cleland kept entertained gave him some details of the treasure the general was bringing—cash and valuables that Bavarian Jews were no longer allowed to keep. She could hardly comprehend how they'd done so well for themselves in the first place. The stacks of confiscated marks were loaded into the train's armored cars, to be sent on to safety in Switzerland, but the jewels and objets would be fairly distributed, unless that Magda Goebbels bitch and Eva Braun creature claimed more than their share.

"There's more." Meaghan smiled. The other four stared at her. "He's bringing approved culture. One textbook factory has provided all the history books for Berlin students for the next two years, the local Department of Education has spent a great deal of money on the venture. And the art, well, simply thousands was sunk into the commission of this art, all to hang in the great halls of power, and schools. Portraits of the man himself, much of it, him, and so many of those around him. So that no one will ever forget the faces of these architects." She stole a sly glance at Brigit. "Or anyway, that's what my man at the Chamber says."

Swefred kissed her and the other three looked away, but they were openly impressed. The train and all in it were a veritable Tutankhamen's tomb. It was ripe for the plunder.

General von Kassell and his twelve guards were early. Most of the expected guests were at a tour of a new school and would not arrive for another hour at least. The small group of SS officers and lesser men assigned to this evening's proceedings were nervous and apologetic, but the general brushed off their concerns, cheerfully untroubled, and said he was quite happy to sit by a nice fire and wait. He did not care for long train journeys.

The lieutenant in charge privately congratulated himself on having lit a fire in the auditorium's opulent antechamber and laid in some extra bottles of schnapps. He'd hoped to purloin them later, but no matter, compliments on his organization would make for a better reward.

The antechamber was an awkward room, oversized, with high

ceilings and heavy velvet drapes that collected too much dust. The general seemed pleased, nonetheless, and busied himself lighting a pipe.

"*Guten Tag*, General," murmured a sweet voice behind him, so that he and his guards started violently.

No one had seen the scrumptious golden-haired girl enter, but there she was, standing by an armchair, her smile an open invitation.

"Pleasant journey, one hopes?" The strawberry-blonde with the enormous green eyes might have sprung up from the antique Persian carpet, but the general was hardly interested in asking questions. He was impressed that these German peasants were so thoughtful and had such very fine taste. The girls were exquisite. They must be Prussian.

The honor guard hovered hopefully, not expecting the general to share, but wanting to be at the ready, just on the chance. Von Kassell noted the looks the girls were giving him, the way they were assessing his figure. He was over sixty, true, but still handsome, and powerful. A warrior to the very core.

"Is this your first trip to Berlin, General?" the blonde queried.

"No, I came to Berlin as a boy," he answered, his tone both jocular and rueful. "It was very different. A warmer place, full of life."

"I agree," Mors put in, astonishing the group. They hadn't heard the door open, but three strange men, wearing swords, leaned against the wall. Von Kassell glanced past Mors to the short corridor leading toward the auditorium. The scent of the suddenly too-silent space made his neck prickle, the way it always had in the heat of battle. Mors was smiling at him, and for a brief moment, von Kassell thought he recognized him, or perhaps it was just that he knew a fellow soldier when he met one.

"If you don't like what Berlin has become, why are you here to help it down this new path?" The tone was polite, but the disgust and malice unmistakable.

Von Kassell only stared, and Brigit suspected he had no answer, or none that he wanted to speak out loud. The Prussians had always felt themselves above the Germans, and having first to give up their own kingdom, and now come round to this new Reich, so much more powerful than theirs had ever been, was shameful. Undoubtedly, von Kassell had some plan to join with Hitler so as to build up the Prussian kingdom again. Mors looked at him with a kind of amused pity.

The guards had drawn their weapons and were only waiting for the general to order them to fire. Brigit and Meaghan each smiled at two men and ran their hands over the close-cropped hair. The other eight guards and the general stood in frozen horror as the vampires neatly twisted the heads, popping them off the bodies and tossing them into the fire.

As the cacophony of yells rose, Mors, Cleland, and Swefred each gave easy, almost careless swings of their swords. Eight heads toppled to the carpet, rolling about like marbles before being squashed by falling bodies. Mors smiled at von Kassell.

"You should be pleased, General. You are to set a good example of what will befall everyone in Berlin if they carry on down this path. You seem like the sort of man who likes to set examples."

Mors stepped closer and von Kassell brandished his own sword with a practiced grace. Mors smiled, and even Brigit did not see how, seconds later, the general's sword was in Mors's other hand. Mors's arms seemed hardly to move, and yet von Kassell's body lay in the center of the room, the head and limbs severed, veins protruding so as to more thoroughly saturate the carpet with blood.

Brigit found the hook that opened the skylight and the five vampires leaped up through it. Only Mors knew the trick of closing it so that it would lock from the inside. They lurked near the auditorium's entrance, watching the guests approach, biding their time for maximum impact.

They had carefully calculated this next step, wanting the terror to build. The first men entered and slid to the floor on the reams of spilled blood, snatching at hands that came loose on contact. The hardier ones ran through the auditorium, useless guns in hand, calling, until they found the antechamber. They yelled for those who weren't vomiting to hunt the assassins, who could not have gotten far. The vampires were counting on a few among them to keep their heads and run for the train, knowing it must also be a target.

Mors could have managed the Nazis and the general on his own, but the other four were determined to be in on the fun. The mission was a group effort, after all, and too little real progress had been made not to want to team up now for such a brilliant show of chaos. Besides, it was cleaner and quieter this way, all the better for what they were about to do.

The train was ringed with guards whose ears were just pricking at the sounds of cries from the nearby auditorium. Each man felt a rush of cold air and had a millisecond to see the volcano of blood spurt from his neighbor before he, too, was slashed to ribbons by the knifelike claws of a sprinting vampire.

The men who came running from the bloody scene at the auditorium saw only the bodies. They paused, hearing a rumble, a whine, and then stared, dumbfounded, as the train exploded.

The fireball sprang into the air like sunrise. The shouts of fear and dismay, as well as the sound of falling debris piercing flesh and setting buildings afire, were pure nectar to the vampires. They held back their laughter as everyone screamed that the saboteurs must be near, there was no way they could escape, and yet no one thought to look up. Mors gave the signal and the vampires scampered away, skipping lightly over building rooftops like gazelles, all the way back to the lair, enjoying the singed air and its ripe promise of a hot summer's journey home.

"It was too inhuman."

There was rueful congratulation in Cleland's tone, because no one wanted to make Mors feel worse than he plainly did. They had never seen him cowed, and it was more terrifying than the realization of their new problem. The cleanliness of the assassinations, the perfect destruction of the train, and the total lack of any clues had led many in the party to whisper that there was something evil among them. It seemed someone had consulted a legend book and found that a few other enemies of Britain had been killed in the manner von Kassell had, and the legends all were sure it was the work of Mors. It was only Mors's brilliant acting, combined with the poor renderings of his face in the German legend books, that kept anyone from realizing who Major Werner really was, but Mors was still compromised.

"It wasn't just the assassination, it was all of it. We did it too well. That's why it's not in the papers." Swefred was gently encouraging. And it was true. When Brigit asked Gerhard about the meeting with von Kassell, because she'd known for weeks that his superiors were going, he turned white and told her something had gone amiss, but she wasn't to worry. Meaghan reported that the Chamber of Culture was devastated, and the Berlin Department of Education frantic, but with so many events planned for autumn, it would be well not to stir any doubt in the general public.

"So the plans are still going ahead," Mors remarked with a bitter smile. "I wonder what role they're expecting my major to play in this little war game of theirs? Ought I be worried they haven't told me?"

Brigit lay a hand over his, running her thumb gently over his wrist. She wanted to enjoy their success more, but three weeks later, it was as though it hadn't happened, and the only result was that they all had to be more circumspect than ever, lest the new wonderings brewing in some minds went wandering to close quarters. But Mors was still a fond member of his group of Nazis, they did not seem to suspect him, and the others reported no change in their circles. As for Gerhard, he was very much the same, and Brigit knew he was no actor, so it must be genuine. That was useful, but the fact that the vampires had shown such force, had taken such a stand, and ultimately achieved so little—that stung.

"We'll have another chance." Brigit spoke with simple authority, knowing it was what Eamon would think. Mors grinned at her.

"Of course. And one thing is certain. They are sleeping far less peacefully. I like that."

As the summer passed, however, Brigit had a bad feeling that they had only spurred the Nazis on to greater ambitions. The German Jews were kicked out of government jobs, Eichmann was given yet more power, and still the vampires came no closer to achieving their goal. The word from Otonia was to keep at it, to not lose faith. They had done well, they were making progress; it was just taking longer than they'd thought. But they should be encouraged: The world was getting nervous and paying attention to Germany, so surely, between their good work and the growing censure of other governments, war could be averted and the Nazis brought down.

For the first time in her life, Brigit knew Otonia was wrong. She admired their fine leader's optimism, as she admired her power, intelligence, and courage, but she was wrong. The Germans loved Hitler, questioned nothing, adored him more than their families and themselves. And other governments? Those that hadn't blinked when the Treaty of Versailles was so flagrantly violated upon the Anschluss? They as good as shrugged when Hitler helped himself to the Sudetenland, yawned when Czechoslovakia went down, and continued to placate and tolerate him. Brigit wanted to laugh, to shake every single world leader and slap them round the head to make them see that this was not the way to avoid war, that appeasement was pointless, that the world was only forestalling the obvious. It wasn't going to end, it was never going to end. The Nazis were hungrier than a new vampire and they were going to eat with abandon the way no self-respecting vampire ever would. Now that they'd been allowed forks and knives again, they could eat even more readily, with refinement, and malice. Possibly, like so many empires before them, they would gorge themselves until they burst, but that would still mean the world had been stripped bare. Humans and vampires would starve together, waiting for life to start again.

Brigit lurked in the shadow of the U-Bahn station door, counting down the seconds till it was safe to go forward to her date with Gerhard. At four other doors, she knew the others did the same. Mors, back to his cheerful, assured self, would wink at her if she caught his eye. From far, far away, she felt loving fingers brush her cheek. Eamon believed in her, in all of them. And that trumped all doubt. Once again, she felt that thrill of certainty. What did it matter that this was all taking longer and seemed more difficult than they'd originally envisaged? They were here. They'd dealt a hard blow, left a bruise, and were continuing to twist their way in like corkscrews, as well as eating steadily, chipping away at the foundation. From them, there would be no appeasement, or mercy.

The world may not know quite what you're up to, but we do. And every day, we learn more. And you, you learn nothing. You seek to plunge the world into darkness, but there is no darkness but ignorance, and you do not even know you cannot see. Master race . . . huh. You will learn indeed. It is we who will be the masters of you, most assuredly.

As Brigit set out for the restaurant Gerhard had named, she held her head arrogantly high and her eyes snapped with anticipated delight. Men ogled her as she passed, but she saw none of them. All she saw were the frightened faces of Hitler and his inner circle as they realized that the impossible had befallen them, and that it was indeed creatures they feared and despised almost more than any other who had found a way to bring them down.

Chapter 9

London. August 1939.

"You're lucky, you know that?"

Padraic collapsed next to Eamon on the grassy knoll, rubbing his belly.

"Why, because I don't have indigestion? Who did you eat?"

"Some drunken arse who smokes too much."

"They all smoke too much. It's the tension, I think. Or maybe they like the taste."

"Well, I don't."

"Nor I. But it's only really bad the first hundred years."

They sat silently, watching the flickering of the lights in the city. Padraic's stomach rumbled and he poked at it in frustration. Eamon grinned and Padraic continued.

"That wasn't what I meant, anyway, about your luck, I mean."

"I didn't think so."

"You hoped so."

"Maybe."

The younger vampire assessed his companion. He went on, hesitating only slightly.

"It's a bit of a bastard, being his second love, d'ye know? I mean, it's awful hard not to feel like there's still some comparing going on. He wouldn't have made me if he hadn't lost Raleigh, of course."

"No, but that's just how these things happen. You wouldn't want to not be here, would you?"

"Aye, no, I'm happy here and that's sure. What would I be otherwise? Some dead and forgotten Irish poofter, right? I tell you this, it was a damn sight easier being a poof in London, even with them not much cottoning to the Irish, than a poof in Ireland. And easier yet being a vampire poof." He studied Eamon again, and chuckled. "Would you have ever believed there'd come a time when it was better to be a Jew in England than a queer?"

"That's the advantage of a long life, you see things change. Neither still have the easiest time, I suppose."

"No, we have the advantage of them there."

Eamon fell silent, impatient for and yet dreading the moment when Padraic was to get back to his main point.

"It must make a difference, it can't not so, knowing that you're the only one she's ever loved."

"You shouldn't think such things, you'll upset yourself, and that does Cleland no good. He waited a few hundred years before he found you. He knew it was real, and you did as well, you know you did. So he loved once before, so what? All that means is he learned how, it doesn't mean he loves you any less."

Padraic nodded. Eamon understood how he felt. That was the trouble with a long separation, it allowed your mind to wander to some dangerous places. Hanging between them was Padraic's unasked question, "Why was there no one else, all those decades?" and it wasn't the easiest question to answer. It was one he'd asked her more than once, as he was learning her, but although she was never less than honest, it seemed as though even she didn't really know the reason. Her sins had been expunged at last and her heart was clean and ready to lay itself open, and that was when she found him.

But first, there was Aelric, and all the years in between.

No one in the tribunal could believe how much taste Aelric had shown in choosing Brigantia, nor how much luck he'd had in such a pick. Despite a temper that could be sudden and often vicious, she took to the dark life with alacrity and was admired by all.

Otonia made a point of tailing the new ones in their early days, so as to evaluate their potential. Brigantia was a preternaturally powerful predator, Otonia found, with an impressive knack for zeroing in on choice prey. When she ate, she seemed to be sucking more than blood; she wanted to imbibe the essence of the world with every kill. This was a vampire who wanted more than the hunt and food. A vampire who needed careful nurturing.

This was where Aelric created yet another problem. A maker didn't have to instruct, but he should be a guide. He should initiate her into the deeper complexities of undead life, its trials as well as its joys. To begin to delve these was the path to a long and prosperous existence.

Brigantia learned to read faster than any vampire Otonia had taught, and she was quick to learn several languages as well. She devoured books like blood.

"Careful, lest you tear through the whole library in a year and have nothing left."

Brigantia grinned and tossed her head.

"I'll just start all over again, won't I, and learn it even better. And the humans will have to write more. They don't seem to have the same passion they did in your day, why do you suppose that is?"

Otonia ran a loving hand over a volume of Aristophanes.

"Times ebb and flow. Life was richer then, but humans don't always appreciate what they have. You wait, though, things will change again, I'm sure of it. Our England will have its excitement, and so will we."

The hungry young vampire's eyes shimmered in eager anticipation.

She was intelligent, far more so than Aelric, but she did not know how a vampire's life could be ended. This was one of the first things a maker was meant to teach, in a loving and tender manner, so as to dissipate the fear. Aelric had no subtlety, but that didn't excuse his failing. It didn't seem right for another to step in on this crucial duty, but Brigantia was reckless, even beyond the scope of new vampires, and the tribunal would prefer to keep her. They'd never seen a vampire who ran through the woods chasing storms, whose wild laugh echoed down through the moors, who could spend hours on a cliff, calling down all her newly learned poetry into the sea and daring the waves to reach out and grab her. She once overheard Mors mutter something about "furious happiness and happy fury" and knew, with a fierce pride and pleasure, he was talking about her. And quite some time later, she discovered he'd talked about her again, to Otonia.

"Marvelous creature, our Brigantia, isn't she? Who'd have thought Aelric had it in him?"

"Everyone gets lucky at least once in their lives."

"Quite a taste for risk she's got. I saw her leap into a whole circle of Vikings to grab one. The others shat themselves. She held down the prey and shot their own arrows after them as they ran. Missed, as it happens, probably on purpose, but the laugh in her was something to hear. I shouldn't be surprised if they heard it in Cumbria."

"Yes, hers is an especially virulent demon. It's not wise, though, for one so young to draw so much attention. Too many will know her face."

"Face like that, they should be grateful."

"Indeed. But it's too soon for a legend. She needs control first."

"And Aelric won't help her there. Couldn't, even if he wanted to. So what do you think, shall I step in and be of use?"

"Yes. Take Aelric on a long journey of distraction so that I have uninterrupted time to talk to her."

"Oh. Well, yes, I can certainly do that. He's terrified of me. It's such fun. I'll take advantage of it, take him on a nature walk. Perhaps drop him off a cliff."

Otonia smiled but said nothing.

On an evening when Brigantia was working in her new garden, Otonia sat down on the edge of the freshly dug earth, pulled a distaff from her robes, and began winding wool.

"Was there any talk of vampires in your human world?"

"None whatsoever, but to be frank, I never paid much attention to what our elders said. Except for the healer. They didn't inspire confidence."

"I imagine that's often the case. But has Aelric told you of hunters?"

Brigantia looked at her quizzically.

"No, I didn't think he had. Simply put, the humans have teams amongst them that learn to kill vampires. It is the same theory as the parties that go forth to slaughter animals, only these are a rather more elite group."

"They actually hunt us?"

"Well, sometimes. Other times, they just protect the village. It rather depends. The Romans were crack hunters, you had to be skilled indeed to thrive in Rome, but it was worth it. Here, they're less focused. Life in general is rough, I suppose, and so they can't be bothered to cull the vampire community too much. Also they go to bed early."

"But . . . I don't understand. They can . . . they can kill us?"

"They can, and they often do."

"I thought it was just sunlight . . ."

"And fire. Although that's a bit slower and considerably less reliable, as they found out when they burnt the library at Alexandria."

"That was to destroy vampires?"

Otonia smiled. "Accounts vary. It's actually quite a story. But no, predominantly it was a political act, with a bit of religious conflict thrown in for good measure, of course. The fact that vampires were using it after-hours was just a bonus. As is typical with that sort of human thinking, they lost more than they gained. In the aggregate. But we got a nice haul." She smiled blissfully, contemplating the library inside the caves, then returned to her theme. "Anyway, a well-swung blade can take off our heads, and there's no recovery from that, as you may imagine."

"I can imagine. But would rather not, if it's all the same to you."

Otonia grinned.

"Well, so their favorite method of execution, it seems, is also the most ingenious. How they discovered it, I cannot say, but it would seem that a sharpened bit of wood, of the correct length, can be driven into our hearts. Quick, clean, and effective."

"Why should our hearts be vulnerable? They don't do anything useful anymore."

"Perhaps that's not as true as we may think. Even if we had scientific wherewithal, a vampire corpse cannot be studied."

"Why not?"

"It disappears."

"I beg your pardon?"

"Unfortunately, you will see yourself, someday. We all do."

Brigantia was already accustomed to, and generally amused by, Otonia's cryptic way of speaking. She liked everyone to wonder about things, and think. In this instance, however, Brigantia sensed her reticence came more from a place of pain.

"So they hunt us, then?"

"Yes and no. They've been known to seek and destroy lairs, but focus on the smaller families. It's why our own caves are so deep—they would have a time getting to us, and we older ones would hear it. The hunters might get in, but they wouldn't survive us. I suspect they know that. They work in pairs, often, and seek out pairs. Carelessness on our part, that's what helps them. Bloodstained shoes that leave tracks. Too much revelry too near human settlement. The like."

Brigantia nodded, thinking of her own revelry and carelessness. Now a bit more of the sunlight of this life was snuffed out. And Aelric should have told her. She wondered why he hadn't. Perhaps it was that delicacy of his, the way he wanted to protect her. Perhaps he was hoping she'd warm to him. She still shared his bed, after all, even though little happened there besides sleep. She knew she could request her own chamber and no one would think the worse of her, but it felt too soon. She didn't want anyone to think she was cold.

To her surprise, Brigantia laid a hand on Otonia's arm, pleading for the reassurance of contact. It was not something she recalled ever needing to do as a human.

"Some hunters must be skilled. It can't only be our carelessness that draws them."

Otonia smiled, and squeezed Brigantia's hand.

"No. As with most men, the ones who are most determined to carry an act through . . . well, they manage."

Several weeks after this conversation, Brigantia was still puzzling the ways and means of hunters, and wondering how it was that they didn't find the vampires in these caves during the day. She wondered how they learned to do what they did and how strong were their numbers. This feeling she had about them wasn't fear, that she could tell, but it was a powerful, morbid curiosity.

Aelric saw that her mind was occupied and unsettled and vainly sought to help.

"What is it, what's wrong? Is it all those books you've been reading? You should come and play more, that's what this life is for, come and have some fun."

In no mood to debate, Brigantia gently and even politely rebuffed him, which should have been a warning. Aelric assumed the slight upgrade from tolerance was warmth and renewed his attempt to soothe and please with vigor. It quickly began to wear on Brigantia, but she didn't want to pick a fight. She tried to keep away from him, but he clung to her like a leech. Her voice grew softer and softer as she asked him to let her be, and still it never occurred to him that she might mean it.

A week later, Brigantia was coming home late from a fruitless prowl when Aelric dropped down from a tree into her path.

"Hello, my Brigantia, bad night?"

She was so astonished, she jumped back, slipped, and fell smack into a dunghill. She would have gotten out more quickly had Aelric not tried to help her, and they were both covered head to toe in it by the time they were back on the path. Another time, in different company, she would have laughed, but a rage was swelling through her like she'd never known, and she was desperate to escape to the sanctuary of the baths.

Mors was lingering in the corridor that adjoined the male and female baths, joking with Leonora. At first, he thought Brigantia had walked into cobwebs and they were clinging to her lashes as though to a cat's whiskers. Then he realized it was smoke. Smoke, wafting from Brigantia's eyes and billowing around her head. A deep flush was rising in her face. Her hair—he could see even through the shit—was reddening and lifting, although there was no breeze.

Aelric was bouncing behind Brigantia, intoning a steady monologue.

"I'm a good listener, I am, you should try me, you should trust me, you owe me that, you do, you know. You owe me that and more. You owe me everything you are, didn't I choose you? Didn't I make you? Didn't I give you a gift and aren't you ever going to show me any real gratitude?"

He leaped in front of her then, arms crossed righteously, and he, Mors, and Leonora witnessed Brigantia's explosion in all its full horror. It wasn't just fangs, and claws, and red eyes. It was something that seemed regurgitated from Hell. Blood-drenched bones burst from under her skin. Then, what no one had ever seen in any vampire: flames shooting from her hair and lashes. She roared, and fire spewed from her mouth. Aelric fainted, and her fiery claw shot toward his throat, but Mors seized Brigantia and threw her into the bath, holding her under the warm water until the flames succumbed and died and he finally saw the bones slide back into place and her skin regain its pallor.

Brigantia sputtered on reaching the water's surface and stood silently as Leonora reached over and pulled a towel around her. Nearly a foot of singed hair fell into dust at her feet and her fingernails were black, but she was otherwise outwardly unscathed. She wiped her face and looked at the filthy bathwater with regret.

"Well . . . shit."

Mors chuckled and Brigantia looked up at him ruefully. She was trembling with exhaustion, fear, and pain, because the fire had burned deep within her, but she felt her own self flowing back into her, even more so when she made a point of treading on the still-unconscious Aelric as Mors guided her to a small, unoccupied cave.

"I suspect you want your own little chamber now, don't you? You'll sleep better."

He waited outside while she changed into dry robes, then came in and tucked her up in bed as though she were a child. He folded her hand in his and smiled down at her.

"Well, little Brigantia. We all knew you were a fiery one, we just never guessed how much."

She laughed weakly and shut her eyes.

"Thank you, Mors."

It was hardly even a whisper, but he heard it. He leaned down and hummed an ancient song into her ear, sending her into a deep and dreamless sleep.

She could not stop being the new self she was coming to like so much, but the feeling of the fire subdued her. Undoubtedly, Mors knew what she did not want to tell anyone else, or even admit to herself, which was that it had been halfway to killing her. Her slow, considered movements the next few days were a result of charred organs painfully repairing themselves. Her esophagus ached too badly to ask Otonia the question to which she already knew the answer anyway. No one else had a true fire inside like that. Other demons could not explode so viciously as to destroy their own hosts. She touched the place where she knew the demon dwelled, wondering why it would do such a thing to her. She'd entertained an idea that it loved her, that it was helping her to grow. Now it seemed it was another thing to mistrust, a thing that, on a whim, could turn against her.

Nothing was said of the incident, and everyone treated her much the same as always. The only difference was that Mors's eyes twinkled sardonically whenever they met hers. Eventually, however, it was he, not Otonia, who offered the explanation that comforted her.

"You were an angry human, weren't you? You were filled with bile, born with it. Times were it simply exploded from you and woe betide anyone who might be within spewing distance."

Brigantia did not ask how he knew such details. She waited for him to continue.

"It's not the demon. It wouldn't be. Your human self was full up of anger when it died. It was too potent to simply be absorbed by the demon. It is its own beast. That's the fire, your physical manifestation of your human anger. Congratulations, Brigantia. You are unique indeed."

There was no way to know if this was all true, but she accepted it. And it helped.

For his part, Aelric kept a wary distance from the creature he'd made and prized so much. Whether it was murder or death he'd seen in those flaming eyes was a distinction that hardly mattered. She was nothing like what he'd hoped when he had taken first her humanity and then her virginity. He'd had a dream of a fun-loving companion who gazed at him with adoration, who showered him in love and giggles and never strayed from his side. Or perhaps he'd wanted something like what Swefred had in the quiet Meaghan, a lover who, though passive and outwardly unsmiling, still saw nothing in the world but the man who never wanted to leave her sights. He was her world, and she his. It was this that Aelric had hoped for, and perhaps the envy of the tribunal, and instead he was back to bedding down alone, while she whom he so wanted to hold and love avoided his eye.

As he became more distant and troubled, Brigantia felt uneasy and even concerned. To her own mild vexation, she could not help occasionally trying to comfort and bolster him. That potent mix of duty and guilt made for uneasy relations.

Something akin to détente was eventually achieved, and Aelric took to hunting with her, even knowing it broke all their laws. He couldn't help it, he was addicted to watching her hunt. A nagging sense of duty, however unreasonable, drove her back into his bed, although it held even less pleasure than before. And it wasn't long before she was irked at his company again. But she was now close to seventy-five and slowly learning control. She also had the respect of the tribunal to revel in. No one could have dreamed Aelric would achieve his centennial, and it was her influence that had done it. These things kept her from lashing out when he was his most childish and exhausting.

"I've always wanted to eat a couple together, haven't you?"

"No."

"Let's try it anyway, don't you think it would be fun?"

"No."

"It would be new, anyway, and you like new things, right?"

"Aelric, I'm hungry. I want to eat alone. After that, there's some new plants that need tending and . . ."

"Ah, see? New."

"Plants. In my garden. Yes, those I like. And you know it. Now go on, hurry up, you'll have a hard time finding anything good to eat if you dawdle much longer."

Aelric fidgeted nervously, wanting to say more, but finally wandered away, leaving Brigantia to meander with some leisure toward the Nessgate alehouse.

It was no hard-and-fast rule, but when selecting a meal, vampires tended to drift toward the gender that might draw them sexually. Since most meals were killed via seduction, rather than terror, it made the process easier, and added color. It was playacting, which they all enjoyed. Brigantia often wondered about that, and determined that it was the vague unreality of undead life that gave them all such a natural turn for drama. In any case, human society being what it was, there were fewer women out in the dark than men. Even prostitutes kept to their brothels, although they were still useful prey, as they lurked by windows and were apt to invite a man inside. Sometimes, those who sought women waited till closer to predawn, when girls might come out to tend cows and poultry. Other times, you just had to acknowledge a bad draw and give it up for the night. Even the newest ones needed to eat only every three days. The older you got, the longer you could go without food. Which, of course, was better for the human population and, in turn, better for the vampires. More selection. They could be choosy.

The alehouse was as raucous as Brigantia expected it would be. Men and the way they changed under the influence of ale . . . it never failed to amuse. It often made the game a bit too easy, but one had to find prey in its natural habitat.

The young man who staggered out early smelled of lust, and was indeed wending his way toward the brothel. Definitely too easy, but entertaining. Brigantia pleasantly waylaid him and raised his hopes, being far prettier and more intriguing than the wares inside the house. She hadn't even asked for any money first before leading him into a dark snicket and running a cool hand up his arm and around his neck. His eyes were closed and he was drifting with pleasure when Aelric surprised Brigantia from behind and broke the spell.

"Any of that left? I'm starving!"

Brigantia whirled. Her prey reeled in pain. Feeling the blood dripping down his neck, he began to scream.

"Vampire! Vampire! Two of them here! Vampire! Help!"

He ran, not well, but it was enough to be heard.

Brigantia caught him quickly and snapped his neck. But it was too late, she could hear the stirrings of the city and smell the fear . . . and the hunt.

Her first instinct was to leave Aelric, knowing she could run faster without him, but in his panic he would run straight for home and that would be disaster. So she seized his wrist and dragged him behind her, running a carefully circuitous path that she hoped would kill the scent.

It was hard going. She didn't know if they would be coming from the city or the outskirts. Perhaps they were among the guards at the walls? How much light would they need to travel? She desperately wanted to stop and think, but Aelric made thinking impossible.

"We can go now, Brigantia, we lost them. I'm sure of it."

"I'm not."

"Well, let's fight them then. Come on, pull that fire out of you—that might well frighten them to death."

"I couldn't pull it out at will even if I wanted to. Don't you understand?" She stopped and faced him. "I have hardly begun. I am not ready to die."

"You could never die."

She wondered if perhaps that was the kindest or most foolish thing he had ever said to her.

There was little time to wonder. They were deep in the woods now, many miles north of the caves. Her thought was to crisscross their way to the river and swim back south. It would be arduous, but there was no better plan. She wished she knew how many men were hunting them, and how capable they were.

Aelric was worse than useless. He talked much too loudly, he wanted to fight, thought it would be hilarious, and what did Otonia know, anyway? Humans able to kill vampires, that was absurd. Insane. A folk legend.

"Perhaps it's we who are the folk legends."

That shut him up, because he could not understand it.

It happened fast, faster than she could have imagined. The shouts were unexpectedly near, and though she was startled, she didn't know why she fell so hard into the bracken.

Seconds later, she realized Aelric had climbed a hill and caught the light and that the hunters had seen him. It was bad luck. Simple bad luck. She herself had tumbled into a shallow ditch and, covered in fallen leaves, was as good as invisible. It was good luck. Simple good luck. She pressed herself deep against the earth, wanting to run and yet prostrate with fear. And she could see . . . she could see only too well.

Aelric fought, and it was not a fight to be ashamed of, but again, his luck was against him. Though he snapped the arm of one man, he left himself free for the other. And here was where it began. There is always a choice. Even if the end is the same, there is always an option for how to get there. Her human self might have stayed with her people and fought the Vikings and either died by a blade or from the shame of sexual slavery. She might have left Aelric behind in that alley when the man screamed, but he was her maker, and she would not have done that. Now, for the same reason, she must step forward. Here was her chance. A blinding moment of pure opportunity. As if in a dream, she saw herself fly around behind the man wielding the pointed wooden stick. She seized his arms, snapped them off at the elbow, dropped them and grabbed his head. Turned it, quickly and with just the right amount of force. The other man, all he needed was another kick to break his ribs and Aelric could feed off him. So easy, really. It was done.

But she didn't move. Aelric turned and saw his death coming and saw she wasn't there. That she was letting it happen. The stunned betrayal and hurt in his eyes pierced her as surely as the wood pierced him, so that she felt its point enter her own heart, felt her body contract. Then, what Otonia had not described: the long, long second before the body crumbled, collapsed in itself, shriveled into dust. A body was there, and then it wasn't. Aelric had been, and now he was nothing. Skin, flesh, bone . . . all air and dust.

"Well done," the hunter with the broken arm congratulated his partner. "Let's find the second one. Must be near."

"No, no, you're hurt. We can't take the risk. Come on, put your arm around me, there's the man, I'll get you back all right."

She waited a long time, till they were more than a mile away, and even then couldn't move. When her fingers did twitch, she was shocked, hardly believing her nerves still had instincts. She crawled to the spot where it had happened. Dragging herself to her knees, she saw a vague outline of a body, although perhaps she only hoped she saw that much. She pressed a hand in the dust and brought it to her face. There was no smell. No taste. Nothing to connect it to anything but dirt.

Aelric. Exasperating, foolish, overeager Aelric. Made but nearly ruined her. His own carelessness finally caught up with him. But those moments, those few key seconds before the hunters came, the bit she couldn't quite see . . . could he have pushed her down into that lucky hiding spot? Could the instinct that chose her have returned one last time to save her? Was she beholden to him for yet another life?

What would have happened to her human self anyway, say she'd run off with no vampire after her? She'd have been long dead by now, certainly. She might have had some adventuring, but she would never have met anyone like Otonia or Mors. She would never have learned to read. Her world had been opened, and Aelric had facilitated it.

And there were those other seconds. The ones she could have used to keep him whole. The seconds she'd used to make a choice, even though she'd hardly registered a thought. What of them?

With infinite care, she dug a shallow hole and swept the dust into it. She made a neat mound and encircled it with stones. Using a twig, she scratched into the mound the words "Aelric was."

Drifting down the river, only her face protruding from the water, she wondered how long the words would last. How many hours before a breeze disturbed them, sent the grains of earth rolling over and through and away into nothing, as surely as Aelric was himself? Was there some record somewhere of words written? Did something in the universe remember? Or was everything just erased, always, and then gone?

But I wrote them. I did. They were there.

It was Cleland who saw her when she drifted in, soaked through and expressionless. He stirred, ready to speak, but changed his mind. He tagged after her to Aelric's cave and watched her go in. He peered through the hangings—she was alone, sitting on the bed, staring.

All those pretty little words. "It isn't your fault." "You mustn't blame yourself." "No one lives forever, that we know of." They dropped around her like a rain that never makes contact with earth. No one else could see those seconds. The little bundles of time. The treasure trove she couldn't see and the one she saw only too clearly. The unused seconds. The heavy chill around her heart and behind her eyes was not the guilt of not missing Aelric, but the possibility resting inside those lost seconds.

Those seconds stayed with her for decades.

England changed. William came and the vampires watched cathedrals go up and the last remnants of pre-Christianity die. They increasingly found that the crosses some people carried or wore could be painful. Otonia was unsure why it was a problem for the pre-Christian vampires, seeing as the Jewish ones had no trouble with crosses and told the most amusing stories of the reactions they got from prey who thought the cross would save them. So the vampires learned new seduction techniques.

The fashions were interesting, as was the architecture. The Normans were pleasant-tasting. There was little good literature or entertainment—those vampires from Greece and Rome still longed for those days and hoped they would come again soon—but York thrived and there was much life to enjoy.

But Brigantia went through it in a fog, still mourning a chance missed, wondering if she'd doomed a vampire she'd never loved on purpose, and what did that make her?

And yet, in the last quarter of her second centennial, still chilled and buried inside those infernal seconds, Brigantia knew she was reaching a time when something must happen. She would either break free . . . or break. As if she'd read inside her, Otonia suggested she might be ready to venture outside herself and find a companion.

She'd been on a hunt, she realized, and for something she hadn't put a name to in centuries. It wasn't going to find her, even though she had hoped it would. She wanted, she wanted, and she needed and she knew even without any suggestions what must happen, lest she lose something in herself forever, or lose the nerve to find it. Otonia might call it a companion, but Brigantia knew it was more. It was her most cherished hope and, though she hardly knew why, her greatest fear. But she touched the newly budding periwinkle in her garden and sensed the promise, somewhere in the earth, of the something, the someone, that might pull her out of the self she didn't always know, or like, and into the self she might finally become.

Chapter 10

Berlin–Basel train. August 1940.

The doctor, his young hunters, the officers, even the friend-seeking nurse and the toadying Kurt, all these annoying humans demanding her attention for one reason or another were horribly draining. Brigit longed for the halcyon days when there was no human interaction in her life, save that which was of her own choice. There were many hundreds of humans she'd admired through the centuries, usually artists of some sort: authors, poets, playwrights, actors, musicians, painters, and on and on. Thinkers. Those who erected beautiful buildings, or opened up minds to science and the possibilities in numbers, or advocated for greater equality among humans. Those who used their brains and energies to improve upon the world. Those who cared. These were men and women whom she could admire and even love, quite genuinely and with all her heart. But she wasn't forced to interact with them. She wasn't forced to play a game of being one of them, dance an intricate dance and hope that no one knew the truth and thus threw her off her rhythm. Everyone stayed in their proper place and the world was balanced.

Now that her belly was full, the whole of her body was yearning for sleep. The demon did all but pull her eyelids shut from behind. She'd caught only the meanest snatches of sleep since boarding, feeling the dangers of sleeping during the day but worried it might be yet more dangerous to sleep at night. How could she sleep at all, charged with duty as she was? The precious cargo in her care, all these watchful men lurking, waiting, preparing, but exactly for what she didn't know. Her worst nightmare, that's what they wanted, and she did not want to be caught sleeping when it hit. It was bad enough she'd had to leave the cargo un-guarded to eat and circulate, playing the game. Sleep felt like an indul-gence. But the aching hunger for rest was snaking through her, and she was going to have to give herself up to it.

Deciding to take no chances, she lay down in front of the compart-ment door. It wasn't comfortable, but it felt like a good precaution.

The raveled sleeves of care won't mend, that's for damn sure, but at least I'll feel better.

Brigit shut her eyes, allowing her body to drift to the deceptively soothing rhythm of the train's steady rumble. She adored trains, even though she'd experienced a pang upon their development, seeing as they tore through the wilderness she loved so much. But travel had always ex-cited her, and trains made it easier. There was, however, that which had always troubled her about travel as well. It seemed wrong that you should be in a place, love it, take of it what you did, but then, when you left, it went on without you, just as it was, neither knowing nor caring that you were no longer there. She had the same feeling about the theater. There were nights she could hardly stand it that a show she had loved was going on with the same energy and excitement, if not more, when she and Eamon were not in the audience.

They had just seen *The Importance of Being Earnest* for the fifth time, and Eamon had pulled her into an alley to lick the ecstatic tears off her face.

"How? How can you stand that it will be on tomorrow, and we won't be there?"

"We've had it. We can't take it from others too much, that would be cruel."

"No, Eamon, really, don't you understand me?"

"I do, but what's your answer, then? To stop time? To be the only one to experience anything, ever?"

"Of course not. I just don't like to be a part of something and not have it miss me when I'm gone."

"We're vampires. No one misses us when we're gone."

"No. But at least we do leave a stamp upon a place."

"We leave empty spaces where souls once stirred."

"We have impact."

"Not exactly artists, but memorable, nonetheless."

She laughed, and thumped him gently on the chest.

The thump near her head woke her with a violent start and a low growl emitted from somewhere above her abdomen, audible only to her, but worrying nonetheless. It didn't matter that she was exhausted and undernourished and terrified. She had to be strong. Stronger than strong.

"Sorry, I didn't mean to wake you."

Brigit looked up blearily. The volatile cargo of which she was taking such care had chosen an inconvenient time to jump down from the top bunk. Or rather, the girl had. The boy lay on his stomach, kicking his heels in the air and gazing out the window. Brigit coughed and rubbed her eyes, determined to resume the role of guardian and open smuggler.

"How long was I asleep?"

"About an hour."

"A whole hour. Marvelous."

"I said I was sorry. Can't you go back to sleep? It's ages before we change."

"No, I should stay up. I'll sleep when I'm dead."

"Is that a joke?"

"Yes, and not a bad one, all things considered."

"Is what a joke?" piped up Lukas.

"Nothing," his sister assured him. "Our guardian is talking like an adult."

It was the bitter irony with which Alma used the word "guardian" that riled Brigit. She felt sorry for the children, but since they were all in the same boat, she thought something that resembled détente might be appropriate.

"I'm bored," Lukas complained, looking somewhere toward Brigit's chin.

"We all are," Alma agreed. "Shall we play with your teddy?"

Lukas looked hopefully toward the door. He wanted to run and play with the other children, but Brigit couldn't allow it. Bad enough she was saddled with the care of these small humans, but she had no intention of losing them. When they weren't immediately in her sights, she insisted that they remain in the compartment with the door locked, and that Alma enforce this rule rigidly. The advantage to being a vampire was that these orders were not questioned. The children might not like her, and barely trusted her, but they knew they were surrounded by enemies, and so they obeyed.

"What was the news you got?"

Brigit hadn't shared the contents of the telegram with the children, it was not their business and the less they knew, the safer they were.

"I told you, nothing important. Just news from home."

"I don't understand why Papa can't send you coded telegrams so we know he's all right."

"We've been through this."

"And it's not dangerous for you to receive telegrams?"

"It is. That's why it was just one."

"Then what was that other paper you destroyed?"

"Just some paper, it doesn't matter."

"It does. You look better. You ate." It was a simple statement of observation. Brigit didn't answer. She would give so much to still be years away in sleep.

"How long to Bilbao, after we change?"

"Not long."

"I thought it would be faster."

"So did I."

Alma went silent, and Brigit was glad. She couldn't bear these conversations, the words that made the situation so much more real than it was. The last few days felt more like a horrific waking dream than anything else. Two children in the guardianship of a vampire was a sick joke, an absurdity, something not even seen through the looking glass. And all the men watching them, all the unseen traps being laid, it was too ridiculous. Yet real.

I didn't have a choice, that's all there is.

Which didn't matter. What mattered now was every moment pulling them to what she hoped was safety. There was nothing to do but hope the foolish hope that she looked like a legitimate nanny, shepherding charges to Ireland. It was no one's business, surely, why a German parent should choose to have their children educated in Dublin, but she would prefer not to entertain the queries.

Not that Ireland was their ultimate destination. Brigit dreaded even the scant hour they must be there, that land of notorious vampire hunts and torture and destruction. She cursed the timing that put her beloved London in peril as much as the bombs themselves. Their escape would have been so much easier had they just been able to travel directly to Calais and then across the Channel. This circuitous route and the uncertainty of the ferry schedule from Bilbao to Cork added to the stores and stores of dread. Undoubtedly, Spain was very beautiful, but Brigit had no interest in holidaying there.

A sharp knock made them all jump. Brigit leaped to her feet and tidied her hair while Alma and Lukas hid their faces behind books.

"Who is it?" Brigit trilled lightly.

"Kurt, Fräulein."

She allotted herself one grimace before opening the door and slithering partly out so as to dissuade him from close inspection. His face was eager, and he spoke with desperation.

"Mine is the next stop, I'll be off for Paris."

"So you will. And a very great adventure it's going to be, I've no doubt."

"I suppose you can't join me?"

She forced herself not to gape, or laugh.

What fools these mortals be.

"That's very sweet, but I'm afraid it's impossible. I have a schedule I must keep."

"But . . ."

He leaned in closer and caught Alma's watchful, interested eye. He stared at Brigit.

"What on earth . . . ?"

"Children. This isn't a pleasure trip for me. I'm paid to take them to their school in Dublin. Their mother was Irish, you see."

Her voice was somber and respectful and gave him to understand exactly what she hoped without the effort of saying more. She didn't want him to study them any more closely.

"But . . . but they weren't with you last night?"

"They were tired, I put them to bed early. Now, if you'll excuse—"

"Wait! Please, won't you come to my compartment, just for a little while?"

The plea in his eyes was laughable. She considered. To kill him would mean questions, because of Eberhard, but she was itchy to finish him off and there would be a lot of bustle at the next stop. She gave him a warm smile.

"Look for me in a quarter of an hour or so."

He smiled gratefully and didn't even think to nod at the children before hurrying off to his compartment to prepare, even though he had no idea what he was doing.

Alma was standing up and her arms were folded. She was not quite twelve, but her strength was tremendous and Brigit couldn't help but respect her.

"Haven't you left us alone more than enough already?"

"It isn't by choice."

"You ate. You don't need him, too."

"This is something different. You don't understand."

"What if I do?"

It was possible she did. The girl was clever beyond her years and highly intuitive. Still, Brigit had no intention of taking a child into her confidence.

"Alma, will you please just sit down and—"

"I heard them talking!"

"What?"

"They were talking about a missing woman. Some horrid ugly cow, they said, and they were sure she hadn't gotten off the train. They were laughing about it."

Of course they were.

"All right, now listen, I need you to tell me exactly what they said."

Alma cast a quick glance at Lukas, but he was now deeply engaged in reading to his bear and paid the others no mind.

"One of those officers, I think it was one of them, was outside the door and said a woman was missing. They wondered who might know something about it."

"I'm sure they did."

It seemed too bald to admit to the girl that she had eaten the woman in question, even though it was understood. However much Alma may think she knew about Brigit's ways, and however wise she was, she was still a child and under Brigit's protection.

That protection, though, was what stopped Brigit. She must maintain the ruse, even though the enemies were close to certain and were only trying to gain absolute proof before snapping the trap. The clouds, the lingering strands of doubt had to remain, the chance that she might be human, and if human, rich and Irish and not someone they could attempt to destroy without expecting consequences. The murder of a privileged, undoubtedly well-connected Irish girl could be just the sort of thing that would begin to tip the Irish away from their warm neutrality and toward reluctant partnership with Britain. Or at the very least, turn them colder toward Germany. It was too great a risk to take. If, on the other hand, she was indeed the vampire they thought, even not knowing what it meant to be a millennial, they still had to operate with care. They had heard of huge massacres committed by a single vampire, and even though this one was a soft-looking female, they wanted to hedge their bets. Their orders were to do it on the sly. The public must not know any vampires had crept back onto the Continent. Furthermore, while they were all prepared to die for the dream, none was willing to die such a shameful death. They wanted to humiliate and torture her and emerge unscathed.

All this she could bear easily enough, but she knew they had their suspicions about the children as well, and that would not be borne. It was foolish of her to hope they did not know whose children they were, or even that the children were Jewish. No, the little girl was right. Brigit could not leave them alone again, not for Kurt. What Mors had told her all those months ago on the train to Berlin still held true: She couldn't kill them all. She abhorred the idea of Kurt and all he represented, but to kill him would only create a blood trail she couldn't afford and would gain her nothing. The worm would have to live, and feed the worms their supper another day, by another way.

Deep inside, the demon prodded her. It was weary of circumspection and care. It wanted action. She closed her eyes, willing it to lie quietly.

The better part of valor is discretion, my eager friend. They both knew there would be time enough for action. Transporting two children marked for death in Germany to the safety of England was certainly action, although none upon which the demon could thrive. It would have to wait. And so would she.

Chapter 11

Berlin. October 1939.

Again and again, they pored over the papers, not speaking, not looking at one another. They had all maintained their disguises and their business, but the shameful weight of failure clung to them like cellophane, and choked just as hard. Poland was occupied and war had begun. True, little seemed to be happening now, but that made no difference. More was on the way, they didn't need Eamon's sensitivity to smell it. They took cold comfort in the humiliation of Chamberlain, and liked the speeches Churchill was giving, but despaired of any of it amounting to anything. Something needed to happen, and every day that passed in inaction felt like another step toward annihilation.

"We should leave. To hell with whatever Otonia thinks and to hell with these bastards and this whole fucking country. We should leave while we still can."

They all stared at Swefred. Brigit's eyes narrowed.

"You're turning into quite the agitator for passivity, aren't you?"

The full force of Meaghan's punch in her jaw was something Brigit had not expected. Meaghan was only about twenty years older than Brigit and her fretfulness and stolidity gave everyone to believe that, millennial or no, she hadn't much vim or strength. So when the blow tore into Brigit's face and sent her sprawling to the floor in agony, it was several moments before any of them could register what had happened. Only when Meaghan, her green eyes tinged with pink and her fangs at full extension, gripped Brigit's ear and flung her around to spit in her face did Cleland jump forward and push her back. He threw Meaghan against the wall and slammed his forearm into her windpipe.

"Whingeing, useless, tiresome bitch! We should send you back to England in pieces!"

Swefred, his face in full fire, seized Cleland's outstretched claw and had nearly snapped it off when a noise like a sonic boom sent them all flying into a corner. Brigit, still stunned, dragged herself to her elbow to stare at Mors. This was what the legends spoke of, with fear and dread. This was what it meant to be a vampire more than two thousand years old. A powerful vampire, filled with fury. His body appeared suddenly colossal, as though it extended ten feet tall, his skull bulged through the skin, his eyes swelled far beyond their sockets, blazing heat and death. He roared again, and Meaghan wrapped her arms around her head. Mors gripped Swefred and Meaghan in one claw and Cleland in another and jerked them all to their feet.

"Remember who we are. We are the millennials of the British tribunal. Who are we?"

He shook Swefred, who gasped, "The millennials of the British tribunal."

"And what does that mean?"

"That we are great and noble and admired throughout the vampire world."

Mors turned to Meaghan.

"Do you disagree?"

"N-no."

"Do you know what it means to behave as a tribunal millennial?"

"I do."

"Do you have any inkling what I will do to you if you ever fail to behave in the manner you should again?"

Meaghan gazed up at him beseechingly, her face contorted with terror.

Mors flung them away from him and turned to Brigit, his human appearance restored. He ran a finger over the large, indented contusion overspreading her jaw and cheek.

"That should be healed by tomorrow night, and you can go and work Gerhard some more. We will get more of their war plans, by and by."

Swefred, though still shaken and wary, was roused again.

"But that's it, that's just it. What can we do? We were supposed to have destroyed them by now, paved the way for a proper government. We haven't stopped them doing anything."

"And if we leave now, we certainly never will. These are men of action and we will be as well! Enough with this excess of self-pity and defeatism! We know who and what we are. We are creatures of power and we are not done yet, we will see this through. What are we, three parts coward? This thing's to do and we have cause and will and strength and means to do it. Never mind twenty thousand men, we leave now and we'll see the deaths of millions of men, good food most of them, and progenitors of more meals, and if our thoughts can't be bloody as regards the Nazis, they'd best turn on the blood we won't imbibe for years if those devils see their plots through."

Swefred nodded, his eyes fixed on his knees. Meaghan pinched her lips together. She stole half a glance at Brigit, then leaped to her feet and marched off to her chamber. Swefred slumped off after her.

Brigit focused her gaze somewhere in between Mors and Cleland.

"Thank you. Neither of you had to do any of that."

"I did," Mors responded, his voice flat.

"I've never liked her," Cleland remarked. "But I shouldn't have, that is . . . ah, hell. You won't tell Padraic, not ever, will you?"

They murmured that no, of course, what was done was finished and need not ever be mentioned again. Cleland surprised Brigit by kissing her on the forehead, then turned quickly and headed for his bedroom. Brigit was sure she saw tears in his eyes, but thought it best to leave him alone.

Mors pressed a cool cloth to her face and knelt so he was looking in her eyes. The look unsettled her, and she realized it had been many centuries, certainly before Eamon, since he'd looked at her with such intensity. It roused a sudden question, which her mind hastily dismissed, but if Mors saw her discomfort, he gave her no indication. He smiled.

"Who frightened you more, her or me?"

Brigit grinned, even though it hurt.

"I think it might be a draw."

He wound a finger around one of her curls and tugged it playfully.

"Come on, get you off to bed. You need your rest."

She made no argument, feeling herself utterly drained. He put an arm around her to guide her to her room.

"Didn't think I knew my *Hamlet* so well, did you?"

"Nonsense, you came with us to the second performance, don't think I don't remember."

"You never forget a thing, do you? Memory like a whole herd of elephants."

"None of us forget anything, you know that."

At her door, he held her hand and looked at her again. For the first time almost since she'd known him, she had the sense he wanted to say something and couldn't bring himself to do so. The question buzzed inside her again and she swatted it back. Desperate to break this unaccustomed and awkward mood, she grinned her ancient, joking grin and poked him in the shoulder.

"Missed a trick, you know. You could have gone for the St. Crispin's Day speech, easy."

He grinned back, their usual relations restored.

"Ah, perhaps, but that one's better saved. We may need it another day."

As Brigit collapsed onto her bed, willing herself to melt into the feathers, she hoped it would not come to that. In her heart, thinking of Eamon, she had more care to go than will to stay, but again, thinking of Eamon, the desire to fight was still powerful. Allowing her thoughts to turn pleasantly bloody, she closed her eyes, feeling the demon inside purr.

Brigit waited until she heard Swefred and Meaghan leave the next night before venturing forth. She took the long way around to get to Gerhard's office. Her face, she could tell even without Cleland's assurance, was its usual pale and pretty self and she felt equal to the task of listening to Gerhard crow incessantly about all the great good that was happening in the world, now that the Führer had given them a taste of Germany's true power.

Something was wrong, however. Whether it was residual tension from the fight, or just impatience with the tedium of this process and what felt like the constant, low spin of wheels, she didn't seem able to work any magic on Gerhard. She wondered if perhaps he'd begun to grow immune to her powers.

"Ah, Brigitte, Brigitte, imagine the day when we bask in nothing but sunshine, all the year round!"

"I don't think the farmers would like that so much."

He laughed condescendingly.

"Come now, my silly girl, I know you have poetry in you, for all your lack of education. Think broadly, *liebchen*, broadly!"

"Describe it more, then. Let me see it all through your eyes."

"Well, you know what the Führer said at the Reichstag, that all Europe will be clean. We will have space, vast quantities of space. There will be nothing undesirable. The Jews, the Gypsies, those are just the obvious stains. I hear, and I oughtn't to have heard this, really, but they do trust me so, that the cleansing of the mentally ill and disabled has begun. One would pity them, but they are a drain on our resources, and we cannot have that. We want nothing but health and vibrancy in our great new world. A child who is lacking in capacity, well, he's as good as inhuman, isn't he? Not unlike a Jew. So, we will have a clean, healthy world in which to thrive. I could weep with joy."

Brigit gaped, hardly able to comprehend the waste he was describing, and his cavalier tone. True, she had never eaten anyone with an actual mental disability—and she suspected fools didn't count—but this was more because they did not wander the streets at night than any prejudice on her part. There were institutions, and surely humanity had evolved enough to treat the less fortunate among them with kindness? But kindness seemed quite beside the point in these strange days.

"Where will they all go?"

"Who?"

"Everyone. Can you really cleanse Europe of everyone—Jews, Roma, communists, homosexuals, everyone they say is an enemy of the state? I mean, does it really matter if there are homosexuals in Sweden, say? Surely it wouldn't dim the light in Germany?"

"What a funny little thing you are. We are talking about grand principles, my sweet. But there, I am being unfair, I cannot expect you to understand. Come here," and he pulled her into his lap and nuzzled her neck.

"But there must be a plan. Isn't there? People do not just disappear."

"Oh, plans, plans, plans. I have a plan right now, would you like to hear it?"

She forced a giggle and put a hand on his chest, holding him at a distance.

"Isn't Germany a bit worried about England? I mean, she's still considered at war, isn't she?"

He waved his hand dismissively.

"England! They've had every chance, you know. The Führer thinks very well of the pure-blood English. They are beautifully Aryan, like your own pretty self. But they will go their own way, stubborn fools. Well, I've not been told all, but I do hear there is a plan to bring them around yet, one way or another."

"Is that really possible?"

"All things are possible. Now, enough of this tiresome chat. It is making you frown and I want to see nothing but smiles."

She plastered a dutiful smile across her face, but inside was fuming. It wasn't just that the demon was hungry, she herself wanted more. He wouldn't succumb to her whispers and she knew it was because she was so roiled and frustrated, she couldn't concentrate.

I'm so close, I'm so close. He knows more, he can give me something to use, why can't I get it? Why?

But the window had closed for the night. There was nothing to do but tell him regretfully that the housekeeper was ill and she must get back early. With a kiss that nearly choked her, she was gone.

Full of dyspeptic temper, she prowled the streets hungrily. There was something about the quiet that night that exacerbated her rage, her itch simply to lay waste to the nation. Five millennials at full throttle could surely do more than Kristallnacht ever did to destroy and foment fear and rebellion. But it could not happen. The possibility of hunters in the country who knew how to destroy millennials was beside the point. No matter what they were capable of, they couldn't take it all down. Likely the Germans would be more devoted to Hitler than ever, believing not only that the infestation was not his fault, but also that he would stop it, as surely as he had begun to stamp out the pestilence that was all the undesirables. Nor was there any way to create such carnage without destroying innocents, and while there was no question that most of the prey they'd consumed over the centuries had been innocent, this would be something very different. Children would die, for a start, and it would all be the sort of annihilation they had come to Germany to prevent. They were predators, yes, but not indiscriminate monsters.

The scent of chaos swirled hot and sudden in the air and she turned to it. Two Gestapo officers with drawn guns were presiding over the arrest of a small group of Jews. Three families, by the look of it. There was a combination of fear and defiance on their faces and in their mien, but resignation bowed their shoulders. Brigit followed the procession, her anger rising. It wasn't death she wanted. It was the triumph of life. Propelled by a curious heat, she caught one of the officers by the arm.

The man whirled with an exclamation, but the warm smile that met his sharp eyes startled him into silence. The group halted, hovering, wondering.

"What are you doing out alone, Fräulein?" the man asked. "And what do you mean by stopping us when we are about official business?"

"What sort of official business requires women and children to be marched away with guns, under cover of darkness?" Her voice was sweet, but insistent. The man scowled. The girl may be a beautiful, perfect Aryan, but she was treading on forbidden territory.

"You had best get home, Fräulein, and learn not to ask questions."

He made to move, but her hand was a vise around his wrist.

"I like questions. And I like answers even more."

He looked right into her eyes and spoke robotically.

"They have been agitating, breaking laws, as though all our work at Nuremberg was up for dispute. They are to be made examples."

He didn't notice his hand was losing circulation.

"The children, too?"

"Bad blood runs in families."

The small group of Jews was too stunned even to gasp as the two officers fell. Blood flowed into the gutter. Supremely unconcerned, the girl handed the guns to the one man who seemed to sense what she might be. She spoke low and authoritatively.

"Go. Get to a train, go, and don't look back."

They obeyed, but even as they disappeared, Brigit was struck by the new scent they emitted. They were the walking dead. She'd achieved nothing, except perhaps a small pocket of time for them to head more certainly toward their end. As she dragged the bodies to a nearby incinerator, she had a sense of herself and the other four vampires, gigantic, linking arms to block the relentless march of the Nazis . . . and being mowed right down. Not easily, perhaps, but inevitably. Even still, she'd never wanted to fight and protect and win in the human world so hungrily. This had all become bigger than herself, than all the vampires, and she was so livid, she thought at that moment she could reach her claws to the German borders and rip the entire land asunder.

Brigit turned the corner and heard the carrying cry of a man. A nighttime rally was under way inside what had been a small, pretty theater. The demon raised its head hopefully, sniffing the air. The man was screaming, a would-be Hitler, assigned to keep the men in the district enthusiastic and on edge. To remind them who they were, and what it meant to be the master race. Men. Men who were being primed for more action. Nothing innocent there. The demon sang and slithered up through her, a cobra dancing to a charmer's music. Now Brigit smiled in earnest.

Yes, my darling demon, I will sate you.

She crept inside. There was one bored guard posted at the door and as he started to order her off, she snapped his neck with a brisk gesture. A giggle swelled inside her, but she held it down, happily ripping off the guard's arms to wedge inside the handles of the double doors, bolting them from the inside.

Reconnaissance, girl, there is a stage door, too.

First, she checked the windows in the cloakrooms. Two men were smoking in the lavatory. They looked around at her in mild surprise, and this time she couldn't help laughing when, after slamming one man's head through the other's throat, the expressions were still frozen on their faces. One was clinging to life, and she pulled off his legs to bar the window. That finished him.

Pausing only to enjoy the scent of warm, oozing blood, she hissed an old enchantment that kept her from being noticed and used her blinding speed to glide through the theater, counting the attendees, assessing the possibilities as she slipped backstage. Two SS flunkies were there, waiting for the orator to finish so they could go home to late suppers. They looked up at her and one started to speak, but she grinned and slammed fully extended claws into both their faces, piercing eyes and brains.

"You haven't seen me."

Their heads snapped off easily and she chortled. This was fun. She helped herself to their guns, uninterested in weapons, but figuring a bit of change and surprise would be a treat for her audience.

Listening to the orator venting his spleen, screaming about the inhumanity of the Jews and how their human-looking skins concealed rat-like bodies, encouraged her to rip open one of the men and pull out his intestines to use for tying the door shut. She was sorry she hadn't kept him alive to enjoy that, but she'd compensate. She'd compensate.

You've been very good, my beloved demon. You deserve treats.

The necessary prep work accomplished, she hovered at the pass door to look at the audience more closely. They were mostly young, but many were middle-aged and tired-looking. Probably they felt they had to be there; it would look as though they were apathetic or worse if they didn't show their faces at these gatherings. Brigit was disgusted that not a one of them dared say a word against all that they knew was happening, and would continue to happen. She knew there were some who didn't completely approve, and their willingness to bow their heads and simply go as the wind blew roused the demon yet further.

Two well-trained Nachtspeere were near the front, and this unsettled her. It seemed they were everywhere now. Residuals from the business with General von Kassell and the train, she supposed. The Nazis didn't really believe vampires had returned to the Continent, but no precaution was being spared. Besides, the Reich had put a lot of effort into training its hunters. Some had been promoted, were being moved into more active ranks. Others were held in reserve until Britain and Russia were Nazi territory and their vampires thus ripe for the picking. In the meantime, they wanted to feel that they were still useful. Which these two were not, or not against her. Their weapons could kill only the youngest vampires. They were no threat.

There were upward of two hundred men in attendance. That was a lot, more than she'd tackled in a long time. In fact, the last time she'd taken on so many was with Eamon, fighting for the Yorkists in the War of the Roses. Though York had turned on him as a human, he still loved the city, and the two of them had been brutal as its loyal soldiers. However, she hadn't been a millennial then. The power that she was feeling now was exhilarating. What she was about to do was something only a millennial could do with the grace and completeness she knew she would achieve. This was going to be easy. So, so easy.

She drifted to the back and bent over a man sitting in the last row. She snapped his neck and watched him slump forward, so that his companion nudged him.

"Come on, look alive."

She bit her palm so that she didn't laugh out loud. Not yet. Her blood was so high, she wanted to scream in ecstasy. She closed her eyes and threw back her head, letting the rush wash over her, regrouping, allowing the heat to give her even more strength.

Three more bodies, still quick, still quiet, each death filling her with erotic giddiness, anticipating that moment, that sweet moment of realization.

The scream.

She had stopped to eat, and looked up from a still-pulsing neck, her fangs at full extension, the tips bloody. Blood stained her plump lips. Her eyes were red, bulging, dripping with delighted malice. Swollen veins bursting from under her skin. Even her curls straightening and rising up from the roots, drunk with energy. That was what the man saw. That, and the livid smile, the talons that had burst through the long fingers and reached for him, snapping his spine as a neat coda to the scream.

And now the wave upon wave of screams, the beautiful chorus, operatic in its heft. She felt as if she were growing taller on its glorious noise, on that rhythmic chaos.

It was a gorgeous, thundering, orgasmic laugh that tore out of her when they rushed for the doors, the stronger crushing the weak in their fear—yes, here was all their great ideal of brotherhood and standing together—the specter of death showing that the basest desires of humanity would always prevail in the end.

When the doors proved impenetrable, so many of them ran up the disused wooden stairs to the light booth that the stairs collapsed, landing them in an absurd heap of limbs and cries. They retreated to the walls, scrabbling at them, screaming for someone to draw a weapon, to kill the beast. Brigit laughed harder, sank a finger into the forehead of the man nearest her and ran it all the way down through to his testicles, which burst through his trousers with amusing ease. He wriggled, still alive, and she picked him up and wrung him like a rag, sending vertebrae popping into the air like corks.

The screams turned into moans and many men looked to the orator, fruitlessly hoping that he might be able to summon some help, there must be help to be had. Whatever this was that had come unto them, it couldn't be real. It could not be something that the mighty Reich could not control.

The orator stood frozen, swaying slightly, as though trying to decide if he'd fallen into some hideous nightmare. Brigit liked that. Men who want to make living nightmares for others should know one of their own. He was only a foot soldier, true, but she was still saving him for the very end. She wanted him to be nothing but fear.

Jerking into action like a rusty biplane, one of the Nachtspeere seemed to remember what he was supposed to be. He snatched the small crossbow from its holster at his hip and aimed with more care than she might have expected, given he was gray and trembling. He fired, and Brigit caught the sharp little stake with its spear-like tip and rolled it between her palms, sending a sprinkle of wood dust to the floor.

Without seeming to have moved, she was upon him, her hand on his chest.

"Didn't any of your training suggest that such a thing might happen? Don't you know how to fight? Or were you absent the day they went over secondary tactics?"

He gulped. She tugged him with a force that pulled his body closer and sent his head flying across the room.

The other Nachtspeere hadn't moved. A trembling hand reached for his weapon. Brigit slithered behind him, laying an arm across his chest, her other hand snapping the stake in two.

"What's the matter, haven't you any backbone?"

She laid her hands on his shoulders and pressed them together, snapping out his spine.

"Yes, there it is. Don't you know what they say, 'Use it or lose it'?"

And she tore the spine out of him like a whip.

There was a moment of quiet among the men who remained, that ineffable moment at the beginning of realization, when they knew how trapped they were, that they were stealing gulps of air in a futile echo of something that is about to have been.

"Yes," Brigit informed them helpfully. "You are the past tense now."

A middle-aged man with a set jaw stepped out from the frightened cluster, and pulled out his crucifix. He began an old incantation for the dismissal of vampires.

Brigit smiled, liking his bravery. She admired his trust in the old ways. And, of course, had there been more of him, and had she been younger, it would have had some effect. In front of all these Jew-haters, it would have given her much pleasure to be Eamon, and show them how little the crucifix could really touch her, but now was not the time to think of Eamon.

She slowed, and felt the glimmer of hope in the room. The catch of breath that meant there was a chance, that this quiet, gentlemanly man, with his little paunch and thinning hair and tired eyes, he could be their savior. She looked in his eyes, reading him. He was a good enough man, ordinary, the sort who did his business, kept his head down, looked after his family, and just wanted to get by. He wanted to enjoy a tranquil life until called upon to leave it. Brigit suddenly felt a new surge of anger. Where was his good-hearted Christianity when all the trouble started, when the words became attacks, when the attacks became banishment, and now, when the banishment was becoming death? How dare he hug his nice life and gentle faith to him and look away from fear and suffering? Even if they were Jews, or Roma, or the disabled, the homosexuals, the communists, the whatever ... where did the Bible say their pain should be ignored?

She interrupted his incantation.

"If all of you had risen up, had said no, had used all these good words, I would not be here."

He stared. There was only the hint of comprehension in him, but it was enough. The smell of shame wafted from his neck. It wasn't enough to sate her, but even still, she would numb the death. She whispered an old language in the voice of seduction, a soft hypnotism and a quick lash.

He fell before the crucifix did.

It seemed to arouse the orator, and he began to scream anew, screaming about the evil among them, how it was real, how it needed to be destroyed, how they would do it.

"How?" Brigit inquired. "How will you destroy this evil?"

She began to sing tauntingly. She leaped onto the backs of the seats and danced across them, whirling like a ballerina. It was mesmerizing and bizarrely beautiful. She pulled out men hiding under the seats as she spun, slashing them through, tossing their bodies aloft with the flair of a juggler.

"Well, go on then, destroy me. What do you have to destroy me? Where is all your might? Aren't I just a sweet little girl?"

She pirouetted onto the stage, pausing in the spotlight, allowing her face and body to revert briefly to its human-looking self, so that they could see. A young man cowering in the wings gasped, hardly believing how beautiful she was. She grinned at him.

"Ever been kissed?"

He shook his head numbly.

She pulled him to her, popped out her fangs, and bit off his face.

A sudden shot startled her. The bullet grazed her shoulder. The man aimed again and she pulled out her pilfered gun.

"If you're going to use a gun, use it properly."

The bullet sank between his eyes.

One of the last remaining men took out a gun and aimed for his own head, but she wouldn't have that. She leaped back into the audience, seized him, and kicked her foot through his stomach instead.

There were three left. She pulled them into an embrace, her eyes locked on the orator's. He could not see what she did, only that as she walked toward him, fresh blood dripped down her coat. He whined, backing away upstage.

"You won't survive, you won't survive," he squeaked. "We'll get all of your beastly kind in the end. You can't stop us. We're too power-ful."

"I wouldn't lay money on that if I were you."

With measured, deliberate steps, she circled closer and closer to him. He clutched at the faded, worn scrim behind him, then shrieked and leaped up it, climbing all of two feet before the fabric gave way with a tired sigh and collapsed him back to the stage in a cloud of dust and thread.

"I do hate to see a theater in disrepair. Such a waste. And you certainly know about waste, don't you?"

She held out a hand to help him up, then gently drew him back to the circle of light at center stage, slowly revolving, for all the world as if it were a choreographed waltz.

"Why on earth would you leave this beautiful spotlight?"

She slid behind him, laid her hands on his cheeks, and tilted his head to look up into the flickering bulb.

"Even a student on his first day at conservatory knows that you play out the climax front, center, and in the light. The audience has earned that."

He was nearly fainting from fear.

"Evil . . . evil . . ." he murmured feebly.

"No, no. That will not do. You're to speak the speech trippingly on the tongue, or not at all. Care to try again?"

Drenched in sweat, he slipped from her grasp to his knees.

"Then I guess the act is mine to finish."

With that, she reached into his mouth, pulled out his tongue several inches, and snapped his jaws shut so that half his tongue flew across the stage. He howled through a mouthful of blood.

"You and your kind. Such a penchant for drama. I rather think this little show is over, don't you? Yes, I believe this was the finale. Isn't it time the lights went out?"

She punted him toward the spotlight. His head went straight through, sending a shower of sparks down onto the carnage.

Brigit dropped a beautiful curtsy and exited stage left, hearing a wave of thunderous applause play her out onto the still-quiet street.

It was with shock and horror that many in the neighborhood saw the charred remains of the theater the next day and mourned those who had perished so dreadfully. No one could comprehend how the gas main could have exploded so violently, how everything and everyone could be burned so very far beyond recognition. Arson would have been suspected, but the power of the destruction was far beyond human strength and capacity. The baffled local officials could do no more to comfort the hundreds of bereaved than to say that sometimes dreadful things happened and nothing could have been done to change it. This was easier to believe than any other possibility.

For her part, Brigit spent that day sleeping the sleep of the untroubled dead.

Chapter 12

London. January 1940.

"Something's wrong besides the obvious."

Eamon jumped. Otonia had sat down next to him and he hadn't even heard her approach. That was the gift of being so supremely ancient. She didn't even bother to seduce her prey anymore, just took what she needed and got on with whatever else she'd set out to do that evening.

"It's not that I don't enjoy my food," she explained. "I just don't want to miss out on anything else."

She dropped a hand on Eamon's shoulder and gazed out at the city. "I hope this lasts."

He nodded, only half paying attention. He'd been brooding for several weeks now, and he knew they'd all noticed but were diplomatic enough to keep a distance. Otonia, however, had picked up on something more, and was determined to head off any trouble before an idea could take root. It was marvelous and terrifying, the way she sensed things, but Eamon was hardly in a mood to talk. This did not seem to bother the ancient leader, as she knew he was listening.

"Funny, isn't it, our way of thinking? Time is so different for us. Quite a luxury, although I suppose we don't always appreciate it. We can spend centuries mulling a problem, and never get to the end of it. Perhaps we should be the ones to write philosophy."

He bristled slightly at her implication. "I'm not thinking—"

"I know."

Her smile was kind, with deep understanding creased into every fold of her skin. Otonia was not pretty; her face was too strong-featured for prettiness. But there was something in her that made you want to look at her again. Her deep voice and intelligent eyes could hold you rapt for hours, or centuries. The others all surmised that these were the qualities that had led to her making, that she had perhaps seduced her maker, rather than the other way around. Hers was also the only face among them, besides Mors's, that betrayed time. To give her just a passing glance, she was frozen in her early twenties, but on closer inspection, the millennia were written on her skin. The breadth of knowledge and experience in her mien was what commanded all their respect, trust, and, it could not be denied, love. Even now, when she knew that Eamon and Padraic, and the millennials in Berlin, all thought she'd made a grave error in judgment and was only compounding it, she made no apology and asked no forgiveness. Should it be needed, it would probably come. Otonia was not one to worry.

She pulled her ever-present distaff from inside the folds of her cloak and concentrated on winding wool so Eamon did not have to feel any eyes on him.

"There is a lot they can do. We still have hope."

Eamon's head hardly moved, but she saw it.

"You like Mors, of course, but perhaps you don't trust him? Not that it matters, since you trust Brigit so completely. And the fact that there were two centuries wherein they might have become more than friends, than brother and sister, but never did, that is perhaps not the same thing as being lonely and frightened and under terrible duress in enemy territory. So you think that when she comes back to you, she'll no longer be your girl. Or not in quite the same way."

Of all the things he was so terrified of losing in Brigit, this was one that had only recently begun to plague him, and he suspected it did so because it was so tangible. He hated it, though, and he hated himself for it even more.

"Worried that disaster might provoke infidelity . . . I honestly don't know if she'd fall down laughing or never forgive me. It's absurd. I feel so . . . human."

"You look human."

He grinned.

"Well, that's something. But we're supposed to be bigger than that. I don't know what's wrong with me."

"There's nothing wrong with you. You just miss the girl who keeps your heart safe."

She rose and dropped a quick kiss on top of his head.

"No one ever said it was easy to keep the home fires burning."

When she had gone, he fell back on the grass and blinked up at the stars.

Home fires. It's more than that, though, isn't it? You've always had so much more in you than that.

He didn't know what possessed him to relive their past in his head—it was as though writing the history in his mind was a talisman and kept her present, even when she wasn't.

You were so angry and so unhappy. Like me, but for such different reasons.

But for all they had later become, he could not trawl through history without remembering how they had started, and what he had lost.

The Jewish community of twelfth-century York was not large, but it was happy and thriving. To be sure, there were some incidents, and people had heard tell of some unpleasantness throughout England, but they had their faith in God, in the king, and in their overall good relations with their Gentile neighbors. They minded their business, obeyed all strictures, and took care not to give anyone much reason to notice them. Most of them worked at the dull and distasteful, if necessary, job of moneylending, having little other recourse. And they were not all wealthy, no matter what some of their neighbors might suspect.

Jacob of Emmanuel and his little family were certainly not wealthy, although things were improving, thanks to Jacob's talent at baking. The family had always baked the bread for their community, but even as a small boy, Jacob showed a deftness and feel for dough that made a bread so delicious, he could never make enough for everyone. It was noticed that even a few Gentile girls ventured into the Jewish quarter to buy bread from Jacob. In very quiet corners it was whispered that this might have less to do with the goodness of the bread than with the remarkable handsomeness of Jacob, and the shocking bravery of the girls' admiration of a Jew was given due respect.

Jacob's looks were a startling thing to the entire community. He was taller than any other man, for a start, and broad-shouldered, muscular from swinging sacks of flour since he was ten years old. His fingers were long and nimble and never seemed to tire, even after shaping a hundred loaves. He had silky brown hair that tumbled around his head and magnetic, twinkling eyes that were sometimes brown, sometimes green, depending on the light. His ready smile was mischievous, and made those eyes snap in a manner that was highly unsettling to every marriageable girl in the community. Then, too, he had a way with words that made him seem far more learned than he was. Those men whose business kept them from household errands like buying bread found reasons to call at the bakery anyway, simply to exchange a few words with the fascinating baker.

Now nearly eighteen, it was expected that he should marry soon. He knew this, and was prepared to do his duty, but he was hesitant. Perhaps he could solicit a girl with some money, but whatever anyone else thought of him, he did not think so well of himself that to reach above his station seemed appropriate. But how could he take proper care of a wife and children when there was his uncle and small brother and sister to care for already, and the money he earned only just kept them?

He would never have dared express his other reason for hesitating. He knew what it would sound like. It was not as though there weren't pretty, spirited girls around, but that he had an idea of something he wanted that he couldn't articulate even when he lay awake and stared out at the stars. More education, that was part of his dream. He was clever, he knew it, and the rabbi was prepared to help him, but the early deaths of his parents made him feel his position as man of the family. His uncle tried hard, but was ailing and found standing for long hours too grueling. So who but Jacob could manage the business and care for them? Still, he would like to learn more. More even than what the rabbi could teach, but he quashed that thought. It sounded disrespectful.

Then there was music. The unspoken obsession. His dreams were always in melody. His thoughts had a singsong rhythm. Music flowed through him when he made bread. Every sound he heard, wherever he went, he wanted to capture and re-create as a song. It was everywhere but tantalizingly out of reach. He often sang out loud, but there was a strength, passion, and uniquely enticing beauty in his clear tenor that others found disconcerting, so he tried not to sing unless he was alone, or in the synagogue. The singing at Sabbath was never enough. He had to sneak outside the nearest church on Sundays and hide, so he could hear more music. It shamed him, this furtive enjoyment of Gentile music, but there was no helping it. He needed the sound more than liquid. He was a man driven, and didn't know what else he could do.

Once, some traveling players had come to town. The Jews were not allowed to attend performances, but when he knew they would be giving an evening concert for a magistrate, he crept to the house, climbed a tree, and listened. Bliss. This was life. He could just see the musicians and feel the pleasure on their faces. The joy in making music. One of them played a rebec. Jacob stared at it. All his life, he'd known things . . . sensed them. He'd known with horrible certainty at the beginnings of their illnesses that his parents would die. He'd known from the day she could toddle that Alma, his sister, would be the sort of child to play pranks and laugh easily and be a beloved friend. He knew now, with absolute certainty, that were he to hold a rebec, set it on his thigh, and touch the bow to the strings, it would obey him. It would spill out every song that had ever spun around in his tireless brain. Longing choked him. The complete impossibility mocking his dreams. The man played, and Jacob wept.

Perhaps there was a woman who could understand all this, perhaps there was a way to have something else, perhaps . . . but these were not good days for contemplating happiness. News was bad. Jews were being persecuted in England, burned out of homes, or sometimes inside them. Or they were put to the sword. Jacob wanted them to be ready. He knew there was a fight coming, and he wished he had a weapon. Fight back, that's what he wanted to do. Die on his feet fighting, if he was going to die. He knew he was strong, but with only bread knives, he had no chance. Still, he was ready to show those who would hound them what real honor was, if it was the last thing he ever did.

But the children, God in heaven, what about the children?

As it happened, on the evening the trouble closed in, York's Jews decided to flee to the castle for protection. There was little choice—houses had been burned and some were killed. But the king's men were coming; they would settle the growing mob and reestablish order. Their lives would go on. So the logic went. Jacob did not really believe that, but what choice was there? There was his uncle and the children, and no way to escape. He hated the idea of running, but these three souls were entrusted to his care. He was outnumbered, and as good as unarmed. There was nothing else to do.

They walked quickly, quietly, eyes firmly on the path and the parapet. A sweet, coaxing voice hissed in Jacob's ear and his head jerked around, but no one was there. Alma and Abram were quiet, Uncle was breathing too hard with the labor of walking to speak. And this was a voice—perhaps he was going mad, along with the rest of the world—but this voice sounded like some of the songs he'd conjured in his head. Music that came from a dream, but nothing human. There it was again. He shook his head to clear it, and to concentrate on prayer. *Shma Yisrael, adonai eloheinu* . . . where was God, anyway?

As they climbed the steps to the tower's great door, it was Jacob, not his uncle, who found each step more arduous, as though a great force were pushing him back. He had the strongest sensation of trying to walk into an ice-brick wall. He paused, only to feel bonds encircling him, pulling him down, away. He pushed his fists into his suddenly hot, throbbing eyes. The world and he were certainly going mad.

"Jacob? Are you all right?" Alma's hand plucked worriedly at his elbow.

"Come away. Come. Come, let me help you."

This time he saw it. Her. But she couldn't be real. It was a ghost, a mirage, standing there on the hill opposite the tower, long, loose hair billowing around her, a hand extended, a promise in her deep blue eyes. Why could he see her eyes? She was too far away. But he could. And he had to go to her.

"Where are you going?"

Oh, God. He looked at them, the two tiny, trusting faces, the older, bewildered one. What was he doing? He shook his head violently, fighting against the rising nausea and bursting veins in his temples. They had to get inside. But the closer he got to the door, the more his feet burned. He felt shot through with freezing needles. He stopped again, desperate to catch a breath.

"You must, you must come. There is no other chance," the voice was urgent, even frightened.

"There is no other chance."

"What?" His uncle and Alma stared, perplexed and concerned. Abram was too sleepy to notice that Jacob was swaying and his voice was rough and strange.

The musical voice had wrapped itself around Jacob and he found he didn't want to break its hold. He knew, too, that he couldn't enter the castle. The ice was impenetrable. He wished he could breathe properly, could think, could determine what they all should do. He swayed precipitously and his uncle put a steadying hand on his arm.

"Stay outside a moment and catch your breath. I'll get the children inside." His uncle couldn't hear the voice, or feel the ice, but even in the poor light he could see Jacob's eyes were wild and his skin flashing white and then red. If he was going to be sick, better to do it outside.

Jacob bent quickly to his brother and sister and kissed each face.

"Forgive me. Oh, God, forgive me."

Alma clutched at his hand but said nothing. He cupped her face, looked in her eyes. Her brown eyes were darker than his, wider, and wiser. They smiled, though her face stayed solemn. She nodded, whether in understanding or farewell, he didn't know. Beloved sister. Best friend. Blood. No! He wouldn't leave them. He would collect himself, and come inside.

His uncle patted him on the shoulder. "You will be all right in a minute. We'll be waiting for you."

And they went in. Even though others followed, Jacob was sure he saw that icy door close hard behind them, sucking them deep inside. He reached for them, but the singing whisper came again. He had to go.

He almost floated toward the extraordinary girl, sure he was walking the walk of a dreaming man.

"No, this is real," she whispered, though he'd said nothing. "Tell them one last good-bye. The children will hear you."

She cupped her hand around his mouth. And as if in a dream, he did as she bid.

"Alma. Abram. I love you. God be with you, always."

He wanted to say more, or perhaps just the same words again, but the sound died in his throat. The girl dropped her cool hand from his mouth and wrapped it gently around his fingers.

"They're not afraid."

Her eyes were honest, and he believed her.

She applied a tiny bit of pressure on his hand, just enough to pull him away from that miserable spot. He didn't know where they were going, but neither did he care.

They were past the city walls, in a moonlit clearing. He looked into her eyes and forgot that barely an hour ago, he'd guided his family out of their home, fighting the urge to wonder if he'd ever enter that door again. Who could think of anything else, looking into these eyes? And though it was insanity to think so, it seemed to him she was the loneliest woman he'd ever seen, and yet lost in love. Despite the chill and the strangeness, he'd never felt so complete in his skin and right in his place as that moment. And not since he was a tiny boy, falling asleep under his mother's hand stroking his hair, had he felt so loved and protected. It was incomprehensible, but he didn't mind. He'd always had an affinity for that which couldn't be immediately understood.

The girl smiled suddenly, a brilliant flash that took his breath away. The energy she radiated glowed hot around her, a beacon of light in the darkness. There was intelligence in those large, lonely eyes, and a lost world, and a world to be discovered. He'd never wanted to touch anyone so desperately. His heart was pounding, he almost felt like it was expanding, pulsing against his ribs. So slowly, he might have been standing aside and watching himself, he raised his fingers to her cheek. The feel of her skin sent a shot like lightning through him—at once cold and hot. Her eyes sparked and he bit back a gasp. He had no idea what the love between a man and a woman was like, but the powerful energy that was now swirling around him, tickling his skin, told him he was on his way home.

Brigantia was terrified. She had smelled him before she saw him, and the scent had made the back of her neck tingle and her fingers ache.

His intelligence, his pride, his courage. His hunger for all there was in the world, and more. And music, music that made her think of sunlight dappling the river, the feel of lying on a hill and staring up through the trees and into a bright blue sky. Two hundred and seventy-four years since her humanity, and the few happy memories of that life were flowing through her useless veins. She pressed her hands to her head, summoning all her concentration. But then she looked up, and saw those eyes.

She buried her face in a tree, trying to think. *This is love. This is the love I thought was just the stuff of ancient poetry and idle dreams.* She peeked at him again. *I can hear his heart beating. I want to crawl inside that heart. I want to be the only one for whom it beats.* She would have to turn him, there was no other option, as a human he was already the walking dead, but turning him meant that heart wouldn't beat, and would she deserve him, deserve this possibility of love? She knew only too well that to turn someone did not mean they rose and loved you.

The Jews were heading to the castle to wait in safety for help. But there were so few of them, and the hatred in the air was so high. If he went in there, he would not come out. She told herself this was his only chance, even knowing she meant it was hers. So with guilt overwhelmed by longing and hope, she sent out the whispering call.

And so here they were. She knew what she had to do. Otonia had explained it. With infinite care, with infinite tenderness, and yet with control.

"What is your name?"

"Jacob. Of the family Emmanuel. What is yours?"

"Brigantia."

"An ancient name."

"Yes. Mine is an ancient family."

She willed herself to stop talking, fearing it would dissipate the spell. She laid a hand on his chest, memorizing the feel of his heartbeat. He laid a hand over hers and her stomach contracted. Otonia had never even suggested it might be anything like this. "And yet with control." Easier said than done.

She was aching to kiss him. It was taking most of her control to fight that urge. It would be wrong, it would be kissing him under the blind canopy, embracing from across a divide. It wouldn't be real, and it wouldn't be love. However long it took, she was going to wait for that kiss, till he was in this place with her.

She reached up to his ear, whispering again. A formula that slipped back to the beginning of their time, and nobody knew when that was. But it was a sweet hiss that hung like a mist around them. His breath was hot on her neck, his arms tight around her, his pulse racing. The demon strangely unwilling to rise—all she wanted was to lie down with him. At last, however, the fierce pounding of his heart against her breast and the feel of his blood coursing under her touch roused the demon, and her fangs slid out from under her gums. More gently than she knew possible, she bit.

Of course, Jacob had dreamed of holding a woman close, and wondered what it must feel like. He wanted to kiss a woman, properly, and no woman had ever made his mouth tingle like Brigantia. But she shied from his lips, her mouth was hot on his neck, and he wondered why he wanted so much from a stranger, or why she felt like someone he'd known even before he was born.

His mind was whirling. He was floating; no, sinking. Was he supporting her, or she him? His blood was pounding so hard, he had no sense of it draining, and was fast becoming a freak of nature as his heart simultaneously raced and slowed.

His one certainty was that his mouth needed to be on some part of her flesh. As though she read his mind, or, happier, shared his need, she slid her hand up his back and around to his face. He pressed her palm against his slightly open lips, drowning in the salty sweetness of her taste and the pressure of her fingertips against his cheek. There was warmth in this small hand. Warmth and wetness, although he didn't notice that, and if he had registered the blood dripping from the swift slash, the injury would have horrified him even more than that same blood dripping down his dry throat.

But he was now far past noticing anything.

For years afterward, it was a small point of pride with him that, although far from the manner in which he'd imagined or even intended, he did, indeed, die on his feet.

•   •   •

There is no consciousness in the dig, any more than there is in a bird's pecking of its shell, or indeed, a baby sliding out of its mother. The dig is just determined, the arduous and painful task of vampire birth. It was not until his head burst through and he shook particles of dirt from his eyes that his brain clicked in and began to work again. She was there, watching, her lovely face bathed in moonlight. He pulled himself out of the grave and knelt on the edge, feeling the need to pant from the exhaustion, but, of course, there was no panting.

He wished she wasn't there, wasn't watching. He didn't want her to see him struggle, gasp for a breath he didn't need. The chill clawing at his back wasn't the night or his own self, but her. Her, and the cold stillness she'd planted inside him. He blinked down into the empty grave, expecting to see a shadow of himself inside all that churned-up dirt. He studied his hands—dirty, but familiar, and wondered where this tingle came from, this sense that each was enclosed in something immense, overwhelming, something that tugged and was determined to possess him. His hands were not his, not anymore.

Food. He needed food. Simple sustenance to fill the hollowness, to settle the mind. A warm meal, a good meal, the essence of life. The bowl of lamb stew that flitted through his mind danced tauntingly before him, its sweet smells dissipating with each imagined sniff, chunks of meat and vegetables evaporating and then the gravy swirled and snaked its way into the ether. Blood bubbled from the bottom of the bowl, blood that had been so carefully drained away and buried, now swelled up to the brim. Blood. An unkosher thing, forbidden, even if it was what some Gentiles alleged the Jews stole to make their Passover matzo. But as the bowl expanded into a tub and invited him to bathe, he knew this was his staff of life now, and he would not shy from it.

Infuriating certainty told him exactly where he must go. Steps retraced, moving backward through space even as he'd leaped forward into a vortex. Pushing against a heavy wall that chafed deep under his skin, all the way back to what had been his home.

And all the while, she tagged behind him. He could hear the buzz of her unspoken thoughts, feel her mouth open and then close, and took some pleasure in her uncertainty. She had pulled him from where he belonged and set him here, on this peculiar precipice, and although an echo whispered that he'd wanted that, that the song which breathed through him when she'd summoned him forward was the song he had always wanted to sing, was meant to sing, his propensity at this moment was not to forgive. The weight of his partial soul was too heavy.

They were there, as he had known they would be. The vultures. Not even vultures, for the bold and determined had raided the homes of the Jews the previous day. These were the weak parasites who were suffered to pick at bones and privileged to keep a morsel of cartilage, should they find one.

The small, shabby house in which he'd been born and lived his short life still smelled faintly of bread. He could open the door and enter, which meant the house knew its people were gone and would not come back. It was stripped bare. Furniture, crockery, linens, the children's whittled toys. Other children had played with those toys on this day. The vision filled him with a rage he hadn't thought possible.

He tucked the rage away for later use and concentrated on the smell. She was in the bakehouse. Searching through the cupboards by the light of a single candle for things overlooked. Already she had found some salt and a dull knife. She was enjoying her luck.

"Go away, this is my spot!" Her cry was an echo from inside the cupboard, her impertinent bottom an obscene protrusion.

"Is it now?"

The voice was pleasant, leisurely, and tinged with sarcasm. Her bottom froze. There was an alertness about it, like a fox who hears the distant baying of hounds. It amused him, and he wondered how much mileage she'd gotten from that communicative round rump.

She backed out quickly and looked up. Yes, he knew her. One of those flirts who sometimes came to buy his bread and ogle his face. Giggle, and even wink. Exactly what she expected from him, he never wanted to know, but if she thought her own face and patronage meant anything to him, she was quite wrong. He was not so foolish as to refuse to sell, because that could have led to trouble, and the entire Jewish community had always been determined to avoid trouble. But trouble came anyway. Didn't it just?

The girl had enough grace to look abashed. She brushed a loose curl out of her face. Flour clung to her cheeks and hair, making her look foolish. She tried to smile.

"You are back. I thought . . ."

"That I wasn't coming back? That I was taking up permanent residence in the castle, perhaps? I, and all my people? Well, why not? We could earn our keep there, certainly. Mop up after the pigs. I suppose that would be appropriate. The animals dirtiest to you tending the animals dirtiest to them. What a charming entertainment."

"No. No, I . . . you don't understand. I'm not like that. Some Christians are, I suppose, but that's not proper Christian behavior, not really. You must believe me."

"Oh, I do. I suppose you only thought that since everyone else had stripped our homes, you may as well come along and see what could be yours. Why should only the people who want us dead get to prosper off us?"

"But you are not dead. Are you all coming back?"

"That would be a sight, wouldn't it? Such a welcome for us."

"I'm sorry, Jacob. I am sorry. And I'm glad you're well."

"Where are my brother and sister? My uncle? All my friends?"

"What?"

"Do you wish them well, too?"

He didn't want to enjoy her fear so much, but he couldn't help it. Such a tiny thing he could do now, such a meager offering to the universal determiners of retribution. The fear emanating from the souls in the castle, as against the swell of fear inside this silly rabbit of a woman. As neither man nor vampire did he believe in the mantra of an eye for an eye, but right now, in this empty room, feeling chaos closing in on the distant castle, he wanted this fear. Perhaps if he had smelled remorse in her, sorrow, if he knew she'd come to salvage in penance and grief and resignation. But she was only sorry to be caught, inside her she knew that her word against a Jew's would be believed, though she was a woman. He could bring no charge against her. He had nothing.

The sureness of her superiority, the blessing of God that let her be born a Christian, the feeling that he and his fellow Jews, hardworking and quiet and decent though they were, deserved the fate storming in on them . . . no, it would not stand. She may only be a trivial symbol of the thinking that doomed them, but it was enough.

He pulled her to her feet and kept an arm on her, smiling that bright, twinkling smile that had haunted so many girls' dreams. The blush overspread her cheeks and neck. How much atonement would be necessary for reaching out to touch a beautiful Jewish man? Let a hand wander through his hair? Let her breasts brush against the thin fabric of his tunic? His fingers ran down her spine, pressing her further into him the lower they went. So this was what it took: Reduce a man to nothing and now he is putty in your hands and will fulfill your desires. She was getting married soon, it wouldn't matter. So many men in town had wanted her, with her giggle and wiggle, but it was this man, this forbidden man with his sensual eyes and that smile, around whom she wanted to wrap herself.

She put her arms around his neck and pulled him toward her, eyes open just enough, hoping to see the delight in his face. Yes, he was smiling again, slowly, a thin smile growing wider . . . she was too frightened to scream.

The fangs were out before the eyes turned red. He felt them elongate and found it a peculiar and exquisite sensation. She struggled, and he enjoyed that, too. The round, wriggling little body. The obnoxious flesh she'd wanted him to touch. She'd wanted his mouth on her, although she would not have been above spitting at his sister.

"You bought my bread, but you would have died rather than break it with me. Still, let's have one last supper together, shall we? Well, your last. My first."

But the sweetness of relief drained from him as he left the house without a backward glance. There was no comfort in Brigantia's watchful presence, no desire to delve his new world. To his surprise, he found himself back at his own grave, half wishing to get back in it, draw the dirt over him like a blanket and stay. There could be only two places he belonged— on this earth as he had come onto it, or in it, disintegrating.

Brigantia stood beside him and he finally met her eye. Now that he was on the same side of the divide with her, the shadow that encircled them repelled him. He felt how she radiated life, even warmth, and there was a sparkle about her and a deep energy that enticed him, much the way her expressive, overflowing eyes were lighting tiny fires under his skin. He could not dismiss any of that, but neither did he want to kiss her.

"You're dead. We're dead. We are the walking dead."

"That is the simplistic definition, but not wholly accurate."

"You killed me."

"Saved you."

The words were arrogant, but the tone placating. Even desperate. She was strong, far more powerful than he, as was the privilege of age, but right now, he had a power she did not, and he savored it.

He was wasting time. He knew where he had to be and his new strength and power meant that he could do all that he'd wanted and more to set the world right. Her eyes were standing in his way.

The speed with which he could now travel was exhilarating and he reveled in it. His body had always been powerful, but this, this sense that he could rip through a fortress, destroy a man with his fingers, it was deliciously frightening and he wanted more.

As the castle came into view, he hesitated, sniffing the air for life. Yes, they were still there. Frightened, but alive. Now he moved slowly, the beginnings of a plan revolving in his mind.

Brigantia's finger brushed his cloak.

"Friend, wait."

"Friend? Am I your friend?"

"I, well, I . . ."

A tiny wave of understanding washed over him. They were family, whether he liked it or not, but really, she was waiting for him to tell her his name. She wanted to address him, and chose the only polite way available, however inaccurate. He appreciated her manners but wasn't ready to answer her. He wasn't ready to let go of Jacob, not when so much of Jacob was still bound up in him and in the castle. If he had no good reason to be cruel to her, he was certainly not disposed to be kind. She waited, patience and hope in her eyes, but once again, he turned from her.

As soon as she understood what he was hoping to do, she was after him in a rush of speed and strength that showed him what it meant to be a double centennial. Her hands were hot on his arms and her eyes fiery.

"You can't, you mustn't."

"You're telling me what to do?"

"Please believe me. I saved you, but there is no saving them. It is too late and there are not enough of us. No one would survive."

"You dare tell me not to try to save my own flesh and blood?"

"They aren't, not anymore."

It was the clinging vestiges of the man, not the demon, who struck her hard across the face. Her hands flew to cover the pink cheek, a faint outline of fingers sketched across it, her eyes wide and devastated. Jacob stepped back, stunned, and gazed at his stinging palm. He had a new relationship with humans, and so the woman he'd eaten was no longer his equal, but this creature was meant to be his family, however much he wanted to deny it. And while he was ready to defend his family against any who would harm them, he'd never willingly caused the smallest injury to a single soul. But that realization steeled him, chased the guilt and horror out of his heart. There was no soul inside the pretty vampire. No matter how many fat tears rolled down her face as she sat on a rock and glowered at him. Anyone could feel pain, that was not the same thing as having a true soul. But a swathe of his soul stretched around his chest, pulled him toward the castle, and it gave him an intoxicating sense of superiority. Whatever else she may have, she didn't have this, a shred of humanity and a cause. Maybe later he could pity her, but for now he had to go.

He knew before he reached the castle that something was wrong, horribly wrong. Worse than he imagined. There was a smell he couldn't define, but as it engulfed his senses, he knew he'd never forget it, that it would permeate his nightmares for years. He didn't register starting to run, to cry out their names; it was only when he hit what he thought was a tree and fell backward that he realized his muscles were shaking.

The vampire, and he knew it was a vampire, who looked down at him was a terrible thing to behold. A bald creature with hypnotic eyes and a powerful mouth set in a cold, cruel, ironic smile. He squatted over Jacob and set a hand on his shoulder. There was nothing inherently unfriendly about the gesture, but fear rose in Jacob's stomach.

"You are the vampire Brigantia made last night."

It wasn't a question, and Jacob was too unnerved even to nod.

"I am Mors. You can ask them all questions about me, and you will get a different answer, every time." Mors paused, and smiled as a dog trotted up to join them and licked his hand. The scene was so incongruous Jacob almost wanted to laugh. He suspected the vampire of sensing as much, because the look Mors fixed him with drove any kind of laughter far away.

"Brigantia has waited a long time to make a vampire. A long time. And I have been her friend, even her brother, all during that time." The words were casual, but Jacob bristled at the subtle warning, even as he paid it close attention.

"There is much to learn, entering this world. Heedless recklessness, that won't do. Not if you wish to survive."

With that, he seized Jacob's hand and jerked him to his feet. It would almost be friendly, except that Mors was gripping the hand that had struck Brigantia and clutched it so hard, Jacob could feel the cartilage disintegrating. He gasped, struggling, but Mors only grinned.

"Dawn is less than an hour away. We're going home now. That's not negotiable."

Jacob knew better than to argue. He wondered if Mors had seen the slap, because he was certain Brigantia would not have told anyone about it. Mors definitely sensed something and was going to brook no nonsense from this hatchling. The power he radiated was intimidating. Jacob desperately wondered if vampire limbs grew back once ripped off and decided he had no interest in finding out.

Inside the caves, Mors shoved Jacob into an empty chamber that he could tell from the scent was next to Brigantia's. A tiny tug inside him told him he belonged in the chamber with her, but he ignored it. Mors studied him, still grinning. His eye slid from Jacob to a dusty book on the table. He picked it up, twirled it thoughtfully, then remarked to its spine: "Some things can't be interfered with. Some things have to just be let go."

"What does that mean?"

"Oh, nothing. Only that human chaos is just that. Human."

"I'm not following."

"No. You're not. Not yet. Sleep well."

It was only when Mors left that Jacob realized how exhausted he was, and how much his hand hurt. It was covered in dark, finger-shaped bruises. He lay down, staring at the dark ceiling, wondering if the sobbing he heard as he drifted into uneasy sleep was the lonely, brokenhearted vampire next door or the frightened family and friends locked up in the castle tower several miles away, praying for a miracle.

Jacob woke with a start, feeling he should not have slept, that he should have kept vigil, that he should be somewhere else. He splashed his face with water and hurried up the tunnel to the lair's entrance, only to be struck with the full force of a late-afternoon sun. He cried out and collapsed, rubbing his stinging eyes with cool dirt. It was only as the pain subsided did he realize his hand didn't hurt anymore. He looked at it: The bruises were nearly gone. The wonders of this new body, its strengths and weaknesses, held deep fascination for him and he could not help looking forward to learning this self, once he had leisure to think.

But I'm dead. I'm dead. I'm a dead thing. What more is there to learn than that? What else matters?

Even as he thought it, some small part of him knew it wasn't true, but he was too furious to care. He sat safely outside the sun ray and wrapped his arms around his knees, waiting for the moment he could venture out.

It wasn't long before he felt Brigantia behind him, her eyes boring into his skull. He resolutely ignored her. Much later, he could feel Mors sitting just behind Brigantia, watching her as she watched Jacob. He didn't give a damn. He was feeling the waves of horrible energy emanating from the castle and bitterly, impatiently counting seconds, even though the familiar feeling told him he was already far too late.

When the sun finally dropped over the horizon, he took off at a gallop. The smell was worse than ever, a gut-twisting smell.

Once again, it was Mors who caught him, and once again, Jacob felt that thrill of fear and wonder at the speed and ability of such a powerful ancient vampire. The look in Mors's eyes was one almost of pity and understanding, rather than anger, and this frightened Jacob far more.

"You shouldn't go."

"I have to go."

"There's nothing left."

Jacob stared at him. Now Mors's eyes glazed over with a kind of resigned fury, the look of someone who'd seen something he did not want to see, but it didn't surprise him because he'd seen so much that should never be seen. Jacob waited, knowing before Mors opened his mouth what he was going to be told.

"The militia came. The mob was excited. The Jews knew what was going to happen . . . because what else could happen? We all know what a promise of mercy means from a mob. Your rabbi was a brave man. They were all brave. He said it would be better to die at their own loving hands than face them outside. The men killed the women and children first and then themselves. There were a few who thought they'd take a chance, no point detailing what happened to them. Then there was a fire. And the Gentiles are happy. They've destroyed all the records of money they owed the Jews. They've burned the last of your houses. I suppose the king won't be pleased, but do you reckon there will be any reprisals? It won't matter anyway. Dead is dead. You should be proud, though, and grateful. Those were good deaths. That matters."

And it did, of course it did, but the cold reality of it wound through Jacob's intestines. How Mors knew all these details he didn't want to even imagine, but he knew it was all true, every bit of it. Mors released him and Jacob could feel his eyes on him as he trudged to the castle to see it all for himself. He sensed Brigantia out there somewhere, too, but all he wanted now was to say one more good-bye.

Cruel black smoke wafted from the ruins. It stung his eyes and he grimly enjoyed the discomfort, feeling the weight of how much he de-served it.

I should have been there. I should have done something. It should have been me.

As he pushed through the scalding, broken doors and descended into the charred remains of his human community, the smell choked him. He sifted through the ash, knowing there was no way to find the pile that had been his family, but unable to stop searching. The scene played out in his mind, as certainly as if he'd been there. Uncle would not have been able to do it, he would have refused, was probably one of the hopeful men who'd stepped out into the mob looking for their mercy. Alma, though, she would have negotiated with whoever wielded the knife, protecting Abram from the full horror of it all.

"Take him from behind, be quick and firm, spare him the worst of it," she would have insisted. And although barely twelve, and small for her age, there was that in her face and voice that made the unwilling assassin obey.

And she smiled at her small brother, and held his hands, and sang the family song, the silly nonsense ditty Jacob had made up when he himself was a child and had teased Alma and Abram with from their cradles on. Abram did not register the blow from behind that pierced his heart, it was too quick, and his last memory was his sister's loving, smiling face and the beloved tune that made them all so happy.

After carefully closing Abram's eyes, with their faint residual twinkle, Alma stood and faced the miserable man with the knife, from which her brother's blood dripped through the cracks in the floor.

"Jacob always said if we had to die before our time, it should be on our feet. Drive it home well."

Jacob saw Alma as though he were standing in the man's body, saw that the little girl had suddenly become a strong, powerful woman, one who could charge through the world and set it on fire with her energy and glow. The moment hung suspended in the air, heavy with beauty and tragic waste. Slow, slow seconds passed as she threw back her shoulders and smiled proudly, ready for the strike. When it came, the light drained from her eyes, from her smile, and she collapsed onto the still-warm body of her brother, enveloping him in one last, eternal embrace.

Jacob stretched out a hand, laying it in the hot ashes, then bringing it to his face, concentrating on the feel and the smell. With both hands, he scooped up more ashes and buried his face in them, running his hands through his hair. He wanted the ashes to seep into his skin, to be as present as this moment and memory would always be.

I wonder if guilt ever washes off?

He could not envision what he might have done; how, as a vampire, he could have broken through the hold and pulled out the children—and what then? Where could they go? He could not have turned them into the animated dead, so what sort of lives could any of them have? But it didn't matter. He wanted to have done something, and he knew it would be years before he could stand up straight again, without this heavy guilt hard upon his shoulders.

When he finally staggered out of the castle, he saw Brigantia hovering, not quite meeting his eye. He could feel her sorrow for him, even her penitence, but he knew he existed because of her desire for love, and however bonded to her he'd felt before she turned him, he could not now see her as anything but the creature who had torn him from his duty. Part of him felt this made no sense, that he was no longer human and so neither the joys nor horrors of humanity should have much weight with him, but yet there was that guilt. He had been a man with deep loving ties to a human family, and that made all the difference to the sort of vampire he now was, and would always be.

She came to him that night, stood awkwardly at the threshold to his chamber, twisting her hands and stammering before finally uttering an actual sentence.

"I didn't want you to die. I felt who you were, what was in you, what you could be, and I didn't want that to leave the universe. Not yet. It belongs here. You belong here. This way, you can grow, you can be so much of what you wished to be. Our world can be wonderful, can be better, in some ways. In a lot of ways. Please, believe me. I didn't want you to die."

"But I am dead."

"No, not really. I know that's how it seems, but . . ."

"And you're dead. You think there's something in me to love, and you want me to love you, but you're dead. You're a dead thing." He relished the tears that welled up in her eyes, the desperate hurt seizing up her lovely features. "Just a dead thing. A cold, beautiful dead thing that thrives on the warm blood of real humans."

He clutched at his still heart, the truth of those words gnawing at him, the realization that this was what he was as well. A dead creature who would never sit in the sun again and, if he were to remain corporeal, would eat thousands of girls like the one he'd eaten the night before. The disgust and hatred made him taste his own lukewarm blood as he closed in on Brigantia.

"A dead thing, a dead thing, a dead thing!"

He pummeled her like a child having a tantrum, fists and tears flying into her body while she stood quite still.

"Dead! Dead! Dead!"

He collapsed in sobs at her feet, helplessly pounding the floor, the word "dead" occasionally sputtering from his lips. He wished he really were dead, was a citizen of that unknown world over the precipice, was not painfully confined to this half-life. Or, if he must be here, he wanted not to care, not to feel, to be as cold and still as his organs. This place, this place of partial humanity, even with the knowledge of a demon rooted inside him, this was incomprehensible torture, with no end in sight.

He had no sense of time passing, only that, some hours later, a new scent floated into him and made him feel a touch of warmth. One eye opened and saw a twist of rosemary and lavender, bound with a vine, lying beside him. He reached for it and drew it up to his nose, inhaling deeply. Sprinkles of sweetness flowed through him. The pain was no less, but he thought he could imagine a place of its being bearable. Too tired to move to the bed, he rolled over, the bouquet tight in his fist, and slept.

Eamon drew a small cherrywood trunk from under the bed. It was inlaid with several stacked trays, all holding small treasures. He pulled out each tray until he had reached the bottom, where the ancient bouquet nestled in a bed of fine Egyptian linen. Except for being dried for preservation, it was otherwise unchanged. By rights, it should have withered centuries ago. But then again, so should they all.

Things exist if you want them to, I think. Love, too.

He smiled down at that first gift, not forgetting that this life was really the first, but preferring the herbs.

I came to you at last. And I've stayed. Once I got here, I never wanted to be anywhere else. I still don't. Whatever happens, that's true. I know you won't forget it.

They never forgot anything. Some of them saw it as a curse, others as a blessing, but it amounted to the same thing. Eamon set the rebec on his thigh and played a curious ancient tune, the silly song he and Alma and Abram had loved so much. He hadn't thought of it in centuries, but didn't miss a single note.

Chapter 13

Berlin–Basel train. August 1940.

They were delayed. Passengers had disembarked, others had boarded and settled, but still the train idled at the Freiburg station. The staff and guards were surprisingly unhelpful. People complained bitterly of schedules and connections and destinations that must be reached by a particular time, and the only response was a maddening smile and the rhetorical query: "Don't you know there is a war on?"

Brigit forced herself to save her energy and sit still, marking time. Each minute that passed with the train not moving meant it was far more likely their change would take place in broad daylight. Even if that disaster could somehow be dealt with, there was the ever-changing schedule of the Ireland-bound ferry to consider, provided, of course, that it was still sailing. The longer it took them to reach Bilbao, the more perilous the situation felt. Brigit knew they could not consider themselves really safe until they were in Britain. Britain, which was at war. Britain, which was being bombed mercilessly and fighting hard to prevent invasion. But still, it was safe, and to get there meant to be home, free.

Spain worried her. She knew Franco was inclined to favor the Axis, and would do whatever he was asked to do to help them along. It might be easier to try to sail from Portugal, but that meant more time on the Continent, and with so many eyes on them, it seemed better to stick to the original plan and hope it worked. Then there was Ireland. Bloody old

Ireland. Ireland, where the art of vampire hunting had been refined to new and horrific heights. Ireland, where any hunter who wanted to be great went for training. Ireland was where Raleigh had been so viciously teased and tortured on his long, slow path to death. Brigit, Eamon, and Mors had sought some vengeance on his and Cleland's behalf, thus assuring that the sight of any of them in Ireland would bring a swarm of the greatest hunters upon them within an hour. Vampires still ranged in Ireland out of sheer spite, and seemed to be thriving. But it was not a place Brigit wished to go anywhere near, even for the brief time they would have to be there to decamp from the ferry to the mail boat bound for Wales. She would not feel so apprehensive if she weren't escorting the children, but there was no point in thinking about that. The children were here, and so was she, and if they wanted to get to Britain, they would have to go via Ireland.

At last they were off again, steaming toward the Swiss border. Brigit saw that the delay meant it would be nearly noon when they had to make their change. And she could not use her speed, because papers were being checked. It was too much to hope that she could whisper ideas out to everyone and bypass procedure. There was no forecast of rain; in fact, Alma glumly reported the sky to be an obnoxiously beautiful blue. Brigit turned the problem over and over. A millennial could endure the full force of the sun for about a minute before the skin started to smoke and crack, she knew that. Even the least bit of shade would help her. The trick was to prevent any of her skin from being exposed. It wouldn't protect her for long, but she might buy herself a few minutes more. Which might be all she needed.

I have the gloves, the parasol, the hat with that dreadful little veil I've always hated. I'll look like a Victorian invalid, but maybe it could work.

Maybe. She was heartily sick of dwelling in the world of maybe. Not so long ago, everything was governed by certainty. That was the privilege of the undead. They knew what their world was, they could thrive well within it, so long as they stuck to easily understood parameters. There was always the possibility of disaster, of course, and the human emotions that never died inside them meant they were prone to both sorrows and joys, but there yet remained that certainty of the world and their place in it. They had only to decide how to spend their evenings and then go forth to enjoy and enrich themselves. Even the knowledge of hunters did not trouble them greatly. They understood that some among them would be weeded out, such was the way of things, but a wise vampire did not let fear govern his life. Undeath freed one to be cheerfully fatalistic, and unfettered. Goals were larger. Brigit pursued books, Eamon pursued music, together they gobbled up all the culture the human world set before them and this, plus the ongoing growth of their love, formed the whole of a happy life. At no point did they find themselves plagued by doubts, or even many worries. Those things they did not have bore little thought, because all they did have made for such everlasting delight.

But now she was stuck in this cycle of guessing games and worry and a fear that had dug firmly into the nape of her neck and wouldn't let her go. Nothing could be relied upon, each minute was wildly different.

It would be nice to breathe easy.

"Why are you smiling?"

Alma was frowning at her in disapproval.

"I thought of a small joke."

"That doesn't seem very appropriate."

"Actually, it's the only thing that is appropriate. Have you never heard of gallows humor?"

Alma shrugged, which Brigit had come to understand meant that she didn't know the term but had no intention of admitting her ignorance.

"It means making a joke of a nasty situation, but doing so when you yourself are the victim. More than that, though, some things in life are just so absurd, you rather have to laugh. That, or die."

"Can you not say that?" Alma jerked her head toward Lukas, who was now playing with a paper airplane Brigit had made him and humming to himself. There was something about the tune Brigit found familiar, but a knock at the door interrupted both tune and thought.

It was Maurer. There was yet more oil in his smile and his eyes were wet. He put Brigit in mind of a fairy-tale monster that grew uglier with each passing day.

"I believe you are changing for Biarritz, yes? Or was it Bordeaux?" The question could almost have passed for sincere, if not for the half wink.

He didn't wait for a response but plowed on. "I thought you would be pleased to know that my orders send me on through the south of France as well. Charming territory, I'm told, a shame the Reich is not occupying it. But no matter. In any event, our two paths will continue the same, for a while, at least."

"Delightful."

He studied her, trying to read her eyes and her steady smile. He knew she was full of questions, starting with why the journey was taking so much longer than it ought to, but she kept her counsel. He glanced past her at the children, his eyes running over them not unlike a vampire unschooled in subtlety. She hated him looking at them. As repellent as she found his attention, she moved so that his gaze was wholly on herself.

"Yes, we all have to keep a close eye on each other, don't we?" He touched the tip of his tongue to his teeth and winked again.

If the children hadn't been there, Brigit would have lost patience, sunk her fingers into his eyes, and pitched him straight through the window behind.

"Thank you, Sergeant Maurer, your eyes are on me, you've mentioned it, and I've not forgotten. I've got a marvelous memory. Now if you'll excuse me . . ."

He yanked her into the corridor and slammed the door shut.

"Look here, my little *lady*, I am offering you some protection, at great risk to myself. You had better start learning some gratitude."

She twisted her arm out of his clammy grasp, thinking he ought to be grateful for the people milling at the end of the car. Otherwise, he'd be dead for sure.

"I'll tell you what, you start earning it and I'll start learning it," she snapped.

"Didn't you hear me?"

"I heard. But I've got responsibilities. I can play games of riddles with the children, but I have neither time nor patience to play them with adults."

She put her hand on the door, but he was by no means done.

"Who are those children? Why are they with you?"

There was something indefinable in his tone. He wanted to know the truth, of course, but she sensed it was almost for another reason entirely. Or anyway, something not in the usual Nazi Party line. She felt a shiver in the base of her spine, even as she looked down her nose and gave him an imperious sniff.

"What is this, rehearsal for the border crossing? Our papers are in perfect order. They've been stamped. Shall I show them to you as well?"

"Impertinence gets you nowhere."

"That hasn't actually been my experience, but I always appreciate advice."

"You should."

Brigit smirked and made to go back in, but he grabbed at her again. This time, she lurched away from him with more strength than she meant to show, but the flash in her eyes was only an icy blue, no telltale red. Still, he was cowed enough to back away.

"Hadn't you ought to be getting back to your duties, Sergeant?"

He hesitated, then muttered something unintelligible and stalked off.

That one, I'm going to kill. He's far too annoying to live.

It was not quite one when it was announced that they were at the Basel station at last. The children stood unnaturally still in their straw hats and gabardine coats that Brigit had brushed to spotlessness. They were nearly as pale as she, and watched as she fit the wide, ugly hat to her curls and made sure her gloves were drawn far into the sleeves of her own smart coat. Alma had tried to speak many times but the look on Brigit's face stopped her. Finally, as Brigit sorted through all their papers once again, she couldn't help herself.

"Exactly how . . . ?"

"Force of will."

"But what if . . . ?"

A twist of Brigit's mouth silenced her. It was enough to know they were all thinking the same thing. The ridiculous joke of it, a vampire treading in broad daylight, guiding two contraband children, all of them clutching to a tenuous disguise at which the Nazis were busily hacking away, determined to find the chink and bear them back to Berlin as examples of the Reich's ultimate power. The dead escorting those marked for death. Brigit smiled, but checked her laugh. She wanted to cheer the children, but it was safer not to look happy about leaving marked German territory.

A young, towheaded porter came in to take their bags and Brigit tipped him handsomely. He grinned at her, liking the pretty Irish girl, about his age, who was so strangely tempting and so out of reach. He looked at her now, fussing with her handbag, the papers, a parasol, and the children and their things and thought she looked like a girl who needed some proper male protection. Being a governess clearly wasn't her milieu, and he wondered how on earth a member of the idle rich had wound up with such a cumbersome task. There was no way the children were any relation, although that was the story that was whispered, and relations a wealthy family did not want to broadcast very loudly. The family was kind, however, and wanted the children well educated, as well as out of harm's way; and so had come this expedient of arranging for the young miss, who in any case must cut short her Continental adventure and return home at once now that war had begun, to collect the children and bring them with her back to Dublin, where, presumably, they'd be shut away in some posh boarding school and essentially forgotten till adulthood. The porter found the ways of the rich amusing, if foreign, but none of it allayed his fascination with the blonde.

"Will you need some assistance getting off the train, Fräulein? I can hold the parasol for you, that you may better tend the children."

Her dazzling smile made him feel rather faint.

"How kind! Thank you so very much, I'd be delighted. As you can see, I'm not used to getting sun. It doesn't agree with me, I'm afraid."

If the children weren't there, he might have found the courage to say that the brilliantly white skin to which she alluded, against which those blue eyes and lipstick-reddened lips were so vivid, was beauty beyond all measure. His mind's eye traced that skin down from her face and under her expensive clothes. Vast regions of marvelous white skin, all waiting to be explored. If only there were a way to change trains with her. However, he would do his bit to be gallant. At least this way, he could congratulate himself at length for his disinterest and gentlemanlike behavior.

All the passengers had to file out for an inspection of their paperwork, and this was handled with an efficiency that could hardly be surprising, considering both the Nazis and the Swiss were overseeing the activities. Brigit had wondered if the two systems might butt up against and thus repel each other, or if each party would be falling over itself in a bid to out-efficient the other, but instead there seemed to be a cold sort of cooperation about the proceedings, with all members respectful, if wary, of one another.

Brigit waited, imagining how painfully her heart would be pounding if it could, almost amused at its inability to give her away.

No, I'm safe from my heart. It's the smoke that might rise from my skin that could give up the game.

This time, she felt no desire to laugh. She couldn't even reach her mind out to Eamon. All her focus was on the ten or so steps to the little inspections building, and the short walk from there to the next train, just over the track. Such a short way, so manageable, and yet so treacherous.

"Look, Fräulein, there is a little bit of shade already. That will be pleasant for you, I am sure," the porter pointed out helpfully.

It wasn't much shade, but Brigit would take what she could get. She lowered her veil, feeling like a knight preparing for a joust. As they were stepping down, however, the doctor wended his way toward them, a purposeful look on his face. Alma could feel the chill even through Brigit's glove, but managed not to look at her. Brigit turned to the porter.

"I'm finding that man to be rather too persistent, and really, I do not want to be delayed in getting the children settled on the train, it is not good for them, they're delicate, as you can see. I don't suppose you can find a way to, er, detain him, and maybe you can then steal a moment to come help us settle in our compartment?"

Exactly how she was able to press another five marks into his hand and brush her breast lightly against his elbow he wasn't sure, but, still holding the parasol, he sprinted to the doctor and insisted on being allowed to be of assistance to the great man, managing to upset several other waiting passengers in the process.

Brigit seized the children, hissing at Alma to lead the way, and barreled forth toward the inspections room, gritting her teeth. Pain shot through every bit of her, even her hair ached. The eager rays assaulted her clothes, her hat, dug around searching for her tightly closed eyes, desperate for a flint on which to strike.

Faster, faster!

The newly erected building was no more than a shack, but stepping into it was like dipping into a cool bath and it was all Brigit could do not to sigh in relief. She desperately needed to sit, would have preferred to curl up on the floor, but forced her shaking muscles to keep her erect and smiling.

There were two inspectors in the little office, both of whom looked as though they felt they'd drawn a short straw in their assignment, though they perked up slightly when Brigit lifted her veil. On inspecting the three impeccable sets of papers, however, one of the men frowned and turned to a pile of notes in a file marked "To Be Questioned."

"What a funny thing that is!" Brigit cried in her most guileless and cheery accent. "Isn't everyone to be questioned? Else what are you here for?"

The inspector stared at her, struck by her twinkling eyes and the obvious artlessness of her manner. He'd heard the Irish could be a bit backward, but this seemed absurd in the extreme.

"Don't you know there is a war on?" he asked with heavy condescension.

That question again! These people have got to learn variety.

"Oh, but that is exactly what I mean! There is a war on, and so everyone must be questioned. Who knows what we might be? Goodness, I should like to hear of your catching a spy. The British think they are so clever, but I have never seen anything to warrant it and would like to see their so-called brilliance handed back to them with interest. I'm not sorry London is being bombed, none of us are . . ."

She stopped at last, the look on her face slightly guilty, as though wondering if she might have said too much, even knowing the Swiss were neutral, like Ireland itself was meant to be, though it was hardly a secret that Ireland was friendly to Germany.

But are you Swiss of the same bent? Or are you merely trying to stay out of trouble, keep the clocks ticking?

The mad chattering seemed to work. The younger inspector, entranced by the pretty, dim blonde, noticed that the people outside were growing impatient. It seemed so unlikely that there could really be any trouble with this girl, or the children under her care. In fact, it seemed to him the only reason she was to be detained was to determine her suitability to care for children when she herself was so clearly in need of guardianship.

The other inspector glanced at the flagged papers. They were much the same as many others, saying there was suspicion the children were Jewish and that the blonde . . . he looked at the note again. It seemed to be written in code. It must be. That, or the Nazis really were as mad as some whispered, and why on earth anyone in the Swiss government should be placating them was a mystery. He glanced at the smiling girl, watched her bend over the little boy and gently wipe his damp nose with her lacy handkerchief and chuck him under the chin. He swore she squeezed the little girl's hand to reassure her. Even if the children were Jewish, he didn't understand the Nazi fuss about Jews. Personally, he had no opinion about them one way or another. They kept banks running, which kept economies in order, and he liked order. The papers the blonde presented were certainly in order, and that was good enough for him. He stamped each one, then noted on the alert that they had been duly questioned and there was no trouble. That cut down on paperwork, which was all to everyone's good. With a friendly salute, he waved them on through.

Brigit had steeled herself, but the pain of the sun seemed even greater as they trotted to the train, and it was with a hot, trembling hand that she gripped the handrail and dragged herself in. Someone took her elbow and helped her into the corridor. She raised her veil and involuntarily released a puff of smoke. The towheaded German porter blinked, startled, and noticed her face was bright pink. He decided it must be a blush, and the smoke, well, perhaps he'd only imagined it. He must have, because her wild eyes promptly focused, snapped, and lit up.

"Well! So you were able to join us!"

"It's highly irregular, but I could not resist such a warm invitation."

The new train's porter deliberately turned away, tucking a bank note into his pocket and smirking as the hungry man guided Brigit and the children to their compartment.

He made a point of showing them all the amenities, even though he didn't know this train at all, and kept glancing at Brigit, waiting for her to send the children to the observation car. Brigit simply smiled placidly, although inside she was roiling. The demon was still cowering in pain from the sun and she was yearning for a cool sponge bath and sleep. The stress meant she would need to eat again soon, but she hoped to avoid that for as long as possible. And she wanted to laugh, even dance—they had done it! It had been so easy! What was a little pain, they had done it! They were in much safer territory now, she was sure, even if Maurer was still following them and there were warnings floating around about who they might really be. It was not far to Spain and it had to be easier from now on, it simply had to.

Careful. Don't get too giddy. Keep me in temper.

The voice was right, but Brigit was still too shaky to listen to her own good sense. She needed the steady hand of Eamon on her for that. It was Mors she was feeling right now, Mors who would be crowing with the triumph of having walked in the sun—in the sun!—and made it back to safety. Looked all the enemies in the eye and winked.

Like I always say, there's nothing we can't do if we put our minds to it.

She smiled at the echo of Mors's cocky voice in her ear, and the porter smiled back.

"Perhaps I could have a quick word with you, Fräulein? Alone?"

She acquiesced, told the children to wait a moment, and stepped out into the corridor with him.

He looked cross.

"I rather meant that you and I should be in your compartment. We have only ten minutes at most."

"I'm not sure I understand you?"

His eyes narrowed, but her face remained perfectly pleasant.

"You, you rather suggested . . . I did you a favor!"

"Yes, for which you were handsomely paid."

"I was expecting a payment of a different sort."

"I see."

She pulled him round the corner into a lavatory and kissed him deeply.

"That sort of payment?" she asked sweetly.

"That, and perhaps a little something more," he whispered huskily.

"Believe me, I would if I could, but I have responsibilities, as you know. And so do you. This is no time for such idle pleasure." She ran a regretful hand down his chest and stroked the top of his trousers. "Don't you know there is a war on?"

He stared, dumbstruck. She took pity on him, even though she was exasperated.

"Oh, here, then." She seized his hand and jerked it under her knickers, allowing him a long squeeze of her bottom. "There's your extra payment, enjoy it, and next time, try pressing your advantage when we're actually on the same train."

She skipped back to her compartment to revel with the children, but the porter had to wait several moments before he was fit to be seen. The man he'd bribed was helping passengers onto the train. He smirked at him again, shook his head, and muttered, "Stupid Germans."

"What was that?" asked the well-dressed man whose luggage he was carrying.

"Nothing, sir."

"I should hope not." The doctor smiled.

Chapter 14

Berlin. February 1940.

"Do you think it's my fault?"

"Don't be stupid."

Mors had cornered Brigit on her way back from another fruitless, exhausting night with Gerhard. She hadn't even sensed him approaching. In the weeks since her massacre in the theater, her strength and faculties had gone into an alarming decline. It wasn't generally discussed, but she could see that the others were suffering as well. Even Mors, she was appalled to note, looked tired and almost haggard. His eyes still sparkled, though, and his smile was as wicked as ever. He turned to her now with a strange urgency and she felt a sudden rush of power. It gave her just enough energy to smile, a question in her eyes.

"Their war machine is heating up again."

The smile drained from her at once.

"Where, what?"

"You must have known. Gerhard—"

"Yes, but I can only find out so much. He's only got one piece of all of it. They really know their stuff."

"Know how to hide it, you mean. From us."

"Us?"

Mors hesitated, then shook his head impatiently.

"I've found out something, but it means a new mission."

Brigit reeled, and he grinned.

"Don't look like that," he chastised. "This will be fun. Just you and me, on a little journey of adventure."

He whirled her around for emphasis and she pulled away impatiently.

"Just tell me what you know."

"That we can bid France au revoir," he smirked, giving her the least merry wink she'd ever seen. "Our friends here are gunning for the French and they've got a damn fine chance of rolling right over them like so much pastry."

"But the Maginot Line?"

He snorted. "Is my point. The French trust it, the Germans know it, and they're just going to slide right around it. A minor detour, hardly noticeable."

"Why should they attack France?"

"Do you need me to explain the thought process that governs domination? Where have you been the last millennium?"

"France isn't weak. And England will join in."

Mors scowled.

"Join in a fight that might make things a lot worse. They've never learned to work together, you know that. The English and French generals will try to score points off each other, they won't focus on strategy. It'll be the Great War all over, only worse, I think."

He paused, and Brigit looked at him searchingly. His eyes wandered around the dark, quiet square, then further, and Brigit felt dizzy, watching him spin back through centuries of human warfare. At last, his focus came back to her. He smiled, but it wasn't his usual smile, and it made Brigit shiver.

"I suspect we are entering the realm of the last chance, my girl. I hope I'm wrong, of course, but how often have I been wrong?"

"Since I've known you?"

But it wasn't a moment for teasing, or levity. Mors was deadly serious and Brigit knew he was right, of course he was. This thing was its own demon, a human-propelled demon spinning with chilling precision to a conclusion of absolutes. The war had paused only so that the Nazis could stretch, sigh luxuriously, grin at one another, and start again. So France was next, and why should anyone be surprised?

"All right," she murmured. "All right. So what can we do?"

"I've got it all sorted. Too easy. I'll be good Major Werner, turncoat extraordinaire, come to call on General Michaud, oh yes, I've already done the proper research! And inform him of the war plans of which I so heartily disapprove. I will have proof, papers they can't dismiss. And I'll have you for extra credibility. We know how the French have a weakness for pretty, plausible girls. I will be eminently believable, *et voilà*: the Germans will get quite a surprise a few weeks hence."

Brigit shook her head.

"Why should he believe us?"

"Oh, now, don't insert cynicism into the proceedings. We know this game. An officer will believe another officer, even if he is a German, and a traitor. Honor among thieves, if you will. Especially if the traitor perceives a possibility of reward."

"We should go to him as Britons, as spies who have worked here awhile and learned something."

"Now you are being ridiculous. Weren't you just fretting about them believing us?"

"Why ridiculous? The British are their allies."

"Yes. And no matter the circumstance, the French will always trust a German before they'll trust a Brit."

Brigit said no more that night and Mors whistled happily all the way back to the lair. But as they finessed the plan over the next few nights, with Cleland and Swefred offering advice and Meaghan more fretful and morose than ever, her apprehension grew. This mission would take only hours, perhaps one day and night in total. And there was a clear target and good information, and yet it all seemed too impetuous, too rushed, too void of details to be anything other than disaster.

The night before they were to leave, Brigit took advantage of being alone with Mors to confront him.

"We're not ready, we need more hard evidence for him, we need to talk more thoroughly, we need——"

"Do you think the Nazis waste much time in talk? They're men of action."

"Men of action, who plan! They plan everything, meticulously, or haven't you noticed? How else have we managed to uncover anything useful?"

"Of course, but what I'm telling you is that we have to go, and that we have to go now. The sooner we get to the French, the sooner they can form a new strategy. They can defeat the Germans, if they just play smart."

"What about us? Why are we even here, except as the exemplars of playing smart, and we are to tumble forward into the ether with only some flimsy pieces of paper to guide us? Who is this general? Shouldn't we try to find more than one? And the French, the French have always had a sense for vampires, the same as they discern good wine. How do we know he won't know about us, what we really are? Why not find some British generals, that can't take much longer, and surely we could do better with them? What if—"

"Brigantia!" he roared.

The use of the ancient name stopped them both. Brigit sat down as hard as if she'd been struck, the stale syllables reverberating painfully in her skull. Mors stroked her head, seeming to know exactly where it was pounding.

"Brigantia," he whispered, the warm fondness on his tongue soothing. "I know, I know, but we have to go now. To wait is to waste time. We'll make the man listen. We have our ways, and you know it. Now, I will be a turncoat major, and you are my well-connected wife whose additional information corroborates my story."

"I look too young to be your wife, better to say I'm your mistress. A hungry young thing."

She spat out the words and took one brief moment of pleasure in the sting they delivered before remorse overcame her.

"A hungry young thing with a weakness for handsome, powerful men."

He smiled, choosing to take her first comment as a joke. Wrapping her hand in his, with his other hand on her waist, he danced her about the room.

"O mistress mine, where are you roaming? O stay and hear, your true love's coming . . ."

If he didn't sing the song in such a funny, un-Mors-like manner, the lyrics would have upset her all over again. But he spared her that. When at last they headed off to their beds, he caught her chin and grinned in encouragement.

"There will be no worry or fear. We're what we are, right? Millennials know no fear!"

But all that sleepless day, and throughout the quiet and tense train journey to Paris, Brigit could think of little else except fear. Her palms were sweating, staining her white wool gloves. Fear. She certainly knew all about the concept, but had spent the bulk of her undead life causing it, creating it, occasionally reveling in it. It wasn't as though she hadn't experienced it at all, but this, this chilly apprehension that seized her muscles, prodded her pressure points, this was alien and unpleasant and felt like a cobweb she'd walked into and couldn't shake away. They could do this, they could zip around Berlin, killing their way into the inner circle, they thought, and they could journey to Paris to try to circumvent a bloodbath, but she couldn't help feeling like a rat in a maze, running thither and yon, but ultimately controlled. Or at least watched. Whichever it was, Brigit hated it. And she could say nothing to Mors. She wouldn't. She didn't want to spoil his happiness.

Brigit pushed the troubling thoughts away and focused instead on Mors. There was something strange, both exhilarating and disconcerting, about being alone, truly alone, with him again. It had been a long time.

His face seemed foreign under his German officer's hat, but it was still happily familiar. Though he wasn't beautiful, Mors was certainly attractive. The longer you looked at him, the less easy it became to take your eyes from him. And if he spoke to you, the hypnosis was complete. His was an astonishingly melodic voice, sensual, enthralling. You looked into deceptively mild green-blue eyes, and the voice ran rings around you, stroked you, pulled you closer, an embrace by a Hindu god. Tucked up in so many arms, you couldn't want to go anywhere else, even if you had the power.

It was not only his face that was so fascinating. When he wasn't briskly, cunningly funny, he told spellbinding stories, tearing into them with the same exuberance as a warm, fresh neck. Then, too, he could be curiously quiet, and those moments were almost more seductive in their frustration. He was thinking, he couldn't not be thinking, but his removal from the center of things, his silence, made him more present and drew more attention than his antics. Those who knew him best, to the extent anyone really did, were sure it wasn't calculated. Mors simply had places in his mind he needed to go, and no one could follow.

What Mors really was, more than any of the rest of them, was sexy. The other males were handsome, of course, and carried about them the aura of danger and mystique that was the mark of undeath, and the deep passion and otherworldly violence that lurked under the veneer of human flesh. But Mors was something else again. He usually adorned his bald head with silver earrings in intricate shapes, and wore several rings that might have been old in Roman times. He'd made himself massive boots out of strange black leather that looked like some magical idea of dragon skin. When asked how he'd managed it, or what it really was, he only grinned that strange, stirring grin. Lips closed, one side curling up toward an ironically cocked eyebrow. How many girls had come out of evening prayers, from pagan times on, and halted, startled at the sight of the sleek-headed man with the twinkling eyes? And he smiled at them, and they floated into the web of that smile. Though he wasn't tall, you didn't realize it, so well formed was his figure. Power, that's what he exuded. It had drawn many men to him as well, and he never minded. He never seemed to mind anything. Life was too good. Brigit smiled. It must be lovely, being Mors.

The next evening, they called at General Michaud's unbecomingly nouveau riche home as early as they dared. A late-afternoon rainstorm allowed them to step out long before they might otherwise have done, and Mors crowed over the good sign and their obvious luck. Brigit simply nodded, clinging to her umbrella and concentrating on the sound of her heels thudding on the damp pavement. The air was slightly humid and felt thick, an acrid smell swirling around the manicured trees. The fabled prettinesses of Paris held no charm for Brigit this evening, and she refused to remember nighttime strolls along the Seine or down the Champs-Elysées with Eamon. Paris had been a springtime pleasure, a place of heavy blossoms and stuffy salons full of exciting new art. The Folies and the Comédie Française and the Divine Sarah and music at once cheerful and melancholy, teasing and tickling the flesh even under heavy fabrics and boned corsets. And, of course, there was the food.

French food had a particularly storied flavor among the vampire world. There was a distinction, a peculiar sort of ferocity and bite to it. An individuality that meant no meal would ever be generic and each would be remembered, would linger like a fine wine.

A je ne sais quoi.

Brigit didn't smile. Each young man who passed her, looking at her with smiling desire, even noting the menacing presence of Mors, smelled like hypocrisy. Or complicity. Brigit suspected she'd spent too much time in Germany to discern the difference anymore.

Or maybe my senses aren't what they were.

Nothing was. She knew that. They all knew that. They didn't discuss it out of some absurd combination of politeness and superstition, but it was true. The armor was melting.

Two girls huddled under a single umbrella were skipping down the path, but slowed to drink in Mors. These were girls who had just left school, were just stepping down the road toward sex, and they perceived the power in the smirking man, even with the lovely blonde on his arm. Mors gave them the merest hint of a wink, never breaking stride. Brigit turned to look at them, not bothering to paste affront and fierce possession on her face. She was simply interested. They looked back at her, curious. Finally, the older one shied from the look and drew her companion away.

"Here we are!"

Brigit blinked up at the house, and Mors's bright smile.

"Yes, here we are."

She hadn't meant to speak out loud, and struggled to take command of herself. She reached up and straightened his tie, blasting him with her own most glittering smile, enjoying the glint in his eye.

"Once more into the breach, dear friend."

He closed his hand over hers.

"Once more."

Then, leaving off any thought of English dead, they hurried up the path and knocked.

A maid answered the door, a plain, unpolished girl, a shade too young to be in service already, and Brigit suspected she came cheap with the house, and was certainly the daughter of someone who was owed a favor. Her eyes locked on Mors, her mouth dropped open comically, and Brigit was sure she didn't hear a single word of his greeting. Eventually, realizing Mors had stopped speaking and was waiting for her to announce them, she dropped a nervous bob and rushed down the corridor.

Unfortunately, the girl hadn't invited them in, so they lingered on the step, affecting nonchalance. A few minutes later, General Michaud strode down the corridor and came to the door. He was small, with a thick mustache and heavy brows. He regarded his visitors with an unfriendly smile.

"Good evening, I'm afraid Berthe did not make clear to me who you are, nor your purpose in calling."

Mors bowed.

"General, I am not at liberty to speak as freely as I like, not when I am out of doors, but be assured my business is most serious and urgent and of great import for you, and indeed, for all France."

Mors hummed low, the throbbing hum so different from Eamon's, but so very effective and deadly. It seemed to have little impact on the general, however, and so Brigit smiled and breathed her own beguiling whisper.

Please work, please, please, please work. Invite us in. We're here to offer you life, not death. Please see that. Invite us in.

The general looked at the German officer and his mistress with narrowed eyes. Finally, he relented.

"Major, do come in."

Mors did, and grinned at the general disarmingly.

"Does that invitation extend to my lovely companion?"

The general looked hard at Brigit, and she knew Mors was hoping as hard as she that this hawk-nosed man, despite being French, was only disgusted by the blatant immorality of the relationship and wasn't weighing other possibilities. He jerked his head.

"Come in then."

Banishing Berthe and her tray of refreshments from the fussy little parlor, General Michaud sat opposite Mors and Brigit and frowned.

"State your business, and be quick about it, if you please. I have a dinner engagement."

Mors leaned forward and plunged deep into his tale with deadly seriousness. Brigit's imploring eyes never once left the general's face, even though he studiously avoided her gaze. She read him hard, desperate to discern whether he was really listening, paying heed, caring. Believing.

Believe us. You have to believe us.

The general took advantage of a pause to light a cigar. After a long moment, he offered one to Mors.

"I appreciate your coming here, Major. I understand it must be at immense risk. I confess I am surprised. We did not think there would be any among the Reich who would not be wholehearted supporters."

"I was. But the current plans unsettle me. With the lands in Poland, and the reunification with Austria, there seems no reason to continue in warfare. I cannot but think it will ultimately bring more harm to the German people than good. I've always liked France. I like her spirit. I think the Continent is stronger with the nations clearly divided where they are properly so, if you see what I mean. Additionally, if I may so say, much of the current policy as regards those in the citizenry who do not toe the exact line is growing displeasing to me. It seems, perhaps, inexpedient."

Michaud smiled, but seemed perplexed. He turned again to the papers Mors had shown him.

"These do trouble me, I admit. Of course, this would not be the first time the Germans had underestimated France. Yes, it often seems most of Europe underestimates France. The British have certainly done so, more than once. And they never seem to learn, I have noticed."

Mors puffed on his cigar and smiled.

"I certainly do not underestimate France. I have a great respect for history. But my country is reaching beyond its grasp, perhaps like England did with Agincourt, however much it may have believed itself to be right. These things do not matter now. I am concerned with the future. I have made my views known to my superiors and they are unpopular to the point that my companion and I are, shall I say, no longer welcome in Germany. Or at least, not without some significant signs of reformation. I cannot, in good conscience, take up a fight against Germany. Not at this time. You understand. We are bound for Switzerland, at least for the foreseeable future, until this unpleasantness is settled. Sir, the papers are yours. I beg you, show them to your fellow officers. Tell them what I have told you. It is unsafe for us to stay in France much longer, else I would join you, but please, you must believe my information is sound. They mean to see swastikas soaring over Paris. The machine has grown very powerful. But it can still be stopped. You can stop it."

The general's eyes slid from Mors to Brigit, then back again. Brigit sensed a slight chill ripple through Mors's skin and she bit back a gasp. She had no memory of him ever being less than wholly certain of anything, but he had no power over this little man and he knew it.

Still, Michaud continued to study the papers and the two vampires hissed their separate but equal siren calls around him, joining the sounds in a chain to encircle his head and seep into his skull, perhaps bending him, at last, to their will.

Seeming to come to a decision, he laid his cigar in a tray and smiled at Mors.

"Excuse me just a moment."

He went into the adjoining room, leaving the door an inch ajar. Mors flicked one of the tacky little ornaments from an end table at the door, pushing it open farther. The vampires watched the general while discussing the charm of the French décor as loudly as they dared. Michaud pulled several books from a large case before extracting one that lay hidden. He skimmed through it, his eyes surreptitiously raking his guests.

"It's a book on vampires," Brigit murmured through closed lips, even though, of course, Mors knew. He gave her a sharp nudge.

Michaud's hand played over a telephone, but another long look at the creatures on his sofa changed his mind. He walked back in and stood over them, hands behind his back, for all the world as if they were troops under his review.

"If you think you are playing me a little game, you are playing with the wrong man. I am nobody's fool. If you are come to kill me, then I'd thank you not to act the cat, but to simply go straight for the target and finish it. I shall not scream, I will give no one that pleasure."

Mors smiled at Brigit, then stood. The scuffle could barely be discerned, indeed, Mors seemed hardly to move, but two crosses and a stake had dropped from Michaud's clasped hands and he was now pressed against the floral wallpaper, courtesy of Mors's fingers.

"If you choose to ignore all that we have told you, General, then I am afraid you are indeed a fool," Mors informed the quaking man in his grip. "Think what you will about us, but know that these papers are accurate. Keep them. Show them to your colleagues. I don't know when the Germans are coming, but coming they are. You are an unusual man, General. You are one to whom my companion and I have brought the chance of life. Take it. And know this. If you choose to, shall we say, toe the Maginot Line, well, be it on your own head. You will never be able to say you weren't warned."

He released the general, who straightened his jacket and threw back his head.

"I think the highest echelons of military command are quite capable of making these decisions. Shall I escort you out?"

"No, thank you."

Mors took Brigit's arm and steered her back down the corridor. She was grateful for his guidance, because the fire in her was rising apace and it was all she could do to put one foot in front of the other. She wanted to kill and laugh at the same time. As they reached the door, Mors flung a hand behind him, snatching the wielded stake from Michaud's fist and sending it to the floor in a dust heap. He turned to the stunned Michaud and smiled.

"My apologies to Berthe, for making a mess she will have to clean."

The smoke was curling from Brigit's eyes. Mors saw it just in time and shoved her outside into what was now a hard rain. She threw back her head, mouth open, and wallowed in the relief of the wetness.

Mors followed her, but couldn't resist shouting back to the general.

"That book might need updating, Michaud. We're too old for that weapon."

The door slammed.

Mors put his arms around Brigit and blew cool air and thoughts around her. He caught more rain in his hands and ran it through her hair. They stood there a long time, completely unnoticed, waiting for the rain to tamp down the demons.

When Brigit was finally cool, and even cold, Mors offered her his arm and they walked back toward town.

"If we hurry, we might catch the last train."

It was Mors's silence on the way back that made Brigit so uneasy. It felt different from any silence she was accustomed to from him. Hostile. Knowing the hostility wasn't directed toward her was strangely not comforting. She hated him being so upset and hated that there was nothing she could do. He had protected and soothed her, but she, what had she done?

I didn't get hysterical. I suppose that's something. I haven't tried to say anything that would ultimately be meaningless.

What was there to say, anyway? The humans were veering toward madness, driving themselves into a forced descent, and whatever roadblocks the vampires tried to set up would be knocked down. Brigit wished she could shake all of them into clarity. It was bad luck that Michaud realized what they were, but surely, surely he must be aware, too, that if they came to him like people, spoke so reasonably, had such proof of the calamity in store for his nation, they must be worth heeding? He feared and despised them, but why wouldn't he also respect them? Still, Brigit knew he would go to sleep that night believing he'd imagined them, and would never ask Berthe if they'd been real.

Plus ça change.

As they crossed the border back into Germany, Brigit thought she could already see the tanks rolling through the Ardennes, the Allied defenses crushed. The bewildered French, Belgians, and British blinking at the might of the German war machine and wondering how they had been so totally overpowered. She wondered what Michaud would say then.

If he's any kind of man, he'll fall on his sword.

It was late when they arrived in Berlin and Brigit was reminded of their original arrival, and how much energy and excitement they'd had, especially Mors. She hated to feel him so beaten, so grim. It was with a shock that she realized it had been months since he'd emitted any true music. Mors was full of music, like Eamon, but his was very different.

Hot. Almost angry. An exciting wail that tore through a body. It was part of what made him so completely Mors. Brigit reached for his hand and squeezed it gently, hoping it might mean something. He looked down at the hand, almost startled, and then surveyed the quiet streets, an indefinable expression on his face.

"I ate a madman once. I wanted to see what would happen. I suppose you never have?"

Brigit shook her head.

"It was like the world turned in upon me, but I saw it all with perfect clarity. Clarity, but also that haze, that fog of waking too early, of being still asleep. You splash water on your face, you stretch and you even start to dress, but you're not sure if it's a dream."

"You're a storyteller, Mors." Brigit smiled uncomfortably, thinking this all sounded too interesting to be true. "You string together words because you like the taste of them. No wonder you've always had the dogs. They just like to hear you talk, and it doesn't matter that it means nothing."

He continued remorselessly.

"I felt all my me slipping away, I was watching it swirl down a drain. Bits of it caught the air and I was running after it, could almost catch it and it was just out of reach. I could see it all, but through the glass darkly, I suppose. Shakespeare understood it only just a bit, with Ophelia, because he didn't get at the fear. The abject terror of seeing the self through the looking glass, but not being able to absorb it back where it once was and ought to be. I've never before understood how clearly we are made, how very separate . . ."

He hesitated and she felt a terrible chill under his skin.

"I saw the demon."

She didn't dare encounter his eye.

"I saw its face. It was my face. Which I thought I didn't remember. My face. But inverted, shattered, like a broken mirror. A child's nightmare vision of a face. It couldn't understand why I was there, how it was I'd turned so far inward."

Mors's voice dropped lower but remained strong and insistent.

"He is so whole and yet so needy, that demon we bear inside us, that friend and foe that gives us our reason. Only I had no reason. The demon, he didn't know if it would come back, and what would he have done then? He can't claw his way out, he dies with us when we go, so he ran desperately around inside me, searching for where I'd gone. I almost wanted to comfort him. But the part of me that could was trapped on that other side. It took hours for me to come back together. I don't think the demon's ever forgiven me."

Brigit concentrated on putting one foot in front of the other, hardly knowing what she was doing. She felt as though Mors had stripped naked before her, but instead of its making him vulnerable, he'd reached out and gripped her throat, smiling that charming, sexy half-smile as his fingers squeezed just enough to warn her how quickly they could snap her head off, should he be so inclined. For a moment, she had no idea who, or what, he was.

"Let's not tell the others the whole story, not yet," he urged, his voice its old self, although the defeat and frustration in it were unbearable. "Who knows, maybe the fool will come to his senses? Or if not, well, maybe we'll break through in the next few weeks. We're getting closer, aren't we? You certainly have done well."

They both knew that wasn't really true, but now was not the time to point out the truth. Nothing had gone as they had anticipated. These architects of the new Reich conducted business in a new way, and one that made such limited saboteurs more ineffective than they could have imagined. Even doors that looked open were closed. Things were conducted so baldly, in daylight with open windows. The nighttime parties and meetings, always frustratingly few and far between, had dissipated even further. The wives who had seemed so pliable instead subscribed wholly to the children/church/kitchen formula and were as caught up in the dream as their husbands.

We didn't count on the determination.

They'd expected a house of cards. Well-built, yes, but a few gusts of discord here and there and the whole thing would collapse. It seemed so logical. They'd all seen empires rise and fall and knew how fragile they really were. How easy, then, to use all they knew, all those lessons from history, and infiltrate, kill the beast while it was still rising. But the beast was bigger than they were. No one wanted to admit it, yet it was so painfully true. Brigit puzzled it over and over. The house of cards was instead a shell game, which it should not have been. For all their power, they were just players in a casino.

And it doesn't matter how many tricks we know. The house will always win.

"Brigit? You all right?"

She wasn't, and he knew it, but they decided to pretend otherwise.

"I'm just tired, that's all."

Which was true. So tired she briefly hallucinated the shadow of a nearby human, watching, recognizing. But she smelled nothing and Mors had reverted to his jolly self.

"Do you know what I think?" His eyes twinkled. "I think the next few weeks will really turn us around. Think of it, they'll be so busy, so focused on what's coming with France, they won't pay as close attention to other details. That will give us ample opportunity. If nothing else, we can break in and stage a mass killing. You're not massacred-out, are you?"

The evil grin was as infectious as ever, and Brigit wanted to believe him. Maybe they did have one more chance. Anything was possible. Perhaps they could get a message about the useless Maginot Line to British High Command. Or indeed, use the energy focused elsewhere to their advantage.

They don't know what we know.

One more chance. Brigit hoped they could use it well.

Chapter 15

London. March 1940.

The energy in the West End was high that evening, and Eamon drank it in with nervous tension. He could barely stop himself from flying down to Folkestone and taking the ferry to Calais and from there go to Berlin. The noose was closing in, he knew it, and he wanted to get Brigit out.

Otonia had agreed that they should prepare to come home. The disappointment in her face was palpable, but she covered it well. After all, they'd always known there was the possibility this wouldn't work. Just because no one had ever voiced it didn't mean it wasn't known. Accepting it was something else again.

"At least they can make one last big push. That will be something. As Mors says, if this attack on France happens, it may give them an edge. Unfortunate, but we must take what we can," Otonia murmured, optimistic and pragmatic to the last.

Eamon had an urge to contact someone connected with the military and give them the crucial information, but he knew with that familiar, horrible certainty that it wasn't possible. Everyone in the tribunal had looked at him apprehensively since Mors's last telegram, wondering how much he sensed and hoping he would tell them what was coming, but he couldn't. His focus was on Brigit, on her coming home. He didn't want to feel anything more.

Even so, he was sure, looking at all the bright streetlights and theater marquees, that he could see them darkening, as though each step he took was one step back in his own history toward a darker, quieter time. A London in its infancy, a city of possibilities, and sometimes menace. It pained him to walk by the men in uniform, some of them so beautifully young and fresh. They were stepping into darkness, too, and they didn't know it.

One young soldier, too young, a boy who had lied about his age to escape a stultifying country life and become part of the glamorous set he thought soldiers might be, struggled to light a cigarette. His studied casual swagger fell away with each failed flick of the lighter. Eamon took pity on him and offered the use of his own lighter, a twinge of guilt flickering through him, this being the lighter he used when seducing prey who liked to smoke.

"Cheers." The soldier grinned. "Want one?"

He held out the pack with easy generosity.

"I'm all right, thank you." Eamon nodded and was moving on, but the boy soldier was lonely and disjointed and desperately wanted to chat.

"How come you're not suited up, then?"

"Ah, they wouldn't have me." Eamon smiled, shaking his head in a sort of sorrow.

Although that would be something to see at the recruitment office.

"Intelligence, is it?" Eamon's questioner was eager, finding something innately intriguing about the handsome young man, so close to his own age and yet so self-possessed and seeming far older. Perhaps there was a friend lurking under the simple politeness, even though the man was so plainly wealthy and cultured.

Eamon made the mistake of looking straight into the boy's hopeful, smiling green eyes. He saw them cold, pale, open, staring without seeing at a misty sky through black trees.

Waste, waste, waste! You unhappy many, stepping into the breach and over the edge.

He pressed his lighter into the boy's slim hand and smiled warmly.

"In a manner of speaking. Now, take my advice and go find yourself a nice girl and have fun. Have a lot of fun. In fact"—Eamon slipped the astonished boy two ten-pound notes—"have more fun than you ever thought possible."

And he hurried away, desperate not to hear any thanks that might echo in his brain for longer than he could bear. He hoped the boy would find a girl, hoped he would know the feel of a woman's skin, grasp an idea of love, have some sweet memory that might keep him warm while his life was ebbing away in that frozen forest.

Even the shortest life is long without love.

And the long life was worthwhile only with love, which was why Eamon often wondered how Mors managed, because he was always alone, except for the dogs. By all appearances, he preferred it that way. For himself, however, Eamon knew to be grateful, to thank the universe for what he had been allowed to enjoy all these centuries. Brigit may have stopped his heart, but she had also opened it.

If music be the food of love, play on.

And they had. Once the music began, nothing could stop it.

Having all the time in the world means one doesn't always notice it passing. Years went by, and still Jacob maintained a wall around himself. Brigantia was certain he knew what she could really be for him, that she was safe harbor, that she was warmth and happiness. But he hesitated to reach out to her. Distance was safer. Times were she felt he was afraid, afraid to push through his own barriers and step into love. There was a comfort, however cold, in the world he'd constructed for himself, and something about leaving it unnerved him.

All the years he was meant to be a wild thing, then, were lost in a fog of contemplation, of guilt, of uncertainty, but it built him an unusual power. Otonia privately thought that Brigantia had chosen better than she knew, that this vampire was the missing piece of her, and she his own lost part, and when they finally locked hands, they would find they were stronger together, even unconquerable. The legend books wouldn't know what to make of them, because this would not be the sort of love that could be confined by words. Otonia, as a great respecter and believer in words, found that unsettling, and Otonia was never unsettled. She did not shy from the sensation, however, and rather enjoyed its novelty. Neither was she impatient. The wall would come down, sooner or later, and the dance would be a wonderful thing to watch. In the meantime, she relished the thrill of anticipation.

Jacob, however, thought he was in stasis. Both Otonia and Brigantia could have told him this was not the case, but they each felt he would do better to discover as much on his own. Just as he would eventually find who he was, and who he would be with Brigantia.

Some paths are more satisfying to walk alone, however frustrating it may be for others.

That was what Brigantia thought, but Cleland, Raleigh, and Mors could not understand her and were rarely as silent on the subject as she'd have preferred. They all thought Jacob—"Is he ever going to give himself a name?" Mors complained—was a better friend for the quiet and humorless Swefred and Meaghan.

"You're quite wrong," Brigantia corrected them. "He's neither quiet nor humorless. Just give him time, you'll see."

She saw Cleland and Raleigh exchange glances, the look of condescending understanding, the amused patience and anticipation of laughing openly at a friend who had trapped herself so thoroughly in delusion but would eventually see clear again. Brigantia wanted to explain that love was a more peculiar creature than they knew, and chose its own maddeningly obstinate path, whether by design or by caprice or just because that was how it had to go. She couldn't tell any of them what had happened before the bite, what she'd felt inside the man and what he'd seen in her eyes. That wasn't something to be shared. It had happened, however, and she clung to it. Nothing else could have taught her patience, except the memory of that hour.

Jacob wanted to rename himself, wanted to step into his skin properly, but the fog persisted, and his body was split. There was so much he strangely loved about vampire life, the power, the ability, the way his mind opened and absorbed all around him. Hunting was an adventure, and for all it followed a formula, it was different every time. He had never seen a play, but still he knew this was the stuff of drama, and that he was stepping into a role, embodying a different kind of human man for each girl, improvising a new script, entertaining and drawing in an audience. The bite was the climax, the blood applause. But once the curtain dropped and he was back to himself, this half-life that constrained him, the body filled him with guilt. There was nothing to be done, but he sometimes thought of the parents or siblings who would find the shell of a girl they'd loved, and be convulsed in sorrow, and he wished things could be different. Rabbits could not weep when foxes carried off their brethren, nor could deer mourn long when their kin were felled by wolves. He was a predator, he did not kill for sport, but to remain alive. It was who he was, who they all were, but that didn't mean he could wholly embrace it.

He was also still unable to accept Brigantia, and the way she'd torn him from his family. He'd kept the herb bouquet, but he still didn't want to meet her eye. One afternoon, sleepless and pulsing with vengeful fury, he stalked into her chamber. She was asleep, and he stood over her, preparing to snap her neck. Looking at her, he grew repulsed. She was so plainly already dead, lying there without breathing. A pale, waxy, unreal thing. A graven image. An accident of nature.

As his hands reached for her neck, her eyes flickered. He hesitated, but she didn't wake. Rather, he could see her eyes moving rapidly under the lids. Her cheekbones twitched and her lips curved in a shadow of a smile.

We dream.

His own sleeps since that night had been so restless, he hadn't registered dreaming. But Brigantia was undoubtedly deep in a dream, and perhaps a happy one. Her cheeks looked almost flushed, rosy, and moist. Or maybe it was a trick of the light.

Her arm was folded up against her head, her palm open. Not knowing why, he laid a finger inside the palm and her hand closed lightly around his. He watched her for several minutes more, then withdrew his hand and went back to bed. That night, his sleep was deep and sound.

The night that would have been Alma's seventeenth birthday, Jacob wandered through the woods a long time, trying not to think. When he came back to the caves, he saw Brigantia in her garden, which was edged by delicately carved lanterns she'd made herself. Her fingers hesitated on a plant, just enough to let him know she sensed his approach, but she didn't turn.

He meant to skirt the garden and go inside, but he found himself stopping, and sitting on a tree stump, watching Brigantia. There was something remarkable about the way she coaxed so much life out of the earth. It seemed impossible that plants should thrive so well under hands that only touched them in darkness. Her fingers were deft, her touch delicate, and he saw how much love she had for those plants, how much passion she channeled into them, even though they were so unnecessary for vampire life, except that their sweetness lightened the air.

Mors, Cleland, Raleigh, and Otonia loved her, and Jacob was sure she loved them, too. But there was something that hung over her and made him wonder what else was lingering under her skin.

"Whom did you lose?" he asked.

She inclined her head toward him, curious.

"When you were turned," he elaborated. "Whom did you leave behind, who missed you?"

"No one." Her voice was soft. "The Vikings slaughtered my people. . . . But even so, there was no one. None of them loved me. Nor I them, I suppose."

Jacob was torn between disgust and pity, but then she raised her eyes to his. It was the first time he'd looked directly into her eyes since that night, and he'd forgotten how deep they were, how much they resembled the Yorkshire sky on a cool autumn day. The honesty in them tugged at his heart. He stared at her, wondering what to say. She smiled shyly, and even though it was a small smile, and a sad one, it still had a potency that warmed him and enticed a return smile that he averted his head to hide.

He murmured something and headed inside, but then he stopped and looked back. She was working again, her head bent low over the sage, and he wondered if she was weeping. He felt a tug toward her, remembered that he'd looked at her in his last human moments and known she was love. It had meant something. It still did, however much he tried to push it away. And however resentful he may have been of her taking him from his duty, he couldn't help seeing that he'd had more than she did. He'd had human love, a family he'd adored, who had adored him. She may now have more strength and knowledge, but he had an advantage. He promised himself he would never wield it.

On midsummer night, vampires roamed even more wildly than usual, as though taunting the dark that came so late and would fade so early. Its brevity could not keep them from tearing into the night air. They would eat the heavy scents, the lush sensuality that rose in the humans, if they did not eat any humans themselves. A vampire could get drunk on midsummer night, a dizzying high that would linger for days.

Jacob had yet to really enjoy a midsummer night, there was something about it that made him feel distant, lonely, and to tread openly on ground so saturated with enchantment and intoxication felt indecent. Tonight, however, he was suddenly invigorated. A surge of the old Jacob polished his skin and brightened his eyes. He floated through the woods, danced his way under the moonlight, found himself on the edge of the Dales, and had no choice but to sing. These were new songs, songs he didn't know he'd been writing, some without words, and all a mix of the two worlds he'd navigated with such trepidation and discomfort, but when united in melody they were bigger than he was, bigger than a human soul, bigger than air. The echo rolled over the land, delving inside anyone and anything who paused to hear it. From the moths and mice, to the men and women, and more.

It pulled Brigantia close, to the point where she felt like she was lodged deeper in him than his own demon. This was music to send indeed, music that made her dizzy, sounds so sublime, it was as though every beautiful sound the earth made had come together in one idyllic chorus. She was soaring, rolling in grass and heather, twirling under a waterfall. She was skipping over treetops, bouncing in clouds, pirouetting across rivers. She was balancing in a brilliant blue sky, floating through a blaze of daylight. The music she loved so much in Mors was dark and exciting and volatile, but this, this was evocative on a different plane altogether. It was what poets hoped to define, or would if they knew it existed. Mors's music thrilled the demon and stoked the fire, but this was music that filled her with glowing warmth, with a bliss so pure and whole, she knew that if she never had another moment of happiness in her life, she would still have this sound to soothe and comfort her, and pull a smile into her eyes.

He saw her, saw how much more beautiful she was with a face suffused with happiness, saw the glint of warm tears clinging to her lashes. The bricks of the wall around him, each from which blinked Alma and Abram's eyes, began to rupture. One of Alma's eyes smiled at him. Smiled, and even winked. Through the chink in the wall, he reached a hand toward Brigantia. She took it, and their intertwining fingers introduced a new song to his repertoire.

"I am Eamon," he whispered. "Jacob of Emmanuel has been dead a long time, and I release him. Eamon is pulled from Emmanuel, just as a remnant, but Eamon is his own creature. I've stepped into him and there is no way back."

"Yes," Brigantia nodded. "Eamon. I think I've always known that's who you were, or who you were going to be. Welcome, Eamon."

"It is good to be here."

She held out a hand and he took it, burying his face in her palm, kissing it with a passion he didn't know he had. He thrilled to the feel of her blood rising, even as they both remembered this was the hand she'd offered up to his mouth on his making. He kissed it in benediction, and she in turn received the kiss with gratitude, feeling his forgiveness and the beginning of something she didn't dare put a name to, in case she might yet be wrong. In his eyes, she saw the shimmering bricks around him, a shadow that clung with a fierce will. His eyes curved toward her fingers, craving their touch, and yet tacitly agreeing that he was not wholly there, not quite ready to take that final step. But he was getting closer.

Hand in hand, they headed back through the deep blue predawn to the lair and exchanged neither a word nor a look as they parted.

A few weeks later, on a close and balmy night, Eamon felt restless and itchy, sensing there was a direction he was meant to walk but not quite able to find it. He lingered by Micklegate, eager to move and yet standing unbearably still.

Brigantia joined him and took his hand.

"I think it's this way," she said, and he followed, sure that she was right.

At the curve in the road, she left him and he went on alone.

The musician sat on a stile, his head hanging heavily over bony knees. The rebec lay wedged between his feet, its gleam a glaring antithesis to his worn shoes and shabby clothes. Even a human could have smelled the despair and brokenness that he exuded with such heartbreaking absoluteness. He looked up as Eamon approached, unkempt hair obscuring eyes that were far too dull, his thin face so much older than his years. Eamon did not surprise him, because after the shock of finding daily life so arduous and impossible, nothing could be surprising. Even when Eamon knelt beside him and touched his arm, he didn't move, didn't wonder. His few flat words came easily, answering the question Eamon hadn't voiced.

"The music just wasn't in me, after all. I wanted it. I chased it. My father had it, but all I had was the dream. I thought it was enough. It was, for a while. A short while. Everything and everyone I loved died, and I'm still here. Except I'm not. I should have sold it, I know," his eyes traced the rebec's silky contours and took on a tiny speck of animation before deadening again. "But I couldn't, how could I?"

"Of course not," Eamon assured him.

The musician's eyes locked on Eamon's then, and dilated in comprehension and even pleasure. This beautiful young man, he had the music. He had that spark, that ineffable quality that can't be taught, that goes beyond talent and skill and is simply innate and will always captivate. It was full inside him, brimmed over, was the gift given him that he would turn and share with the world. Whether for an audience of one, of hundreds, or of air, this man would make music that would seep into the earth and stay.

The musician smiled slowly, and it looked as though it pained his lips to curl upward, but he welcomed the pain. He handed the rebec to Eamon, who took it with proper reverence. Despite the tremble in his fingers, it was exactly as he knew it would be. He laid it on his thigh, touched the bow to the strings, and spun out a melody that held despair at bay as it told a curious, charming little story.

When he stopped playing, Eamon stared down at the instrument, wondering how he'd ever been without it.

"You're a vampire," the musician said simply.

Eamon stared at him in astonishment. The musician shrugged.

"Music like that, expressed like that, you should be panting, your pulse visibly throbbing. You haven't taken a single breath."

Eamon smiled. He couldn't help it.

"The rebec is yours." The musician smiled in return, and with real delight. "As it was meant to be. It plainly loves you. It's a living thing, in your hands. Me, I want no dark gift. I ask only two things in return. That you find a way to make the music touch the world beyond your own, and that you send me away with ease, and a song."

Eamon understood, and played a melody that blanketed the musician, tucked him up in a cozy bed and sent him into a happy dream from his childhood. The hands on his face were his mother's, tender and loving, and the turn was swift and sure, so that the smile stayed on his face above his broken neck.

Brigantia helped Eamon bury the musician, feeling his pleasure in the guiltlessness of the death and the completion of one part of his journey.

That dawn, he stepped inside her chamber. They said nothing, they knew there were to be years of endless conversations. He looked at the bricks of his wall, which were now almost transparent. The sound of them cracking and finally, completely, collapsing, was one he would store for a different song. Alma's face lingered briefly, suspended in his mind's eye. She smiled and nodded, fading to one small flicker and then slipping away under his skin to rest in her own private corner of his partial soul. His hands extended to the creature who had touched him more deeply than he'd even known, long before she'd ever laid a hand on him.

"Brigantia," he breathed, tasting each syllable with care.

But she shook her head, a strange smile on her face. He waited.

"Not anymore," she said, "the name of a goddess no longer fits. I think, with you, with us, I have to . . . I have to be . . ." her eyes were filling with tears and she struggled to command herself. He stroked her palm and she clenched both his hands in hers and gazed at him intently. "Yours is a human name, and there is a thread yet of humanity in you, and always will be. And to be with you, properly, the way we're meant to be, I have to be more and less than a goddess. I have to be something closer to human. The goddess name was presumption, perhaps, but it fit then. It doesn't now. Now I am Brigit, I have to be, there's no one else I could ever be. You and I, we are equals, each making one half of the other. So I step down from the goddess and into Brigit, and as surely as you and I will learn Eamon, we will also learn Brigit."

He kissed a tear from her cheek, slipped a hand around her neck to look deep into her eyes.

"Yes," he murmured. "The education of a lifetime."

And they kissed at last, a kiss that seemed to have neither beginning nor end, because it was always meant to be. He pulled her hair loose around them, ran first fingers and then face through it. Her mouth traced his ear, his neck, the shoulder she gently laid bare. They took great care tugging at each other's clothes, letting hours pass as threads slipped away to reveal oases of skin, vast acres of terra incognita to be explored over centuries. Their inexperience was a patient guide, leading them to sweet spots in wrists, the crooks of elbows, the shallows of necks. There were deeper shivers to enjoy as first fingers and then tongues discovered the delicious sensitivity in nipples, in inner thighs, and all that lay between. The impossibility of their physiology, of bodies that were predominately shells and yet still generated such heat and moisture, an impossibility that allowed him to slip deep inside her and carry them on a long, long journey into the heart of ecstasy, this was the unspoken benevolence of the dark gift. The demon took pleasure when the body bathed in eros, and it was generous enough to allow the relic of the human inside to fall into the warmer, sweeter bath of love.

All throughout that long, rapturous day, they mapped every inch of each other's body, discovering their own selves in all those commingled molecules. Every sigh and cry and drop of sweat was precious, each whisper imprinted deep upon the psyche and lodged in silent, yet swollen, hearts. As tongue entwined with tongue, the separate entities ended and a new creature emerged. They were wrapped in a binding that was unique and had more power than either of them could ever possess on their own, however long they both should live.

When at last there was a place for words, Eamon took her hand again and pressed it to his heart.

"You are my blood now."

"And you are mine," she promised.

A few hours later, she suddenly laughed.

"Tell me," he smiled, winding a lock of hair around his hand and kissing it.

"We are meant to have received a curse from Hell, and yet here we are, touching Heaven."

They settled into each other's arms, preparing to sleep.

"Yes," she said again. "Heaven. We must cherish this thing. Honor it, and protect it. Love it. As we will cherish, honor, protect, and love each other. And I do, Eamon. I love you. I love you."

"And I love you. My Brigit. I love you. You are the music. You're everything."

They wiped each other's damp eyes and slept the sleep of the blessed.

It was exactly as Otonia had imagined. The true union, without barrier, of the ones they now all called Brigit and Eamon, was a force to be reckoned with. It was a phenomenon that Mors, Cleland, and Raleigh observed with bemusement and awe. And indeed, it was not written about in the legends, because few humans could believe such a thing could exist anywhere, even, or perhaps especially, in the dark and inhuman world of the vampires.

Once, when Eamon was off hunting, Mors came to Brigit in her garden. She handed him a trimming of lovage.

"Explain it to me, my dear old Brigatine"—she noticed he hadn't yet used the name Brigit—"my brilliant and powerful brain cannot wrap round this puzzle. Cleland and Raleigh have a great love, and whatever else you want to say about Swefred and Meaghan, less said the better, generally, you can't deny their love. Leonora and Benedict, Althius and Allisoune . . ." He ticked through the tribunal's couples in a singsong recitation. "And yet somehow you and your Eamon are peculiarly peculiar. What 'tis, old girl?"

Brigit snapped off a sprig of parsley and nibbled it thoughtfully.

"You're asking a question for which there is no answer."

"Isn't that the sort of thing you like about me?"

She laughed, pulling his dog out of the burdock.

"Ah, Mors, what isn't there to like about you?"

"Well, now, that is a good question. One for which, perhaps, there is no answer. Or rather, if we're being completely honest, one that there would never be enough time to answer."

She reached out and squeezed his hand.

"True enough, my friend, true enough."

Brigit and Eamon did not question what had grown between them. They tended it carefully, as though it was a delicate plant in Brigit's garden. They talked of everything: books and poetry, music, the funny quirks of humans, remembrances of things past. But Brigit was circumspect about her history. She was secure in the knowledge of Eamon's love, but not ready for him to know about Aelric, or the fire. For his own part, Eamon did not mention the guilt that clung to him, the path his mind occasionally walked toward Alma and Abram. They would both be grown up now, he realized with a jolt. Grown, married, with children of their own. What would Alma look like? A beauty, no doubt, like their mother, with untamed dark curls and flashing eyes. Marriage and motherhood would not have suited Alma, though, not the girl she was under her sweet smile. Alma would want what Brigit had, the chance to read, to run, to explore. But then, if she didn't know such a chance existed, would it have mattered? Eamon couldn't stop himself wondering about her, wishing he could reach back through the vortex of time and pull her through it.

He also wanted to know about Brigit's birth as Brigantia, and how she spent the 274 years before she found him. She told him a few stories, funny stories, usually involving Mors and often Cleland and Raleigh, but he watched her dance away from details and questions, her eyes averted, although never so quickly that he couldn't see the clouds, and wondered if it was really so awful as that. He knew she trusted him, and suspected that her refusal to delve the past so thoroughly had something to do with a sliver of mistrust of herself.

The truth did come at last, however, and was spurred in a manner none could have wished. It would have come eventually, but it was hastened by death.

For their five hundredth anniversary, Raleigh wanted to visit Ireland and the place where he'd made Cleland. Cleland was more wary. Raleigh had found him in a prison cell, awaiting his torture and death after having been forced to witness that of his lover that day. It had been a good joke on the tribe to discover the empty cell, and a better one when the pair revisited the tribe that night, after Cleland's rising, but Cleland had no sentiment about Ireland and would have been just as happy to hear it had sunk into the sea. Raleigh missed the music, and the action that could be found there, and thought that now, as an old and powerful vampire, Cleland might find that to enjoy and thus eradicate some of the bad blood of the past. Raleigh was a vibrant, fun-loving vampire, and it was hard to deny him anything. When Mors, Brigit, and Eamon decided that they would like to holiday in Ireland as well, Cleland gave in.

Eamon was immediately struck by the music in Ireland. It was so lovely, so plaintive, so evocative. It seemed to call out over the sea to long-vanished lovers, promising eternal fidelity.

"Music like that, it could reach the one who'd gone away and pull him straight back to his beloved's arms." Brigit sighed, and Eamon nodded, pulling her into his own arms.

Mors liked the Irish girls and the wildness. Raleigh liked the old spots and the entertaining stories he could tell of various exploits, only half of which they believed. Even Cleland began to relax and to pick up strands of happy memories. There was something in the air that unnerved them all, made the demons restless, but the dizzying chill of the wind excited their senses too much to care. They had heard that the hunters in Ireland were particularly refined, but they were not fresh young things, easily picked off. They must be immune.

Why they'd ever thought such a thing was absurd, because even Mors was in more danger than he knew. Some Irish hunters knew how to dispatch a millennial. They were heading toward an ancient site that was meant to give luck to all who entered it. Raleigh had been there once before and was running ahead, shouting at Cleland to hurry up. His voice changed midshout, and Mors snatched the other three and used his own special powers to bear them into the forest, somehow keeping them silent, even with only two hands. They never questioned how he found a cave, he simply deposited them there and left it to Brigit and Eamon to hold Cleland down while he went back for Raleigh.

He rejoined them alone, his face gray, his eyes those of an old, old man. He took Cleland in his arms, put his hands over Cleland's ears, and rocked and sang to him throughout the rest of that night and the next day. He, Brigit, and Eamon sat in helpless horror, listening to the hideous screams that rhythmically punctured the air, the long, slow end of Raleigh. They hadn't known a vampire could be tortured, and it was only years later, reading a gleeful account by a hunter, that they learned he'd been confined to a box and exposed to short bursts of sunlight through the day, burning chunks of him off bit by bit. It was only when he begged for the hunters to finish him that they did, but not quickly. They wanted the fun to last.

Brigit never believed that Raleigh had begged. That was just a flourish to make for a better triumph. She told only Eamon that, though. Among her and Cleland and Mors, Raleigh's name was not mentioned again.

The hunters had searched for them, but Mors knew how to get them home. It was not fear that any of them felt, not really, just fury. That Raleigh should be cut down was bad enough, but the torture bespoke something else, something deeper. Vampires viewed hunters with respect, and naturally kept their distance, but these men seemed more like beasts than their own selves, and Mors and Brigit were determined to avenge their friend.

Otonia had called for a communal gathering by the river. Eamon knew it was a sort of memorial, but Otonia did not want to say as much. Cleland had not spoken a word since they'd returned and was under watch. Otonia clearly hoped that this reminder that there was love and friendship here, that many of them had experienced loss but had recovered and found love again, might start him on the path to acceptance. Brigit made him a special bouquet of herbs for healing and remembrance and Mors and Eamon each had new songs to share.

It was Meaghan who threw a bitter golden apple into the circle.

"At least you tried to do something," she congratulated Mors and Cleland. "We all know someone who didn't lift a finger to help when her maker was staked."

Even Otonia was shocked. Meaghan so rarely spoke to anyone but Swefred, and rarely loud enough to be heard, and why she should want to lob such a vicious insult at Brigit was unfathomable. Swefred simply gaped at her, and so no one tried to intervene when Brigit turned to her accuser with steaming eyes.

"If memory serves, you were not there, so you don't know," Brigit hissed through clenched teeth.

"As though anyone had to be there!" Meaghan scoffed. "You despised Aelric, that was hardly a secret, you were relieved to see the end of him. You broke the code, you ought to have been chastised, cast out, and yet here you are, happy and in love, as though you deserve it! I'll tell you what I think, I think the wrong vampire was killed over there in Ireland, and if . . ."

The fire exploded. The circle, too. Mors was closer to Cleland, and seized him as he hurtled toward Meaghan with a yowl of fury. Leonora, the only other one who had seen what could happen to Brigit when so roused, had her hands full quelling Swefred, who was raring to pounce on Cleland. Eamon felt he must be caught in a nightmare, seeing the massive flames pouring from his beloved's eyes, ears, and mouth. Even Otonia's terrifying bellow, which silenced the others, did not stop Brigit from gripping Meaghan's wrist, but the flames were overwhelming her. Hardly even thinking, Eamon threw his arms around Brigit, ignoring the hot pain, and tumbled them both into the river.

They rode the current for a long time, Eamon holding Brigit underwater till her skin felt smooth and cool. Her eyes were closed, and he sensed this was as much out of a fear of looking into his as out of sheer exhaustion. He laid a hand on her belly. It was cool and still. The fire was gone.

It was nearly dawn when Eamon carried her back to the lair and was grateful to get inside their own cave without meeting anyone. She was still sopping wet and he took up a few towels and began to dry her hair.

"My name was Hilda," she began, and only a slight rasp under her words betrayed that she'd nearly been suffocated by her own self earlier that evening. Slowly, with infinite care, she told him of her human life, and Aelric, and what had become of him. The whole while, Eamon sat quietly, drying her hair.

Evening had fallen by the time she'd told him of the seconds that she remembered with such horror, and those first few miserable years under their shroud. She paused, realizing how tired and thirsty she was, and finally allowed her eyes to meet his. The question in them tore at him, and he kissed her several times before whispering that of course, of course it changed nothing.

"Or if it does, it's only that I love you more, now that I am beginning to really know you."

And it was true. Aelric and the fire, these things were all a part of who Brigit was. They had formed her, grew her into the vampire who had sensed the possibilities in him. To love her meant to love the negative qualities, too, as well as that in her past that shamed her. Eamon cared about none of that, only that she was his, and he wanted to know more and more of her. Each detail was a note in a song he decided would never end.

So, like Scheherazade, she spent every night over the next several months telling him the whole of all her days leading up to him, remembering details she hadn't known were stored inside her. The stories opened up her life, and she found herself fascinated and rather liking this curious creature who was now called Brigit.

Eamon was opening as well, and they studied him with equal fascination. Music constantly poured forth from him, more, now that there was more to sing about. He pulled them out of Brigit's stories, her laugh, her tears, the wind. Brigit loved each one, each more nourishing than any blood could ever be, and when he sang, she curled around him, head on his shoulder, hands folded over his heart, letting him transport them.

Meaghan was too shy to apologize, so Swefred did those honors. It was when they'd returned from a journey of vengeance to Ireland. Cleland was speaking again, and could even sometimes be seen to smile. Brigit felt he'd enjoyed the close brush they'd had with death, the knowledge that they were now wanted vampires. The Irish hunters might have followed them to England, but the Black Death refocused their concerns on the human world. Eamon's sense of the coming plague and suggestion that they shore up animal blood to keep them nourished, along with Mors and Brigit's hard work in stealing pigs and sheep, made Meaghan feel guilty.

"It was the fire, too," Swefred explained. "She hadn't meant to provoke that. We didn't really believe that old story, you know. She knows you didn't let Aelric die on purpose. She was just upset that night, frightened. She'd had a nightmare that it was me instead of Raleigh, and she knows she can't do without me. She oughtn't to have taken it out on you, and she is sorry."

Brigit had long since stopped caring, but was pleased. The community was at peace, as it should be.

One night, shortly before the outbreak of the War of the Roses, Brigit and Eamon sat at the top of Bootham Bar, watching the quiet city engage in its nightlife.

"We're going to leave York, I think. All of us. In a decade or so. Go somewhere bigger, richer."

Brigit was used to these occasional pronouncements.

"Will we miss it?"

He hesitated. The remains of the homes in which he and the other Jews had lived were long vanished, and the hulking tower where the Jews had died was still a wart he circumvented whenever he traversed the city. But the countryside was beautiful, the new architecture in the city pleasing, and there were happy memories here. The hillside where he'd first looked into Brigit's eyes, and so many other places, these they would miss. However, they prized adventure over nostalgia, and he sensed good adventures ahead.

"Not really. We'll be too busy."

"You'll hold it all for us anyway. Isn't that what 'Eamon' means, after all? 'Wealthy guardian'?"

"And I am certainly wealthy."

He kissed her ear.

"And I'm a guardian. Of you, of us, of . . ."

She touched his face, sensing his tiptoe into dangerous territory.

"Of old souls," he finished. "Old, old souls."

"That seems a lot to protect. More like a job for two, really."

"Yes. Yes, so it's lucky I have a partner."

They were silent for a long time. When Brigit spoke again, it was with soft regret.

"I haven't got a soul, of course."

"You have more and less than a soul, I think."

"What does that mean?"

"I don't know. We'll have to spend the next several hundred years parsing it."

They laughed. He nuzzled her neck, her shoulder, nipped at her breast, and pressed his lips to her palm hungrily as his fingers crept up her clothes, seeking warmer, wetter climates. The moans that soon emanated from the top of the bar made the humans quiver in their houses. The dead were awake, and speaking volumes.

What they didn't say was that Brigit shared Eamon's soul. That scrap of soul was a voluminous thing, and powerful enough to cradle them both.

Chapter 16

Basel–Bilbao train. August 1940.

"You were singing again."

Brigit rubbed her sore eyes and gazed at Alma, flummoxed.

"I what?"

"Sometimes you sing in your sleep. You were doing it again, just now."

"Was I really? Anything in particular?"

"Nothing I've ever heard before. They're usually . . . pretty, though. The songs. Can't make out the words, most times."

Brigit suspected this was because some of the songs were sung in medieval English, or, if later, with inflections that had long since disappeared. The children spoke excellent English, but humans could not be expected to understand the bulk of Eamon's lyrics.

"Pretty," though. Yes, I imagine the songs are at least pretty. Whatever I'm singing in my sleep is probably downright ethereal.

She was still managing only snatched minutes of sleep here and there and would have preferred to avoid sleep altogether. Sleep was dangerous. The issue of food was rearing its vexing head again and she was determined to wait until they were in Bilbao to take care of that. No more meals on the train, and she would resist the temptation of what might be available on a French platform. It was, however past time the children ate. Brigit thought that it might be safe enough to bring them to the dining car, that it might look less strange than confining them to the compartment and ordering soup and sandwiches, as she had on the German train. She didn't trust the Swiss or French, either, but felt they must be at least somewhat safer and wanted to play up her role as supposed nanny.

Lukas was delighted to go to the dining car and confided to his sister that he was going to order stew and eat three hot buttered rolls. Alma assured him that sounded delicious. She also reminded him, to Brigit's great relief, that the dining car was a place for very, very quiet conversation, and it was best that a big boy like himself concentrate on his meal and speak only when their guardian or she, Alma, spoke to him. He nodded solemnly, anticipating the momentousness of the experience with pleasure.

The white tablecloths and steady clinks of silverware did not disappoint him. Brigit sensed that even Alma was elated. Her parents would not have deemed her old enough to be taken to a fine restaurant until this year, most likely, and even the Jewish-owned eateries were virtually gone from Berlin. Brigit felt a sudden swell of delight for the children, imagining the life they would have in London, free of being marked as undesirable, able to go to theater and concerts and films and restaurants. The delight was quickly singed with a pang. They would do all this with their aunt and uncle, not their father. Not now, anyway, and more than likely, not ever.

Well, no one ever said life was fair. Or kind.

They were seated in a corner and Brigit found herself enjoying the supervision of the handling of cutlery and the careful use of butter. A war was on, after all, and wherever they were, nothing must be wasted. The children ate their food with slow, considered pleasure. Brigit had to force herself to eat, the meat sliding down her throat only serving to make her more ravenous for real nourishment. The demon was wretched, but it simply had to wait.

Alma's eyes rolled up above Brigit's head and widened just enough that Brigit whirled around before she could control the response. She didn't know what upset her more, that the doctor was smiling down at them with such venom, or that he'd seen the apprehension in both Alma and herself.

"Well, Fräulein, what a pleasure to continue our journey together."

"Doctor Schultze."

"And you have brought your little charges to lunch, how delightful."

Brigit loathed the sneer in his voice. Its only use was in assuring her that his quarry was all three of them. He must be certain of who and what the children were, and seemed unpleasantly certain of her as well. For the thousandth time, she cursed the stupidity of a situation that made it impossible for her simply to kill him as the demon implored.

The children finished their food and lay their cutlery across their clean plates. Brigit dabbed her lips with her napkin and smiled at the doctor.

"It seems as though the children are done eating, so I must get them back for the little one's nap."

"Nonsense, they have not had any pudding. I am quite sure that young man there would love a nice bit of gâteau."

Lukas's eyes lit up and he was about to announce that he would indeed, but Brigit broke in loudly.

"I have some chocolate waiting for them already, thank you."

Schultze was about to argue, but Alma was on her feet and helping Lukas fold his napkin. The hovering waiter coughed meaningfully; there was another family waiting to be seated. Brigit forced her smile to look regretful, rather than triumphant.

"Enjoy your coffee, Doctor."

He hesitated, then caught her as she stepped into the corridor. The children lurked just ahead, nervous.

"So sorry, Fräulein, but I cannot help noticing the little boy looks pale."

"First me and now the boy! Really, Doctor, I know it's your profession, but you seem obsessed with cheek color."

Brigit laughed, but Schultze's face was grave. Only a small spark in his eyes gave him away.

"I can forestall my coffee for half an hour to give him a brief examination. Surely his nap can wait that long?"

"I suspect that he's only pale because he's overtired. Traveling is exhausting business. I can take care of him very well, thank you, but I do appreciate your concern."

Lukas yawned obligingly.

"There, you see?" Brigit chided the doctor. "Now really, I must ask you to let me tend my duty."

She raised her voice just enough that a pair of busy, matronly women on their way to coffee stopped to enjoy the scene.

"After all," Brigit continued, laying on the melodrama for her audience's benefit, "his mother entrusted him to my care. She was very particular about his sleep schedule. The poor lamb is hot and overtired and an examination will only frighten him. Please, sir, will you let me get the boy to bed?"

The women were properly shocked.

"Keeping a child from his nap! For shame, what sort of business is that?"

The doctor held up his hands, fending the women off.

"I am a doctor! I only noticed that the boy was looking pale and offered to examine him, quite free of charge."

Brigit tossed her head, insulted.

"Are you insinuating that I would not be able to pay for medical services? Or, perhaps, that I would ask for some sort of discount?"

While the women might have swayed under the authority of Schultze's being a medical professional, their shared umbrage at his implication incited a verbal fusillade under which the doctor promptly sank. He slunk back into the dining car and the women turned to Brigit with an excess of solicitation. They patted and praised and encouraged her and guided her back to her compartment under a constant stream of chatter so fast and shrill, Brigit could hardly decipher a word. She was grateful for another large yawn from Lukas, even though it sent her defenders into raptures of tender concern, because they at least avowed to hurry away, though they first had to advise Brigit at length as to the best means of getting a child to sleep properly in the afternoon.

They bustled off just in time. Brigit realized she had been so distracted by the doctor, she hadn't been paying attention to the sunlight, and the rays were just creeping up to the windows on their side of the corridor.

"Well, that was eventful," Brigit said with more sarcasm than she knew was appropriate. She supposed she should be thankful they weren't waylaid by Maurer as well. He wasn't working with the doctor, she knew that now. His plan was separate, special, and, she suspected, just for her.

"We are almost there, aren't we?" There was a pinch to Alma's voice.

"Almost."

"And we will get on a ferry?"

"Please don't worry."

"Brigit."

Brigit had been pawing through their papers again, obsessively assuring herself that there would be no trouble in Bilbao, that they would indeed be let on the next ferry bound for Cork. The sound of her name arrested her. Alma had thus far managed to avoid using it. She looked up at the little girl and saw the uneasiness in her face. Alma looked down at the drowsy Lukas.

"He is looking pale."

It was true, Brigit realized with a flash of fear. She'd noticed his overall listlessness, but put it down to the heat and the strangeness and the confinement. Now, however, his color was definitely off. Even as she looked at him, a greenish tinge was spreading over his cheeks.

She got him to the toilet just in time. Alma stood behind them, arms wrapped around herself, her lips pressed together in a thin gray line. When Lukas finally finished vomiting and accepted a tin cup of water from Brigit, he began to cry.

"I liked my lunch so much!" he howled.

Brigit rubbed his back with an awkward, unpracticed stroke.

"That's all right, quite all right. We'll get you feeling better and then you'll have an even lovelier supper, I promise."

He continued to cry, sounding pained, and Brigit thought his little body felt too warm. She laid a hand on his forehead and he whimpered. Even through her own chill, she could tell he was running a fever. Her first fleeting thought was that the doctor had done something to make the boy ill. She would not put it past him, past any of them, but neither did she think it was possible. It was just a pleasant coincidence for Schultze, who must not know—no one must know—that Lukas was indeed unwell. A full examination would mean the discovery of his circumcision, and that would be the end of all of them. Brigit would defend the children, as she had been charged and sworn, so the end would be spectacular, but she had a very different end in mind for this journey.

And I've temporarily lost my taste for the spectacular.

"Do you think it was something he ate?"

Alma was twisting her hands. Her face was nearly as white as Lukas's.

"I hope so."

The sun would still be high and fatal at the next stop. Even if she could risk being seen buying medicine in the station's shop, she simply couldn't go out. Possibly she could feign a headache and ask the interfering women for some aspirin, but she had no idea if it would help Lukas, and was leery of even the slightest confidences. The only remedies she really knew for illness were herbal, and she hadn't brewed a concoction in more than a thousand years.

Nor do I know what I'm dealing with.

She kept her cool palm pressed to Lukas's forehead, hoping it gave him some relief. With any luck, whatever was troubling him would pass quickly and no one would be the wiser. Or, if he was still ill when they got off the train, she could pretend he was asleep. Once they were settled on the ferry, it wouldn't matter. But there were a lot of steps to take before they were on that ferry and at sea.

Brigit wrestled down her worry. Alma was upset enough, and if she sensed how Brigit was feeling, she might lose her control. So Brigit smiled.

"We'll manage. You'll see. Screw your courage to the sticking place, and stick close to me. Lukas will be fine, as will we all. I promise."

"And if you're wrong? If they catch us?"

"Well, we won't make any of it easy for them, will we?"

For the first time since they'd agreed to this journey, the hint of a real smile played across Alma's face.

Half an hour outside Bilbao, and Lukas was only worse. He'd vomited several more times and his skin was waxy. Even without a thermometer, Brigit could tell his fever was dangerous. He lay on the bathroom floor, drowsy and delirious, and Brigit and Alma were sponging him down with the lukewarm water Brigit desperately wished was colder. He barely blinked when they both jumped and gasped at the sound of a sharp knock at the door.

"Stay here," Brigit whispered, shutting the bathroom door firmly behind her, grateful for the pretense of privilege that had allowed them to claim another private compartment with a bath. Money didn't help everything, but it was certainly useful.

She knew before asking that it was Maurer at the door. The demon's head rose, and she couldn't blame it.

"Ah, Sergeant Maurer." She smiled, leaning against the door frame. Her voice was friendly and casual, but she was taken aback by his appearance. He looked flushed and his upper lip was damp with sweat. She could tell by his smell that he hadn't bathed. It was with a strangely hunted look that he glared at her.

"Never mind, never mind, where are those little brats?"

"I *beg* your pardon?" Her eyebrows raced to the top of her forehead.

"Let me in," he snarled, pushing past her. She laid a restraining hand on his wrist as hard as she dared.

"They're having a bath now."

"This close to arrival?"

"We'll be catching the first ferry we can and I didn't know if there would be another chance, now if you please . . ."

"Good, keep them in there. This won't take long."

And he launched himself inside, slamming the door shut behind him. He seemed to relax and gave her a knowing smile.

"You could have kept me out. You could throw me out physically, if you wanted. Isn't that right?"

"I have no idea what you're talking about. All I know is that I didn't ask you to come in and yet here you are."

"No idea what I'm talking about . . . Do you take me for a fool?"

Yes. But don't you take me for one, little man.

"Sergeant Maurer, please . . ."

"We each have something the other needs."

"I doubt that very much."

"Stop it!" He smacked the wall with more force than she knew he'd intended, and she enjoyed the look of pain that flitted across his face.

"Sergeant Maurer, you seem upset."

He glared at her with mingled loathing and yearning.

"We haven't much time. Although believe you me, I can make more, if necessary. There is some flexibility. I think it would be better for you, all of you, however, if you just accommodated me now. You do that, and then I can assist you."

"I really have not the pleasure of understanding you."

He clawed for her again, growling. She slid away from him.

"I know who you are, do you understand that? I know who and what you are."

The desperation in his voice fascinated her and she listened with courtesy, which he took for tacit agreement.

"I've made a study of you, of your people. I know what you can do."

"Not much, it would seem. What do the Irish do but try to fight the British, drink, and dance jigs?"

"Stop, stop, stop!" he was nearly tearing at his hair now and she watched with flattering concern.

"You have power," he whispered, and the entreaty in his voice was almost sweet. "You have a gift you can give me. Share with me. I want to be stronger, I need to be stronger, it's my only chance. You do this for me, and I can get rid of them, I can make sure you travel safely. I will have more strength, don't you see? And you, you need me. You don't know what you're dealing with, and you are compromised. Give me, give me what you have."

She gaped at him. It was inconceivable he should be asking to be made a vampire.

"I . . . there is no gift."

He seized her shoulders.

"There is, there is! I have read about it, and all the old folk say so. You can bestow some of your power without turning us. It's in all the books."

Brigit swore she could feel the demon rolling around inside her, laughing helplessly. The humans so often managed to get important details wrong.

"My dear Sergeant, you can't believe everything you read."

"But my grandmother always said—"

"Or hear."

He glowered at her, every inch a sullen adolescent. His movement was swift, but the strike of a man who needed more physical adeptness. It was just an ordinary stake anyway, and he had no intention of driving it in, he only wanted to frighten her. She glanced down at the stake, then at him, curious.

The conductor's call echoed down the corridor. All those who would be disembarking at Bilbao were advised to be ready. They were ten minutes from the station.

"Well, Sergeant Maurer, this has been delightful, but I must get the children in order."

With a sudden civility that astonished her, he slipped the stake back in his pocket and nodded to her.

"You do what you must do. But be aware, Fräulein, that I shall as well."

"Marvelous."

He stalked out of the compartment without giving her another look.

Alma opened the bathroom door, her face ashen.

"Is Lukas any better?" Brigit asked, more out of polite hope than any expectation.

"No. But what will you do about him?" She jerked her head in the direction of Maurer's departure.

"I'll take care of him. That's what I do, remember?"

Alma looked uncertain, but nodded. They hurried to dress Lukas. Brigit bit her lip at the sight of his color, then drew some rouge from her bag and made him up with care. If he didn't look truly well, he at least looked less ghastly. Alma's face was wan and ashy, and Brigit rubbed some color into her cheeks as well. Alma couldn't resist looking at herself in the mirror and Brigit wondered if she was letting herself imagine what she would look like in a few years, when she would put on makeup every day. Just now, she looked disappointed, because the light touch Brigit had applied meant she only looked like her own healthy self.

"What about me, do I need any color?"

That almost-smile flitted across Alma's lips.

"No, you're all right."

The station was shaded and it was late enough that Brigit, once she'd fitted on her big hat and gloves, felt no fear on her own account as they disembarked and headed for the ferries. She carried Lukas, keeping his head nuzzled in her neck, and it seemed not unreasonable that the little boy would be sleepy in such unaccustomed heat, and after such a long journey.

At first, Brigit was sure they would be all right. The bay was so tantalizingly blue, and she squinted, sure that she could see the coast of Ireland all those miles away. She could hold out on a meal a while longer when they were this close.

A dock man stopped her with a wormy smile.

"So sorry, señorita, but the last ferry has just left."

"I thought there was an evening ferry?" she demanded, outraged.

"No, señorita, not tonight. But there is a pensione just over the road. Shall I call someone to assist you with your luggage?"

"I . . ." Brigit was flustered. "Yes, all right. But tell me, please, what time does the first boat leave in the morning?"

"Tomorrow morning?"

"Yes, tomorrow morning." Her teeth were clenched and Lukas whimpered as she tightened her grip on him.

"Have you the proper boarding passes?"

"Of course. We arranged those in Berlin."

The man shook his head, his smile wormier than ever.

"I'm afraid those won't do. You will need Spanish passes. They ought to have mentioned it. Undoubtedly the war makes them distracted."

Brigit stared at him. She was suffused with fury, but couldn't really be surprised.

"Very well, where can I get proper passes?"

"The shipping office. They are closed now, but open at nine."

With a sinking feeling, she inquired flatly what time the ferry left.

"Nine o'clock sharp."

"But there is another?"

"Oh yes. The schedule is a bit erratic, as you understand. The Germans and their war, you see. We must work around them. The shipping office can give you all the information you require."

He grinned as a porter arrived with the luggage.

"Will you be needing anything else, señorita?"

"No . . . yes, where is the shipping office?"

"Ah! It is that little building just over there." He pointed, and Brigit could see only too easily that there was no shade around the office, and that it would only be accessible intermittently. She was tempted to ask if the weather was forecast to remain sunny over the next few days, but didn't dare.

"Lovely. Thank you so much."

"My pleasure, señorita."

He gave her an oily bow and waved her toward the pensione. She and Alma walked slowly, each consumed with the same questions. The only thing Brigit could focus on was the need to be inside, to have a door shut behind her, to be concealed from all the many pairs of hostile eyes she could feel burning into her flesh.

Chapter 17

Berlin. April 1940.

One week after their return from Paris, Mors had a new swagger to his step, and no one could blame him. The Nazis indeed became more pliable with distraction. Their focus was so wholly on the upcoming rout of France that they became careless, and so more plans were uncovered and several more deaths "arranged." Thanks to Swefred, the vampires could drop in forgeries of conflicting plans and thus create confusion, but to their dismay, the disorder was soon resolved. Mors chose not to be bothered. He was too busy trying to send copies of plans to warn officials in Britain and the Scandinavian countries.

"Knowledge is power," he assured his companions. "When they know that for which they must be prepared, they can plan accordingly."

All the while, they were also planning their own departure. They did not want to count on the French and British heeding their warning about the Maginot Line and thus considered that travel through France would be nearly impossible.

"Never mind that, we'll just go around." Mors dismissed all concerns with an airy wave of the hand.

"I don't think we need to go that far," Cleland opined. "Our papers should get us through France if the trains are running. It's getting across the Channel that I worry about."

They were all very worried on that point, less for themselves than for Britain. They'd discovered the plans for Operation Sea Lion and knew that if France fell, their beloved Britain was next. It was inconceivable that Britain should be attacked and that they themselves would not be there to defend it. Mors had acquitted himself with a brilliance that was renowned through the vampire world when Napoleon had thought Britain could be tangled with, and he was itchy for the chance to prove himself again.

"Don't be too itchy," Brigit warned. "We want to avoid all this, remember?"

No one had forgotten, but as the weeks passed, their anxiety mounted. Less and less was going according to plan. Nothing they set out to do seemed to have any effect. Each of them but Mors complained of feeling tired, even weak. As though they were burdened with an extra self slung over their shoulders.

"Come on, come on!" Mors exhorted them. "Ambition should be made of stronger stuff than this! It's all a matter of belief. Believing in the thing will make it so."

Brigit believed, but she knew that wasn't the problem. She was frantic to comprehend what was really going on in both the party and herself, but it was taking all her energy now simply to go forward. Gerhard was being malleable enough, even amiable, and she had uncovered many useful plans via his caresses.

If only I could be sure they'll be used properly.

Therein lay the rub.

Denmark. Norway. Valiant countries that stood hard, knowing they stood no chance. And then the big battle, quickly begun and quickly over. The day France fell, the vampires huddled around the wireless with ashen faces. Long before photos and film were shown to the elated German public, they could see it all far too clearly. The swastika adorning the Arc de Triomphe with such brazenness, the newly subject French raising their arms before a gleeful Hitler. Brigit wanted one of them, even one, to hurl himself into the motorcade and forfeit life before liberty in the hopes of taking the oppressor down. Even if someone were to throw a rock, or an egg. Invective. Anything but this meek acceptance. These were the people who had mustered the vehemence and resolve to see the blood of their own royals spilled, from children to crowned king. And they had danced and cheered around the severed heads as though they were maypoles. How was it that, less than two hundred years later, they should consent to being governed by a new, harsh, foreign king? The British they scorned so deeply had allowed a German king to rule their realm. Since when did the French want to emulate the British? But there they were, allowing it to be so. The vampires determined to think no more of France, for which they now entertained only the bitterest contempt. As Churchill, a man they were starting to love, pointed out, the Battle of France was over. The Battle of Britain was soon to commence.

The evacuation at Dunkirk pleased them all, but they knew it wasn't enough. They each redoubled their efforts, hoping against hope that there might yet be a chance.

"I bet we could disable some of the Luftwaffe," Mors suggested. "How hard would that be?"

"We'd have to kill the guards, break in, and then suss exactly how to damage hundreds of planes. Do we even know where any hangars are?" Brigit wasn't against the idea, but thought it impractical.

"I believe I'm close to finding out," Mors assured her.

So that was their plan, and they knew they had mere weeks to carry it out. They would have no choice but to be successful, both to save their country and to avoid trying to get home to defend her via Ireland, which was perilous for all of them, especially Brigit, Cleland, and Mors— or they would have to find a boat that would take them up to the Scottish islands and work their way southward from there. It all involved far too much potential for sun exposure. But they were going to get home. There was no question of that.

"I'm in desperate need of a Pimm's Cup," Mors complained. "And this may be the last summer they have Wimbledon for the duration, so I refuse the miss the finals." The others begged him not to make such jokes. He waved off their squeamishness with disdain.

"Please! That's like begging a fox not to steal chickens," he rejoined.

Brigit and Mors were working their particular contacts to uncover hangars. The need for speed was perversely slowing them down, and they were getting sloppy. They couldn't help it. The Luftwaffe had already begun engaging the RAF over the water and there was little time before the battle over the land began. Most of the hangars were well outside Berlin and the risks involved in getting to them were too great, especially with the nights being so short. Swefred was trying to procure them a car, but Brigit was sure from something that Gerhard had once let drop that there was not just a hangar on the outskirts of the city, but a bomb-making factory. Such a tantalizing pair of targets was not to be dismissed, and Brigit was thus chipping away at Gerhard's secrets with renewed vigor.

Increasingly, however, with her diminished strength, it was impossible to trick him into believing they'd had sex. She confided as much to Cleland. It was different for him, as his quarry were several women. He wouldn't feel sullied in the same way, but he understood.

"I'd have more energy if we did do it, I'm sure, I'm sure I'm spending myself unnecessarily, trying to tease him with visions, but I just can't bear it. I hate him touching me, even through clothes."

"Of course you do. Hold hard, Brigit. It's not for much longer."

"But every night is such torture!" She knew she was whining and hated herself for it. Cleland squeezed her hand.

"You could ask Meaghan how she's managing," he ventured.

"I could," she conceded. "But there's no comparison. She gets resurrected in Swefred every dawn. He must be keeping her stronger. They look better than us, don't they?"

She spoke with some trepidation, but knew from his face that she was right. The two of them were looking worn. It wasn't something anyone outside their own circle would notice, not without very careful study, or knowing where and how to look, but they could see it in each other.

Cleland opened his mouth to answer her, then snapped it shut and pulled her close into a tight embrace. She was astonished, but grateful. They held each other a long time. Finally, he muttered into her neck: "It won't be much longer now."

Brigit's decision to believe Cleland was making this night with Gerhard pleasingly illuminating. She'd purloined a bottle of excellent schnapps from her invalid aunt and about half of it was sloshing inside her jolly young man, who, in consequence of having at last received a promotion, had also made the monumental decision to buy a bottle of champagne and was too happy to realize he wasn't sharing much of it with his dear little mistress.

"We are on our way, we are on our way!" he crowed, dancing her around his superior's office. This was strictly forbidden territory, but it was a night for throwing caution to the winds.

"And where are we going?" Brigit asked.

"Anywhere your heart desires. Paris, then London, then perhaps New York. The world will soon be Germany's oyster. Isn't it marvelous?"

"I'm breathless with excitement."

He grinned and dove for a kiss, ending up with a mouthful of curls. She laughed mercilessly. He scowled, but then decided to laugh as well.

"You're a cruel, cruel little girl, and you must be punished accordingly."

"Oooh, 'punished,' eh? Well, well, I'm not so sure about that."

"But I am. I am very, very sure."

His mouth was on her again, hot and hungry. She kept her eyes open and scanned the room, noting the oak file cabinet and rococo desk that, to her shocked delight, were not locked. Another long swallow of champagne later, and Gerhard had to stagger off to the toilet, admonishing Brigit to be a good girl while he was gone.

She worked quickly, riffling through the various files with a practiced eye. Munitions stored here, munitions manufactured there, details for British bombing raids, which she made note of, but nothing for their own more immediate purposes. Large shipments of arms prepared for Poland and other . . . Brigit paused and looked more closely at the papers. She read and read again, still not registering exactly what she was reading.

"What are you doing?"

Gerhard's voice was cold with fear and anger, but she didn't care.

"Why do you need so many guns for countries that have already been subdued?"

A twinge of power in her voice made him forget her espionage. He answered, a sly smile on his face.

"For cleansing, of course."

"Cleansing?"

"You are an artless, naïve girl. Yes, cleansing. It is never enough to scatter a people out of a country in which they do not belong. They still exist, don't they? The earth must be properly cleansed. I have told you this many times. You have no memory."

"Jews. You're going to shoot Jews." It wasn't a question, but she was still incredulous, and disgusted with herself for it.

"It's all planned. Very clean and quiet. Round them up, march them away, have them dig their grave, then finish them off. They go into the earth and will fertilize the land. A use for them at last. Mind you, I do think it's insufficient. There are such a lot of them . . ."

He kept talking, but Brigit tuned him out. She could feel the fire rising.

No. No. No.

The demon helpfully tamped the fire down. It sensed an interesting turn of events and wanted to be more than ready.

"Why are you doing this?" An unfamiliar taste rose in Brigit's throat. She suspected it was bile.

"Don't you want to live in a clean world?" His eyebrows were raised.

"I don't think you know the meaning of the word."

He took a long swallow of schnapps, glaring at her. A slow laugh worked its way up through him as he staggered toward her, dripping menace.

"You couldn't know all we know. I suppose you think you're very clever, but you are like a little girl playing at a game. The Third Reich, we are not to be played with. It is perhaps time you learned that."

She wondered how long he'd known she was a spy, and what else he knew about her.

"You owe me, I think," he informed her as he downed the last of the schnapps.

"Owe you what?"

"What you haven't given the way I want it."

He twisted her hair and jerked her up against the wall. Both she and the demon were too impatient to use any verbal tricks. She tore herself out of his grasp and was about to strike when he slammed the side of his pistol into the softest part of her head. It would have knocked a human unconscious, but it shouldn't have felled her. The fact that it did made her howl with rage into the carpet, giving him ample opportunity to flip her around and tear at her clothes. Buttons went flying into corners. She stared at his deranged face, too stunned to fight back as he tore the chemise from her shoulders and struggled with her bra. What the hell was wrong, where was her power?

Oh. Oh, Eamon. It's the food. Of course, so simple. The food. It's too tainted. It's blunted us.

A cold hate pumped through her body harder than blood. Hate for the Nazis, for Germany, for all the Germans who enjoyed the world that they were paving in other people's blood. And hate for Gerhard, for this slimy, hungry little man so desperate for a fuck. If she were a human girl, he wouldn't marry her, not even if she became pregnant. She wasn't connected, had no money. He was seeing a new empire, a world of German princes and dukes and barons. He was going to be a noble and feel the adulation of the peasants. She was just a primer from which to learn, and entertainment.

Her eyes were swimming in a red mist, but he didn't see. He was on a different journey. His hands squeezed her breasts painfully and to her horror, she could feel something like lava oozing from her nipples. She tried to pull a cooling song into her brain, but everything in her had stopped working.

Eamon! Eamon!

But her mind may as well have been screaming "Demon! Demon!" because that was what responded. It had waited a long time with this petty human and was famished. Its tongue flicked through her ribs, its claws tickled her skin from behind.

Gerhard's scream roused her. He'd burned his hand on her breast. She couldn't fight the demon anymore. Either it or Gerhard would win, and she trusted the demon more.

The fangs had never emerged so slowly, each muscle seemed to creak as her face contorted and the demon broke out from under. It chortled at Gerhard's whitening eyes, thrilled in his gasps and shakes. It reached for him, wanting to touch the terror, wanting to feel the pounding heart at which Gerhard clutched and beat. But just as the talons sank into his chest, Gerhard's body seemed to turn liquid and slipped from Brigit's grasp.

She stared at Gerhard several minutes, losing all her chances in her astonishment. It was impossible, it was not fair, there was simply no way that he had died of a heart attack. True, he had been drinking, but Germans were meant to be able to hold their drink. And true, too, he hadn't expected his little whore to be a vampire, but Nazis were meant to be made of sterner stuff. The demon pounded at Brigit's chest, but there was nothing to be done. He was gone indeed.

We did kill him, anyway. We frightened him to death.

The demon was not placated, but there was no time. She was going to ransack the office for papers and make it look as though Gerhard had been working with a spy who turned on him. She wasn't entirely sure how this would be accomplished, but she was determined to yank the confidence out of these monsters masquerading as men.

Half an hour later, she found what she had been looking for. The location of a hangar, a small one, but more than compensated for by the large nearby factory building bombs, so many bombs. She committed it all to memory, then swept through the office like a dervish, sending every paper flying. It would take them hours to tidy it and days before they could be sure everything was accounted for. Even then, they would not rest easy, because if nothing had been taken, did that mean that all the information was safe? And if not, what on earth was to be done?

It was late, and she should be going, but she couldn't stop staring at Gerhard's body. This horrible human had been a part of her life for a long time. There were humans she'd met fleetingly over the centuries and liked, usually at the theater, but this had been different. This had been something she hadn't known since before her making. She knew he wasn't a fair representative of the human race, but as she gave his body several unsatisfying kicks, she felt with absolute certainty that the vampires were the superior ones, no question.

Gerhard's death and all the troubling questions it raised were as good as front-page news in the inner circle, and Mors ate it up with glee. He was also pleased that it meant Brigit's nights were now free to further finesse the plan. He'd learned there were only days before a serious bombing campaign was to begin, and they wanted to strike as close to the opening salvo as possible to create maximum alarm and chaos.

Swefred found himself at a standstill as well. He'd prepared several immaculate sets of papers for their journey home, covering all possible circumstances, and had worked his own marks to their limit. He volunteered to assist Brigit in her planning, pilfering what information he could on the best means of sabotaging machinery and bombs. They worked quickly and quietly. Even meal breaks were hurried affairs. Brigit had little appetite, but focused on what SS officers she could find, reasoning that if she wouldn't be nourished, she could at least chip steadily at Hitler's prized forces.

Late one night that first week in August, when darkness had settled at last, the five vampires set out on their final attempt to shake at the foundation of the Nazi establishment. Only Mors was high and excited, the others felt weighted down by their sense of failure and were apprehensive about the journey home. As they neared the target, however, the thrill of the impending chaos they were to wreak rallied them. Their plan was twofold. The planes in the small hangar would be attacked first, the rationale being that a plane took longer to build than a bomb. The factory was only about three hundred yards west, although in totally open space. And there was some worry about the fire they would create in the explosion. However, Brigit and Swefred had discovered that both a sewer line and an entrance to the U-Bahn abutted the factory's courtyard on either side. They were thus guaranteed a quick, clean escape.

The hangar was not under guard, and its locked doors were easy to force, but opening them even the tiny bit necessary for slipping inside made an awful racket.

"Leave them open," Mors ordered. "It will be easier to hear anyone approaching."

There were barely fifty small planes in the hangar. Knowing the Luftwaffe had more than four thousand planes at their disposal, many of which were on their way to Britain now, did not raise anyone's spirits, but something was better than nothing and they silently set about their business.

Brigit enjoyed the mindlessness of the work, the rote opening of the engine, snipping of wires, and the rewiring that would result in explosion. They didn't hurry, concentrating instead on getting the job done properly.

It was nearly three in the morning by the time they were finished, which was plenty of time to tend to the factory, but Brigit still inwardly cursed the timing that meant they hadn't been able to set out until after nine. It was monstrously unfair that the Nazis should enjoy the convenience of the long summer days when planning their attacks. If she didn't know better, she would say they'd planned it that way on purpose.

Mors held up a warning hand as they approached the door, but it was hardly necessary—they could smell lurking humans as easily as he. Mors signaled that there were nine men several yards from the entrance. That seemed nothing to worry about—their speed would have them halfway to the factory before the men could even shout. But they all smelled the approach of more men, could sense them on rooftops all along the route to the factory. Nachtspeere. The ignorant creatures they looked on with such derision, viewed as so impotent before their own selves, nearly every one of them, it seemed, was outside, waiting. And they had abandoned their small crossbows for much larger ones, fitted with oil-tipped arrows, ready to be dipped into fire. They even bore axes. The vampires were beside themselves, trying to wrap their minds around the incontrovertible fact that the Nachtspeere had tracked them so effectively. But then they caught the unmistakable stench of Irish hunters. Cleland and Brigit clutched each other and Meaghan swooned against Swefred.

They know. They've known. Not for long, maybe, but long enough.

There was no time for such reflection. They retreated to the center of the hangar where they were absolutely sure they couldn't be heard.

"I don't give a damn how they know and not one of you had better dare ask," Mors began. "What can we use in here that's a weapon?"

"We could rewire a plane and fly out," ventured Swefred.

"We damaged them too thoroughly," Brigit answered, wondering if the men outside knew that, too.

"We haven't got the time to tunnel out, and they've got the perimeter surrounded," Mors muttered more to himself than the others, who didn't need to be told anyway.

"I don't smell a man who could kill a millennial," Cleland said. "I don't like those axes, but if we're at top speed, and run zigzag, even a top hunter won't have that kind of aim."

"And it's still dark," Meaghan added in a confident voice that surprised them.

Mors glanced at the east-facing high windows at which more men with torches were stationed.

"Not for much longer. The weakness is the entrance. There's no way out without being seen or heard. Even at our fastest, we're going to bottleneck at that damn door." He drummed his fingers on his head. Brigit realized that he was panicking. She'd never seen Mors panic, and her own demon went icy. Cleland and Swefred were waiting for Mors to continue. It was only when she caught Meaghan's eye that she saw someone who knew their only choice and was resigned to it. The two females nodded to each other grimly and Brigit spoke.

"We have to wait. Till just before dawn. Get them as tired and tense as possible. We'll blow clouds of confusion en masse, it should be just enough. Like Cleland said, we'll zigzag. We know how to get there, it's not too far, we'll allow ourselves two minutes. They won't expect that. We can even create an idea of decoys. Mors, you're still strong enough for that. They'll have been ready so long, they'll be spent. It's not a great chance, but it's all we've got."

"And the bottleneck?" Swefred wondered.

Meaghan grinned and showed their last hand. The bomb they were going to use to destroy the bomb-making factory.

"If we blow up the door, they'll have a harder time seeing us leave."

Mors chucked Meaghan under the chin.

"Perfect. Can't have all our hard work going to waste."

"So we get outside . . ." Cleland prompted.

"And leg it with violent swiftness." Meaghan finished, and there was no argument.

A few minutes before dawn and all was deathly still and silent. The vampires could sense the exhaustion of their would-be predators and were pleased. They themselves were high with anticipation. Brigit had to acknowledge this much, that imminent action and danger provoked excitement. They'd been so careful, so steady, for so many months. Now they had to use all their strength and power. The demons were ecstatic. Brigit just wished she didn't feel so drained. She wasn't frightened, however. She had no fear of hunters, be they Nachtspeere or Irish, would not give them the gift of her fear, and anyway was concentrating too hard on what she had to do to feel anything even remotely like fear.

Boldness is my friend. And Eamon's at my back. His energy will push me faster than I've ever run before.

Mors cast a pleased and loving eye around the little band of compatriots and set off the bomb. The explosion set up a screen of smoke and fire that, together with their mingled hypnotic whispers, gave them their initial shield. They bolted from the hangar and ran.

The wind sang in Brigit's ears and she was suddenly exhilarated, the closeness of the air around her convincing her she was actually going to run into the future at this dizzying speed. She could hear the shouts of the men, see arrows and axes whizzing by her, but she was too fast and clever for them. There was the courtyard of the factory, there was the entrance to the sewer.

Oh no. Oh Eamon. We're the little foxes.

The entrance was blocked with chunks of cement and crudely nailed boards. With one eye on the fiery arrows and spinning axes the hunters continued to lob at her, she tore at the barriers. She knew without looking that Cleland was on the other side of the courtyard, doing the same. The light was pale purple, just on the edge of turning pink, but Brigit began to smile. Clearly, even the Irish hunters who had come especially for this didn't know the strength of a millennial. The barrier came down just as Meaghan sprinted up beside her, an ax unnecessarily appropriated to bust them in to safety.

Cleland had broken down the blockade to the U-Bahn entrance with ease. He waved at Brigit and Meaghan, then took up a fallen ax and hurled it up into the fray.

"You'll have to try harder with your slings and arrows than that!"

To Brigit's delight, she saw a man's head bounce down into the alley.

Mors was running leisurely, confident in the shield of his longevity, his closeness to safety, and his easy ability to outmaneuver the enemy. He caught the axes that were thrown at him and launched each one back in a graceful arc that didn't miss a single target. The hunters were beside themselves with rage. A dead man dropped his bow and arrows, which Swefred caught. He was in the courtyard, mere feet from them, and took a rare chance. He let loose a volley of arrows at a line of men and they all fell like ninepins. Meaghan laughed and applauded and Brigit screamed with joy.

Another set of arrows soared toward Swefred and he ran backward to catch them up and repeat his triumph, even though the sun was peeping over the horizon. Mors bounded past him and Meaghan had just opened her mouth to call Swefred back when an ax swung with unexpected strength for a human caught him just below the knee, striking the lower leg clean off.

The humans cheered uproariously and held their fire, eager to see what the great vampire would do now. Meaghan's screams gave them only more pleasure on which to get drunk. Mors was holding her and Brigit back, the sun was coming and it was too late.

Swefred knew it, too, because he didn't even try to hop to safety.

"Meaghan!" he yelled. "Stop screaming, don't give them that satisfaction."

Meaghan fell silent instantly, her eyes locked on Swefred's. His skin was crinkling and turning black, smoke curling from under his hair and nails, but he smiled.

"I love you, my princess. One more for them, all right?"

With that, he picked up his severed leg and whirled it around to get the blaze roaring. He threw it at a cluster of hunters and knocked them all down.

The final conflagration came with blessed speed, the flames consumed him greedily and then, realizing there was nothing left to feed them, disappeared in a burst of orange smoke.

Brigit caught Cleland's eye. She could see him wanting to run across to them, to help them control the hysterical Meaghan, but he couldn't move.

A flaming arrow flew right at Brigit's eye and Mors grabbed her arm and jerked her behind him. It gave Meaghan all the advantage she needed. With one furious twist, she was out of Mors's grasp and in the courtyard. Mors clutched Brigit to him and they stared, helpless and fascinated.

A long, low, weird cry emanated from somewhere deep inside Meaghan, something that had once soared down across the Scottish Highlands, penetrating the mist. It was a piercing buzz and it dazed and froze the crowd of hunters so that they stared numbly as Meaghan took up a hogshead of fuel, bust it open, and began to whirl, dousing the factory, the buildings, and all the hunters in and around them in cold gasoline. Even then, they didn't budge. She whirled harder, her arms outspread, her eyes facing a blue sky she hadn't looked at so openly in centuries.

Then Brigit understood the secret of Meaghan's demonic life and longevity, the magnet she used to draw in prey. Her emerald-green eyes, always wide and limpid, swelled and turned liquid, so that a man knew if he walked toward them they'd envelop him like a clear lake on a hot summer's afternoon. Even Brigit was not immune. She would have moved forward to bathe in those eyes, were it not for Mors's firm grip on her. The flames took full hold, but the eyes took on a life of their own, rising well above the fire, refusing to be swallowed. With one last, hard, fiery spin, Meaghan exploded, and the flames shot round in a perfect circle, catching the gasoline-soaked hunters and buildings.

Fireballs leaped from the factory and all its surrounding buildings in a deafening display. The bombs inside went off, sending even more fire into the sky and down the surrounding streets. Ball after ball of fire bounced toward town and the ashes of dead men were all dwarfed by the ashes of two millennial vampires.

Mors bore Brigit deep into the sewers, outrunning flames and sharp debris. Brigit didn't even feel them move. Meaghan's eyes had finally burst and sent green marbles of liquid in a hot shower that had landed on Brigit. The feel of Meaghan's eyes on her skin doused every other sensation.

It was a long time before either of them moved or spoke. A sound, an echo of the explosions far above them, roused Brigit suddenly, reminding her that they were alone.

"Cleland!" she cried.

"He's all right. He had to run through the U-Bahn tunnels, that's all. He's fine. Fine."

"How can you be sure?"

"Because I am. He's Cleland."

"Mors, please. Don't protect me."

"It's true. He's been my friend for fifteen hundred years. I would know."

"How? Even you aren't that good."

"But Cleland is. He's got too much life in him to die. Not here, not now, and not alone."

Brigit nodded, clinging hard to the belief. Mors smiled at her.

"I don't know if cowards die many times before their deaths, but it certainly does seem that the valiant never taste of death but once. Would you have ever imagined we'd say such a thing about Swefred and Meaghan?"

She shook her head, wishing she could brush the droplets of eyes off her skin. She was proud of the dead couple, proud that they'd created a new legend to awe the humans, but it was Cleland she was thinking of now, hating that he was alone, fighting off the thought of any other possibility, and wishing with all her power that she could reach out into the darkness and pull them into the circle made by herself and Mors. For the first time since leaving England, she put Eamon completely out of her mind and concentrated all her energy on Cleland.

Cleland. Sweet, strong, wonderful friend. Don't be dead. Don't be gone, a pile of ash, caught up in the remains of all those horrid Nazis. Don't be debris, blown through the air, part of the smoke. A shadow, a problem of theirs solved. Be alive, my dear friend. Be their headache, their disaster, their doom. Hurt them, hinder them. Be their nightmare, and then come home. To Padraic, to Otonia, to Eamon, to me, and to Mors. Your family. Be strong, be brave, and Cleland, whom I love so well . . . be.

Mors was humming a lullaby that dipped into her brain and blew away the buzz. Only minutes ago, she thought she could never achieve peace again, but now she was drifting into sleep. Mors wrapped himself more tightly around her and they slept for hours.

Brigit woke and blinked, readjusting her eyes to the sewer's poor light. Mors was already awake and on his feet, stretching like a yogi, working his muscles and even breathing so as to focus his power and energy.

"What are you doing?"

"Getting ready."

"Where are we going now?"

"No, my dear friend. Not we. I've had a long think and there's only one sure path for each of us now."

She sat up very straight.

"What are you saying?"

He spoke with deep seriousness.

"It stopped being about vengeance, or even our food supply, quite some time ago. You knew that. We all did. I want to see an end to these Nazis. They'll eat the world if they're not stopped. I'm not going to sneak back to Britain with my tail between my legs, and anyway, we haven't the time to waste. It's quicker for you to go on your own and less dangerous, too. On your own, you'll make it easily."

"But . . . but what about you?" None of what Mors was saying was the least bit comprehensible.

"Rumor has it, the Nazis have their eye on Russia. The idiots. I don't think they know what a Russian winter is. I'll pay Moscow a call, rally up the comrades a bit. Their problem is relying a tad too much on that snow of theirs to slow invaders up. I'd like to give the bear a bit more teeth than that." He laughed, shaking his head. "Yes, I'd like to see the Nazis exit, pursued by a bear."

Brigit was in no mood for such jokes.

"You dare say such a thing, you dare even think, you . . ."

She flew into him, punching and kicking with what little strength she had left. Mors subdued her quickly, folding her limbs underneath him.

"It's my way, Brigit, it's my way. You know me. I don't want to leave you, why would I want to leave you?"

"But you said . . ."

"It's what I have to do. You won't travel safely with me. They know my face too well. You, wonderful girl, you're going to live. I need you to live, and thrive. You're going to get home to our London and . . . and to Eamon."

The crack in his voice pulled her straight into his eyes. There it was, the love that he had kept so carefully tucked inside him, hidden. He didn't have the strength to hide it anymore, and didn't need to if he was going away. The sharp edge of that unrequited love sliced into Brigit's heart. He pulled away from her eyes, not wanting to be tempted to speak what she already knew, however much she didn't understand it.

"Why? You had so many, many years after Aelric and before Eamon. Why didn't you say something?" She spoke with the full weight of hypocrisy, knowing that to have become the lover of Mors would have meant there would be no Eamon, but the idea that Mors had loved her all this time and, perhaps, forgone any other love in his life because of her, shredded her insides to ribbons, and she had to know why.

He pressed his face against the sewer wall. She moved to stroke his arm and he pulled away from her. His hand slowly crushed a loose brick into dust.

"Mors, I . . . I . . ."

"Oh, Brigit," he croaked, and reached for her. He turned her to face him, her hands wrapped in his. The rims of his eyes were pink and his whisper ragged.

"Don't you see? You were always the perfect one for me, but I was never the perfect one for you."

The heavy truth of that bit into her. When she was Brigantia, their energies were far too similarly high and angry and potent. One fire would have burned out another's burning. They'd have been the greatest legend of all, but they would not have lasted. Or she wouldn't. Mors was not made for dying, but she, without the more balanced temperament given her first by the seconds before Aelric's death and then by Eamon, she would not have stepped into the possibility of infinity. Mors would have given her much, but he could never have tempered her, have given her leisure for reflection. The energy in her was so powerful only because she gave it room to breathe. Her pursuit of knowledge, her passion for the arts, her communion with herbs—in as much as Mors would have encouraged all this, and of course he himself indulged in the arts and loved knowledge, they would instead have drained each other. With Eamon, she reached for the stars, but with Mors, she might have sought to touch the sun, and thus burned.

Thinking of the sun brought her back to the dark sewer and Mors's new intention.

"Please, Mors, my dearest friend. Don't go to Russia. If we have to travel separately, all right, we'll travel separately, but I have to know you're going home with me, you're going back where we both belong and can now do the most good. You can't go to Russia. Even you can't survive white nights."

"Oh, now, Brigit, can you really be underestimating me?"

She smiled despite herself.

"But Mors, please. England needs you. I need you."

His glance slid to his knees and he spoke flatly.

"And what about what I need?"

Brigit was pierced. She'd loved Mors like a brother, given him so much, second only to Eamon, but he had never suggested there might be something in the world he actually needed. She wondered if this reckless plan was the answer, that he needed to constantly brush up against his own death to feel alive, if he couldn't have love.

His eyes, those beautiful green eyes, so different from Meaghan's and so wholly magnetic, found hers again. She didn't register them coming closer, half-shutting, the lashes brushing her brows until his lips were on hers. Their arms were so tight around each other, there was no telling where one set ended and another began. As they kissed, Brigit felt herself spinning back through centuries, through all of Mors's happy dreams, dreams that involved her and the merry adventures they had behind his closed eyes. Deep in his mind's eye, he was her maker, it was he who enfolded her in the dark kiss and then, the next night, opened her body to his and channeled that fire in wave upon wave of unending lust. Suddenly she was drinking, a sweet, sparkling liquid coursing through her, filling her up, sending her bouncing and floating through ether with an unheard-of potency. It was better than being drunk, because she was in complete control.

He pulled back lightly then, pressing his forehead to hers, coaxing her eyes into his, a hand stroking her cheek. She gasped, realizing what he had done, and wildly wondering if this was where fairy tales got the notion of resurrecting kisses. He'd gifted her with a new strength, a power only a double millennial could wield, and with that weapon and the echo of Eamon's music, she would have the capacity to get home.

"But Mors, you need that! You have to need it more than me."

"For now, I have everything I need. I do. And I've got plenty of strength in reserve. I grow it like you grow your herbs. I'll be all right, trust me."

"I'm begging you. Don't leave me alone."

"Brigit. If there's one thing we've all known for centuries, is that as long as Eamon's somewhere, you're never alone. They've started attacking our England proper. I hear it. One mission failed, so now we've each got a new mission. We wanted to interfere with the humans, so this is where we are. And you and I, we're vampires of honor, we're going to see it all through to the end. It's not in the stars to hold our destiny, but in ourselves. Isn't that right? Now, look at me."

He folded her hands against his chest and stared intently into her eyes. One tiny heartbeat fluttered under her palm and then went still again.

"That's it. Look at me and promise me one tiny thing. You won't go forgetting this silly old mug, okay?"

Her eyes traveled the circumference of his intriguing, endlessly attractive face. That beloved half-smile, the cocked brow, the dancing eyes. She laid a hand on his cheek, then wrapped her arms around him, nestling her head into his neck. His arms went tight around her again, and she could feel a cool sigh down the back of her blouse. She stroked the back of his smooth head, wishing she had Eamon's gift of feeling what might be coming, or Mors's own powerful confidence in the future, but she had neither. So there was no choice, then, but to hope that some bright night, back in a peaceful England, Mors might come singing through the darkness, a dog by his side, ready to join their community again, and with new stories to tell.

When her tears started splashing onto his neck, he slowly pulled away from her. His own eyes were wet, but he winked, and tugged a strand of hair from her head. He tucked it somewhere in the depths of his clothes, chucked her under the chin, and strode off down the tunnel, whistling an old, old tune. It echoed for a long time.

The sobs drove her first to her knees, and then facedown into the dirt. She cried until she was nearly choking on mud made by her own surprisingly hot tears. She found herself wishing for Otonia, for something like a mother, for a memory she didn't even have of someone into whose unconditionally loving lap she could crawl to howl and beg and beat with fists until at last she was limp. Someone who would rock and stroke and assure her that the whole world hadn't collapsed upon itself even though they both knew this was a lie.

Isn't that the job of a parent, to tell a child a beautiful little lie so that she can sleep? That's the contract between parents and children: The parents tell the lie, pretending it is truth, and the children pretend to believe it.

Finally, there was nothing left inside her and she lay quiet. She wondered how long she could lie there before her body dissolved into the dirt. She wondered what was happening in the world above while her own precious world was crumbling, and cursed every desire any of them had ever possessed for trying to make a difference in that human world.

"Eamon, oh, Eamon. Eamon, I'm lost. I'm lost, and there's nothing left, and I don't know how to get home."

There was no answer. She felt nothing except cold, the coldest cold she'd ever felt in her life. She almost fancied she heard footsteps, but the cold and misery and exhaustion had overwhelmed her. She couldn't concentrate on the sensation. She was empty.

It was only the tip of the stake, a stake wielding the definitive power of death, pressing under her left shoulder, just behind her heart, that roused her.

"Hello, Brigit. Or should I say, Brigantia?"

Chapter 18

London. August 1940.

Eamon awoke with a violent start, a gasp singeing his throat. Cold sweat pooled under his arms and his hair was damp. He knew he'd had no nightmare; he didn't even register dreaming. Something terrible had happened in Berlin. Was still happening. Brigit was alone. Brutally alone. More than alone: She was in danger. He tried to reach out to her with his mind, feeling his way toward comprehension, assuring her that he was with her in spirit, but he couldn't see the path. He touched the sketch of the two of them, gazing into her eyes. The longer he looked, the more he could see them imploring him to extend a hand to help her home.

The Amati was in his hands almost without his realizing, and the music as good as played itself. Song after song after song, but Eamon didn't hear any of them. His mind was extending forward into a dark tunnel in Berlin, wrapping itself around the beloved who needed his protection, and backward through centuries, tugging all the music into his fingertips.

Others took care of preparing false papers, gathering German clothes, drawing up lists of important officials. Of the five vampires chosen for the mission, only Mors threw himself headlong into the arrangements. The others were free to do as they pleased in the days before they were to leave.

Brigit and Eamon had not discussed it, had made no plans, but found themselves quietly traveling. There was no itinerary, no order. Nor was there any question that their first jaunt was to Bankside.

It was moments like these that gave them pause, contemplating the curiosities of their existence. To traverse the area where the old theaters had once thrived: the Rose, the Swan, the short-lived Hope, and, of course, the Globe—it felt like walking on dreams. They themselves had been there, in their heavy silks and feathered caps, the jewel-encrusted hem of Brigit's skirt lightly skimming the path. They had been glanced at through corners of eyes with some envy, perhaps occasionally some suspicion, but the whole of their own attention had been solely for what took place on the stage. There was danger in theatergoing, what with the open air and afternoon shows, but that was no deterrent. London's recurrent fog hung like an amulet over them, allowing them to see a new clarity. True, they had first discovered Shakespeare on their regular, surreptitious visits to the castle at Whitehall, but it was here, in these purpose-built playhouses, before a cross-section of London's people, that the words took true flight. The vampires reveled in language that began to touch on what they thought no human could see, not unless they lived many hundreds of lifetimes, and stepped into places they could not reach. Those playhouses were the site of thousands of hours of immeasurable joy.

But there was nothing left. Tenements where the Globe had stood, an alley to the Rose. And themselves, with their memories. Brigit knelt and touched the cold cement.

"The ghosts sleep under here. They may rise again."

Eamon held out a hand to help her up.

"Will we go to the theater, the first night you come back?"

His lips were pressed to her palm, his eyes warm and teasing. She grinned.

"Perhaps the second night."

They strolled past Queen's Hall, thinking of concerts, so many concerts. Music permeated almost every corner of London for them. And there had been times, more than once, when they'd detected the distinctive sound of Eamon's melodies in someone else's work. It pleased them.

What other musicians might regard as plagiarism, they regarded as a promise fulfilled. They hoped it would never stop.

Brigit needed to explore the countryside, damp and dark though it was. They traveled down to Hampshire, to Chawton, to Jane Austen's house, where what Brigit considered the most perfect book she had ever read had been written. The afternoon was wet and raw, but that suited them, and in fact, they had the house to themselves save for the tiny, elderly woman who took their admission money and apologized several times for the chill. They had been here twice before, the first time shortly after the book's publication. Having found out through some investigation who the anonymous author was, they actually tried to secure an invitation to a dinner the Austen sisters were attending in the village. They failed, but Brigit was happy simply to see the sisters walk out of their home. She liked the way Jane Austen walked—a woman comfortable in her skin. They visited again when the house was made a museum. It was unchanged, which pleased them.

As they wandered through the rooms, absorbing the good energy, Eamon studied Brigit. She looked very smart in her navy wool suit with the pink blouse underneath. Her hat was navy with pink ribbon trim, and a matching handbag dangled from her wrist. Not much more than a hundred years ago, she had walked through these rooms in an empire-waist dress, her hair piled on her head, a cloak over her shoulders. How much and yet how little changed, and they themselves changed only their clothes.

They loved their constancy, but they were preparing for a break in the pattern. And unspoken, barely even thought, was the knowledge that the break might be irreparable. That to visit once more places that meant so much to them was to solidify each memory, lest that be all either of them was left with.

Back in London, at Claridge's, they indulged in a dance. They'd come here many times, but Eamon's favorite memory was of them learning to Charleston here. He smiled, thinking of Brigit's freshly bobbed curls bouncing around her head and her short, sequined skirt swirling about her thighs. She moved with a grace a ballerina would envy, her legs flying around her. As Eamon watched, it seemed to him he'd never appreciated those legs as much, and he was glad for the radical changes in fashion.

On this night, though, not twenty years later, there was much less exuberance in their dancing. Happy Londoners twirled around them, but Brigit and Eamon moved slowly, marking each step, carefully noting every moment of this new memory.

The boat from Folkestone was to leave the next evening. They had one day left for each other.

It was like the first time they made love, all those centuries ago. Brigit concentrated on memorizing the body she knew so intimately but rediscovered every dawn. The fullness of his lower lip, the length of the finger that traced a path down her thigh, the firmness in his belly. Each plane of his body, so happily familiar, was new terrain, and she explored it with infinite care and gusto. She thrilled like a green girl to the shudders he couldn't control as she stroked him, first with her hands, then her tongue. She pinched and teased each nipple, storing the resultant gasps for use all the lonely nights to come. His hair tickling her breast when his tongue circled her own nipples, the pressure of his tongue between her legs, this was a hundred years of love in the space of twelve precious hours.

Eamon, too, was memorizing the partner who had penetrated him with her being as much as he did her with his body. The magical rhythm of her hips, rising and falling as they rode him. The way her back arched, pressing her breasts even more tightly against his chest as he entered her, first slowly, teasingly, and then with gradually increasing urgency. The pressure of her fingers on his back, on his bottom, in his hair, and intertwined with his own. Their lips on each other's, open, almost breathing, groaning with ecstasy as they climaxed together. As the shadows outside grew longer, Eamon carefully ran his hands over every last inch of her, resting finally between her legs, slowly and gently stroking his favorite button there and loving her sighs and murmured assents and the way her body moved in time to the touch. He stopped, holding his hand tight to her as she gave over to the quaking thump of the orgasm, feeling the whole of her opening pulsing warm and wet under his hand.

She pulled him to her, wanting every bit of his skin on all of hers, wanting pore to melt into pore. She dove deep into the eyes that had pierced her so many years ago, even before she'd really seen them.

"Wherever else I may go, for however long, I am always here," she promised. "You are my heart. No stake could ever be strong enough to pierce that."

The large, beautiful eyes grew wet.

"No. And you will not be from me, because you carry me inside you. I will protect you, as surely as you protect me."

They wanted to say so much more, to find new words to express everything that had never been properly said in all this time, but Otonia's soft call came through the door. It was time to go.

Little was said before the group went to Folkestone. Only the five of them, plus Eamon and Padraic, were going all the way there, it was too dangerous otherwise. Otonia kissed them all on the forehead, even Mors, who looked graver than Brigit had seen him look in several centuries. No one said a word on the train, nor on the walk to the dock. Meaghan and Swefred boarded first, then Mors. Brigit turned to Eamon, her heart full but her eyes dry, choking on the realization that this was happening, that she was leaving that which she could not possibly leave, with no immediate return in sight. She felt as if she were ripping herself in two, that she could not possibly be of any use in Berlin because only a small piece of her would be there.

The warning bell sounded. Cleland was halfway up the plank and sent Brigit a carrying whisper. Eamon nodded, and nudged his frozen beloved toward the boat.

"You are going forth to conquer in a mighty way. The whole world will have new songs to sing when you are done. And you will be home with me soon," he swore.

She touched his face, the skin of his cheek a cool purr under her fingers. She had no words of her own anymore, there was no way to speak anything inside her. For one crazed moment of near amusement, she wondered how they had ever managed without poetry.

"My bounty is as boundless as the sea, my love as deep; the more I give to thee, the more I have, for both are infinite."

She turned from him quickly and ran onto the boat, knowing that if she looked in those eyes one more second, she would never be able to leave them.

Halfway across the Channel, she raised her eyes to the low-hanging stars and smiled, hoping Eamon could feel it.

Yes, infinite. Like our own selves.

Eamon played on and on and on. He knew she would hear it, or at least feel it. If his music was there, not just in her but all around her, she could not be alone, could not feel fear, could not be in danger. There were hundreds of years of songs to play and he would know when it was time to stop.

Chapter 19

Bilbao. August 1940.

The clerk in the pensione gave them what he optimistically referred to as a two-room suite and Brigit knew he was charging her twice what it would normally let for, but she hardly cared. It was stuffy and shabby and barely clean, but she didn't care about that, either. Lukas was deteriorating more every minute, and Brigit was consumed with terror for him.

They'd gotten inside and bolted the doors without anyone realizing that the boy was anything other than tired, or so Brigit was choosing to believe, but this was small comfort. Lukas was even hotter than he'd been on the train and barely conscious. Possibly it was already too late for a doctor, even if they could take that risk. It didn't take much reading of history to know that children could sicken and die within hours, and Brigit, so intimate with death, felt that cool shadow lurking near the lightly breathing boy. Another enemy she couldn't fight, not that she didn't intend to try. To lose Lukas would be to lose everything, and more. The boy was going to live.

"What are we going to do?" Alma's face was twisted in fear. Brigit saw a demon of a very different sort clawing at Alma, showing her Lukas's death, their capture, Brigit's public execution, and her own long journey back to Germany and the certain horror that awaited her there. Brigit seized Alma's cheeks and looked the girl hard in the eye.

"We're going to nurse Lukas till he's well, and then tomorrow,

246

we're getting on the ferry for Ireland, just as planned." The ferocity in Brigit's voice stunned Alma into something like acceptance.

"How, though? How can we nurse him? We haven't got anything. We don't even know what's wrong, besides the fever." Alma was quite right, and Brigit hated it.

"I'll find a way."

She couldn't think of anything that might work, however. They were being watched, and whereas on the train it had been difficult for their enemies to try to compromise the children on her brief jaunts out of the compartment, this was a far easier spot for them to attack. There was no leaving the children alone, even for a moment. Nor could she send Alma out for the herbs she knew might help. The only real option, asking someone in the pensione to run an errand, would be courting questions at best—and possibly far worse. They were stuck.

Brigit loathed Lukas's pallor and sweat. She dabbed his brow impatiently, almost hating him for putting them all in this precarious position. As the hours passed, however, her sympathy grew. He was only a frightened boy, after all, in a strange place, with not even a human for a caretaker. He knew his own weakness, that he was just a child, not as fast and sturdy as his sister if speed and strength were needed. None of it was his fault, he could not help being merely six. He would not be six forever. Or so Brigit hoped.

His breath grew raspier, and Brigit felt colder and colder. That too-familiar fear was weaving its slithery path up through her intestines. He couldn't . . . she couldn't lose him. But he could. And she could. This thing could happen. Here, in this dim, shabby room, in this arid hour of the wolf, he could slip through the shadows and disappear like so many billions of children had since the dawn of humanity. And she was helpless, powerless, had nearly no resources for holding him here in the human darkness. Like so many billions of mothers, she was doomed to hunch sleepless over a fitfully sleeping child, and will him to wake at the end of the night. And stay.

Mothers at least had God to beseech, and from whom to glean some cold comfort. She had her distant Eamon, the burning fire inside, and her fierce, furious relationship with dusty death.

Is it me? Is it spending so much time in my company that is draining the life from his little body? Is death contagious? To one yet so fresh, so recent to life, is he maybe in his way as close to the precipice as I? And if so, what the hell can I do to pull him back?

What a terrifying thing it must be to be a mother. Brigit decided it must be one of the most frightening institutions in the world. These horrible sleepless nights urging your child's soul to stay enveloped in the body you grew inside your own, coupled with days of instruction and concern, mingled with all the other work a woman must undertake. Then that feeling of some cautious relief as the child passed into adolescence, possibly safe from some dangers, but now prime prey for Brigit and Eamon and their kind. It seemed unlikely there was ever any reprieve from worry.

That Lukas was a paradigm for the children who grew into food was an idea Brigit shrank from, knowing full well that if she let herself dwell there even for a moment, she would never enjoy a meal again. She would be like a farmer who loves his cattle and swine, but eats beef and bacon nonetheless. That was the way of things. It was how it had to be.

She lay a finger on Lukas's neck. His pulse was racing. Fury welled up inside her, making her want to grab both children and simply swim their way to England. A strangled sob reminded her that Alma was huddled in the corner.

"Don't cry. It won't help."

"You have to send for a doctor!"

"That would be handing a victory to Doctor Schultze."

"What! Why . . . him? How do you know he's even in Bilbao?"

Brigit knew she'd said too much, but sensed it was wisest to trust the girl with the truth.

"He's following us, Alma. And he's not the only one. They want to keep us on the Continent, and you know it. It's mostly luck that's gotten us this far."

"So I just get to sit here with a vampire all night and watch my brother die? Is this what my father entrusted us to you for?"

"Alma, please. Don't you think I would do more if I could?"

"Can't you hypnotize one of these men around here, make them do it?"

"That's not exactly what I can do. And anyway, I'm not at full strength."

"Well, something! Do something! Do something!"

Alma shrieked and flew at Brigit, beating her with small, sharp fists. Brigit seized Alma's hands in one of her own and clamped her other over the girl's mouth.

"Don't attract attention!"

She could see Alma's eyes screaming that she didn't care how much attention she attracted and amended the order.

"You will upset your brother."

Alma quieted at once, but her eyes still snapped.

"I can cast no spells, not the sort you hope for, nothing out of a storybook, but there is one thing I might try. It's a risk. You must prepare yourself. It may not work."

"Prepare myself?"

She only understood when Brigit didn't answer.

"Go and sit with Lukas. Shut the door and don't you dare open it, not one crack. I don't care what you hear."

Their eyes locked and Alma silently obeyed.

Brigit no longer gave a damn about questions. She rang for a night porter.

The youth who answered the call had the same knowing, condescending smile that was making Brigit itchy to lay waste to the entire city. But his eyes flicked over her figure with hungry appreciation and when she smiled at him, she could feel his knees go weak. Her spirits rose.

"I was wondering, could I ask you to run a small errand for me? It's not safe for me to go out alone, not so late, and there's no one I can trust." Her voice was warm and melodic, a gentle purr that made him lick his lips nervously.

"I am not meant to leave the premises, señorita."

"It is very urgent. I do not think it will take you long."

She carelessly pulled out several bills from her calfskin fold, taking care he saw their numbers. He gasped, and she knew he was imagining all the stupid things he could buy with that amount of money.

"Truly, dear señorita, it's not possible," he protested, but it was clearly just for show now.

"All I need is rosemary, sage, sorrel, and a lemon. Strawberries will do if need be. I am sure you can accomplish this easily?"

"My deepest apologies . . ."

She wondered fleetingly if proper nourishment, combined with that store of Mors's gift, would be enough to cajole him, whisper an idea, anything to keep her from having to do the obvious. There was no point wondering, however. His blood was hot and this would not take long. Better to save her strength for where it was needed. She sank to her knees before him, her eyes wide and warm.

"Dear señor, I am begging you."

And beg she did. It took even less time than she'd thought, and it easily sealed the deal.

He was back with the herbs in ten minutes. Also a very sweet-smelling lemon.

By midmorning, Lukas was regaining color. He was still feverish, but Brigit hoped that perhaps it might be passed off as discomfort in the Spanish sun.

What's my excuse?

Alma had finally fallen into a fitful sleep, and Brigit was disinclined to wake her. The day was hot and bright and even the heavy coverings she had would not be enough to shield her, not for the amount of time she needed protection. What she would like was to use the sewers, if she could find an entrance, but it meant taking the children down there and the nascent motherliness flowering in her made that impossible. There was no choice, then, but to wait until late afternoon and hope that was late enough, while still in time. She ordered eggs and paella from the sour-faced waitress.

If only the kitchen could send up something to feed me.

That afternoon, they set out for the shipping office, Brigit carrying Lukas as before, grateful for the drowsiness that kept him quiet, and clutching Alma by the hand. She couldn't hold her parasol, but the horrid hat and veil, along with her gloves and scarf, kept her skin from any errant rays. There was barely a foot of shadow in which to walk, and the heat seared inside her, but she didn't care. They made it.

The shipping clerk smiled when they walked in, and Brigit thought she saw him almost wink until he remembered himself.

"You must be the Irish girl seeking passage to Cork," he remarked.

"Business is clearly slow here in Bilbao."

He laughed condescendingly.

"No, no, only there are too few blond beauties who come this way now, and with two children in your care, well, everyone is likely to know who you are."

"Good, that should make things more convenient." Brigit smiled, knowing full well that he was going to find a reason to deny them passage.

"Yes, but I am afraid the convenience is solely my own. Apparently there was some confusion about your papers at the Swiss border. Officials from Germany are on their way now to sort it all out with you. Absolutely routine, of course."

Alma's hand went clammy, but Brigit tossed her head and glared at the man.

"What utter rot! If anything is the matter, surely it is Irish officials who should be seeing to the trouble, not Germans."

"I am only passing on the message, señorita."

"I see. Well then, pass on the message that I wish to send a telegram to Ireland about the appalling treatment I am receiving here."

"Please, señorita. We only want to help. It is merely a matter of the correct stamps. There is no reason why you cannot be on a boat tomorrow night, or the next day at the latest, if you simply cooperate."

"How dare you speak to me like this? The Germans have no authority over me."

Sweat beaded on the clerk's brow. He stood, but as he was a good three inches shorter than Brigit, this was hardly impressive. She didn't much care for his glare, though.

"No, señorita, they have no authority over you, perhaps, but these children you are taking to Ireland with you, they are German, are they not?"

He looked hard first at Alma, then at Lukas, and then, with great deliberation, at the chipped plaster statue of the Virgin Mary on the corner of his desk.

Brigit thought he ought to thank the statue she had a child in each hand, because otherwise she would rip him straight down the middle.

"I see. Well, I expect this absurd muddle will get straightened out to my satisfaction directly, else I shall have to register a number of complaints, and I guarantee you, I know how to make trouble."

"I have no doubt." He smiled, smug.

There was a bit more shade to cover them on the way back to the pensione, a blessing Brigit was in no mood to count.

"I thought Spain was supposed to be neutral." Alma's voice was thick and Brigit saw she was close to tears.

"These things are often more complicated than that," Brigit told her.

"They're really coming for us." Alma sounded much younger than she was. Brigit realized it had only been the girl's anxiety over Lukas that had kept her from fearing for them all before now.

"Don't forget, to get to you, they have to go through me."

Alma nodded and Brigit was pleased to see her shoulders straighten slightly.

She'd been so concerned, she almost hadn't registered what she was smelling, but now she discerned the familiar scent of a sewer, one that could be accessed mere yards from the shipping office. It was a slightly more circuitous route back to the pensione, but she detected another entrance there, quite close. She still recoiled from the idea of taking the children down there, but she knew a mother would do what had to be done.

It meant they could be in the office first thing in the morning.

The clerk was shocked to see them at nine. Brigit knew the Spanish had only fleeting beliefs in vampires, which was reasonable, because no vampire would want to linger in such a sunny country. More likely he'd been told she was one of those idle rich who never rose before noon. If she hoped the surprise would win her any favor, however, she was quickly proven wrong.

"You will have to come back this evening," he insisted. "The authorities will be here then and you can discuss the problem with them."

Brigit hesitated, then pulled out her calfskin fold. She lay several notes on the desk, her eyes boring into the clerk's.

"I would rather discuss it with you now, and be on the ferry before they arrive."

He gazed at the money for a full thirty seconds, his mouth slightly open. For good measure, she slipped off her diamond watch and laid it in the center of the pile. His hand inched toward it. Brigit hissed a whisper, urging him on, but whether she was too sapped or his fear of repercussion too great, his hand jerked away as though burned and he spoke to her in a clipped voice.

"It is not possible, under no circumstances. I have strict instructions."

The money and watch were swept away and the words that slithered into his ear turned his blood cold.

"You may find yourself sorry to have been so subservient."

He knew a real man would not let her get away with that, would say or do something to remind her of her inherent inferiority, but in fact he'd never felt so terrified, and it wasn't until the door was shut behind the threesome that he was able to breathe again.

"I told you, I told you." Alma was almost hysterical. They were in the sewer and the dim light and dank surroundings did nothing to assuage the girl's despair. Brigit could hardly blame her. She had no idea what was in store for them, or how they were finally going to get the hell out of this broiling city with its foul air. She was so hungry she was on the verge of losing control, a realization that frightened her more than the meeting they would have to attend that evening.

Eamon! Eamon, help us.

She knew he would feel the call, start the music again. She hated to set him back on such a task, but there didn't seem to be anything else.

"Papa did everything right, it was all right. Why is it going wrong?"

"I don't know."

"He knew we had to hurry. And we hurried! But it didn't help, did it?"

We ran with violent swiftness and now may lose by over-running.

She only squeezed Alma's hand, wishing it could be some comfort.

"What do you think they're going to do to us?" Alma's voice was soft and trembling.

It was another, colder voice that answered, freezing them to the spot.

"I would worry more about what I am going to do to you."

Maurer.

It was a mark of how weak Brigit was that she hadn't smelled him. She cursed herself, cursed the stress that made her need more food than should be necessary, cursed the Nazis and every man and woman who bowed and scraped before them, happy to stay alive on their knees, rather than standing up and dying on their feet.

She would not let him see her weakness. He had no weapons with which he could overpower her, that she could tell, but he wielded a gun and she knew he was only too eager to use it. Even worse was that strange, hungry drive of his, that determination that had led him so far off his course, led him even to track them into the sewers. This was not a man swept up in the ardor of orders. This was a man who had struck out his own twisty path, whose unpredictability lent him a danger all his own. Keeping her eyes drilled on Maurer, she handed Lukas to Alma.

"Hold him tight, and stand behind me," she commanded.

Maurer laughed, a cold, high bark.

"It's far too late for them. And you, too. But I like it, I like that little rat babies trying to escape like rats should die like rats."

He fired the gun without even taking aim. Alma was too frightened to scream, and it was only Brigit's grunt that told her they were all right, that Brigit had caught the bullet. She pulled it out of her hand and dropped it to the brick floor. Alma hoped Maurer couldn't see how hard Brigit was shaking.

He grinned, seeming pleased with the turn of events.

"You are indeed powerful, just as I knew. What are you doing, wasting all that lovely power on these little roaches?"

"Do set yourself straight, Maurer. Are they rats or roaches? Shall we give you a moment to collect your thoughts, or do you need to go back to indoctrination school?"

He shot again—and again Brigit caught the bullet, but her hands were bubbling with blood and melted lead and hot black residue.

"If I didn't know better, *Brigit*, I would say that you were looking a bit peaked."

"I'll take your word for it."

"Perhaps what you need is a bit of sun."

He seized a chain and jerked it, loosening the slats from a grate above. The fierce morning sun hit Brigit's bleeding hand and she howled and dropped to the floor. Maurer shot again, but Brigit flung herself over the bullet, smashing it underneath her stomach even as she groaned in agony.

"Can't you just leap on him and kill him?" Alma begged in a squeaking whisper.

"I'm weak. I need food." Brigit grunted, dragging herself to her feet.

"Your devotion to these vermin-spawn is rather touching." Maurer smirked. "But my superiors won't mind if I bring them back dead."

"Don't lie, Maurer. We wouldn't have gotten this far if that were true."

Maurer waved away her comment, intent on his main point. "You, my dear, are worth far more. You and I can still strike a bargain."

She staggered toward him, eyes on the gun.

"Over my dead body."

"Think about it, Brigit." He grinned, jerking loose another slat. The sun scalded her flesh and she screamed, falling back to her knees. Why she had thought this path would be safe, why she hadn't worn gloves, was all beyond her—the joke of her overconfidence. Maurer made to shoot again, but she flung her handbag at his wrist so that the shot caromed off the wall and echoed down the sewer.

"Give it up, Maurer. You must see that this won't end well."

"Oh, but I think it will. I have right on my side, and that is rather the difference, don't you see? I'm Aryan and human. They're Jews and you're a vampire. All the laws of nature are on my side."

He squatted so he could look in her eyes and winked. The wink was a loathsome thing. Brigit thought it was not just the poor light that made his eyes look bile-green. There was already something inhuman fermenting inside him. He reeked of envy and resentment for her power and anyone who had ever enjoyed her.

Jealousy is indeed a green-eyed monster.

Brigit held his gaze, marshaling her strength.

"Is it the same bargain you want? The impossible one?"

The burst of hope in his eyes made him look even less human.

"Not impossible. You lied to me. But tell the truth now, and you shall have my protection."

"From whom?"

He laughed, incredulous.

"This is no times for games, my girl."

But she sensed something and wriggled herself another inch closer to him.

"Do they know you're here? They don't, do they? You've wandered well off your path."

"And with what you can give me, I can go back and go further. Much, much further. So, do we have a deal or don't we?"

"But with what you think I could give you, how far could you really go? Wouldn't you be dismissed from your rank? They have a strict non-vampire policy in the SS. I don't think they'd grant an exception for a partial."

"That's not what I . . ." But his patience was sapped. He flung his arm out wide and aimed another bullet at the children. The scream that ricocheted through his head was Brigit's, because, although she had leaped on him and forced his wrist up, the bullet had loosened another slat, bringing more sun down upon her bare skin. She rolled him away from the patch of sun, her hands slipping against his flesh. The demon was riding hard inside, a knight coming to help. She twisted the gun out of Maurer's hand and went on twisting until his hand popped off.

"No!" he howled. "The laws of nature . . ."

". . . are a bit more complex than those of man." Brigit finished the sentence through glinting fangs.

Maurer squealed, long and low, pushing at her with his bleeding stump, shaking his head in denial.

"No! No, no, no. They're Jews! And you're a vampire! It's all of you who should die, not me. They're Jews! You're a vampire!"

"Right on both counts, but I'd say it was rather a Pyrrhic victory. Tell me, Maurer, will anyone miss you?"

Knowing the answer garnered him no sympathy. Brigit sank her teeth into his neck and drank slowly, savoring the meal, foul-tasting though it was. Maurer's shrieks resounded through the sewers and it was only when Brigit registered the accompanying shrieks of the children that she clamped her hand over his mouth. She continued sucking him dry, even as she started to sob, hating that the children were seeing and hearing this, but helpless to do anything about it. She had to eat.

When he was empty, she flung his body hard against the wall with a scream, then doubled over, still sobbing, her face buried in blood-soaked hands. Alma's touch startled her. The girl prodded a moistened handkerchief between Brigit's fingers.

"You can't go back to our room looking like that." Her voice was low but steady.

Brigit suddenly realized she could feel Eamon, feel the music in her. She allowed herself a breath, and was whole again.

I'm all right, my beloved. Thank you. I'm all right.

Alma and Lukas were staring at her with awed eyes. The boy's face was tear-stained and even the rims of Alma's eyes betrayed some telltale pinkness. They were calm, however, and Brigit was grateful. She hauled herself to her feet.

A sudden clatter made them all jump. It was only a slat that had been dangling loose and finally dropped, but it shed more light on Maurer's body. Brigit glared at it. The screams had been loud—nightmares in broad daylight—and it was perhaps a wonder the police hadn't already tracked them down. She seized Maurer's foot and jerked him into semi-darkness. But she still wasn't satisfied.

"Brigit?" Alma ventured.

"Walk," Brigit ordered in response. "Walk. I'll catch up to you."

As the children trudged down the sewer, Brigit searched Maurer's uniform, stripping him of his identification card. She doused it in blood and shredded it, then dropped it in his wide-open mouth. Then she stomped her foot through his face, sending the card and all his teeth into his stomach. She twisted her toes into each of his fingers on his remaining hand and the one she'd snapped off, feeling the tips disintegrate into powder under her alligator pump. Brigit was far past caring if the authorities determined his death was the work of something supernatural. She simply wanted everyone to have to work that much harder to identify him. Content at last, she rejoined the children.

Safely inside their room, Brigit busied herself with bathing and dressing, taking extra care with her hair and makeup.

"That horrible man, he was nothing, wasn't he?" Alma asked, obsessively brushing her own hair till it shone. "They've got something worse planned for us tonight."

"Maybe," Brigit conceded. "But I feel far more equal to it now."

On entering the office again that evening, however, a scant two hours before the ferry was due to set sail, Brigit was uneasy. Maurer had twisted himself far from the party doctrine and into an insular world of his own half-madness, yet he knew her, knew at once who and what she was. And so had others. She supposed it was just the stories, the rumors, the intensity of the Nazi obsession with all things occult and supernatural, the paranoia—this was what had ended up raining hell down upon the millennials. Her pretense still held. It had to. And for this next hurdle, she would just have to play even harder at being human, and trust her talent to get her through yet again.

Alma assured her before they left that she looked flawless, white and bright and sparkling. A young, thoughtless beauty with a giddy snap in her eye and merry, teasing smile. So confident that all would go well, she'd had their luggage brought down to wait by the dock. With her lovely clothes and perfectly turned-out look, they would have to know already to guess what havoc she'd wreaked on one of their own a few hours earlier.

Perhaps, if they do know, they don't care. They haven't got much room for rogues in the Nazi Party. Rather a shame, really. Could have worked to our advantage once.

There was no ruse of normalcy at the shipping office. Rather, the officials clearly hoped to cow her with their show of pomp and force. She and the children were guided into a large private office and told to sit. Two minutes later, Doctor Schultze strode in, beaming.

Oh, excellent.

"Fräulein! How can it be that you are here in the lovely Bilbao and yet taking no sunshine?"

She was given no opportunity to answer. The ubiquitous henchmen, Weber and Lange, were with him, and she could smell the hatchets hidden in their jackets. There were also two Spanish officers, hulking, unsmiling men whose icy eyes rested on the children. The last two men interested Brigit most of all. One, another Spaniard, was small, but with an intimidating air about him, a busy, official sort of man. The other was tall, blond, with an ironic smile. A hunter. A good hunter. Irish. She sensed various tricks up his sleeves and took special note of the sword he wore around his waist. Brigit remembered the French swordsman called in specifically to behead Anne Boleyn. She could fight all these men easily on her own, but with the children there . . . she fixed her eyes on the doctor.

"Well, you shall be very pleased to hear we have already straightened out the little problem with your papers. It is not bureaucracy keeping you in this charming spot."

"Imagine my relief," Brigit assured him with a sniff. "What is it then?"

"Doctor's orders." He smirked.

Brigit's arm instinctively tightened around Lukas. He was much better, he looked almost well. Surely no one could believe he must not be allowed to travel?

"We are all in excellent health. Our papers prove as much besides."

The little official spoke then, his voice an absurd chirp.

"The children, perhaps, yes"—and her heart sickened as she saw him sneer at each child in turn—"but it's you who raise the question, se-ñorita."

"Me!" she cried, glaring at her accusers.

"Yes!" The doctor pounced, ecstatic. "We suspect you of having a very dangerous and contagious blood disease. I have alerted the Irish authorities and they agree that you must be given a complete examination before being allowed to enter Ireland. They have sent Owen here." He waved a hand at the Irish hunter, who scowled. "He is to make sure nothing untoward gets on that ferry."

Brigit glared around at the leering men. It would be so pleasant to lash out and kill them all if she could be sure the children would be unharmed. But then what? Grab the children, head for the ferry, and from there . . . where? She couldn't board without the tickets she didn't know how to falsify. Her mind reached the dead end her pursuers intended.

They must know she would not let them capture her, but they had no intention of letting her out alive, not with the children, too.

The doctor opened his medical bag and removed several instruments. The stethoscope he saved for last, dangling it playfully, his eyes bright with malicious glee. He walked toward her with annoying deliberation.

"Now then, my dear girl, if I could ask you to remove a few layers of clothing . . ."

"I demand a nurse!" Brigit snapped.

The doctor sneered, but the other men looked uncertain.

"I refuse to submit to any sort of examination like this, about which my government will hear a lengthy complaint, without another woman present to guard my virtue." Brigit was haughty and indignant, but also a terrified young girl, raised in a strict Catholic home.

The Spaniards and even Owen were abashed. They were all good Catholics themselves, and the realization of what they'd been about to allow troubled them. None of the Spanish men really believed the wild accusation that this entrancing creature was not human. They were willing to accept the possibility, hence going along with this bizarre arrangement, but if indeed she was exactly as she appeared, a privileged young lady, the resultant time in confession would be unpleasant. As for Owen, he felt sure this was the vampire Brigantia, but something about her, perhaps it was the children, made him waver. No, a nurse must of course be present, and it was shocking that the doctor had not insisted upon it himself.

"Oh very well, very well, fetch a nurse then!" Doctor Schultze snapped. "Not that it will make any difference."

Brigit wasn't sure what she was doing, only that she needed more time. She closed her eyes and reached out to Eamon.

Eamon, my heart. Hear me, help me. Have we not always said your music makes the skin breathe, has the power to start a heart beating? Eamon, I know you're there, I know you're playing to comfort me, but it's something more I need right now. Please, please know what I need and please find the power to save us all.

For the agonizing seventeen minutes that elapsed while one of the men went to fetch a nurse, Brigit repeated her plea, sending every neural force in her out over the water and deep into the castle. She could not have been more grateful for Mors's gift, knowing it made the message that much stronger and clearer. Eamon would hear it, would know what to do, but would it work?

The room was eerily silent, and Brigit was grateful. Deep inside her, Eamon whispered, *"I'm here. Listen."* She opened every closed pore and listened as though she'd spent the last millennium deaf.

The music melted inside her. She could feel it worming its way through her flesh, tickling a path into the silent stream of her veins. The still heart began to stir, a bear waking from hibernation, sniffing the air. Brigit fought to keep the exhilarated smile from her lips as her heart gave one tentative beat, then another, then another. She felt the music in her fingers, clumsy as she'd ever been when toying with any of the instruments, she was suddenly a master puppeteer, with her own veins as a marionette. A dam unblocked and the blood dripped gingerly, then faster, a river running free under the power of music that indeed knew how to stir blood. The heart, the arteries—Brigit wondered what other of her organs might dive into the novelty of a working circulatory system.

I am an organist indeed.

She would like to see any maestro have more power than she did right now. She yearned to tell Alma what was happening, how Eamon was rescuing them, but she only smiled at the ashen girl and removed her coat and jacket and rolled up her sleeves when the nurse came in and nodded to her.

Doctor Schultze was trembling with heady anticipation as he approached his prey at last. His smiling eyes were hard on Brigit's and he laid his plump, stubby fingers on her wrist.

"Well, well," he intoned with heavy sarcasm. "What haven't we here, isn't this . . ." He paused, frowning.

Alma swiveled to Brigit, just in time to see her nostrils flare slightly with the effort of holding back a guffaw. She was otherwise quite placid, politely interested in the results of the doctor's examination.

The doctor kept his hand tight on her wrist. The other men exchanged glances and the official coughed.

"Will this take much longer, Doctor?"

"I . . . I . . ." Doctor Schultze sputtered.

The nurse, who had been recruited unwillingly from her hospital job, impatiently seized Brigit's other wrist. She held it for a moment, then stared at the doctor.

"I do not understand, señor," she began, and the other men, especially the hunters, leaned forward eagerly. "It is a good, regular pulse. For what else are you looking?"

The doctor thrust his hand at Brigit's neck. The other men edged forward as though to stop him and the nurse exclaimed, but he wanted to feel that pulse. He glared at her, his fingers digging into her neck.

"This is not possible," he growled.

"I beg your pardon?" Brigit inquired, sweetly polite.

"This is not possible!"

He tore at her blouse, wielding his stethoscope like a stake, but now the nurse and the Spanish officers pulled him away with shouts and expletives.

"Check for yourself then, check her heart! Whatever magic she can wield, she cannot make a dead heart beat, she cannot!"

The little official nodded to the nurse, who grunted with exasperation, snatched the stethoscope, and held it to Brigit's heart.

"Breathe, señorita," she instructed tenderly. The women looked at each other, a collusive glance understanding the passionate stupidity of men and their own inability to change it. Brigit took a deep, slow breath. And another, for good measure.

The nurse handed the stethoscope back to Doctor Schultze and spoke with deep disdain.

"A perfectly strong, healthy girl. May I return to my work now?"

The official, red-faced and furious, was about to dismiss her when the doctor howled, pointing at the children.

"They are Jews! They are Jews trying to escape Germany! Their father is a known criminal, the entire family is to be arrested! You dare call yourself good Catholics and let little Jewish rats go to spread their germs abroad?"

Brigit stood, buttoning herself up. She was still focusing her energy on the charade of her body and sensed it was wiser to remain silent and let the doctor tie his own noose.

"Now, Doctor," the little official remonstrated. "Their papers have been checked twice and all is in order. Or perhaps you think the Swiss and Spanish are not as thorough in checking papers as you Germans?"

"Never mind papers, never mind! There is proof, better proof! Pull down the boy's trousers, you shall see he is circumcised."

Brigit's heart leaped ahead of her control, pounding so hard she thought she might faint. The nurse looked at her again, a long, searching look. Then she looked at the children.

"Well? Do it, woman!" Doctor Schultze looked like he was about to strike her.

The nurse sneered at him and lied blithely.

"And what if he is circumcised? My own son had to be circumcised at three, a urinary infection; these things happen. These healthy people have business in Ireland, and I have sick people to attend in my hospital. Good day to you, gentlemen."

She nodded warmly at Brigit as she swept out the door.

Brigit knew better by now than to feel relief as they boarded the evening ferry. No sooner were they settled than she could hear the vitriolic shouts of the doctor outside. She took the children to the railing and saw with a sinking heart that he and his men were being allowed aboard the full boat, even though the little official was arguing strenuously, hating the extra paperwork that was now being foisted upon him.

"It's a whole night and a morning before we're there." Alma fretted.

And it's Ireland.

Brigit shook her head.

"I'll take care of it. There is ever more to me than he thinks."

Oh, Eamon. I hope that's true.

She hadn't slept in days and knew she dare not blink for the next twelve hours.

The doctor, Weber and Lange, and the lurking Owen joined Brigit and the children on the deck. The two parties glared at each other in the dimming light.

"Well, Fräulein," the doctor began, barely suppressing his rage, "it seems our paths continue together yet a little longer."

"Yes," Brigit said, her voice low and melodic. "Won't that make a pleasant night for us all?"

Chapter 20

Berlin. August 1940.

"Turn over," the man urged, prodding her with the stake.

Brigit did, blinking mud out of her eyes. The stake, mounted in an elegant old crossbow, had a smell that made her nauseous. Its core was two intertwined hairs of a long-lived vampire couple who had died together, at this hunter's hand. The only sort of stake that could fell a millennial. From it, her gaze traveled up to the man's face. A haggard face, older than it ought to be. The brown eyes were tired, but there was warmth in them. The energy he radiated was one of sweetness, something not expected in a powerful hunter. Brigit was intrigued.

To her astonishment, he smiled, and extended a hand to help her up. After a moment's hesitation, she took it. She was unsteady on her feet and absently brushed the dirt from her face and clothes, strangely uncomfortable.

"It doesn't matter," he told her. "You can bathe and change later."

For one brief, bewildering moment, she thought he was preparing her for a public execution, although that was not the way of true hunters, which this man certainly was. He had some other plan she couldn't fathom. The stake was only to get her attention and keep her from fighting. Or perhaps he hadn't expected her to be alone. Mors could not have felt this man coming, but she was suddenly, wildly glad he was gone.

The hunter's demeanor was almost friendly, but still wary. He gestured with the crossbow for her to walk in front of him. He knew his lore well. She wouldn't run. No millennial would die from a blow to the back.

They walked a long way in silence. Brigit was too tired and hungry to talk and the hunter seemed lost in thought. At last, they reached a staircase leading into a cellar, which in turn led into a small, warm house. The hunter bade Brigit sit and sat across from her, laying the crossbow on his knee.

"I am Leon Arunfeld. Ours was one of the legendary hunting families."

"Was?" Brigit asked.

"In Germany. Prussia, before. The records will be expunged, I believe."

He excused himself and went into the kitchen.

Brigit stared around the room, too dazed to wonder why she was there. A tantalizing smell wound up her nostrils and the demon twitched pitifully.

Leon reentered, bearing a tray of tea. He smiled at Brigit and poured her a warm cup of blood. She blinked, took it, and sipped. Bliss. The best food she'd had in months.

"I've been saving it. Warmed over, but still potent, I should think. It's mine."

Her mouth dropped open and he smiled.

"I do some pharmacology, too. Did. I know about slow lettings. I've been planning this moment for a while."

Brigit set aside her cup.

"You know who and what I am, and I you. This isn't just a mad tea party, I'm sure."

Leon smiled, opened a door, and beckoned. Two children came into the room. The little boy kept his head down, but the girl held hers arrogantly high and was quite equal to meeting Brigit's eyes.

"I waited too long," Leon told her, as casually as though they were talking about the weather. "I was very foolish. They had coerced me and my wife to help train the Nachtspeere and promised us security . . ."

He trailed off and looked away, his face pink. Brigit sought to spare him further discomfort.

"We know. The refugee vampires told us about it. You were placed in an impossible—"

Leon held up a hand to stop her.

"Don't try to exonerate me." He looked at the children and gestured for them to leave the room, waiting until the door closed to continue. "They wouldn't let me send them out on the Kindertransport. The children are the best leverage the government has over me and they know I know they'll stop at nothing." He took a sip of tea and stared Brigit hard in the eye. "They said a vampire killed my wife, my Lena. It wasn't true. I could tell by the wounds. They killed her, and probably knew I knew. I said nothing, of course, because that was when I saw how foolish I'd been to stay. Wicked, even. I did much of their dirty work for them and lost my dearest love in return."

"But I don't understand. What did they have to gain by killing your wife?"

"They knew by then that I was wavering. I had cleared the way for some of my neighbors to emigrate. Under the guise of flushing out vampires, I warned more Jews. The Nazis wanted to show me they meant business. And Lena was pregnant. If they knew that, well, one less Jew coming into the world was probably just a bit of gravy."

Brigit wished she'd held her tongue. She gazed around the room, her eyes automatically skimming the rows of leather-bound books on the shelves. At the very top were legend books, dozens, going back several centuries.

"When did you find out about us?"

Leon's lip curled in an unsettling facsimile of Mors's own half-smile.

"I had my suspicions, once I heard about General von Kassell and the train. And that mess in the theater. Millennials, of course. I knew there were still some in the Russian far east, but this was all too elegant, too artful to be anything other than the work of the British tribunal. I could not understand it, so I refused to believe it until it was proved."

Brigit sipped at the blood, listening hard.

"You will have been told the Nazis recruited several true hunters. One was a bit more zealous than I might have expected. Likes the party's line. Knew his Irish lore and it was Cleland, of all vampires, that he recognized. Dumb luck on his part. And since others must be with him, who else but Brigit and Mors? Swefred and Meaghan were a bit of a surprise, though. Well, so I volunteered to track you all, drew up a plausible plan that would end with very public deaths, good examples. It wasn't easy. But I am the best, so they trusted me."

"Public deaths. Like what happened yesterday?"

"You did well, but they saw you and Mors come back from Paris. They knew you must be planning something big. It took them a while, but eventually they guessed. They are clever, the Nazis. I had to be a part of it. I didn't want to, but there was no choice."

"How did the Irish come to be there?"

"Oh, they rather like the Nazis. My colleague gave the word and they came to help. They knew the Nachtspeere couldn't manage with just two true hunters to help."

Leon leaned forward and smiled in earnest.

"I'll tell you this, your Meaghan cast a killing blow. There are perhaps only four Nachtspeere left alive of the entire squadron, and Ireland's ranks have been badly damaged. She deserves commemoration in your world."

Brigit returned his smile and hoped that Meaghan, wherever she was, knew what she had done.

"How did you manage to escape?" Brigit wanted to know. The man was wholly unscathed.

"I slipped away in the commotion, once Swefred was hit. I saw what was coming and knew what I had to do."

Struck with another idea, Brigit gripped his hand.

"Cleland! Did you see what—"

But he was already shaking his head.

"It was you I needed to follow. I'm sorry. I don't know what happened to Cleland."

Brigit sank back in her chair, her hand pressed to her mouth.

I will not weep for him until I know tears are warranted.

Then she realized what he'd said.

"You needed me?"

Leon stared at the floor for several minutes, his shoulders slumped. Bitterness emanated from him. At last he looked up and spoke flatly.

"I need you to guide my children to England. My sister is there. I'm done, a blind man could see that, but they might get out, if you help them."

Brigit gaped.

"You . . . you want . . . you want a vampire to take care of your children?"

"Not just a vampire. The great Brigantia, later Brigit. A millennial of the British tribunal. If anyone can give them safe passage, it's you. I have all the papers ready, I have clothes and money, and the children are packed. The main thing is getting on the train undetected. The house is watched, but there are several good routes through the sewers they don't know."

"But I—"

"Can protect them."

Brigit wanted to laugh. The sheer absurdity of it was too much. She admired his forethought, even appreciated his trust, but it was ridiculous.

"I'm sorry. I can't."

"You came here to help."

Hunter and vampire looked each other hard in the eye.

"We came to avenge our kind." Brigit corrected him.

"Oh, yes. Destroy those who would so systematically, wantonly, destroy you. But then that changed. Then you wanted to obliterate the Nazis for the good of humanity."

"And if so? What difference does it make? We failed." Brigit drained her cup and glared around the pretty little room.

Leon was quiet for a long time.

"So. You have to go home, and I've made it easy."

"Easy!" Brigit exploded. "A known vampire escorting the Jewish children of a known—and doomed—hunter? Preposterous. And I couldn't protect them with my full abilities, not when I'm playing human. That's been our problem all along. Or anyway, it was one of them. We've had quite a few problems. But no, if we're done then we're done, and I'm going home via stealth, not in the open and not with baggage. I'm sorry, but I have too much to lose."

"Yes. A reason to get home." Leon examined his crossbow, a slim, fine piece of craftsmanship. "Eamon, of course, is not a millennial, else he would have been here as well. His strength is great, certainly, but he remains easier to destroy than you, if assiduously hunted."

He looked hard at Brigit to see that she was listening.

"You know we are less concerned with older vampires, as they don't tend to wreak quite as much havoc as new ones. Too much work, not enough reward. And, of course, these are difficult times. Still, arrangements could be made. If necessary."

Brigit ran a finger around the edge of the cup, imagining it dissolving into invisible molecules.

"So, blackmail."

"If you'll forgive the crudeness. They are my darlings, my blood. I must have them safe. They must grow, and thrive. Even if I won't see it."

Brigit's mind raced. Eamon. She would protect Eamon with everything she had and more. And he was so strong and so careful. It must be an empty threat. She and Eamon could destroy hundreds of hunters if they had to. She could not be a guardian to human children.

"Meet them properly," Leon invited, calling the children back in.

She didn't want to. She'd never had any interactions with children and was not interested in starting now. But there was no choice. She looked at them. Handsome little things. Unformed, and full of possibility. They intrigued her.

Leon laid his hands on each child's shoulders as he gave their names, thus preventing awkward attempts at handshaking that no one wanted.

"This is Alma, and this is Lukas."

Brigit was drawn to the girl, with her flashing, contemptuous eyes. The eyes were enormous, the color and texture of rich dark chocolate. The girl stood on the precipice between childhood and adulthood, the glowing energy inside her only just beginning to take hold.

"Hello Alma," Brigit ventured.

As the name left her lips, she flushed hot, then cold, and clutched at the edge of her chair. Alma. A name she'd never spoken, and hadn't even heard in centuries, but knew only too well. Alma, and a small brother. Jews marked for death. The longer Brigit looked at Alma, the more she saw Eamon. She looked deeper into the eyes, feeling them open, feeling herself sucked through a vortex back into her own history, to the gaping wound in the sky above the smoldering tower in York.

What wound did ever heal but by degrees?

She tore her eyes from Alma and back to Leon. It was impossible that he should know, but it didn't matter. She was his chosen one.

"When do we leave?"

The bath was glorious. Brigit closed her eyes to better enjoy the water, and to think.

They tracked us. We failed.

The Nazis were advancing by the hour. Meaghan and Swefred were dead, Cleland missing, and Mors walking into suicide. The Nazis may as well have known all along, considering how little the vampires had really accomplished. Brigit supposed their initial certainty was simple hubris, and the expectation that they were above such follies was more hubris.

We need humans, but they don't need us. Human nature will always be stronger than anything we can muster. They rule the land. We simply roam it.

If they'd known about Leon, they might have joined forces with him. Human allies might have made all the difference. But it was something they had never thought of, not even for a moment.

Brigit wiped her eyes and dried herself, slipping on pajamas and a robe. They were not to leave till tomorrow at dusk, and she was looking forward to some more food and rest.

Leon spent the whole of supper detailing the operation, showing her the papers he'd carefully prepared, the maps, the schedules. He apologized for the need to go through Ireland but expected they would be there only an hour at most and this was not enough time to alert hunters, let alone one who could handle a millennial. Brigit sat numbly, letting it sink in.

After supper, Leon put Lukas to bed and Brigit and Alma regarded each other across the table.

"Is it true vampires don't prey on children?"

"Yes."

"Why not?"

Brigit grinned.

"Because they're in bed when we go hunting."

She could feel the girl fighting a smile and suspected she didn't want to be put at a disadvantage, which any sort of warm relations might be. Brigit studied the fierce young human, rather liking that she didn't want to be obedient. Alma clearly knew what she had to do, knew the family was at the end of its options, but that didn't mean she had to be friendly. The girl was obstreperous at heart, and Brigit liked her for that, even though she could feel they were more adversaries than not.

In any case, it was true, vampires did not eat children. A child's blood had no scent for them. It was like a raw ingredient. A human had to be nearer sixteen to become appetizing. To eat a child would not only be tasteless, but also a violation, an intrusion into the development process. There was a sanctity in the coming of age, and to feed on an unformed creature would be as improper as to eat fowl still in the shell.

When Leon returned, he showed Brigit his masterwork, a telegraph system he'd set up when things began to be bad and communication tricky. She hated the thought of Eamon and Otonia receiving the information she now had to send, but it was a relief to know they would be thinking of her, and that Eamon, in return, would be sending her everything she needed to accomplish this one last mission.

All that strange day, in that strange house, Brigit slept fitfully, seeing the faces of Mors, Cleland, Meaghan, Swefred, and Eamon circling her head.

"It's all right, it's all right," they whispered. "You're going home."

Home. Yes. Please, Eamon. Please let me get there. With these children.

The good-byes were hurried; it wouldn't do to linger and tears were out of the question. But Brigit took Leon's hand in both of hers and looked him in the eye.

"They will be my family, beyond what you've falsified in these papers. I will protect them and I will see them to safety. I swear it."

He kissed her hand. She took each child by a small hand and, her head high and eyes glowing, boarded the train.

Chapter 21

Ferry to Ireland. August 1940.

Eamon's fingers were bleeding, but he didn't notice. They remained nimble, dancing over the strings, coaxing out every melody he'd ever had in him. A cloud of song to comfort, to fill, to shield. He could feel it working. The only question was when he would have to stop so that he could travel. Brigit and the children would have to be met in Ireland, whatever the risk. She would need his corporeal self there, and she would have it.

He had a few more hours before the train left for Wales. The sweat mingled with his blood and made a puddle at his feet. He kept his eyes closed, concentrating only on the music, ignoring the sprains creeping up his wrists, the skin rubbed raw from the chin rest.

Otonia drifted in silently, laid an ice bag on his neck and stuck a straw in his mouth so that he could swallow a mug of warmed-up blood. He barely noticed.

It was only later, when he was sprinting for the train, that he realized she'd saved him a step. Two days of nonstop violin playing with no sleep would have forced him to hunt, and there was no time to lose.

Brigit decided the only safe course was to stay on the deck so that they might be in someone's sights throughout the journey. It would look odd, a guardian keeping children awake and outdoors all night, but even on the open water, the air was sticky and humid, and she could argue the children would sleep better outside.

Lukas she kept in her arms. He was still frail, even a bit warm, and she wasn't going to let anyone see that. She also hoped it gave him some comfort. At least he got to sleep, which was more than could be said for herself or Alma.

"Try to at least close your eyes," Brigit urged Alma, tucking her up in a deck chair, but Alma was adamant.

"You're staying awake and so am I."

Brigit was grimly pleased to note that they weren't the only ones lurking on the deck as the night wore on. This part of the sea hadn't been disturbed by U-boats, but that didn't mean people weren't uneasy. It was a long night's journey into day, and many of them wanted to stay awake, as though that somehow guaranteed safe passage.

The doctor and his posse set up camp on another set of chairs across from Brigit and the children. They pretended to play cards and smoke, their eyes tight on their quarry. For their part, Brigit and Alma looked only at each other, the sea, and the stars.

Shortly before midnight, Owen left the group and headed inside. Ten minutes later, he came back, taking care to catch Brigit's eye and wink as he passed.

"I'm so looking forward to getting home, aren't you?" he asked, without waiting for a reply. He rejoined the other men and soon they were all laughing.

Alma shivered. Brigit patted her arm.

"Courage. Perhaps I'll get the chance to see he doesn't get home."

Alma nodded, staring out at the black water, her arms wrapped tightly around her. She looked at Lukas, who was sleeping peacefully, hesitated, then climbed into the chair with Brigit and leaned against her lightly. Brigit started to put her arm around Alma, then changed her mind, pointing to the stars instead.

"Look, look at that. That's Leo. He was a very powerful lion, but Hercules killed him. They had to honor him, though, so he was put in the sky. He's fierce, which is why he dominates the hottest summer nights. A fire sign, and very brave."

"Fire?" Alma asked. "That's bad for you, isn't it?"

"If it was only fire, yes, but Leo governs the heart and spine, so I have no fear under Leo."

Alma thought about that awhile.

"What about Orion?"

"Oh, Orion. Orion has a whole universe to protect. I think he's learned to accept me. No, it's a brave o'erhanging firmament up there. It's been my friend a long, long time."

Her murmur turned into a low hum and Alma's eyes fluttered, then closed.

A chill wind rose and the boat swayed. The sea was growing choppy. Owen produced a bottle of whiskey and took a long drink, then offered it to the others. The doctor frowned, but Brigit thought she heard Weber tell him that a drink was medicinal on a rough night. She smiled, remembering ancient drinking songs, wondering why it was that men back to the beginning of her time so loved to extol liquor and its quixotic powers in song. She hummed one of the old tunes and watched as many of the tired, anxious men waiting out the night fetched bottles from inside and started up a party.

Two hours later, the wind was colder, the waters choppier, and every man on deck save the doctor was drunk. Their carousing had awakened Alma, though Lukas still slept. The three were huddled in a dark corner and Brigit had warned Alma to stay silent and alert. She herself was delighted. With faculties so dazed, her enemies were becoming prime targets. The demon was dancing a jig.

The irritated doctor was also becoming seasick, much to Brigit's amusement. A very drunk Spaniard offered his assistance. The doctor tried to shake him off, but was promptly overwhelmed. He was given a wide berth as he lurched over the railing and stayed there a long time, the Spaniard patting him and speaking bracingly.

"Come on, gents, let's get inside and wake some ladies!" another Irishman cried, and the others trotted after him. Brigit grinned.

Men just never do change.

The three hunters didn't notice the indisposed doctor, or the absence of the others. They had their arms around one another and were singing a hunting song in German and Gaelic. Brigit had heard it before.

The world sleeps sound, but we stay awake
Tracking the scent of the vampire's lust
We lure him in, we wield the sharp stake
And dissolve the monster into dust.

Brigit stood up slowly and told Alma to close her eyes and try not to listen.

A gust of wind and a wave crashing against the ferry muted the sound of Lange falling into the water, his neck broken. Weber, assuming his friend had only fallen, shouted into the water while Owen scouted for a life buoy. But when the Irishman returned, Weber was gone and a drop of blood slid off Brigit's finger and onto the damp deck.

Without a word, Owen drew his sword. Brigit braced for battle, but felt the defeat even before she heard the triumphant voice.

"Leave her, Owen. Leave her for now."

Doctor Schultze, still very green, was holding a knife to Alma's throat. He smiled. As horrified as Brigit was, she could yet feel some pride that Alma looked less frightened than contemptuous of her attacker. She kept Lukas's head pressed tightly to her chest.

"Now then, Vampire, we can speak freely at last," the doctor said, gesturing her closer. She approached him reluctantly and the frustrated Owen joined her.

"You are certainly an impressive specimen." The doctor nodded to Brigit with professional appreciation. "Although of course we were always going to win. I admit, I thought our last recourse was going to have to come later, when we landed, but this is far preferable. I will look most brave indeed."

"Hang on," began Owen, but the doctor interrupted him.

"You can share the plaudits, of course. Germany values its Irish friends. The vampire can be killed in Ireland. All I ask is to study the creature."

"Study me?" Brigit was cold, but perplexed.

"They are promoting Mengele above me," the doctor said, and Brigit detected a whine. "If I bring them detailed knowledge of vampire physiology, they may reconsider. They are very respectful of scientific research."

Brigit had no idea who Mengele was, or what position Schultze was after, she was only interested in distracting him.

"I can save you the trouble of dissection." She improvised. "Except for my fangs, talons, and the viscosity of my blood, I will look like any dead human inside."

"I will see for myself." The doctor snarled. "I shall not touch your heart, but simply explore until I am satisfied. One assumes you can endure pain."

"A live dissection. Of course. How charming. But I'm more concerned about your plans for the children."

Both Schultze and Owen appraised her.

"I do believe you mean that," said the doctor at last. "Why would a vampire care about little rats? Are you hoping to keep them as pets?"

"Obviously, whatever my hopes were, they're now dashed. What are yours?"

Schultze shrugged.

"They go back to Germany as an example. Their father was quite the troublemaker, even after the Reich tried to be kind to him. What waste. And trying to send his dirty spawn to Britain in care of a vampire, disgraceful. Perhaps he did some good in his time, but a vampire-free Germany no longer has need for vampire hunters."

"Leon Arunfeld is a great hunter, though."

Brigit didn't dare turn. There was scorn in Owen's voice, and she sensed it was for the German attitude, rather than Leon.

Schultze shrugged again.

"So a rat can hunt vermin, well and good, that is no excuse to reward it."

"You speak a bit too light of the art of vampire hunting."

Brigit inched back, feeling the space she would need.

"Great respect, great respect," Schultze intoned, though the condescension floated under his words. He was bored. "Now, I shall have to lock the rats in our cabin and notify . . ."

"The girl is a firstborn. She'll be a hunter. We don't waste good hunting stock."

"You may take that up with the Führer if you like, but I have my orders."

Brigit laughed, a tinkling melody that dazed the two men.

"I never thought I'd hear such a thing, the Irish being so desperate to get a German hunter in their mix." She fixed Owen in a sweet, sympathetic gaze. "So the rumors are true. The Irish are losing their vampire-hunting vigor. What a shame. Undoubtedly it's all the drink that does it—"

The drink and the fury certainly did it for Owen. He launched himself upon her, but the deafening battle-wail he meant to emit never worked its way past his intention. His own sword lopped his head clean off and sent it soaring into the sea. Its tip was under the doctor's chin before the latter could even blink.

"Drop the knife, Doctor."

He wasn't going to, he wasn't going to relinquish his prize, but the sword slipped under the knife and slung it into the air just as he sliced into the girl's neck. Alma's skin was only grazed, but the demon was fully roused.

Pressed against the railing, thin trickles of blood wending down his neck from each of Brigit's talons, the doctor still tried to wield an upper hand.

"What do you think will happen, once we are all missed from the ferry? Do you really think you will be allowed to continue on your journey?"

"You fell overboard. The sailors who would normally be watching for such incidents are now watching for potential U-boats," Brigit reminded him, winking a red eye. "These would be the hazards of traveling in wartime, you see."

Her confident, lilting tone unhinged him further. He scrabbled at the claw holding him so firmly, with so little exertion.

"We are being expected in Cork. When they see we are not there, you will have signed all your death warrants."

"And here I thought you'd taken care of that for us already. Isn't that what you Nazis are renowned for? Efficiency?"

He was sweating now, twisting in her grip. Brigit was strongly reminded of a wolf chewing his leg to get free of one of those horrid traps humans liked to set. She didn't want to keep him alive, but she did want to know what exactly was awaiting them in Cork. She smiled to urge him on.

"All right, Vampire, perhaps we can arrange a bargain." He hurried on, taking note of her gleaming fangs. "I can call off the posse at the dock, you can go free, just let me take the children back to Germany."

"You were about to kill Alma."

"No, just hurt her. I only wanted to subdue you. So, it is a bargain?"

"How large is this posse?"

He didn't answer. She poked a talon under his ear. His breath came out in one long exhalation of astonished pain.

"What will you gain, killing me?" He meant to sound defiant, but the demon drank in his fear.

"Very likely nothing at all," she conceded, "except hopefully the lives of these children. What will you gain, taking them back to their deaths?"

"Reward. And the assurance of doing well for the master race."

That phrase again. The doctor was short, rotund, with mouse-brown hair and piggy eyes. He had conviction, though, Brigit had to allow him that.

Schultze was smiling now, tasting a bright future as though Brigit was going to release him.

"In a world without Jews or vampires, or other undesirables, there will be so much good. And we will prevail. You see how you tried to stop us and did not succeed. Good triumphs over evil. It is the way of the world. Your England shall not stop us invading. You British will soon see your king on his knees, bowing to our Hitler. It is only a matter of time."

She shook her head, smiling.

"No. No, you're quite wrong. That precious stone, set in the silver sea? You think it's small and weak and can be tamed, like Napoleon did before you. But no. My England never did, nor never shall, lie at the foot of a proud conqueror."

The doctor was bemused, but relaxed. That he was still alive meant that Brigit was surely playing him, was going to accept his offer. She had too much to live for. She wasn't going to sabotage it.

"Let me have the children, Brigit. They were never meant to be. We are simply righting wrongs."

"Is that what you think you are doing?"

"I think of myself as curing a cancer."

"How benevolent. But I do not understand you. You would see them dead, they, who have souls, and you would think yourself a hero for it. It's a tale you would tell your grandchildren, dandling them on your knee. You could douse their light and feel strong, and yet somehow, I'm meant to be the soulless, evil one. No, I do not understand you."

Dawn was breaking, and the Irish coast was in sight. It was an overcast, misty morning, and Brigit was happy for it, even though safety was still such a long ways away. Death might be standing on the shore, beckoning her to his side again, and this time forever, or perhaps to snatch the children from her grip. Death would accept the doctor but take the three of them as well; it had no qualms and no quotas, just its steady stroll through the sentient world, collecting as it went.

To kill the doctor would, indeed, achieve nothing. They'd meant to break the spine of a beast, and they'd hardly touched it. Their fight had turned out to be merely fragmentary. It was the human fight that was going to matter now, the only one that had ever mattered.

Still looking at the looming coast, Brigit slowly drew her talon across the doctor's throat and pitched him into the water. It was drizzling. She extended her hands, watching the blood drip off them. The wind grew stronger as they approached Ireland.

Hey, ho, the wind and the rain.

Alma joined her at the railing.

"What happens now?"

"We change for the mail boat to Holyhead and then catch the train for London." Brigit was calm and matter-of-fact.

"Will they follow us?"

"I won't leave a trail."

Eamon crept from his hiding place on the mail boat. He found being a stowaway distasteful, something for which he was too old, but there was no choice. He knew he could do more good assisting them onto the boat from where he was and couldn't risk the clouds breaking. Still, he was itchy to be on the dock. He could sense the waiting hunters, smell their weapons and their hot blood. Two were after the children, which made no sense, but the others were even more frightening in their way. They didn't care what they killed on their path toward ending the reign of Brigantia.

Brigit took her time identifying the luggage and arranging for it to be transferred to the mail boat. She was cool and unruffled, and the talk that was flying around of four missing men didn't bother her.

The border patrol, too caught up in the excited rumors, stamped their papers with an absentmindedness Brigit almost found disappointing. She was hot for another charade. She and the children repaired quietly to the waiting room.

The rain had stopped, but the clouds hung firm. For once, Brigit was not concerned about the sun. She was seeing an echo of last week's cataclysm. Men climbing the roofs of the dock buildings. They were armed with bows and arrows, and fire. Their three selves were the only passengers set for Wales, so there was no hope of human camouflage. She couldn't believe they would really strike down the children in this ignominious fashion as well, but then she saw the two men outside the waiting room. Nazis. They were in suits, not uniforms, but she knew them by the scent. Nazis. There to return the children to Germany. She was briefly bewildered, then remembered that the IRA had courted Nazis, offered to spy, tried to help them with plans for the invasion of Britain. The enemy of their enemy appeared to be their friend, and many Irish had little love for Jews anyway, so hardly cared what became of them. Now Brigit saw what Doctor Schultze had meant about what was waiting for them here. Of course all these slaves to ruthless ambition were still working together. It seemed utter madness to Brigit, as though the Irish were inviting foreign roosters to rule the coop, but madness was the order of the times.

Or perhaps it's shortsightedness, or maybe even just stupidity. Or they simply don't care. With devotion's visage and pious action men do sugar o'er the devil himself.

The ceaselessness of the violence, the keenness to let ever more blood . . . that order for guns, for so many guns. Brigit swallowed a sob as she had a flash of hundreds of thousands of dead, mountains of dead, the millions of humans who had died under fire since she'd first walked the dark earth compounded in one outpouring of pure horror, the sort only man could inflict upon itself. The obsession, the need to destroy, the opposite mark on the land. She could only hope that this excess of energy and resources they were wasting in an effort to cut down her and the children would stand as a paradigm, that their obsession with death would eventually bring about their own destruction.

But not soon enough. Oh, Eamon, we failed so completely.

The whispered answer in her head made her gasp.

No, not at all. You're nearly there. I'll help.

She'd known Eamon would be there, but feeling him so close, so truly close after so long, filled her with as much terror as longing. Would they see him, would they turn on him? If she had to fight for both the children and Eamon, how could she ever . . . ?

They will all survive. There is no other option.

With that, she took out her handkerchief and wiped first Lukas's face, then Alma's.

"It's nearly time to go."

Alma's eyes were too white around the irises.

"They still want us."

"Yes. We're of high value to them."

"Why can't they just let us go?"

"Human nature is a funny thing."

Alma's face crumpled. She looked tiny, a toddler frightened by a nightmare.

"Papa says that millennials can run fast if they have to. A mile in the space of a heartbeat."

"Not quite that fast, but that's the general idea."

"That means you could get away. You could get away and leave us here."

Brigit felt her hand rise to smack the insult out of Alma's mouth, but remembered just in time that the girl was exhausted and terrified and still just a child. She gripped Alma's jaw instead so that she could look directly into her eyes.

"I am a creature of honor. I swore a solemn oath to your father, and I swear now by all that you hold holy, by the love that binds me to Eamon, by the strength in all my brethren here and gone, you are as surely my charge as if you were of my body, and I *will* see you to safety."

Tears sprang up in Alma's eyes and Brigit dabbed at them hurriedly, hissing at her to control herself, that they still had to look calm and untroubled, even if they were walking straight into slings and arrows.

But how? How are we going to do this?

She was exhausted herself, weak and worn and frightened. She was at a tremendous disadvantage. If there was time to think, to plan, if only she and Eamon could actually talk . . . but the boat would leave in seven minutes. There was nothing for it. They had to go.

Once again, she hefted Lukas into her arms, although now he was quiet and still from fear, rather than illness or exhaustion. She would have liked to carry Alma as well, to be more sure she could guard the girl, but they could not look so suspicious until the end. An idea was growing in her, a possibility, the possibility of the speed Alma had mentioned . . . and something more. A way to send the children to the boat while she remained on the dock to see this thing through to a bloody end. Combine her own strength with that of Eamon and Mors and use it in one quick, benevolent gesture to the human race. She knew it was a defiance of nature, whose laws she respected. That power was for vampires alone. But maybe, just this once, she could bend the laws that bound her.

Nature was certainly on their side in so far as the cloudy sky was concerned. They strode under it boldly, basking in pretended entitlement, trembling under the façade but too proud to let it be seen.

The Nazis waited until she was at the brink of the short pier leading to the waiting boat. She could just make out a shadow of Eamon, hovering near the railing. The two men flanked her.

"Hand over the children now, and perhaps you will be spared much pain."

The various hunters and men just along for the fun of seeing a vampire killed, and in daylight no less, quivered with delight. They couldn't hear the conversation on the ground below, but they knew how it was going. Most of them didn't mind the idea of killing the children as well, since they were only Jews and it was in such a good cause, but they would rather not.

Brigit looked from one man to the other. They marked her hesitation, took out pistols from inside their jackets, and cocked them. To her grudging admiration, hovering hunters tossed each man a sword as well.

Alma's palm grew sweaty in Brigit's.

Eamon. We need music again. Not to calm the savage beast, but to arouse it.

He met her eyes. They were at exactly the same distance as they had been that night, 750 years ago. He winked, and she winked back.

And so they began. A low hum, a whisper, a song of juxtaposition and contradiction. Wave upon wave of rhythm to intoxicate and yet soothe. An aural heat to cool. To create an invisible fog. It was a song composed of melody so ancient and powerful, the planet had nearly forgotten it. Stirring a memory in dirt deep beneath the ugly buildings of the port, the earth sighed and stretched luxuriously. The rolling earth shook the men and they looked around, nervous.

Each note vibrating through Brigit and Eamon seamlessly wove together to make a tunnel, through which reached the vaguest essence of a smoky hand.

The flaxen rope through the labyrinth.

She nodded to the Nazis and bent to Alma, as though kissing her good-bye, and pressed her hand to the girl's heart, whispering into her ear.

"Take Lukas by one hand and grab hold of that large hand. It may look like an illusion, but I promise it's solid. Keep tight hold of it and you will get to the boat. Eamon will take care of you."

"What are you doing?" Alma breathed, trying to hide her panic.

"Go!"

And Alma obeyed. To anyone else, they were gone in a blink, but Brigit saw them holding the hand, saw them pulled swiftly to safety on a wave of ancient music, saw Eamon receive them, scratched and coughing and crying from the pain of a path they weren't meant to cross. She had a brief moment of satisfaction in the reunion before she turned her attention to the men flanking her.

All right, my demon. Let's create the sort of chaos that could wake the dead.

The demon smiled at her. It reached out and took the fire into its mouth, where it would keep it, under control.

If only Mors could see this.

The Nazis were stunned to receive broken noses at the hand of the creature between them, and could hardly comprehend how the children had escaped. One of them still held his sword and swung out at Brigit, clipping her thigh. She ignored the pain and crushed his wrist beneath her foot as she seized the sword and plunged it into his heart. The other Nazi screamed to the hunters to do their duty.

Arrows flew down at Brigit. She whirled desperately, batting them away with the sword while begging Eamon to remain where he was. This was her fight now.

"Which of you will come and fight me like a man?" she bellowed into the throng. The men hesitated, wanting and needing that fight, but knowing, too, what it might mean.

From the boat, Eamon, Alma, and Lukas watched in stunned silence. Eamon kept a hand tight around each child's shoulder and they welcomed the touch as though it were familiar. He hummed steadily, a calming, joyous little tune that made them think perhaps they were not watching their guardian engage in a fight with several dozen hunters, while the sky threatened to brighten.

With guttural battle cries, the hunters leaped to the dock to take on the vampire eye to eye. This was what they were meant to do, after all, destroy great evil at close range. Filth could be disposed of at a distance, but evil of this magnitude must be looked in the face and smiled on before it was vanquished. None of them had ever even tried to take down a millennial, but they were many, she was one, and they knew how to fight.

Brigit had never studied the art of battle, but she had Mors inside her now, and a man did not become a general of the Roman Republic without knowing some tricks. Her mind emptied, she concentrated only on the hot music inside her, a tune that whirled her this way and that, dispatching men in a frenetic ballet. She heard their shouts, felt blades cut into her limbs, even her torso, but she was too possessed to allow the pain to slow her. Heat was rising, inside and out. The sun and the fire were coming.

"Now, Brigit! Come now! The boat is leaving!" Eamon shouted.

The remnants of the fog Brigit and Eamon had created meant no one on the boat, save the three most concerned, could see what was happening on the dock, and the sailors methodically went about their duty so that the mail could go through.

Brigit paused. She could escape now. No self-respecting Irish hunter would tread upon the province of the British hunters to stalk a vampire, it was only that she was Brigantia and had dared breach their border that they fought her with such venom. But then she caught the scent of Nachtspeere. Weber and Lange hadn't been the last; there were some here in training, and some that had been sent ahead in case all else failed and this was necessary. Irish hunters siding with Germany, and Nacht-speere. To finish them now meant the Nazi purge of vampires was con-fined to the Continent, and thus as good as done. She had gone to Germany to avenge her kind. She had come to care about the fate of humanity itself, but this was the end of the circle. If she had failed to stop them from killing humans, she could make one final strike on be-half of the vampires and see more of their strong young men fall, their dazzling hope for the great Aryan future diminished.

With a roar that reached far back into history, Brigit whirled and swung the sword, taking no pleasure in the necks it sliced through like sausage links, feeling only that it was an act of completion that was too late.

A hunter leaped on her from behind, the shock and his weight knocking her to her knees. She spun, and smelled the furious zeal and the sure power of the stake, not the one Leon had used to make his point, but one forged hundreds of years ago and saved for the chance to wield with such certainty and precision.

On the boat, Eamon turned the children into him, pressing their faces to his chest. They would not bear witness to this, nor to the redness rising in his eyes. His Brigit was in danger of shuffling off her almost-immortal coil, and there was not a thing he could do about it.

The tip of the stake pierced Brigit's breast, she could feel flesh pull-ing away, as though making a path for the weapon that was meant to fin-ish this unnatural body. But Eamon was in the heart that stake intended to touch and thus shatter, and Mors was alive somewhere, pulsing under her bones. She clamped her hands around the stake and squeezed so it splintered and crumbled. Her hand flew through the hunter's shocked eyes, sending brains soaring across the dock.

Hazy sun rays poked through the clouds. The boat was unmoored, was beginning its slow chug toward Wales. The remaining two hunters, feeling their advantage, ran toward Brigit as she stumbled to her feet.

The blood from her many wounds still oozed down skin that was starting to steam and crack in the coming sun.

No.

She staggered down toward the dock, her eyes swimming with furious tears. She could not possibly be about to die.

One hunter shot a stake at her with a crossbow. It pierced her hip and she yanked it out, disregarding the pain, wishing that the smoky hand would come back for her.

"No, Eamon, no . . ." Her voice was a plaintive squeak, an echo of her own self. She took another few steps and slipped in brains, landing hard on her back.

The hunters yelled their delight, weapons aloft. They made to jump on her. She saw their eyes, saw that they were tasting triumph, that she was nothing more than a finished thing.

"Nooooooo!" she bellowed, seizing each man as he closed in, finding strength in their malice and certainty. With another ear-piercing cry, she ripped out their hearts and squelched them in her fists. She shook the residue from her fingers and ran for the plank.

The boat was gone, the sun was brightening, and Eamon was crouching, clutching the children and crying out for her in a silent plea. She had not saved those children, not come this close, only to be stopped now. With a scream of defiance at the sun, she dove into the water. She kicked hard, pushing herself almost to the bottom, exulting in her burst of strength, in her complete independence of the need for oxygen. The salt was torment on her open wounds, but she didn't care, she swam like a creature possessed.

It was Alma's voice she heard when her head broke water, Alma shouting that her aunt had fallen overboard. And though none of the boatmen could remember any of the passengers boarding, two of them rushed to the side and pulled Brigit aboard. One man threw a heavy blanket over her; the other pulled her into the little office where an emergency medical kit was snapped open and her congealing cuts and bruises inexpertly but kindly tended.

Brigit didn't give a damn about any marks upon her body, they would heal in hours. She craned her neck, frantic for a sight of Alma. When she saw the girl, she clenched her almost too hard.

"Are you all right?" she asked in a squeak.

"Yes," Alma panted, still shaken from her trip through the tunnel and the interminable last five minutes. "Yes, we're all right. All of us."

The boatmen had no idea what the child meant, but were pleased to see the beautiful blonde relax.

"The waters here can be a bit rough," one of them commented. "It was lucky you were able to make it back on board."

On the whole, Brigit agreed.

Chapter 22

London-bound train. August 1940.

The sky was bright in Holyhead, but there was shade on the dock, the station was sheltered, and the train would terminate at Kings Cross that night. Brigit's clothes were still damp, but she otherwise bore no visible mark of what she had just endured, and the little group garnered no notice. Eamon waited until Brigit and the children had their tickets before joining them on the platform. At last, he and Brigit could look at each other and embrace.

Lukas stared openly at the vampires with their arms wrapped so tightly around each other, but Alma, after watching a moment, turned and looked at the track instead, anxious for the train to arrive.

The train was full of soldiers and heavy with cigarette smoke and careless chat. They finally found a quiet compartment and Eamon swung their bags into the hold. He smiled at the children and held out two bars of chocolate. Brigit tsked.

"They haven't had a proper breakfast, they'll be sick, eating that now."

"The trolley will be round in a few minutes, it'll be all right."

"Please?" Lukas begged.

"No, wait until you've had some milk and sandwiches first. You don't want to be sick again, do you?"

Lukas grumbled and stuck his head around the blind that Brigit had closed so he could look out the window.

She and Eamon exchanged amused and sad smiles. The one thing they could never share. It was something a female vampire rarely thought of, but they all knew their demons lodged in the womb, in the most comfortable and reasonable empty space inside.

After the children had eaten, and Brigit escorted them to the tiny lavatory to wash up, they all settled in the cushions. Lukas slept. Alma struggled to stay awake, watching Brigit and Eamon.

Brigit seemed a very different creature. She was still alert, aware of the daylight outside, but more concerned that Alma and Lukas be safely delivered into their relatives' hands. Alma knew they would be all right now. England would cradle them. But Brigit wouldn't rest until she'd seen the job through to the very end. She was, however, more relaxed than Alma had yet seen her. Her head fit perfectly in the hollow of Eamon's neck, her hand rested against his heart. His own hand caressed hers, his other arm tight around her, fingers on her elbow, his cheek leaning on her head. Their eyes were half-closed, looking at nothing. Alma remembered seeing her parents like this once, caught in a moment of wordless conversation, the picture of a love so deep, it was almost painful to witness.

When they crossed the border into England, Eamon nudged Brigit and smiled at the children.

"Welcome home."

Home. It was Brigit and Eamon's home, but Alma suddenly registered what she hadn't allowed herself to think since the day her father told her what he was planning. She would probably never set foot in Germany again. The land of her birth was foreign, hostile territory now. It didn't want her. If she was to live, her life would be here. She would make it a good life. She would do her father proud.

Her eyes found Brigit's. Cleared of fear, concern, and pretense, Alma could see how amazingly old those sparkling young eyes were. There was a lost world inside them, wild places, great unknowns, clear air, and a starry sky that roared out over a wondering world. There was laughter and love and something that had to be called humanity in those eyes. It made Alma's scalp prickle, and she turned away.

As she did, she accidentally looked at Eamon and saw tears sparking in his eyes as he drank in herself and Lukas. He radiated a peculiar warmth, and his soft smile made her want to smile in return. She could feel him wanting to say something, even to reach out to her, but he would not be so presumptuous. She found herself liking him for that.

Brigit wished she could know what Alma was thinking. She wouldn't ask, she respected the girl's privacy, but she wanted to know. She wondered if Alma looked at Eamon and saw a tenuous thread to her own history, understood that he had done as much as she herself had done to see that Alma and Lukas had come to this place. What Owen had said was true: Firstborns do become hunters. There was immense power in Alma, and strength, but Brigit saw glowing light behind the dark eyes, too much light to be confined solely to the darkness.

Will I see you again? And if I do, will it be in the moment before I die at your hand? Or would I see you as you cut down Eamon? He and I have saved you, but that does not make us human. We are still your natural enemy. Or do we have a bond now, you and I? Your life is about to unfold before you. What path will you take?

The conductor came through to see that the blackout curtains were drawn. There was no bombing tonight, or not yet, but this was the new order. The soldiers' songs were louder, defying bombers and the probability of imminent death. Soon, too soon, they'd be in the throes of battle. They would sing while they could.

Alma and Lukas changed into fresh clothes and Brigit supervised one last wash. They were all silent as they pulled into the dimly lit station, the boisterous soldiers pushing around them, shouting and laughing. Brigit helped the children down the stairs and they kept near her, looking for the couple who must be looking for them. Brigit didn't realize she was trembling until Eamon laid a steadying hand on her shoulder.

A woman who Brigit saw must be Leon's sister approached them. She turned and called to her husband, who was farther down the platform. He hurried to join his wife. They avoided the vampires' eyes, bending down to greet the children.

"Alma, Lukas, we are so happy to see you." Their aunt spoke in slightly accented English.

Lukas clung shyly to Brigit and his aunt bit her lip. Brigit knelt and put her hands on the boy's shoulders.

"This is your auntie and uncle, Lukas. They will take superb care of you and you will be very happy. Go on, now. Let them take you home."

He hugged Brigit and she hugged him back, longer and more tightly then she meant to, feeling his little heart beat against her, strong and healthy.

His aunt sucked in her breath, and as Brigit nudged Lukas to his new guardians, she saw them brush at him, as though wiping off filth.

Brigit nodded, standing awkwardly and backing toward Eamon. Alma stood between the two couples, hesitating. Her aunt extended a hand.

"Come, dear, we've got to get a taxi yet and it's difficult in the black-out."

Alma took a step toward her aunt, then hurried back to Brigit and took her by the hand, pulling so that Brigit knelt to her and they were eye to eye.

"Thank you."

Brigit smiled and touched the girl's round cheek. She feared seeing her again, but ached at the realization that she would not see the woman emerge from under the child. She knew that woman would be some-thing incredible to see.

Alma didn't move and Brigit leaned closer and whispered to her.

"There are three things in this world that make a life whole. They are perhaps all the same thing. Happiness, peace, and love. If you have them, you have everything. I wish these things for you, in abundance. Them, and a long life in which to enjoy them. Go well, Alma. Go well."

Alma's mouth was quivering. She nodded, touched her lips quickly to Brigit's cheek, then turned and ran to join her family. None of them looked back.

Brigit and Eamon watched until the family rounded the corner to the taxi bay. Eamon slipped his hand in Brigit's and guided her outside.

London under siege was a chilling thing, and Brigit pressed closer to Eamon, not feeling that she was, indeed, home. The city was fright-ened, huddling under the blanket of darkness that brought no protection. The blackness reminded Brigit of the world she'd loved hundreds of years ago. But she'd lost her taste for it. She liked a world where lights twinkled in the streets. She straightened her shoulders, ready for yet another fight. She was going to see that world come back.

Eamon turned her to face him. She'd seen too much, he registered with a pang, noting the aching and sadness etching her features. She knew without having to ask that there was no word from Mors or Cleland. Her fears and disappointments hung heavily on her shoulders. But she was still his Brigit. He touched her cheek and saw the ancient sparkle. There was a new beauty in her face, new terrain to explore.

"In all the years to come, I don't think I can ever tell you how happy I am that you've come home."

Brigit couldn't answer. Her heart was too full. She wished they could step two hundred and fifty years into the future, into the greater safety of Eamon's millennial, but like so much else, it was impossible. There was no choice but to treasure the present.

They kissed, and Brigit concentrated on the kiss. A kiss without beginning or end, a sweet elixir sweeping them into endless joy.

We still have this. And it is everything.

"Come, good lady, the bright day is done, and we are for the dark."

She smiled. Tomorrow, she would hear all the grim news of the war and what was happening in England and abroad. Tomorrow, she would tell everyone all the disheartening details of the last week, the last month, the last year. Tomorrow, she would join the vigil of hope for Mors and Cleland. But for tonight, she and Eamon wrapped their arms around each other and headed off home through the dark.

𝕬𝖇𝖔𝖚𝖙 𝖙𝖍𝖊 𝕿𝖞𝖕𝖊𝖋𝖆𝖈𝖊

The typeface used for the title page and chapter headings in this book is Fette Fraktur, a German blackletter (also called a "Gothic Script") typeface, designed by punchcutter Johann Christian Bauer in 1850. Popular in advertising, it was considered a symbol of German identity and was initially embraced by the Third Reich until it was banned in 1941, when it was decided its letterforms were *Judenlettern* (Jewish letters). Some suspect the ban was more due to the typeface being hard to read by citizens of occupied countries. It was often employed by Allied forces for use in anti-Nazi propaganda.

Acknowledgments

First, I must thank and pay homage to all my history teachers—and then apologize. I like to think that if history is written by winners, it's reinvented by fiction writers.

Of course, there are more people to thank than could possibly be mentioned here, and if I have forgotten anyone, I hope they feel free to shame me at the appropriate juncture.

On the business side, I must thank my amazing agent, Margaret O'Connor, whose patience, hard work, and awesome cheerleading continue to go above and beyond; my brilliant editor, Hilary Teeman, whose every change and suggestion were both spot-on and enlivening; and my great manager, Steve White, whose belief in me got me . . . here!

A zillion hugs and everlasting gratitude go to: The fabulous Allie Spencer, who told me that this character and story turning around in my head couldn't be anything but a book—thereafter, it was all systems go; the awesome Stephen Smith, who was a tireless giver of insight that brought me even deeper into the world I thought I knew so well—and who sometimes makes me laugh till I feel pain in places I didn't know existed; the divine Christy English, who not only helped me tap back into a specific joy in the work that I'd let slide as life got in the way, but also reassured me during some dark hours that Brigit would always be my beacon; and my darling "twin," Melinda Klayman, who is a sharp critic

ACKNOWLEDGMENTS

but has always believed in me and knew I'd find my way even when I was well off the path.

Big thanks, of course, to my mother, who will remind me that she very kindly never asked when I was going to get a real job.

Many friends at the Writers Room in New York were a tremendous help. I have to single out Tim Kirkman and Jerry Weinstein, who took a lot of abuse and actually seemed to enjoy it. And shout-outs to Eamon Hickey, Dana Liu, Colin McPhillamy, Manjula Menon, and Tony Perrottet.

I also have to single out nitpicker extraordinaire Martin della Valle, whose patience and skill with the fussiest little niggles deserves a medal, and Amy Morton, title exploration goddess.

Others who were amazing along the way include Emerson Bruns, Katey Coffing, Amanda Kirk, Robb McCaffree, Alisa Roost, Michael Santora, Sophie Sartain, Anne Marie Schleiner, Beth Seltzer, William Shakespeare, of course, for helping make the vampires so eloquent, and, for providing endless inspiration, Stephen Sondheim. But that's another story altogether.